Lula
does the Hula

Samantha Mackintosh

EGMONT

EGMONT

We bring stories to life

Lula Does the Hula
First published 2011
by Egmont UK Limited
239 Kensington High Street
London W8 6SA

Text copyright © 2011 Samantha Mackintosh

The moral rights of the author have been asserted

ISBN 978 1 4052 5653 7

1 3 5 7 9 10 8 6 4 2

www.egmont.co.uk

A CIP catalogue record for this title is available from the British Library

Printed and bound in Great Britain by the CPI Group

Hello and aloha, gorgeousnesses!

There are hints in this book of my murky past. Like the time my friends and I went caravanning in the summer holidays. Carrie's dad dropped us and the caravan off, and as soon as his exhaust fumes had wafted away we'd struck up a friendship with the boys in a nearby tent.

They were gorgeous and fun and all you could wish for in next-door holiday mates.

Except they never had teabags.

Not a problem until they WALK IN UNANNOUNCED when, you know, a person could be GETTING DRESSED! All, like, 'Have you girls got any tcab– Oh, hel-lo!'

'Erk!' I shrieked. 'Out! Out!' But it was too late. All that boy talked about for the rest of the holiday was 'Sam's Specialities'.

I did my best to pretend it never happened.

But not so long ago, a million miles and a million days since that campsite, I walk into a live-music gig, and what do I hear across the crowded room?

'SAM! SPECIALITIES!'

Yep, the boy from the tent. Oh HOW? Why? Whyeee?

I hope this kind of thing doesn't happen to you, but if, like me, you're a bit of a Lula and constantly suffering total humiliations, keep your head held high, your best friends close and your spiky hairbrush-slash-pepper spray at the ready . . .

Big hugs,

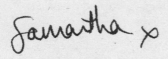

Read the first Lula adventure/rom-com/tale
of total humiliation

'A hilarious, hectic, full-on diary saga'
Julia Eccleshare, lovereading4kids.co.uk

'Laugh-out-loud funny' Bookseller

'Girls will wish they are Lula' thebookbag.co.uk

'Extremely exciting' chicklish.co.uk

'So much fun' goodreads.com

Find Lula's blog at www.lulabooks.co.uk

Who's kissing, who's missing and who's making
complications for our favourite girl next door?

For my mother

Chapter One

Monday 5 a.m. Some witchy instinct has woken me up

My boyfriend is dead. Apparently.

I kissed him goodbye two weeks ago and will never ever see him again. He did not die of natural causes. Oh, no.

Everyone says it's my fault. Most of the village of Hambledon where I live think I'm terribly jinxed – that's the reason all the boys I go out with end up in A&E sooner rather than later. And no one has seen my one true love since we first kissed.

Ohhhh, that kiss . . .

Um. Where was I? Oh, yes. So my boyfriend is dead.

But I know better.

In the pitch black of early, early morning, the start of summer just a breath away, I grinned happily to myself and stretched. It was the perfect start to the day, that velvet dark, the gorgeous luxury of a cosy bed I didn't have to get out of just yet, the feeling that something wonderful was going to happen. I didn't give a flying fig about the dead-boyfriend rumours.

Total silence.

Thank heavens I lived out here in the annexe rather than the main house where my littlest sister Blue yodelled at the break of dawn more often than not.

Still, I guess I was getting a wake-up call, regardless. I smiled in anticipation.

The phone shrilled right on time. I grabbed the handset, but before I could speak a warm voice was in my ear.

'Hey, sleepyhead.'

I grinned and clicked on the bedside light, squeezing my eyes shut against the glare. 'Hey, yourself. What's happening in London town?'

Before he could reply I was squealing like Miss Piggy on Prozac as something shifted under the sheets next to me.

Could it be I was not alone in this bed?

'NYEEEEEP!'

A panicked voice came down the phone: 'Tallulah? Lula? What's going on? *LULA! Answer me!* Oh, geez, oh, man, I'm gonna hang up and call 999!'

I catapulted out of my bed, across the room and squinted back at my tumbled duvet and scattered pillows, phone still in my hand.

'Wait!' I hissed into the handset, watching for another movement from under the duvet.

A dark-haired head lifted from my pillow and sighed.

Oh, frik.

It was Boodle . . . Boodle had spent the night with me.

The gorgeous voice from the phone interrupted my *I'm gonna die, I'm gonna die* thoughts:

'Lula? Lula? You okay?' asked Jack.

'No,' I replied. 'Not really. It's Boodle. She spent the night.' I got back into bed, shoving Boodle the Poodle over so I could get my snug nest back. There was the sound of muffled laughter from the other end of the line.

I coughed, sternly. 'Apart from me dying at the hands of my sister when she discovers her dog has decided to move in with me, I'm fine, *thanks.*' I said this last bit in a sarky voice to disguise the lie. The one about me being fine. No way was I going to let my boyfriend of only a fortnight know that I had anxieties, AND issues, AND maybe even some highly charged emotional baggage.

With Jack interning in the city with Channel 4 these last two weeks, the old rumours of me being a wEiRdy witch girl who damaged every boy she ever went near had started to resurface. So not fair! It took a lot for me to get my first kiss and prove There Was No Jinx – you'd think I could put all that behind me! But no one in this village was ever going to forget I had a history of injuring boys and a witchy grandmother, even if Grandma Bird was six foot under. It doesn't help that crazy stuff always happens to me, but still. People shouldn't jump to conclusions. People should stop muttering stuff every time they lay eyes on me. I have exceptionally good hearing for a girl who loves loud music, and I can hear the whispers:

Where has Jack de Souza disappeared to?

The city?

Nuh-uh – I don't believe it. I bet he's lying in an intensive care ward somewhere . . .

I heard he died.

Yep. He's a goner. Should have stayed away from Tallu–

'Hey? Tallulah?'

I was jolted out of my memory banks. 'Uh! Yeah?'

'So what do you think?'

'Erm . . .' I said, scrunching my knees up to my chest and pulling the duvet round me. 'Sorry. I missed that. I'm not quite with it at 5 a.m. Pen's been moaning about you waking the house up every morning, actually.'

As soon as the words were out of my mouth, I wished I could hit the rewind button.

'She has?' Jack sounded worried. He should be. My little sister is fierce, even for a fourteen-year-old. 'It's just that your mobile is never on. Or you never answer it. Should I stop calling?'

'Noonnoonoonoo!' I said in a panic. Jack laughed. Oh, GOD. Why did I have to be the uncoolest girl in the world? I coughed. 'What I mean is, I'll remember to charge my mobile. I will. I really will. It's just that I can't find my charger, so I have to keep using Pen's, but she won't let it leave her room, so I end up either not charging my phone, or else forgetting that it's charging in there, or –'

'Okay,' said Jack easily. 'It's just I don't wanna pee

Penelope off. She's the type that would take revenge.'

'Yes,' I said with sad certainty, thinking I was already in for it, for sure. 'Calling on this landline number is fine.'

'I don't want to wake up your family, though.'

I smiled. What a considerate boy. 'Don't worry. I pick up the extension out here really fast.'

'You do.' I could hear the grin in Jack's voice. 'You cannot *wait* to speak to me.' Before I could bluster a response he said, 'What's happening in Hambledon?'

I sighed. Life in this town slash village had no way of competing with what Jack must be doing in the city. 'Well, Dad's writing a really bad song at the moment. So awful. The worst is he says he's inspired by our young love.' I flushed. FRIK! I'd just done it again! I'd said the love word. While referring to us.

'Love, huh?' said Jack, and he laughed. 'Yeah.'

Okay, hold the phone. Just pause there for one smidgeony second. What does 'yeah' mean? Oh, frik. If only I had the phone on speaker right now, and Alex right beside me. She'd know for sure.

I coughed again, desperate to fill the silence. 'So, um –'

'So, um,' mocked Jack. 'Can't wait to hear the song.'

'Oh, the song,' I babbled. 'Be happy to wait. It's bliddy bliddy badly bad. Though knowing my luck it'll be in the top forty by tomorrow.'

'Good,' said Jack. 'I'll be back by then.'

And, shamefully, at the thought of my brand-new, first-ever, totally awesome boyfriend being back in a matter of hours, *I squealed.*

Then, *NO, TATTY LULA!* I yelped to myself. *DON'T SQUEAL AT THE LOVELY BOY!*

'Sorry,' I murmured. 'I thought I saw someone at my window.'

Which wasn't a total lie, but I'm a courageous type and flitty shadows at my bedroom window have me reaching for my spikiest hairbrush, not doing ninny squealing. 'Are you coming back on the train?' I asked. 'Today? What time? Should I, um, meet you at the station?' A vision of *Casablanca* flooded into my head and I liked it.

But – oh, woe! – that vision was dashed.

'Nah. I'm gonna drive in with Jazz at noon today, and go straight to the journ department. Could I see you this afternoon maybe? I'll text you when I know where I'm gonna be after school.'

'Driving?' I said. 'With Jazz?' I think I sounded quite calm, but spinning round and round in my head was: *JAZZ? WHAT THE FRIK? JAZZ? JAZZ?*

'Sure,' said Jack. 'You sound squeaky . . . Don't you want me to drive? Have you had a witchy premonition about ice on the roads or something?'

I laughed. Well, I did my best to laugh. 'No no. I – I just hadn't realised you were there with Jazz.'

'Seriously? Didn't I –? Haven't I –?' He spluttered to a halt. 'Whoa, weird. I guess I've just been so into hearing what's up in your neck of the woods that I haven't really said anything about her.'

'Are you saying I do most of the talking in these break-of-dawn sessions?' I teased, trying to sound light-hearted.

Jack laughed. 'You've got the most to say. I've just been work work work.'

'With Jazz.' *Oh, now why couldn't I just leave that alone?*

'Yep,' replied Jack, oblivious. 'She came up to the city last week. She knows a lot of media types, which is good. Her dad, y'know, *owns* newspapers and whole channels. She's got great connections. You remember her, right?'

Yes, I remembered her. You, dear reader, probably won't, because she drifted in and out of my last adventure with scarcely any mention. She was part of a posse of Jack admirers, all hanging around him at the cinema the first time we met. Even then I got a hostile vibe from her. A sense that she wanted Jack for herself.

Oh, boy. I felt a prickle of unease that I tried to squash immediately. No frikking way was I going to turn into a mad psycho jealous type. No way.

'Jazz . . .' I said, bright and breezy. 'Sure I do. Shouldn't she be back on campus already for the start of term, though?'

'Nope,' said Jack. 'We're doing the same course, so she's kind of joining me in this special project work I'm doing, and Channel 4 are keen for us to keep it moving together. Our profs and tutors have said it's all good.'

'Oh,' I said. 'All good.'

But it didn't feel all good at all. Noooo. Not good AT ALL.

Chapter Two

Monday, sun slowly rising

So there I am, scrunched up over the phone, trying to concentrate on what my boyfriend is telling me while I worry about whether he really is my boyfriend, actually.

He was still wittering away about the delights of Jazz, so in the next available break I tried to change the subject. 'Hey, where are your digs? I think Mona told me, but I've forgotten already.'

Mona is Jack's superhot sister, remember? And she's still going out with Arnold – the geek I turned into a god with a mega makeover (if I say so myself. Okay, not quite a god. Quite fit, more like).

'We've got a house at the bottom of Mason. Just down the road from Mona's dorms.'

'We?'

'Yeah, me, Jazz and Forest.'

'O-oh,' I stammered. 'Wow. You live with Jazz.' Pause. 'Um. It's great that you can see so much of her and still work well together, yeah?'

'Yep,' said Jack. 'And she makes a mean three bean salad.'

Three bean salad, I thought. *I bet it's frikking mean. Like the rest of her.*

Stop it! Stop it! Be lovely!

But before I could extol the virtues of beans (are there any?) there was a hammering at my door.

'Who's there?' asked Jack straight away.

'You can hear that?' I jumped out of bed, holding the handset to my ear with my shoulder and grabbing the canister of pepper spray (long story) from my bedside table.

'Course I can hear that! They're gonna bash your door down! Don't open! It's got to be –'

'Pen!' I finished, opening the door, spray still at the ready. Ha! So there *had* been a face at my window. 'What the –?'

But before I could get a word out she'd shoved me in the shoulder with a baseball bat (where the hell did that come from?), knocking me back hard against the wall where she pointed my mobile at me like it was a Glock semi-automatic.

I was so discombobulated I let the phone I was holding fall to the ground, promptly stepped on it and my left leg skidded out from under me. I went down like a tonne of bricks, falling on my right hand and slamming down the depressor for the pepper spray.

A little unfortunate . . .

Because Pen got a faceful as she stormed in through the doorway.

*

Even by my previous record of inflicting grievous bodily harm on people this was pretty bad. Pen got one glancing strike to my head before collapsing in a screaming, blithering, raging heap.

'You –! You –! You – you – you –! HEEELP! HEEEELP!'

I sprang to my feet, my eyes stinging like billio as I tried to read the side of the pepper-spray canister. Should I get water? Would that make it worse?

'WATER!' shrieked Pen.

'Oh frik! Oh frikly frikly frik!' I whimpered, spinning round to face my teensy kitchen. I grabbed the kettle and lunged back to Pen.

All the while a little tinny voice was coming from the phone: 'Lula? Tallulah? Hey! Are you okay? Lu–'

Then I threw the water at Pen's red, streaming face, the phone fizzed and died in the deluge and within seconds my mobile rang.

You will think less of me here, but I'm afraid I snatched my mobile from the floor where Pen had thrown it, thankfully far from my healing waters, and headed for my bathroom, leaving my sister howling in the doorway, scrabbling at her eyes.

I'd only got a bit of the spray in my face, but it was super stingy and the warm flannel I swiped over my eyes was bliss.

'Hello?' I croaked into my mobile. 'Jack? Is that you?'

'No,' snapped Alex, obviously in her News Reporter

zone. 'This is no time for love, Tatty. The police are swarming all over Frey's Dam, and I can't get in there to get stills or clips for Jack's Channel 4 stuff. You have to help me trespass. Now.'

Chapter Three

Still Monday morning, though I wish it wasn't. Hiding in the bathroom from small but scary sister

'What?' I said, still clutching the flannel. 'Wh–'

'Oops,' said Alex. 'Gotta go. See you in five.'

'Wha–?' I yelled, but the line was already dead.

My bathroom door slammed open.

And standing there looking totally nutso was Pen.

Her eyes were red and enraged, her hair dripped in rats' tails around her grim face and she had her pointy finger out. The pointy finger was shaking with fury.

I was shaking with fear.

'Two things!' shrieked Pen.

I flinched and sat down hurriedly on the edge of the old claw-footed bath.

'Firstly! Boodley slept with you again!' she said, stabbing the finger at me.

'Sh-she did?' I stammered.

'*Again!*' continued Pen, taking a step closer. 'After I specifically told you she's *my* dog! You want her to be your dog, YOU pick up the poos!'

'Wroarf,' came a voice from behind Pen, and in padded Boodle the Poodle. You should know that Boodle is not a poodle, but the hugest Newfoundland known to man.

'Oh, right,' I said. Then added stupidly, 'Couldn't this have waited till breakfast? It's, like, the middle of the night.'

'Exactly!' yelled Pen. 'The middle of the night and still your boyfriends PHONE and TEXT and MESSAGE and, you know, if we had a FAX MACHINE, they'd be MACHINING too! How could you leave your phone in my room? *Again?!* I'm sick of it! I've had no sleep! I'm going crazy! I –' She interrupted herself to shove me in the shoulder and I fell back in the bath, my head gonging against the side like Big Ben. I scrabbled about like a beetle on its back while Boodle padded over to drool on my knees.

Yuk! And ouch!

'Hey!' I yelled, suddenly furious. 'Take a frikking chill pill, Penelope! Just listen to yourself! *I! I! I!* It's all about you! For your information I have ONE boyfriend and it's not MACHINING, you cretin, it's FAXING! Which solicitors do a lot of! If you had any chance of becoming one, you'd know!' My little sister Pen, in case you've forgotten, is fourteen, but acts and sounds like a forty-year-old. She wants to be a solicitor with every cell of her being, so this was a low blow.

'Solicitors *email*, mainbrain!' yelled Pen, and with lightning speed she got a handful of my hair and twisted, showing me my phone:

14

Which she then threw on my chest. 'You!' she hissed. 'You're ruining my life! Look at my eyes.'

'Eeeee!' I squealed, my legs going limp. 'Let go! Let go!'

'*Look!*' hissed Pen.

I squinted obligingly through watery orbs. The girl had a demon grip and I needed a quick release.

There was silence while I stared into Pen's big green eyes. They looked extremely red and watery to me.

'They look extremely red and watery to me,' I said.

'*And?*' she spat. 'AND! Look! There are rings! Deep blue rings from no sleep!'

'Not my fault!' I whimpered as she twisted harder. 'Let go. Please.'

'Angus loves my eyes!' yelled Pen. 'He says they're my best feature.'

I winced. Yikes.

'If my best feature goes . . .' continued Pen. I saw something flicker across her face as her voice petered out. Then her grip on my hair slackened and she pulled me out of the bath with a tired sigh.

I could have headlocked her right then, but . . . well, she looked so sad. And small. I knew more than most that loving a boy is the first rung on the long and treacherous ladder of insanity. It looked to me like my

15

sister could be halfway up already.

'Oh, Pen, Angus adores you,' I said warily, gently rubbing my scalp.

Pen was about to say something when the door to my annexe smashed in. I was on my feet instantly, my most abrasive loofah at the ready, and Pen was yelling for help, clutching a mini-manicure nail file behind the bathroom door: 'POLICE! POLICE! WE'RE BEING ATTACKED!'

Footsteps thudded into the annexe and I made for the bathroom doorway, scratchy loofah raised. 'Stay back, Pen!' I hissed.

'WHAT'S GOING ON? LULA?! LULA?! WHERE ARE YOU?'

Pen came out from behind the door, her face grim. I groaned and rolled my eyes at my sister, who replied with a headshake and a sigh that puffed out her cheeks. 'Dad. In here. You scared the bejeepers out of us.'

My father lunged into the doorway looking frantically from me to Pen, back to me. He was holding a tennis racquet in his left hand and the carving fork in his right. His hair was all squashed up on one side and a mad fuzz on the other, but worst of all he was naked from the belly button up.

'YOU WERE CRYING OUT!' yelled Dad. 'FOR HELP!'

'Ew,' said Pen, staring at Dad's hairy torso. 'Dad! You've got to Veet! Like, seriously.'

'Calm down, Dad,' I said. 'It was just Pen attacking me.' Dad lowered the racquet, but the carving fork stayed poised and there was still a crazy look in his eye.

'PEN?' he gasped. 'ALL THAT NOISE WAS PEN?' His chest began to heave.

'Dad,' I said, 'you need to stop shouting. You'll wake Next-Door Dan up.'

Dad's eyes bugged out a little and he lifted the carving fork ever so slightly.

'Uh-oh,' said Pen. 'Boodle, let's go.'

'Mrwoh,' said Boodle, shaking her head. She pawed at my elbow and looked up at me with big pleading eyes.

Pen stared at her dog in shock and horror at the betrayal. 'OH THAT'S JUST GREAT!' she yelled, her eyes all shiny, her cheeks bright red.

'Put the nail file down, Pen,' I suggested. 'Let's all just take a deep breath here.'

'YOU SEE?' she shrieked at me. I widened my eyes and shrugged helplessly as Boodle pawed me again. 'YOU SEE?' she screamed at Dad. 'DID YOU SEE THAT? SHE'S TAKEN CONTROL OF MY DOG! WELL –!' She was looking desperately at Dad and I was dismayed to see there really were tears in her eyes.

'Pen,' I started.

'Well –! Well –! FINE!' And she stamped out of my annexe, pausing only to sidestep Dad's hairiness. He turned to follow her and I wasn't far behind.

'Wait, Pen!' I called across the courtyard. 'You need to know that Boodle –'

She stopped in her tracks and whirled round. 'Oh, so now you're going to tell me about my dog? *You* are going to tell *me*? About *my* dog? Don't even!'

'Boy, oh, boy. This is not good,' bumbled Dad. 'Girls, come on, it's 5 a.m., it's the middle of the night.'

CRASH.

A window in the wall way above the annexe roof slammed open. In the fast fading light of the moon I could just about make out the sexily shaggy head of Next-Door Dan. 'What,' he rasped, 'is going on out there?'

'Oh, great. Priceless,' said Dad, squinting up. 'The boy next door is about to tell me off for noisy behaviour. I can't stand it.' His shoulders sagged and he plodded to the back door of the main house across the courtyard. 'My own children. Bringing me to my bloody knees.'

'Hey, Spenser.'

Dad stopped and looked warily upwards at Next-Door Dan's window. 'Sorry about the noise, Daniel,' he ventured.

'Good tunes last night. At the Guilty Felon.'

'You think?' Dad's face brightened. 'It was all new stuff.'

'I liked it. Especially that catchy one about . . . uh . . . *my heart's gonna boil* . . . y'know?'

Pen snorted. I wrinkled my nose. Dad is a sought-after songwriter, but we all live in fear of his next totally ditzy number-one hit. How can such an amazing poet – a university professor, for goodness' sake – write such crazy stuff, and how can the crazy stuff *always work*? It's mad.

'I think that one's going to be big,' said Dad, shambling back over. 'EMI want it for a funky rap-pop duet with two of their latest signings.'

'Yeah?'

'Indeed. But I need to work on the . . .' Dad trailed off, lost in a world we couldn't hear just yet. Thank God.

'Is it true you're playing at the Port Albert Regatta?'

Pen clutched my arm. The biggest inter-school rowing regatta was not a source of excitement for us, but the after-party was legendary. Kicking off with a fancy ball, it degenerated as fast as you liked into the district's biggest mosh pit. Dad getting down with the moshers was too terrible to think about.

'Please no,' I whispered, blood draining from my face.

'Oh absolutely yes,' said Dad happily to Dan. 'A few weeks to go, but I'm ready already. Hawaiian theme this year. Luau. Can't wait.' His voice raised in happy trilling as he sashayed back into the main house, bumping his sizeable hips to either side. '*Boiiiiil your heart . . .*'

Chapter Four

'How'd the gasket fit, Tallulah?' asked Next-Door Dan. 'Perfect?'

'Oh, yes,' I said, grinning up at him. 'Dad helped me. Oscar's one happy motor. Now I've just got to put his engine block back in, and –'

'*Quiet!*' hissed Pen.

'What?' I asked.

'Firstly, no one's supposed to know about your motor-mechanics obsession; secondly, *naming* that useless car makes you sound even more crazy!'

'It's dawn,' I retorted. 'No one's awake to hear this casual conversation!'

'*He's* awake,' replied Pen, flinging a dismissive hand in Dan's direction.

'I'm harmless,' said Next-Door Dan hurriedly. 'Like, totally. So you'll save me a dance at the regatta ball, Tallulah?'

Pen and I both looked at him blankly.

'The luau, or whatever it is?' he continued, hesitant.

'Erm,' I said, my shock and stupefication switching to unconcealed delight at being asked. 'Actually I'm kind of seeing someone now.'

'So I hear,' said Dan.

'Huh,' said Pen, clearly irked at not being asked herself. 'You're just like the rest of them, Next-Door Dan. All happy to dance with the freaky witch girl now that you know you're safe. Now that Jack has lived to tell the tale. Join the queue.' She glared up at him, and he leaned back into the window a little.

'No, no,' he said hastily. 'Always knew there was nothing wrong with Tatty. No jinx there. Just weird coincidences . . . all those terrible accidents. How's the dude with the fingers?'

'Huh,' said Pen again, her arms crossed, staring up at Dan with her aggro squinty eyes. '*Without* fingers, you mean.'

It was probably too dark for Dan to recognise the danger signs. 'The Hambledon boys are after you, then, Tatty?' he continued. 'Are you playing along while your Jack is away?'

'Yes,' said Pen at the same time as I said, 'No.'

Then I said, 'How did you know he's been away?'

'Ohh.' Dan waved his hand around. 'Everyone knows he's been a big hit up in London with Channel 4. Since the little exposé.' He eyed me. 'Hang on, does that mean you haven't seen anything of him since . . . you know . . .'

'Since she snogged him? No,' said Pen.

'Pen!'

'So she's had a one-night stand, and her man has vanished from sight,' said Dan thoughtfully, leaning further out of the window again. 'Interesting. Very interesting.'

'Don't,' I said, my cheeks flaring with colour. 'Don't even go there.'

'Nothing's happened to Jack de Souza,' said Pen, examining a fingernail by the light of the rising sun. 'He calls Tallulah before dawn each day.'

'Maybe nothing's happened to him only because he's kept his distance. Or may—'

'Goodbye, Dan,' I said with as much dignity as I could muster. 'Goodbye, Pen.' And I crossed the courtyard to get to my annexe door.

I had stuff to think about.

I pushed my door closed with an exhausted sigh and wasted no time in filling my kettle for some hot water to drink. My mind was whirling with worries — Dad seemed happy enough to be performing at the regatta, but any performance is stressful, ultimately, and the last thing I wanted was for him to be stressed, given his recent problems . . .

And Jack . . .

No! I shook my head. He was absolutely *fine*. I was not going to start stressing about him.

Outside I could hear Pen saying something sharp to Next-Door Dan and the rumble of his laugh before she hauled Boodle's hairy ass inside and slammed the door to the main house behind her. I grinned, despite myself. Pen had all the middle-sister issues I'd missed out on, and her feisty attitude could be really funny.

The grin was wiped from my face when my annexe door whacked open, yet again, smashing a chunk of plaster from the wall.

A slim vision of keep-fit glamour was framed in the dawn haze.

'Alex!' I shrieked. 'Geez! What the frik?'

'Why aren't you dressed?' hissed Alex. 'We need to go! Now! What's Next-Door Dan doing talking to Pen? Did you hear them? Are you making tea? Go get dressed!'

'Stop, stop!' I said, flapping my hands at her. 'Listen to yourself! Bossing me around like that! How much white tea have you had today?'

'Not much,' said Alex, jittering from one foot to the next. 'That stuff's full of antioxidants. Packed full. Full, full, full. So how about Frey's, huh? You need to help me. We've got to go in the back way, and I've no idea how. Police all over the road at the front. Hopefully they've cleared off from the dam, though, so we can get in there and see –'

'Firstly,' I said firmly, 'we're not going anywhere now. There's no chance we could get up to Frey's and back and still have time to get ready for school.'

'I've brought my bag,' said Alex. 'And there's time if we run. Running is the only option. That way we look like we're exercising.' She bolted up to my bedroom and my running bra, leggings and a manky T-shirt came sailing down the steps. 'Put those on!'

I sighed and shook my head. The thing with Alex is there's no wiggling out with that girl. Once she's decided, she's decided. Better get this over with.

Alex and I stretched our hamstrings outside the front gate. Opposite us were the remains of the Setting Sun Retirement Home, charred and still smoking, though every timber had been doused three times over since it burned down two weeks ago. Between my side of the road and the other was a three-metre bank of waving grasses, at the top of which was a tree stump on which I perched whenever I waited for pick-ups from friends. Which was often because friends did not come to my house; I went to theirs. My house was gnarled and flaky and unravelling at the edges, with help from my chaotic, untidy family. It was embarrassing. Even Blue was starting to drop raisins in places that no vacuum cleaner would ever reach. You'd think with all Dad's number-one hits we'd have money to spend on the place, but apparently not.

On my tree stump this morning was Mr Kadinski. He usually sat in a rocking chair on the veranda of the Setting Sun, but . . .

'Hey,' I said. 'You're more conspicuous out here.'

'Even with the hat?' His usual fedora was pulled low over his silver hair, bright ice-grey eyes sparkling beneath.

'Especially with the hat,' I said, going into another stretch and gesturing to Alex. 'This is my friend –'

'Alex Thompson,' said Mr K, holding out his hand and gripping Alex's in a firm handshake. 'I like your writing.'

'Oh!' said Alex, going all pink and stuttery. 'Th-thanks, Mr Kadinski.'

'We're going for a run,' I said, pulling my arms behind my back. 'Gotta hurry, actually.'

Mr Kadinski nodded. 'Hmm,' he said. 'Frey's Dam is cordoned off, so I'm sure you won't be heading that way.'

I grinned back at him and he winked. 'Oh, boy,' he said. 'Another adventure. Make sure you check your postbox when you get back.'

'Wowzers,' I said, looking over at the rusty box on our front gate. 'Postie's up early.'

'I'm not sure it was him,' replied Mr K. 'Five a.m. is not our postman's style.'

'Nooo,' agreed Alex, raising an eyebrow at me. 'So who's been dropping letters off at dawn?'

I stood up, hands on hips. 'Oh, Alex,' I sighed, shooting a look at my watch. 'Go and get it. Between you and Mr K –'

'I was hoping you wouldn't be able to wait,' said Mr K, a triumphant smile chasing round his lips.

'*Me?* Oh, please.' I turned and looked at our postbox. There was something protruding from the mouth of it, and it flapped insistently in the cool morning breeze.

I laughed at Mr Kadinski. 'You are unbelievable. You saw some person dropping off something at an unlikely hour and you just can't leave it alone. Who was it? What did they look like?'

'Even the secret-service training didn't help me get a good look at him,' he said with a twinkly smile, tipping the fedora right back on his head. 'The mornings are still too misty.'

'Ouch,' I said, watching my friend reach into the postbox, pricking her hands on the thorns of the rambling roses that had totally taken over. 'You okay, Alex?'

'Oh, boy!' she muttered, standing there holding a piece of paper, oblivious to the scratches. 'Oh, Tatty. This is not good.'

The letter wasn't in an envelope. Just half a piece of ruled A4 paper, with holes punched in the side, ready for a lever-arch file. Alex scrambled back up the bank and shoved it a centimetre from my nose. At the bottom, near the tear, someone had scribbled:

ThE BirDS will DiE

A cold chill ran down my back and raised hair all over my body. I looked over at Mr Kadinski waiting.

'How did you know?' I asked. 'How do you always know when something terrible is going to happen?'

Chapter Five

Monday 6 a.m., outside my house examining an anonymous letter

'Though, strangely . . .' I said, scrutinising the death note, 'strangely this doesn't bother me. It doesn't feel like a threat.'

'Oh!' yelped Alex. 'Oh, so *now* we're getting all second sightish, are we? Ha!' She turned to Mr K. 'Let's bag it and take it straight down to the police station.'

'Hmm,' he said, putting on a suede glove and taking the note. 'You're right to be cautious, Alex. Leave it with me.'

With that he wandered a little down the road and disappeared into a thick hedge. Alex was speechless. I did one last pull on my quads and pointed up the hill. 'Trust him. Let's get going.'

Alex stayed speechless all the way to the top of Hill Street, where it peters out into a dirt track that meanders into the woods and then stops. She didn't speak when we headed into the trees, and didn't utter a word even as we ran through Coven's Quarter, a clearing where ancient stone seats sit quietly in dappled sunlight. Two weeks ago this spot nearly got bulldozed, but it was safe now, and I felt a lifting of my heart as we thudded through the dry leaves and pine needles to crest the rise on the other side. I'd have been devastated if Grandma Bird's witchy meeting place had been flattened. There's definitely something about it that's good for the soul – well, mine, anyway.

A few minutes more of puffing and panting up the hill, and that's where we hit a line of red and white tape, cordoning off Frey's Dam. Through the trees we could just make out the glinting water, and with the rustling of leaves in the breeze came the sound of voices and radio transmitters.

'Damn,' said Alex. 'They haven't gone yet. There's no way we're going to be able to get down there. We're going to have to come back tonight.'

'No point,' I replied, trying to get a better look through the trees. 'Jack will be back by this afternoon. *With Jazz.*' I couldn't keep a snarky tone out of my voice when I said her name.

'Aw!' groaned Alex, ducking under the tape and sidling up to a big boulder. 'I *soo* wanted to get him inside info! He would have loved some images of all this!'

I crept up behind her, awed by the sight of every one of Hambledon's police officers thronging the ground below. 'What the hell's going on?' I whispered.

'Dunno,' murmured Alex. 'Who's that down there?'

I crept up behind her to take a look. 'Oh yeah, I see. It's that homeless guy. Grandma Bird used to talk about him a lot. She saw him up here mostly – he doesn't go into town.'

'Parcel Brewster?'

'Yep, that's him. He looks really upset. I bet the police are saying he has to move out of his shack. It's just there on the north ridge somewhere. Do you think it's a crime scene?'

'I have no idea. Geez, Tatty. Maybe someone's died a violent death – held beneath the surface by a jealous husband mad with rage and –' Alex looked at me sharply. 'What? *What?*'

I tried to stop laughing. I was not a rude girl. Usually. 'Alex, you sound like a tabloid hack, not an investigative journalist. *Jealous husband mad with rage.*' I got the giggles again and Alex punched me. 'Sorry! Sorry! Come on, let's get going.'

Alex followed me without argument, but made up for her lack of conversation earlier. Sadly, it was all about me: 'What's with the *Jazz* attitude?' she asked straight away.

I blushed. 'Sorry. That was really childish. I don't know. Turns out your cousin Jack has spent the fortnight with the woman, plus he lives with her! Did you know that?'

'Don't let it bother you. Jack doesn't *like* like her. He respects her commitment to journalism. She's got amazing connections and the most fantastic zoom lens you ever saw.'

'Oooh,' I said. '*Zoom. Lens.*'

Alex threw me a *come on you're bigger than this* look and changed the subject. Kind of. 'So we've been back at school two weeks, you've had your first kiss, refuting all those idiots who thought you were terribly jinxed and would never be kissed . . .'

'Yes,' I said, smiling a little.

'Yes, well, let's just keep it refuted, yeah?'

'Yeah,' I agreed. Wholeheartedly.

'Nothing happens to Jack. *Nothing*. And he has to stay your boyfriend for a while. Okay?'

'Okay,' I said meekly, though I didn't feel very calm as an image of my boyfriend flashed into my head, leaving me breathless, and it wasn't the running that did it: tall, very tall, and very, very handsome with thick floppy hair that was chopped short at the back, but which fell into his beautiful dark eyes; dark brows; general dark broodingness that had my pulse racing at all hours . . .

Alex was saying something about Jazz being very attractive.

'*What?*' I demanded. 'What are you saying? I thought you said Jack didn't *like* like Jazz. What's going on? What's *really* going on? What have you heard?'

My friend huffed impatiently. 'Forget it! It's no big deal! It's just that Tam said she heard from Gianni Caruso – you know, the guy with the fingers –'

'Yes, the guy with the fingers. When is everyone going to forget about that?'

'Um . . .' mused Alex. 'Like, *never*? Would you forget someone skating over someone else's hand and slicing their fingers off? You, Tallulah Bird, the cause of Gianni Caruso in microsurgery for four hours –'

'Okay, okay,' I said. 'Look, there's the track through there. Nearly home. Gianni Caruso said . . .?'

'He said that Jazz and Jack spent a lot of time together in Big Mama's last term –'

'That's before anything happened between me and Jack.'

'Exactly. Like I said –'

'But –'

'But nothing. What you *do* need to know is that Simon Smethy said to Jason and Jess that it was, like, totally weird that no one had seen Jack since you guys were kissing up at Frey's that weekend.'

'Simon Smethy!' I shrieked. 'I'll kill him! I swear I will! He started the jinx rumour for real last time! He's ruined my life once already! I –'

'Calm down!' yelled Alex. 'Just calm down, Tatty. You'll have a coronary or something.'

I took a deep breath. 'I'm calm. Very, very calm.'

'Yeah,' said Alex. I could hear she didn't believe me. 'So the thing is once Jason and Jess were done discussing the weirdness of Jack disappearing –'

'HE HASN'T DISAPPEARED! HE'S IN THE CITY!'

'Caaaalm, caaaaalm,' hissed Alex. 'Otherwise no more information.'

'Caaaalm,' I agreed. 'But if people are talk–'

'Tatty! Don't make me smack you on the head!'

'What? *What?*'

'I will handle this. Don't you worry. Think of me as your micro-manager – putting fires out wherever they appear.'

'Fires? How can you talk about fires? I –'

'Enough! You're sounding like a crazy person.'

'Sorry, Alex. But you know how I feel about Simon Smethy.'

'He blames you for what happened with his hair.'

'That was nothing to do with me! Nothing! He –'

'Forget that. We've got priorities because now school slut and rumour-mongerer-in-chief Jessica Hartley is all interested and curious about you and Jack. We've got to nip that in the bud.'

'How?' I hated how I sounded all needy and helpless.

'Don't know. Leave it with me.'

At last we'd arrived back at my front gate. I bit my lip. 'Alex,' I said. 'This term is not going to be totally about me, yeah?'

'Yeah . . .' said Alex, looking uncertain.

'I'm not the only one with issues. Carrie's got the twins who drive her nuts –'

'Well, sure, but –'

'Tam hasn't had a boyfriend since Year Eight, and . . .' I tilted my head to the side, considering. 'And neither have you. What's up with your love life, Alexandra?'

Alex flushed. 'Funny you should ask . . .'

'I knew it!' I punched the air and continued on down the path to the annexe. 'You don't binge on white tea like that unless there's a boy involved.'

'You know me too well,' mourned Alex.

'Who is he?' I asked, stepping into the dark cool of the annexe.

'Gavin Healey,' announced Alex with no hesitation.

I was surprised. 'Ha! Well! Alex Thompson going for brawn, no brains. Riiight. Plus he's in college. What is he? Nineteen?'

'Oh, Lula, be quiet,' said Alex, but she was grinning and embarrassed.

'Wait!' I hissed. 'Has something happened already?'

'Noo,' denied Alex.

'But something's planned,' I concluded. 'Hey, I thought he was going out with Emily Saunders.'

'She dumped him,' said Alex. They were supposed to go off to Port Albert together on Friday night and she didn't even bother to turn up.'

'Harsh,' I said.

'So now he's mine,' said Alex, happily flopping into my armchair. 'Hey, I'd better get back.'

'No no no,' I said. 'Why the sudden interest in Gavin Healey? How did you even get talking to him?'

'Oh . . .' Alex flapped her hand dismissively. 'I was

researching a piece on Cleo Cosmetics, you know?'

'Oh yeah?' I hustled up my steps to get a bath running, then jumped back down. 'The factory up on Tillerton Way?'

'Factory!' said Alex. 'Don't make it sound so industrial! How amazing is it that we have a cosmetics giant on our doorstep?'

'Not so much,' I said.

'Yes so much!' argued Alex. 'They're set to take on Estée Lauder! Clarins! Clinique!'

'Hardly,' I said.

'That's what you think.' Alex bent to retie her shoelace. 'With Flavia Ames as the new face of Cleo, it's going to take off like nobody's business. She's designed the whole colour palette. Fresh, funky, fantastic.'

'Huh.' I was still unimpressed. 'How does this relate to Gavin?'

'Oh, yeah. Well, when I was there to interview Leonora Sanderson –'

'Ooh.' Now *that* I was impressed by. 'The big boss herself.'

'Exactly! Well, Gavin was just driving up with his granddad.'

'His granddad works there? Doesn't he do something with . . .'

'Hazardous waste disposal,' said Alex. 'Apparently, Flavia didn't like the latest version of Torrid Talons – too red – so they had to get rid of forty tonnes of chemical waste, and Healey's Expert Disposal has the contract.'

'Gavin is in refuse collection,' I said. Pause. 'You met him in his dump truck.' Pause. Grin from Alex, still bouncing up and down. More pausing. 'You seem excited by this . . .'

'Oh, I am,' said Alex, positively glowing. 'Tatty Lula! Sometimes they clean up crime scenes!'

'Ohhh!' The penny dropped. Now I saw the attraction – for Alex . . . not me, obviously. 'That doesn't creep you out? That would totally creep me out. You're mad, Alex. The boy could have' – I dropped my voice several levels and drawled – 'bloooood on hiiis haaaands.'

After a thousand more questions that she refused to answer, Alex whirled out of my place, leaving me with a load of bossy instructions about my own life (obviously hers needed no help from me, ever) and a feeling that I needed to seriously refuel. Across the courtyard from my humble dwelling is the back door to the main house – direct access to the kitchen: yeeha. It was still unlocked so I shoved it open and bounced straight into the heart of the home.

Usually I'm not up so early. Usually no one is up so early, except Blue, and she heads to Mum and Dad's room, never downstairs. Though we'd already been awake, it was safe to assume Pen and I would have gone straight back to sleep like sensible people. So I couldn't blame Dad for nearly having a heart attack when I slammed in with a bright hello. I couldn't blame him for not returning my cheery greeting, but I could blame him for a lot of other stuff.

'Oh,' I said, looking down at a green box he clutched in his hands.

'Good morning again,' he said quickly.

'Oh, Dad. No.'

'It's not what you think.' Dad put the box on the table in front of him and sat down on one of the rickety wooden chairs. Though the table was crowded by a gazillion dirty plates, bowls, glasses, a collection of pebbles in an old biscuit tin and a lipgloss of Pen's that had seen better days, the box was all I could see.

Chapter Six

Just two weeks ago Dad had told Pen and I that he had been going to Alcoholics Anonymous meetings because his drinking had got out of hand. He'd announced that he'd dried out and intended to stay dried out. But here he was looking at his secret supply like it was a lifeline he couldn't do without.

'I was just about to pour it down the sink,' he said, not looking at me.

'Okay.' I took a tentative step towards him. 'Did you need some help with that?'

His face tightened. 'No,' he said shortly. 'I think I should do this alone.'

But he still wouldn't look me in the eye, and I felt a familiar surge of anger simmer inside me. The house was silent around us, maybe just a murmur of Blue talking to Mum somewhere upstairs. The ticking of the clock above the kitchen doorway muffled by a myriad things hanging from the kitchen rafters – a chicken claw included. Weird for most, but for me, with a witchy grandma laid to rest, it was peaceful and familiar and I wanted it to stay that way.

'Give me the box,' I said, and walked over, my arms outstretched.

Dad didn't reply. His big strong frame was hunched at

the table, his fingers tightening on the green cardboard, staring down at it. I saw a tear fall from the shadows of his face, shielded by his thick, unruly brown hair, still all mussed up. It landed on the box, darkening the green to black, then another fell, and another.

My throat tightened so hard it hurt. I bent to hug him round the shoulders, resting my cheek on his head. He didn't smell of alcohol. Not yet. 'I love you, Dad.' His shoulders shook. 'Come on. I'll help you pour it out.'

It seemed like nothing was going to get my father to his feet, but when we heard Blue try a soprano yodel, and Pen began shrieking, '*Oh, for heaven's SAAAAKE!*' he took a shaky breath and pushed himself away from the table.

I grabbed some kitchen roll, ripped off a square and handed it to him. He shuffled to the sink and blew his nose hard, then balled the tissue up and wiped his eyes. He took a shuddering breath.

'Okay, T-Bird.'

'Okay, Dad.'

'This is very Hollywood,' he said, a smile touching his voice. 'Daughter forces derelict alcoholic has-been to quit the devil drink.'

'I'm a hero,' I said drily. 'You want me to open the box?'

'So Hollywood,' he sighed. His hands moved to the lid, then stopped.

'You're embarrassed.'

My father's jaw clenched. 'I guess I am.'

'You should be, Dad. And I'm not going until you've poured every drop of that down the sink.' I reached over and pulled the lid off the box. Dad blinked at the waft of alcohol. 'Start with the vodka, then the beer.'

But he was already lifting the clear bottle of liquid and unscrewing it. He tipped it up and I ran the tap, then reached out and flipped the window over the sink open. When he'd finished with that, I got a plastic bag and put the bottle into it, then the next and the next.

'I'll walk Boodle later tonight,' I said, not looking at him. 'How about I dump these at recycling on the way? I'll take the box and cup too.'

My father handed them over without comment. He looked exhausted, but not broken, like I'd seen him before. He met my eyes and gave me a wobbly grin. 'Thanks, T,' he said.

'I'm proud of you,' I croaked, tearing up, and he grabbed me in one of his suffocating hugs.

'Love you, T-Bird,' he whispered back. 'Go get rid of the evidence.'

Boodle barked from the courtyard outside, and Blue began thundering down the stairs yelling something about where best to wee if you were a fairy with wings that got in the way. I grabbed a banana and went back to the annexe, feeling like I'd been awake a whole day already.

Chapter Seven

Monday morning, on the way to school
Usually I walk to school, but Mum had hit a maternal streak and insisted on dropping Pen and I at the front entrance, even though we begged and pleaded.

I'd been desperate for some head space to think about that note, and why I didn't feel freaked out by it, and I really needed to think about Dad too – walking to school would have been perfect. Now I was all stressed and grumpy.

'Why are you doing this to us, Mum?' asked Pen, when we'd both slumped on the back seat in despair. 'We are being very adult and clear about this situation.'

'Yeah,' I said in a belligerent tone, even though I was trying to stay on Mum's good side. 'This car is louder than Blue's morning yodel, and looks like sh–'

'Tallulah,' said Mum warningly. 'Blue, you okay back there?'

Blue was sitting in a booster seat at the back, keeping far away from Pen, who was in a *delightful* mood after the morning's antics. Blue was wearing her fabulous cloak, which meant she was in a certain frame of mind. Only four-year-olds can get away with fabulous cloaks, but I had a feeling Blue was going to work the look right the way through to forty.

'I'm hungly,' replied Blue. 'Why can't Aunt Phoebe come with today? It's her turn to be bad twoll.'

Aunt Phoebe is actually Great-aunt Phoebe, my grandma's sister. She came to live with us to help look after Blue when Grandma Bird died a year or so ago. She's a very cool and sophisticated lady, but she can do murderous troll like no other.

'Aunt Phoebe is helping the old people move today,' I explained.

'But they moved before this day!' noted Blue.

'Yesterday. Yes, they did,' I said, turning to look at her from the front seat where I wished I wasn't sitting. The whole town could see me up here in the snotmobile. 'But old people take a little while to get organised sometimes.'

'They were ver ver quick moving the first time,' said Blue.

'Yes, *because their house was burning down*!' snapped Pen.

Boyoboyoboy. I pitied Penelope's classmates today. And I didn't think she should be talking so offhandedly about the Setting Sun – the old folks' home – burning down.

'Aunt Phoebe won't take long helping them, Blue,' said Mum, pulling hard on to Beaufort. The car screeched on two wheels, and though we should be used to Mum's crazy driving we still squealed like excessively squealy things.

'Noooooooo! Nyaaaaargh!' We all slammed into the left

side of the car, except Mum who had the steering wheel to hang on to.

She straightened out and revved between gears. 'It's so lucky the house next door was up for rent.'

'Very convenient,' muttered Pen, shuffling back over to her side of the car. 'Except for the neighbours – *i.e. us!* – who have to help the aged up and down the garden steps!'

'That house is bigger than our house.' Blue was solemn, working it all out. 'Lot of space for old people.'

'A lot,' I agreed. 'Almost a twin of the Setting Sun. Not so many chimneys, though.'

'It's *dark* and *gloomy* and *dirty* and *foul*,' said Pen.

'Geez,' I said.

'Then Aunt Phoebe will pobly be helping a long time,' observed Blue.

'Hmm,' said Mum, checking her watch and skidding to a humiliating halt at the school gates. 'I think you may be right, Blue. I hope no one minds you spending the day with me at the office.'

Mum's office is at Hambledon University's library, in the historical sector. She's an expert on local history and has to catalogue weird stuff all the time, like old farmers' diaries and meteorological records and ancient knickers. Okay, so maybe not the ancient knickers, but weird stuff nonetheless.

I got out the car and banged the door shut. The window fell down and I think Mum swore. Even though it was the start of summer, a moving vehicle needs insulation at the best of times.

I opened Blue's door and kissed her sympathetically on the cheek while Mum tried frantically to roll the window up. 'I hope it's not too boring for you,' I whispered.

'I'm going to find stuff to colour in,' she whispered back. Frik.

I hoped Mum was ready for a whole lot of rainbowed artefacts.

'Babe! Here! Over here!' I looked up as the car roared away to see Jessica Hartley waving madly at me. She was at my shoulder in a nanosecond. Uh-oh. 'Why won't you talk to me about your boyfriend? I hear he is soooo hot,' she breathed in my ear. 'How come no one's seen him yet?'

I flinched. This was not going to go well. This required micro-management, of which I knew nothing. Where the hell was Alex?

'Um . . .' I said, blushing furiously.

'Tatty!'

I looked over the road and there were my guardian angels.

Alex's long dark hair hung thick and sleek to the middle of her back. She made even the school uniform look chic with effortless ease. Carrie's hair was a lighter brown, and cut expertly to her shoulders. She was taller than Alex, about my height, and exuded calm at all times. Tam was pale and delicate, with tawny hair that waved from whatever clips and bands she tried to restrain it with. Carrie had her arm firmly gripped, looking left and right for an opening in the traffic. While we were all sure Tam could probably take care of herself, we'd never take the chance – her dreamlike state was too convincing, and we'd never forgive ourselves if she got mowed down by a twelve-wheeler truck while working out backing tracks in her head.

'Guys!' I shrieked with relief, and flung my arms wide. My schoolbag whacked Jessica in the solar plexus and she doubled up. 'Oops! So sorry, Jess! You okay?'

Jessica heaved for breath while Carrie, Tam and Alex dodged a school bus to make it to my side. They grabbed my hands and pulled me through the gates, calling, 'Come on, Jess,' in a polite offhand way as we headed quickly to the school hall for assembly.

'Were you not listening to me this morning?' hissed Alex.

'Tatty, Jess tends to start rumours and –' began Tam.

'Let's get her inside,' said Carrie.

'I know, I know!' I muttered back. 'But Mum dropped us off at the school gates and there was nowhere to run.'

'Don't overreact, guys,' said Carrie. 'Jessica is actually a good person.'

'Yeah,' agreed Alex. 'Good hair, good boobs, good eye for a story. And not just her own story. Jess has ruined more than just her own reputation. For the next few weeks we are all charged with micro-managing this here nincompoop's reputation.'

'Hey!' I said.

'Because she sure as hell can't manage it herself,' finished Alex.

'It's true, Lula,' said Tam, and she gave me a comforting squeeze. 'The jinx rumour caused us all a lot of stress. We don't need any of that again.'

'Well,' said Carrie. 'At least this is a girls-only school. Here, we can cope. Can you imagine if the Hambledon High boys were in with us?'

My friends heaved a collective sigh of relief at this small mercy, and I have to say I shared their sentiments, but I shook my head at them anyway. 'You're a bunch of old women,' I said, and found us four chairs together in the Year Ten section somewhere near the back. 'Let's hear what the head has for us this morning.'

Helen Cluny was sitting right in front of us. Her mum's Chinese, and Helen is tiny too, with black hair in a short pixie cut. Her dad owns Cluny's Crematorium, so she's a good person to know at Halloween, and a good person besides.

Next to her was Matilda McCabe. Matilda I was never quite sure about. She was a little shorter than me, but she made me feel small and fragile next to her solid strength. Everything about her was blocky, even her mouse-brown hairstyle, and she had a no-nonsense personality to go with it. Her dad is Dr McCabe, who I'm always bumping into because he's had to patch up a lot of boys that I nearly kissed.

Let's not go there.

Helen turned round. 'Mr Lang is looking peppy,' she observed. We all nodded. She was right. Our headmaster was up on the stage rocking backwards and forwards on his feet as if he'd just downed a vat of Ribena.

When the hall was full and the second bell rung, Mr Lang cleared his throat. Everyone quietened down.

'Ladies,' he started, 'welcome to our first school assembly. I'm sorry it's taken two weeks to get together. There's been a lot of recent upheaval, which I'll get to in a minute. Right now we've got a few housekeeping points, and some of the staff will help me out here . . .'

He droned on for a while. Teachers trudged up and down the steps to the stage to tell us about clubs and sports for the term and where to sign up. Alex bumped my arm when Mrs Baldacci got up to urge us to try out Dance Club, but I shook my head.

'*Please*, Tatty!' she whispered urgently. 'Don't make me go on my own! Besides, aren't I micro-managing your ass?'

She had a point. And Dance Club was only an hour a week. 'Fine!' I hissed. 'But your micro-management had better work! I want to be normal!'

She nodded sagely in a *leave that with me, darlin'* way, but for some reason I felt a little uneasy. Maybe because Mr Lang was calling Mr van der Merwe up on stage. Mr van der Merwe is our PE teacher. He's a big, hairy and scary Afrikaans man from South Africa, who had been in the Olympic team way back when. He took no nonsense, and drilled the Hambledon Girls' High rowing squad till their hands bled.

How people pronounce his name was always a tedious issue with him: 'Not *van*,' he'd roar. '*Van* like you say *fun*, okay? And not *Merwe* like *merwah*; it's *maaaairvah*, like *hair*, okay? And *vvv* not *w!*' We nodded and did our best, but it wasn't long before he was Mr VDM, and then, predictably, just plain old VD, but not to his face, obviously.

'Ladies,' said Mr Lang, 'I must have your careful attention now. As you all know, state education is always at the mercy of budget cuts and the like. Despite seamless efficiency from the staff here at Hambledon Girls', and the same from teachers over at Hambledon Boys', both schools have had further crippling budget cuts. We have been forced to consider dispensing with some of the classes, clubs and sports that we provide. This would be a terrible blow for the future of the school as more and more of our individuality is whittled away.'

I looked at Carrie. She was frowning. I could see Tam wasn't paying much attention, but Alex had taken a notebook out of her blazer pocket and she'd already jotted down a headline:

Education
We Don't Need No Budget Cuts

Mr Lang was still rocking back and forth on his heels, but he now held his hands importantly behind his back. 'In order to prevent this from happening, we have spent the half-term break and the last two weeks in meetings with our brother school –'

Tam jolted to attention.

'– and have decided that by combining certain classes and activities, we can keep our options open.'

There was a whole lot of excited chatter. Jessica Hartley, at the end of our row, was fanning herself with her hand and going quite pink.

'We will be trialling this for a term only, starting today, and if there is any' – Mr Lang paused – '*any* silliness from you ladies, we will have to reconsider.'

More excited chatter, though slightly subdued.

'I would ask you to remember the good name that this school has and to do everything to uphold it. We are not a co-educational school and never will be. Please continue to learn responsibly.'

There was a smattering of applause from the teachers

standing along the rows of chairs in the hall.

Mr Lang smiled quickly and ended with, 'I need to take a call from Mrs Pantoffel now. I leave you with Mr van der Merwe, who will be explaining rowing-club sessions in light of this announcement.'

'Girls,' Mr VD began. 'This term I had arranged for Boris Weinstührer to row in and coach a number of boats.' He waited. No reaction. He flicked out his hands in frustration. 'Boris Weinstührer! German schoolboy gold medallist!' No reaction. Mr VD sighed and shook his head. 'Well, we nearly lost out, but thanks to the combined forces with the boys' school, Boris is on his way with an exchange programme, and we will share coaching sessions with the boys.'

Now there was response! Jessica Hartley had actually *screamed*.

'Thank goodness you don't row, Lula,' muttered Carrie. 'Water, boats, boys . . .' She shuddered.

I, too, was thankful. 'Why's Jessica so excited?' I asked.

Carrie shrugged, but Tam leaned over. 'She's in the squad!' she whispered.

'Jessica does a *sport*?' I was incredulous. 'No!'

Matilda McCabe turned to give me a hard stare. 'Jess is good,' she said. 'She's seven-man – rows right behind me.'

'Er . . .' said Alex. 'Seven-man?'

Matilda sighed and shook her head at our collective

stupidity. 'Seven follows eight, the leader of the boat, and all the bowside rowers follow seven.'

'Right,' I said, and rolled my eyes at Alex.

Mr VD was still talking: '. . . Don't think you can suddenly sign up for rowing now that there are going to be boys,' he said in his thick, stilted accent. 'No chance. That is not going to happen. If there is a space in the boat, I will recruit.'

Jessica Hartley looked even more pleased. From what I'd heard of Hambledon Girls' rowing squad she must be the only one under ninety kilos in the crew, so things were looking very bright on her getting-lucky horizon.

'Other combined classes will be art' – my stomach lurched – 'and Latin.' Carrie looked stricken. 'Also the languages: French, Spanish, German, Italian.'

There was more excited chatter and Mr VD looked displeased. 'Quiet! Quiet down! Time for classes, please.'

The whole school filed out amid much noise and racket. Matilda was moaning heatedly to Helen.

'What's wrong, Tilly?' asked Tam.

'I don't want to be bussing around with boys for our training sessions,' complained Matilda. 'We're the best squad on the water this year, thanks to VD, and if there are a load of louts around, Jessica is going to be totally distracted.'

Helen nodded. There was no disputing that Matilda was right.

'Maybe the rowing boys will be fugly,' I suggested, over their shoulders.

Matilda turned and frowned at me. 'The Hambledon boys are fit.' I gulped and nodded, but she wasn't finished. 'Fit and smelly and disgusting. We're going to be seeing a lot of phlegm and smelling a lot of bad odours.'

Sheesh. Let's hope the same wasn't true of their artists.

Chapter Eight

Monday afternoon, in the schoolyard

The sun had finally come out and after a massive school dinner the four of us were sitting in the sun, sleeves rolled up for maximum UV exposure, faces tilted skywards. 'That chocolate sponge was so good,' I commented.

'How you fitted three helpings into that little belly of yours is a mystery,' said Carrie. She rolled her socks down. 'But it's a good sign that you got chocolate in some form at school. Could be your terrible luck has changed forever, Lula.'

'Could be,' said Tam, and rolled her socks down too. 'Now all you need is Jack to be a real boyfriend instead of just a one-night stand.'

'Be quiet,' I moaned. 'All anyone at this school wants to talk about is my boyfriend.'

We all grinned. The girls knew how pleased I was with myself to have a boyfriend. I elbowed Alex. 'Tell us about Gavin.'

'Gavin who?' asked Carrie.

I glanced at Alex, startled. 'No way! You haven't told them?'

'Haven't told us what?' asked Tam, starting to look hurt.

Alex looked flustered. 'I've been waiting for the right moment,' she said.

'Do you mean Gavin Healey?' asked Tam. 'Tasty. How'd you sneak that little relationship under our radar?'

She raised an eyebrow at Alex and Alex blushed.

'I've never seen you so red,' I said wonderingly.

'Oh, shut up,' said Alex. 'He does crime-scene clean-ups. His work is fascinating.'

'Gavin Healey,' said Carrie, 'is not fascinating. All brawn, zero brain. What were you thinking? Dump him.'

Alex yelped in outrage.

'Carrie!' I said, astonished. 'This is not like you!'

Carrie sighed heavily. 'Sorry,' she said. 'Probably it's just his granddad I don't like. He came round once to take away our asbestos garage roof, and he gave me the creeps. He's not a nice man.'

'Gavin is not the same as his granddad,' asserted Alex. 'Trust me. Gavin is . . .' She trailed off.

'Huh,' said Tam, looking at our friend closely. 'I bet your mum doesn't like him. I bet that's it.'

Alex went red again and climbed to her feet. 'Come on, you passion-killers. Time to get some lessons with the boys,' and she laughed in an evil throaty way.

'Oh, frik,' I said. 'Mr Lang is going to rue the day . . .'

*

Art was the last lesson of the day, and my favourite, though I don't know why. I'm useless at it. You've got to walk over the road to the art centre, because the school ran out of space a few years ago. It's actually an old house with lots of the rooms all knocked together to make big, airy studio spaces. There are three storeys with verandas all round, each divided into different departments: painting, graphics, textiles, ceramics, sculpture. Very, very cool. My subject is painting, which I regret because I'm not very good. Mr Tufton says I've got hands like bunches of bananas and he can't help coming over every so often to fix stuff and show me why what I've done is so terrible.

Mr Tufton is small, with monk-like hair – all baldy in the middle – and a full-on beard and moustache. For such a little guy, he's seriously loud, and every so often he does something totally mad, like eating flying ants out of the air when they swarm on rainy afternoons.

There are only three of us in my painting class. The other art girls do fun groovy stuff with dyes and clay and inks. *Why oh why did I choose painting? Hopefully the boys are all doing graphics.*

I got to the studio and Mr Tufton was sitting disconsolately at a painting table.

'Hi, Mr Tufton!'

'Oh, God, it's you.'

I sighed and dumped my bag at an easel. The thing

with Mr Tufton is he means what he says.

A shadow appeared at the door. 'Hi, Mr Tufton!'

'Hi, Delilah. How'd you get on with the still-life?'

Delilah Goldsmith smiled happily and pulled out a brilliant watercolour sketch of a pile of marbles.

Mr Tufton kissed the tips of his fingers and flung them wide. 'This!' he proclaimed. 'This is why I teach!' Delilah glowed and chose the easel next to me. Why does she do that? I'm convinced it's so her stuff looks even more fabulous than it already is. Next to me, anyone would look like Michel-frikking-angelo.

Then in came Grace Mutsapho. She's from Kenya, and totally stunning. She glides everywhere and transfixes people with her intense stare. She is so good at art it's scary.

'Grace!' cried Mr Tufton. 'What have you got?'

Grace slipped her bag to the floor and produced a sketchbook. She ruffled the pages, then found what she was looking for. She pointed with a long, elegant finger.

Mr Tufton sighed dramatically. 'Fabulous, Grace. You're an inspiration.' He turned abruptly, stalked over to the table where he'd been sitting earlier and threw himself down, stretching back with his hands clasped behind his head.

We stood at our easels expectantly. He said nothing.

'You two,' he said at last, gesturing to Grace and Delilah, 'have inspired me. We've been asked to enter several pieces for an exhibition at the Port Albert Regatta. People will see our work! What an opportunity!'

We all stared at him, waiting. He lay there frozen for a while, then, 'I must think,' he announced. After another beat he shouted, 'Do what you like!' And promptly fell asleep.

Grace and Delilah were unfazed. They got out some paper, clipped it to their easels and were soon scratching away. I hunted for a chair to sit on while I decided what to do. But I was feeling even more uninspired than usual. Tufty had reminded me about the regatta. I'd forgotten to ask Dad whether he'd be nervous about singing there. If he were nervous, would the pressure of this show push him off the wagon? What if he felt he just had to have a drink? And another and another . . . No. I gave myself a mental headshake. My father had come a long way, and I had to give him the benefit of the doubt.

At least there was no doubt that I would not be having an embarrassing painting in the exhibition. Tufty would save all wall space for Grace and Delilah. And the next good news for the day . . . *Looked like there were no boys for painting class!* Fantastic.

So. Back to painting. What was I doing again? Oh, yeah. Coming up with ideas. Exasperated, I flung my arms up into a big stretch, but rapped my knuckles on a shelf. A blocked canvas dropped off it and landed on my foot.

This is the kind of stuff that happens to me. Good thing they're not heavy. I picked it up and saw it was blank.

'Hmm,' I said. Grace and Delilah were absorbed in their work. I tiptoed over to the art-supply drawers and pulled out a load of oil paints. Not being sneaky, you understand, just didn't want to wake our inspired yet exhausted teacher.

Delilah peeked round her easel. 'Tatty! What are you doing? He'll go nuts!'

'I've always wanted to try oils,' I whispered back. 'Now's my chance!'

'Tufty says no oils till you can do the acrylics! And you're the worst of us all!' Delilah was looking stressed.

'I hate acrylics. Tufty'll never know,' I said.

'I have nothing to do with this!' hissed Delilah. 'Nothing at all!'

'Oh, Delilah,' drawled Grace. 'Tallulah is an oil painter. Can't you see? Her poor soul has been starved with all the acrylics.'

'Yeah,' I said. '*Starved.*' And squeezed out a load of blue paint. 'So beautiful,' I murmured to myself. I'd just found the perfect brush and dipped it in when the door slammed open.

'Sorry!' came a familiar voice from outside. 'Is this the painting studio?'

Mr Tufton jolted awake. 'Quiet!' he yelled, and shifted around before falling fast asleep again.

I hurried to the door. 'Don't tell me you do painting!' I said quietly.

'Watch that brush,' replied Arnold Trenchard. 'Oil is a devil to get out.'

I looked at my friend in consternation. 'You do painting?'

His hazel eyes sparkled, and I sensed the other girls in the studio appraising his tall lean physique as he slouched in the doorway.

'Well?' I demanded.

'I do.'

'Frik!'

'Nice, Tatty Lula.' Arns ran a hand through his tufty auburn hair and raised a dark eyebrow at me. 'Thanks for the welcome. What's with the grumpy teacher?'

'Dunno. You coming in?'

And so it ended up being the best art lesson ever. Arns and me muttering away to each other, stifling giggles, while I swathed blissfully with the oil paint.

'Hey,' I said at one point. 'What's going on at Frey's? You should know, seeing as how your mama is Sergeant Trenchard, best police officer this hamlet has ever seen.'

Arnold shrugged. 'I've already told Alex everything I know. That homeless guy cornered some dog-walker, scared the bejeezus out of them, and demanded they get the police up there. He had something he wanted to say.'

'Ooh,' I said. 'No wonder Alex is interested.'

'Alex is interested because she wants to show her big cousin Jaaack' – he drawled my boyfriend's name and dropped me a sultry wink; I blushed – 'that she's just as hot at being a journo as he is.'

I grinned in reply. Arns was right. He had that uncanny way of knowing people without even knowing them at all, if you know what I mean. Maybe something he got from his mum.

'But there's another reason the police were up there,' continued Arns.

'Yeah?' I mixed more white into the blue and pasted it over what I'd done. Not bad.

'Yeah. Apparently, someone's gone missing. A girl. You must know? Since Friday night.'

'No!' Delilah's voice right at my shoulder made me jump. Her eyes were wide as she stared at Arns. 'Who? How come this whole village doesn't know about it?'

'Her parents thought she was away for the weekend, apparently, with a girlfriend. But she didn't turn up for breakfast this morning, so they rang the friend and she said no, Emily had planned to go to Port Albert with Gavin Healey, that she was just the cover.'

I heard Grace move out from behind her easel. We all looked at each other across the studio. 'Seriously?' said Grace. 'You're not having us on?'

'Gavin Healey,' breathed Delilah. 'Do you think he's done something terrible to her?'

'No,' I said sharply, feeling as if I'd never be able to take a full breath again. My heart was hammering and my hands felt cold and clammy. 'I'm sure he's not like that.'

'Who is he?' asked Grace.

I told them what I knew, without any mention of Alex. I'm sure I didn't make much sense because all I could think was that Alex needed to know this – now! – but what would she do when she found out, if she didn't know already? What kind of person *was* Gavin Healey? A murderer? Rapist? Abductor? No . . .! I trailed to a finish, my mind a total jumble.

Arns looked at me intently. 'I'm sure an announcement will be made in school tomorrow,' he said. 'For people to come forward with information.'

We were quiet for a long time, everyone getting on with what they were doing. It was a lot to take in, someone going missing. Especially in a tiny town like Hambledon.

In the distance, we heard the final school bell go, and Grace moved round to our easels with casual ease.

'I knew it,' she said, looking at my canvas. 'You better put that away to dry, and clean your brushes. A good artist knows when to stop.'

'Hn,' I said, and stepped back from the easel. She was right. The painting was finished. 'Cheers, Grace.'

'See you tomorrow,' she said, and she and Delilah headed out.

'What are you doing now, Lula?' asked Arns.

'Going to see Jack at the editing suite. He's back from the city.' I couldn't help it. A huge grin flooded my face and I could feel my eyes doing something all sparkly. Arnold winked at me and I blushed. Again. 'He should be finished the Coven's Quarter follow-up. And about ready to load it on to the ftp site for Channel 4,' I added hurriedly.

'You're going to watch it now?'

'No, silly, with all you lot at his digs later. Remember? Pizza, prime-time viewing?'

'Yeah, yeah. Just checking.'

'You going to get Mona?'

Arns smiled happily. 'I am.'

'You guys are cute,' I said, grinning back at him.

'We are,' he said. 'Thanks to you.'

'Yes,' I said proudly. 'I am truly amazing.' I considered him for a moment. 'So . . . lucky you doing art and Latin with us girls . . . next you'll be rowing.' We slung our bags over our shoulders and walked out into bright sunshine, leaving Tufty snoring gently behind us.

Arns shrugged. 'Yeah . . .' he said, and held the gate for me. 'About that . . .'

I laughed. Even though Arnold was not the spindly

misfit we'd thought him to be, I could *not* see him hauling oars with seven muscle-bound smelly phlegmsters.

After a bit of friendly pushing and shoving that actually saw me fall down two steps – mortification! – Arns moseyed off to find Mona at the PSG dorm buildings and I tried to call Alex. No reply. Frik. I texted her:

Have you heard about Gavin + Emily Saunders? Call me!

Then I took a deep breath and headed for the journalism department on the Hambledon University campus . . . with a thudding heart and jelly knees that I'm ashamed to say had nothing to do with Gavin Healey and everything to do with Jack de Souza.

The university campus is quite separate from the rest of town, so it was odd to be in school uniform trudging its trendy streets. I felt a little out of place, even though I'd been coming here to see Mum all my born days. Maybe because I'd never got to know a student before, and now that I did, now that the most gorgeous of them all was my boyfriend, *now* I felt weird about being a schoolgirl when I came up here.

Shaking the feeling off, I pushed through the glass double doors of the journalism department and looked around. It wasn't busy and no one looked at me strangely. And when

I asked a guy where the film-editing suite was, and he told me where to go without batting an eyelid, I wondered why I'd felt uncomfortable. There was a big red light on outside the door, but I pushed it open anyway and stepped into the darkness. Two figures sitting in front of a bank of TV and computer screens, with panels of buttons and keyboards at their fingertips, turned round.

I recognised Jack's profile straight away and my stomach lurched in a way that left my insides all shaky.

'Hey, gorgeous,' he said quietly. 'Perfect timing. It's just loading now.'

'Cool,' I said. I looked around and found a chair near the door. 'I'll just wait here.'

'Could be a long wait.' The voice next to Jack was harsh and abrupt. I remembered it straight away. Jazz. She swung round in her seat to stare at me. 'This site is a little busy just now. It's slowed right up.'

'No rush,' I said, and leaned forward, my hand outstretched. 'I'm Tatty.'

'Yes,' she said. And though I couldn't see her eyes looking me up and down in the dark shadows of the suite, I knew her meaning. Jack was head down, tapping away at a keyboard. 'Thing is,' said Jazz, 'maybe it's better if you wait outside. Could be a little boring in here with us journos.'

A surge of anger crashed through me. 'Thing is,' I said, echoing Jazz's tone, 'I don't find Jack boring at all.'

Even in the gloom I could see Jazz stiffen with surprise. Good. She thought just because she had a couple of years on me that she was a couple of years smarter? Yeah, right. Bring it on, sister.

I looked over to Jack, expecting him to laugh with me, or say something to put Jazz in her place, but he was still tapping away. He clearly hadn't heard our exchange at all. I felt a prickle of unease nudge at me, but I batted it away. Even though Jazz was tiny and beautiful and looked a little like Keira Knightly, I was the one Jack had kissed in the moonlight. It was me he wanted to be with, not Jazz.

Right?

Chapter Nine

Alone with Jack at last

'I can't believe I've just filed my second national news story in the space of a month,' said Jack, pulling me close as he waved goodbye to Jazz, zooming off campus in her black Golf GTI.

'You're pretty amazing,' I replied, punching him lightly on the arm.

He grinned, shoving his hair behind his ear, still looking at the disappearing GTI.

'You sure you didn't want to take that lift with Jazz back to your place?' I glanced at Jack uncertainly. He was wearing a charcoal-coloured T-shirt that fitted closely, very old and faded jeans that hugged him in all the right places and when he looked down at me, and smiled, my heart jumped so hard I nearly stopped breathing. He has the most kissable lips in the world, and the most intense chocolate-brown eyes. I'd like his long black eyelashes for myself, but not his nose, which is a little craggy and just perfect for him.

He turned into me, his arms linked loosely at my lower back. 'A lift with Jazz? Now why would I do that?'

'It's pretty uncool to be seen walking around with a schoolgirl, right?'

Jack took me by the hand and we started walking to North Road. 'Oh no you don't, Tallulah Bird. We're not going anywhere *near* that issue.'

'What issue?'

'You know, that I'm a student; you're a schoolgirl. I just want sex, drugs and loud parties; you need to do homework and turn the lights out at nine. No way.'

'Well . . .' I slowed down and glanced at his face. 'Is any of that true?'

'Yes!' he proclaimed. 'But not all of it. And, anyway, who cares? I like you and . . . you like me, right?'

I grinned. 'Right.'

'I just feel a little disorientated,' admitted Jack. 'I've been stuck in the city forever, then in that stuffy building all of today and it just feels strange being in the real world again.'

'I bet,' I said.

'Like,' said Jack, 'did Jazz really just say, "*Jack*, do you want a lift back?"?'

'She did,' I said.

'She's going to be so embarrassed when she realises how rude that was, you know, not saying "Jack and Tallulah".'

'Sure,' I said. 'Maybe she just forgot my name.'

I regretted adding that, because Jack said, 'That's it. Yeah. I didn't introduce you two properly, did I? I guess she's just feeling a bit out of it too.'

'Hn.' What I really wanted him to say was: 'That Jazz is

a despicable specimen of humankind! So repulsive! So vile! I never want to set eyes on her or her fantastic zoom lens ever again!'

Yep. I had a feeling that wasn't going to happen any time soon. But I wasn't complaining because instead Jack took my hand and locked his liquefying eyes on mine.

Then he paused, and his gaze dropped from my eyes to my mouth. He took a step towards me. 'You're so beautiful,' he said, his voice quiet, and I would definitely have laughed out loud at this, but his lips were already brushing against mine, his arms pulling me close. I could feel his heart pounding beneath my hand as the kiss deepened, and my insides melted.

Oh. Wow.

When we got to Jack's place, Jazz's GTI was under cover at the side of the house. We squeezed past it to get to the back door just under the canopy.

'You don't go in the front?' I asked.

'Forest lost the key before we even moved in,' said Jack.

'Forest?'

'My housemate. Big guy.'

If Jack was calling someone big, he must be huge, and *huge* just about sums up Forest Johnson. But not in a fat way. Oh no. All six foot five of his muscled frame was gracefully reclined on a saggy sofa in front of the telly.

'Susie,' he said as Jack walked over to him. They did a complicated handshake. Forest grinned, his teeth white against his ebony skin. His voice was low and rumbly with a lilt of West African French maybe. 'I been watching this telly, but nothing. Where you at?'

'Dude,' said Jack, turning back towards me and the kitchen that opened into the living area. 'It's only on at seven, like I said.'

Forest heaved a deep disappointed sigh. 'Right. I'll stop watching, then. This is so depressing. Just a loop playing over and over about some missing schoolgirl.' His eyes lit upon me. 'Hey, did you know her?'

'Do,' I said. 'I do know her.' I said to Jack over my shoulder, 'I can't believe I forgot to say to you – a girl from Year Twelve has gone missing. Emily Saunders. Did you hear about that?'

'Geez!' said Jack, frozen in the act of taking out juice from the fridge. 'Seriously? What do you know?'

I told the two of them the sketchy details, omitting the info that Alex was dating the guy who was supposed to be away on the weekend with Emily. That was for her to say. I checked my phone – still no reply from Alex – and tried to push it all to the back of my mind, telling myself that Emily was fine. She was an oddball. She probably gave Gavin the boot and took off for some remote me-time. I wouldn't be surprised. But I kept that to myself too. Jack was pensive, but Forest seemed to shrug it all off. He said, 'Good thing the coppers around here are halfway decent, eh, Susie? She'll be okay. They'll sort it,' and he unfolded himself from the saggy sofa. When he came to stand next to me in the kitchen, he dwarfed everyone in the room. 'You must be Tallulah,' he said to me. I nodded and shook hands. He grinned, then asked Jack: 'You bring drinks?'

'I knew there was something I forgot,' replied Jack. 'Arns is bringing the pizzas with Mona, isn't he? I should have asked him to bring drinks too.'

I brightened, and dived into my schoolbag. 'Actually,' I said, 'I brought two cartons of juice. It's my favourite –'

A light tinkly laugh came from the living-room side of the kitchen counter. I looked up to see Jazz standing with her hand over her mouth, like she was trying to hide her embarrassment for me, holding up a bottle of champagne. She had changed from her skinny jeans and tiny T-shirt into a plunging halter-neck. And when I walked over I saw that her denim skirt was very, very mini. The worst was that she looked sensational. Her long black hair cascaded down her back and her eyes were beautifully made up. Frikly frokly frak.

'I think the boys will be more interested in the Veuve Clicquot,' she said to me.

'Not likely,' said Jack. He took the pomegranate juice

69

from me and unscrewed the lid straight away. 'I want to be fully compos mentis tonight,' he said. 'Save that for later, Jazz.' He opened a cupboard, pulled out some glasses and began pouring juice.

'Sure, Jack,' crooned Jazz. '*Later*.'

It was a serious act of will for me not to narrow my eyes and pull my lips back in a tiger snarl, but Forest must have seen something in my face.

'I hear you're a special lady,' he said to me.

'Er . . .' I replied.

'Jack tells me your grandma was a witch.'

'Yes,' I said, and Jazz snorted quietly. She'd put the champagne bottle down and was staring at me in a scary psycho way with her arms crossed.

'My mama's got some voodoo,' noted Forest.

'Whoa,' I said. 'Guess you were a well-behaved kid.'

He boomed with laughter. 'You got some witchiness from your grandma?'

'No,' I said, 'definitely no.'

Forest laughed again. 'That's what you think, missy. Got to have some magic to pull this guy here.' He slapped Jack on the back, and Jazz's face turned to thunder.

Jack's grin faded when he caught sight of her expression. 'Oh, Jazz! I'm sorry – you want some juice too?' he asked, handing us our glasses.

'No thank you, darling. I'm saving myself for the

bubbly, *later*,' replied Jazz, the thunderous face fading to a flirty twinkle.

Jack's mobile rang and he pulled it out of his back pocket. 'Excuse me,' he said, and stepped out of the back door.

I noticed that Forest and Jazz were staring at each other. And not in a good way.

'Careful, Jazz,' said Forest.

'Oh, I'm being *very* careful,' she whispered. '*You,*' she shot me a look, 'you're the one who needs to watch out. Wouldn't want your headmaster hearing how you've been drinking with students.'

I was struck dumb.

How unbliddybelievable was this woman?

Forest took a step towards Jazz. He was so close to her that she had to tip her head right back, which she clearly didn't like. Her hands went to her hips, and she leaned away. 'You mess with the witch girl, and you mess with the voodoo man,' he rumbled. 'Jack might be blind to your games, but the rest of us know what you're all about.'

My jaw had dropped now, for sure.

'Oh, I doubt that,' breathed Jazz. 'You think you can intimidate me? A brainless pile of brawn and a pathetic schoolgirl?' She strode over to the telly and pointed a finger at an armchair just as saggy as the sofa. 'See that chair, *Tatty* Bird? That's Jack's. The chair next to it is mine. That's my place, next to Jack, and that's the way it's going to stay.'

I raised my eyebrows. Could this girl *hear* herself? Sheesh.

Forest laughed and clapped me on the shoulder. 'You should know I'm not brainless,' he said, smiling at me. 'Just a little forgetful.'

Suddenly Jack yelled from outside: 'AAAAAARGH!'

It sounded like he'd been run over twice by that hulking GTI.

'JACK?' I shrieked, bounding outside. '*Are you okay?*'

Please let the jinx not have come back!

Yes! He was upright.

Yes! He had all his limbs – fingers, toes, everything.

I bounced up to him and gripped his biceps, staring into his face. 'What happened? Is everything all right?'

He smiled at me as Forest loomed in the doorway behind us.

'Man,' he said to Jack, coming over to clap him on the shoulder. 'Your girlfriend worries about you.'

Jack kissed me on the forehead, grinning from ear to ear. 'I gave you a fright?' he asked, and shoved his phone back in his pocket. 'Sorry, Lula, but guess what! Another story!'

'Oh,' I said, burying my freakish fears with a relieved sigh. 'Emily Saunders? Still not found?'

'Whoa!' laughed Jack. 'You do have second sight!'

Jazz tinkled a derisive laugh from the doorway as Forest nudged past to go back inside. 'Oh, hardly,' she smirked, her voice all sweetness and light. 'I've just had a call about this from my contact at the police station. No need for Talluley's guessing games. I'm on it, babe,' she lilted.

Jack chuckled uncertainly at her tone, but glancing down at me his smile widened. 'Well, Jazz,' he said, and pulled me close. 'Lula's the best Hambledon High contact to have. If anyone's going to find out anything about Emily Saunders, it's going to be Lula.'

He pulled me into a warm hug, and while I didn't want the moment to end I just had to murmur, 'Alex is probably your best informer, and I'm not sure I like being called Talluley.'

'Mm,' said Jack, dropping a kiss on my temple that raised goosebumps over my entire body. 'Not great, but Jazz is cool when you get to know her. I wouldn't want the girls in my life not getting on.'

I didn't reply, mainly because I was concentrating on not falling over in a dead faint as Jack's lips moved to mine, but just as my eyes closed I caught sight of Jazz watching us with narrowed eyes, and my goosebumps just got bumpier.

Chapter Ten

Monday night, Channel 4 breaking news

The theme tune for Channel 4 News was already going full blast when Bingley Clarendon's bright red pizza van pulled up in the drive with a screech and the parping of a horn.

The passenger door slammed open and Mona jumped out and sprinted for the back door. She burst in. 'Is it on? Is it on?'

'Where are the pizzas?' asked Jack. I was pleased he had his priorities straight.

'Hey, babe,' said Jazz, lazily getting up from her chair right next to Jack's. She bent forward and enveloped Mona in a *you're practically my sister* hug, and reclaimed her chair.

'Pizza coming!' said Mona. 'Have I missed it? Arns and Bingley took so long to come get me!'

Jon Snow was saying something about another outbreak of bird flu and wearing a tie that would work well with Blue's fabulous cloak. The telly fuzzed for a second, melting the tie, but came back in focus when Forest clapped it expertly on the top right-hand corner.

'Bingley was allowed to sign you out from the dorms?' I asked.

'Long story,' said Mona, 'but I'm here now.' She threw

herself down in Jack's chair and stared at the telly intently. 'Those poor geese,' she said.

'Mona!' said Arns from the doorway. He could barely see over the top of a pile of pizza boxes.

I laughed and went to take a bunch from him, reading out the toppings as I went. Jack was crashing around in the kitchen sorting out knives, forks and plates, and Forest was getting in everyone's way looking for glasses. They were joking around, but I could see Jack had one eye on the telly the whole time.

'Is it on yet?' asked Arns.

Jack checked his watch. 'Eight minutes. Bathroom break – door doesn't lock, don't come crashing in.' He jogged out the room.

'I can't stay much longer after that,' said Arns. 'Got to get back to work with Bing.'

'No!' said me and Mona together.

Bingley Clarendon hove into view behind Arns. 'Who wants the bill?' he called.

'I got it,' I said, and pulled out the money from my little zip purse. Mum and Dad were treating us all – they were seriously impressed by Jack's piece, and insisted on paying for a viewing party. And who am I to disobey my parents?

'Oh, how sweet,' said Jazz, rising slowly from her chair again and coming over. 'Talluley's spending all her pocket money in one go.'

Bingley Clarendon glanced at Jazz. And couldn't look away. 'Oh,' he breathed.

'This is Jazz,' I said, mustering some manners. 'Jazz, this is Bingley.'

'Bingley,' she said distinctly. 'Well, Bingley, I hope you make good pizza.' She pulled out a marguerita, claimed a serviette and got straight back to her chair.

Bingley swallowed. 'I do,' he said at last. 'I make excellent pizza. He shot a look at Arns. 'But we're done for tonight, aren't we, Arns?'

'Whoohoo!' yelled Arns with a delighted grin at Mona.

'We're gonna stay for the celebration,' continued Bingley, gaping at Jazz. He hefted a barstool out of the kitchen and shoved it right up to Jazz's armchair. 'The *whole* celebration,' he declared.

'Great,' said Jazz, taking careful bites of her pizza and dabbing at her cupid-bow lips after each one. 'Just great.'

'Bingley, you're the best,' said Mona, all happy and shiny. 'Come sit here with me, Arns!'

Arnold loped over with an enormous box and squished into Jack's armchair with Mona.

Jazz pinched her lips in discontent at Jack's chair being taken, but made a big effort to smile nicely at Mona anyway.

I was about to claim the saggy sofa with Forest when a familiar roar and loud hooting interrupted Jon

Snow's wrap-up of the bird-flu crisis.

'Nooo,' I moaned.

I heard car doors slam and the piping of an excited child.

In came Mum, Pen and Blue.

'We thought you needed pudding,' cried Mum, wielding Ben&Jerry's Phish Food.

'Anne!' Jack looked really pleased to see Mum. 'You're going to stay? It's on in three minutes.'

'Oh.' Mum looked at her watch. 'We really need to get back for Blue's bathtime. I've Sky-Plussed it at home.'

'I don'wannoo bath,' said Blue. 'I'm ver ver clean.' She held out her hands, covered all over with bright felt-tip marks.

'I –' started Mum, but she was interrupted by another screech of tyres outside.

'Someone's driving recklessly,' said Pen.

We all craned our necks to see out of the living-room window. The claw marks across the bonnet of the car outside left me in no doubt. 'Bludgeon's here,' I announced.

'You. You know someone called Bludgeon,' remarked Jazz, like it was the final nail in the coffin of how ridiculous I was.

I didn't answer. I was too busy staring out of the window, incredulous: rammed into Bludgeon's car was his brother and Pen's boyfriend, Fat Angus, then Alex and Carrie and Tam and Mr Kadinski. How had they all ended up together? And how *on earth* did they all fit into that clapped-out death trap?

'Mr K made it!' I cried. 'I thought he'd be stuck with the wrinklies over the road!'

'Lula,' reprimanded Mum. 'Have respect for the elderly, please. Come on, Pen, Blue, time to go.'

'Stay,' said Jack. 'Please.'

'Please, Mum,' asked Pen deferentially. She'd seen Fat Angus and gone all glowing.

Mum looked at me. 'You don't mind?'

'Course not,' said Jack. 'Sit next to Lula on the sofa. Pen, you squish in there too and make space for Fat Angus. Forest, chairs, man. We need more chairs.' He grabbed the remote for the DVD player and pressed record, turning the volume up slightly too.

Forest disappeared and came back with a bunch of wooden dining chairs, a little swivel stool and a massive desk chair that looked dangerously twirly.

Jazz didn't move a muscle. She was draped back in her seat, chin up, gazing at the telly through half-closed eyes, with Bingley gazing at her, eyes wide open.

'Ugh, fat person,' she murmured as a news reporter came on screen. 'Stick with radio, woman.'

I looked to the telly, and saw a perfectly gorgeous reporter talking about budget cuts at local schools. Sheesh. Jazz had body-image issues, clearly.

Forest set out the collection of chairs as Bludgeon's carload flooded in, talking and joking and helping themselves to pizza.

'Alex,' I hissed. 'Did you get my text?'

'Later,' she said, out of the corner of her mouth.

Someone put the ice cream in the freezer and I got up to pour more drinks. Jazz ignored everyone except Jack, passing the occasional witticism to him as he walked by, and he'd chuckle back, still keeping an eye on the telly.

'And after the break,' announced Jon Snow, 'we have the news where you are. In the south *more* breaking news from the historic town of Hambledon – who would have thought? – and up north . . .'

Forest flung himself back in the desk chair and it scooted a metre or so across the living-room carpet. Blue giggled. Forest opened his arms, and Mum gaped as Blue climbed up to sit with him in the chair. 'Well, I never,' she muttered, settling herself into the sofa.

'Lula, move your lardy ass,' said Pen clearly. 'There's absolutely no room for me to breathe and Angus still needs to sit here next to me.'

Jazz laughed softly.

Pen's eyes darted from her to me to Jack. 'Oh boy,' she said, and whispered in my ear, 'The path of true love never did run smooth.'

'Tell me about it,' I murmured in reply, watching as Jack

tried to sit on the little swivel stool without falling off. He looked across at me and winked, shrugging his shoulders with a wry smile.

Somehow Fat Angus got on the couch, and Bludgeon too, so I peeled myself out to sit on the floor, and cunningly scooched over next to Jack. He got off the stool straight away and we sat together on the floor, fingers linked, looking up at the telly. Alex braved the stool and Carrie, Tam and Mr K perched on the dining chairs behind. Sixteen people all rammed into the living area, but it was completely silent as Jack's segment came on.

It was brilliant.

So, okay, I'm biased, but I've not seen a news item that packed so much atmosphere, tension and story into one punch, and it was beautifully done. The final frame had Jack looking seriously into the camera and I wondered if every girl's heart thundered as mine did.

'This is Jack de Souza, reporting from the town of Hambledon for Channel 4 News.'

I squeezed his hand hard, and kissed him on the lips, even though Mum was right there. 'Wow,' I said to him.

His face lit up. 'It was okay?' he asked.

Jazz got out of her chair and said, 'It was good, Jack. We make a great team.' She came over and smiled down at him, a lazy, sexy smile that smouldered from ear to ear.

Jack grinned happily back at her and said, 'Hopefully

that's not the end of it.' He jumped to his feet, pulling me with him. 'I can get stuck in to a piece on Emily Saunders tomorrow,' he said, and hugged me close. 'I spoke with the producer earlier.' I caught Alex's eye over Jack's shoulder and she raised her eyebrows and flicked a look over at Jazz. Carrie and Tam had the same expression on their faces.

Jack and I pulled apart and Jazz went in for a hug of her own. She rubbed his back in long, slow movements.

I moved away to step into a circle with my friends, who were all watching Jazz in horror. 'Have you *ever*?' I asked. 'Let's hope this isn't going anywhere ugly.'

'Could be the micro-management needs to move into macro-management,' said Alex.

'Could be,' agreed Tam.

'Thank goodness we're here this time,' said Carrie, 'instead of stuck in London. He has no idea, does he, Tatty?'

'No idea at all,' I murmured. 'And the worst is — they *live* together!'

'No!' said Tam.

'I want to see her room,' said Alex with grim determination. 'We'll need all the intel we can get.'

'She's a dangerous woman and she must be stopped,' said Tam.

A dark shadow loomed over us.

'Eek!' said Carrie.

'Who you calling "freak"?' asked Forest amiably. Blue

was at his side, holding his hand and begging for another ride on the twirly chair.

'Freak? No, no,' said Carrie, looking terribly nervous. 'Not – not me.'

'Just kidding,' said Forest. 'I have that effect on women.' He laughed a little.

'Oh,' said Carrie. 'Yes.'

I was startled. Carrie – cool, calm sophisticate – looked a little smitten. She flicked her chestnut hair over her shoulder and stood straighter.

'Forest is our *friend*,' I said clearly.

'Yes,' said Blue. 'He's getting me pizza. We're weally hungly.'

Forest smiled down at her, then looked at Carrie, Tam and Alex. 'You *need* a friend with that devil woman Jazz around,' he said. 'She's been after your mate's man forever. Now that there's finally real news in Hambledon, she's got an in at last. Those two have been working long hours together.' He shot me a look, hoisting Blue to a hip, and I went hot and prickly with a flash of irritability at everyone implying that Jack would be dumping me any second for someone older, hotter and altogether more desirable.

'Jack is totally into Lula, though,' said Alex through a mouthful of Pepperoni Special. 'Jazz hasn't got a chance.'

'Sure,' agreed Forest breezily. He looked at me again and winked. 'Right, Bluebird, ham no mushroom?' He shambled off to the kitchen counter, with Blue ordering him around, and they began putting oddments of pizza slices on to an enormous plate.

'Wow,' said Carrie, gazing after him.

'Don't even,' I said, giving her my look.

'No getting involved!' commanded Alex.

'Geez!' Carrie hissed. 'I'm only *admiring* him! And you're a fine one to talk, Alex Thompson. You spent the weekend kissing Gavin Healey! He's suspect number one in the missing Emily Saunders case! What do you have to say about *that*, hmm?'

Alex's forehead went all creasy and complicated. 'Gavin is sooo not a suspect,' she whispered back. 'He was syphoning the Cleo Cosmetics stuff into drums out at their factory all weekend! He has, like, a thousand alibis!'

'Oh,' said Carrie. 'Sorry. I didn't know.'

'Yes! Well!' said Alex, very high up on a very high horse. 'Forest is another matter entirely. We could need him in our Jack Loving Lula campaign, and we don't want him all angry at being heartbroken by you, or loved up and unfocused.'

'Hey, I –' began Carrie, outraged.

'Besides,' I added, 'he's a lovely guy, but he'd drive you nuts. He lost the key to the front door before they even moved in.'

'But it's hanging on the side right there,' said Carrie.

We all turned to look.

She was right. There was a key hanging on the side of the door. 'Whoa,' I said. 'Maybe you'd make a great couple.'

Carrie flicked her eyebrows up, like, *well, yeah, maybe.*

'He *is* seriously hot,' mused Tam. 'Like, seeeriously. And obviously good with kids.'

'*Kids?*' hissed Alex. 'Tam! Would you listen to yourself? Geez! Come with me NOW. We have work to do.' She grabbed Tam, and dragged her off to take a look at Jazz's room. I'd had enough industrial espionage in the last few weeks to last me a lifetime, so Carrie and I kept an eye on Jazz. She was standing possessively at Jack's side while people thronged around him. Every now and again she tried to lay her head on his shoulder, but she was too beautifully petite and he too rangily tall. Even so, they looked good together. Very good.

'I think I need a Malteser,' I said faintly. 'Maybe bag of.'

'Bag of nothing,' said Carrie firmly. 'You're far more gorgeous than she is. That long snaky hair gives me the creeps, and those mean, squinty eyes . . . Why does Jack let her hang around like this?'

'Look at her stomach,' I groaned. 'That belly button. Totally perfect.'

'Like I said,' sighed Carrie. 'Stop with the Maltesers. Yours is totally perfect too, but it won't be if you don't kick that chocolate habit.'

Suddenly Pen broke from the crowd. 'Mum wants to get going, Lula. Let's leave before that Jazz cow gets to make any stupid comments about little girls' bedtimes.'

I nodded. Good thinking from Pen, though it hurt that I'd not had any boyfriend/girlfriend time with Jack. Checking around for my schoolbag I spied Alex suddenly appear on the far side of the living room. Her eyes darted left and right and she had a slight stoop to her walk. Geez. Could she look more like she'd just ransacked a person's room? I beckoned madly, praying that Jazz wouldn't see her, and Alex scampered guiltily over to us.

Tam approached like a normal person, shaking her head at Alex.

'Well?' asked Carrie.

'You don't want to know,' said Tam. 'Only that Alex needs to brush up on her spy skills if she's going to make it in the real journo world.'

'Not true!' cried Alex.

'You didn't even see the sheer undies!' hissed Tam. 'Or the' – she dropped her voice, looking at us each in turn with a *you're not gonna believe it* face – 'other accessories.'

'Other accessories?' I squeaked in panic.

Alex flapped her hand hastily. 'Don't scare her,' she said to Tam.

'Accessories?' I whispered again, my hand on my pounding chest. '*Accessories?*'

85

'Stop saying that,' said Carrie to me. 'Specifics,' she said to Alex. 'We need helpful specifics.'

'Beautiful room. Ready for luuurve action,' said Alex in a despondent voice.

'Like, totally,' agreed Tam. 'You're going to need chocolate, Lula. You know, to get through this.'

'Frik,' I said.

'She doesn't need chocolate,' said Carrie.

'What's ready for luuurve action?' asked Pen. 'What room? What do you mean *accessories*?'

'Never you mind, Penelope,' I said. 'Let's tear Blue away. We need to get going.'

'Can we get a lift?' asked Tam.

'No probs,' I said, and sighed in the direction of Jack. There was no way I could get near him now.

'He's a bit tied up. You can have a loving farewell another time,' said Carrie, guessing my thoughts.

'Yes,' I said. 'Is it rude to go without saying goodbye?'

'Well, you haven't even said hello yet,' said Mr Kadinski, appearing in front of me. He looked over at Alex. 'I haven't had a response from the police about the note, so you've got to stop leaving me messages, Ms Thompson.'

'Oh!' said Alex, disappointed.

'What note?' said Tam. 'How come no one is telling me anything any more? What's going on now?'

'Oh, I've decided it's nothing,' I said. 'Some joker left

a note saying "The birds will die" in our postbox this morning.'

'But that's not a joke! You *are* the birds!' squeaked Tam. 'Tallulah Bird, Blue Bird, Pen –'

Mr K held up a hand and Tam stumbled to a stop. 'But there's also bird flu hitting the country everywhere. Maybe it's to do with that . . .'

'Oooh, you're good,' said Alex. 'Superagent brain extraordinaire.'

'Well,' he said, 'I'm retired you know. Don't want to be doing superagent stuff any more. Ohh . . .' He trailed off, looking at the telly. Then, 'Jack!' he called. 'Turn it up, could you?'

People quietened down as a local reporter came into view at our very own Frey's Dam. Behind her were the figures of Hambledon's police force, who seemed to be hanging around, rather than collecting evidence or arresting people. What was this all about?

'. . . and police are refusing to comment,' she said, her voice echoing around Jack's living room, 'about the disappearance of Emily Saunders. This was the meeting spot, apparently, between the seventeen-year-old and her nineteen-year-old boyfriend, who cannot be named at this time. But the boyfriend denies ever coming up here and it seems this area is not yielding any evidence. We've not seen anything bagged or tagged today, and a local resident who lives very near to here cannot be found for questioning.'

'Who would that be?' wondered Mum. 'Do they mean Parcel Brewster? They can't mean Parcel Brewster . . .'

'We're all local to there,' said Pen.

Fat Angus looked adoringly into Pen's face. She didn't notice, still frowning at the telly. 'You're so clever,' he breathed.

Carrie, Tam and I rolled our eyes, but Alex looked pensive.

'By *boyfriend*, they mean Gavin, right?' I asked her quietly. 'Seriously, are you not worried?'

'I was.' Alex gave me a wry smile. 'But I went down to see Sergeant T at the police station this afternoon, and she –'

'No!' I exclaimed. 'She told you stuff? Isn't that, like, against police –'

'Hey! Give me a chance! I was waiting outside her office and I heard her tell one of the officers to leave the Gavin Healey investigation and review existing evidence instead.'

I raised my eyebrows. 'That's a convenient bit of eavesdropping.'

Alex flushed. 'This investigation is all they're talking about . . . And she did catch me with my ear to the door.'

'*No!*' My eyes were big. How could Alex be this calm? 'I would have *dropped dead* of embarrassment!'

'Hey,' she said, looking at the telly. 'Isn't that . . .?'

I looked over at the screen and saw that a familiar face had butted into view alongside the news reporter.

Arnold caught my eye. 'It's Esme Trooter, isn't it?' he asked.

'Yep,' I replied. Esme was Hambledon town-crier extraordinaire, and she was saying something about squatters' rights. 'What is she on about?'

'I wish I could hear,' said Jack. 'Do you think it's relevant?'

'I've come across her before,' said Jazz. 'She's just an old windbag.'

I could feel Mr K bristle beside me, but he kept quiet. Jazz was saying something else.

'Really,' said Jack. 'You have those kind of contacts? Do you think Channel 4 would go for that angle?'

'Definitely,' said Jazz. The news was over and someone flipped to a music channel. Jazz looked irritated. She pointed to her ears and shook her head at Jack, then gestured outside to the garden. The two of them went out before I could call to Jack that I was going. As they went through the French doors on the side of the living room, I saw Jack trip over the raggedy carpet, his head angled at the sharp edge of the door.

'Eep!' I said, but Jack steadied himself just in time and bowed out into the moonlight.

Mr Kadinski was watching me. 'Don't worry about that boy. He's not going to get hurt. There's too much other stuff going on to be concerning yourself with that.'

I nodded. 'I know. But I still have this feeling, like I've got to stop something terrible happening to him. It's because of the whole jinx thing I think – I just can't believe it's really gone away . . .'

'You don't need me to tell you that's ridiculous.'

'I know.' We walked into the kitchen and I picked up my bag, and huffed out a sigh. 'Bye, Mr K. You'll get a ride with Bludgeon?'

He nodded and smiled. 'Look, Lula. How about Bludgeon and I keep an eye on your boy?'

'Really?' I felt a load lift from my shoulders. 'You'd do that?' Then, 'Hang on . . . You're working with Bludgeon now?'

Mr K rubbed his chin, and it made a raspy sound. He tilted his fedora back and chuckled. 'No, not working *together* exactly, but we share information.'

'Huh,' I said, and looked at him sceptically. He winked. 'Mr K,' I said finally, 'if Jack could stay unharmed, I'd be such a happy girl.'

'We don't want people talking about jinxes now, do we?' he asked, his grey eyes sparkling.

'We don't,' I agreed. 'Though mostly I . . . well, I just want him to be okay.' Mum was looking for her keys. It was about time to go. 'Actually, I *am* going to say goodbye to him,' I decided finally.

Mr K nodded. 'See you soon. I'm over the road if you need me.'

'So am I,' I replied. 'But not for help on the stairs. The stairs you can manage on your own.'

'You know me too well,' he said, and went to where Bludgeon was blushing while Fat Angus and Pen had their own fond farewell.

I stepped outside and stared into the garden. I couldn't see Jazz and Jack anywhere. Where were they? Then someone turned on a bathroom light and a bright rectangle flooded out a good way across the patchy grass. Jazz and Jack were sitting on upturned buckets, very close, talking intently.

Suddenly my throat hurt.

'Come on, Lula,' said Pen, appearing at my shoulder. She followed my eyes out to the far reaches of the lit rectangle. 'Hm,' she said. 'Time to go.'

I swallowed, the sound loud in my ears. 'Definitely,' I said, and stepped back into the house. 'Definitely time to go.'

Chapter Eleven

Thursday morning. Girl still missing. And girl still missing her boyfriend: two whole days without seeing or hearing from Jack

Okay. So that's not strictly true. I've had a text. But A TEXT, people? I'm feeling unloved. Then feeling bad about that, because really the priority should be Emily Saunders, and being supportive of Alex, who had told people now that she was seeing Gavin, and everyone was looking at her like she was a serial-killer's assistant.

Oddly, this did not seem to bother her. 'Oh, pfff,' she said. 'They're still talking more about you than they are about me.'

'You cruel girl,' I said. But my heart wasn't in it. We were walking to our last class of the day and I was heading for the school gates to go over the road for art. Not even that was going to cheer me up.

'Oh, Lula,' said Tam, putting her arm round me. 'I don't like to see you so sad.'

'Me neither,' I said, and I whimpered a little, though I know that's pathetic.

'At least you got a text. What did it say?' asked Carrie.

'He's got another story to film,' I said in a self-piteous

voice. 'And lectures till five every day, so he's got to work nights to get the story going.'

'Nights with Jazz,' said Alex.

'Alex!' said Tam. 'That is not helpful!'

'Flirt with someone,' suggested Alex. 'Always peps me right up.'

'Alex!' cried Tam again.

Mr Tufty was not pleased to see me. Which wasn't any change, but still. It felt different to be ridiculed in front of a boy.

'Oh, no,' he said when he saw me. 'Can you take the easel in the corner? I can't cope with bananas today.'

I blew out a sigh.

Arns was just behind me and said, 'Jeepers creepers.'

'Who are you?' barked Mr Tufton.

'Er . . . Arnold Trenchard,' said Arns. He walked uncertainly over to Mr Tufton, who was standing legs astride, arms crossed. He was in full assertive, ant-eating mode today, that's for sure.

'Portfolio? Sketchbook?'

'Er . . .' Arnold began rummaging in his bag. He pulled out an A4 spiral-bound sketchbook a lot like Grace Mutsapho's, but more bashed about. 'These are my own – I mean, I don't usually . . . I'd rather not –'

Mr Tufton made a sound like, 'Ftshh,' and snatched

the sketchbook. He slammed it on his painting table and flipped the cover open. Then, fists planted either side of it, arms straight, he bent his head to examine the first drawing. I was curious and came out from behind my easel.

'You,' yelled Mr Tufton to me, 'get back. I'll talk to you later.'

I gulped and cowered behind the wooden board on the easel, and shakily took out a small roll of oil paper from my bag. I pinned it carefully to the board and snuck a look at Arns and Mr Tufton. They were standing exactly as they were before, but Mr Tufton had turned a few pages.

Grace and Delilah came in and took up their positions, only Delilah set up a few easels down from me, which made me really start to worry. Oh, geez. Tufty was clearly really peed off about me using the oil stuff. The only other thing I knew for sure about my painting teacher was how much he hated inactivity in his class, so I rummaged quietly in my bag and pulled out a box of oil pastels that Darcy, my older sister, had left for me before she went back to the Yehudi Menuhin school of music. They were for my birthday a fortnight ago, but I only got them yesterday because my parents had forgotten all about them.

I found the cellophane tag and pulled it gently. The wrapping came off with a rustle and suddenly Mr Tufton pushed away from his desk. It shifted on the floor with an ominous groaning sound. I held my breath and took another peek. Arns had shoved his hands into his pockets and was looking straight back at his new art teacher.

'So,' said Mr Tufton, folding his arms. 'You have talent.'

'Er . . .' said Arns.

'But you need to loosen up. Why so uptight? It's like you're hiding something. Don't be ashamed of your creativity. I want to see it all. In this class, you will become something special. Like Grace. Like Delilah.' He threw a hand out at each in turn.

'Er . . .' said Arns again.

Tufty saw me peeking out and yelled, 'You! No oils till I say so! Back to acrylics!'

My heart sank. 'I've got some new oil pastels today . . .' I ventured.

'PASTELS?' roared Mr Tufton. 'Put that crap away! AWAY! Acrylics! Paint him!' He gestured at Arns. 'And you' – he gestured at Arns – 'paint her.'

'Who?' asked Arns. He took a step away from Mr Tufton and looked back at me, panicky.

'Yes,' said Mr Tufton. 'Paint her. That'll sort you out.' He whirled round to Grace and Delilah. 'Good work on Monday, girls, please continue. See you all later.' And he bounded out.

There was a frozen moment, then Grace began to laugh quietly.

'I need a drink,' said Arns weakly. 'I don't feel so good.'

*

After a few minutes of Delilah being sensible and bossing us around, Arnold and I were seated either end of the painting table, with desktop easels in front of us, charcoal sticks in hand. We'd agreed never to show each other the portraits. It was just going to be better that way and, once that was decided, we were back to our easy chatting.

'So Mum got a call yesterday afternoon from Parks and Green Spaces. They found bird flu up at Frey's Dam,' said Arnold.

'Whoa!' I said, and my charcoal stick snapped. 'First Emily Saunders goes missing, then there's bird flu there? That's mad. Doesn't that whole area fall under Cluny now? I wonder what he has to do about it all . . .' I got up and began gathering tubes of acrylic over near the sink.

'Hey,' said Arns. 'Sit back down. You can't just get up when you feel like it!'

'Oh,' I said, 'sorry. Give me a minute. So that's a bummer for Cluny. Does he now have to pay to get all the ducks and stuff tested?' I got back on my chair and began squeezing paint on to a palette.

'Dunno,' said Arns. 'Move to the left, please.'

'The sun's burning my face there!'

'Well, you shouldn't have sat there in the first place.'

'C'mon, Arns!'

Delilah cleared her throat. 'Can you two stop moaning

and whining at each other? Some of us are trying to work.'

I rolled my eyes and shifted left. 'You've got five minutes!' I said to Arnold, more quietly. 'And you can start saving for my chemical peel from now.'

'What's a chemical peel?'

I rolled my eyes again. 'Dude.'

'What? Tell me.'

'A peel takes all the old sun-damaged skin off to reveal gorgeous new skin below.'

'You've already got gorgeous . . .' Arns trailed to a halt.

I flushed. Grace began laughing again.

Arns looked at me. 'You do have good skin.' He put down a piece of chalk and went over to get his paints.

'*Muchas gracias*,' I said, and was pleased he wasn't looking at me. The sun was making me feel all hot and uncomfortable. Grace came out from behind her easel and pulled the muslin drapes across the window. It was still light, but now I wasn't being blasted.

'Thanks,' I said to Grace.

'Sure,' she said, and paused at Arnold's easel. She glanced from his work to me, and back to what he'd drawn. 'Interesting,' she said.

I put down my paintbrush and stood up, darting a look over at Arnold, still at the sink, pouring water in a jar.

'No, you don't,' he said, without even looking. 'We have a deal, remember?'

'Huh,' I said, and sat down. The acrylics I'd mixed were already starting to dry. 'Hurry, Arns, I need to paint now.'

'Don't rush it, Tallulah,' said Grace. 'That's your trouble.'

'They dry too fast,' I moaned.

Grace leaned out from her easel and considered me. 'Then you need to cheat, darlin',' she drawled. She picked up a small bottle of taupe-coloured gel from the table next to her and lobbed it over. I caught it and examined the label.

Mix with acrylics for oil-like properties.
Slows drying time. Gives viscous quality.

'Wow, Grace. So it could be like painting with oils.' I grinned back at her. 'Thank youhoohoooo!'

'Don't let Mr Tufton see. Mix it in now and you won't feel so stressed with the brush in your hand.'

I did as I was told and threw the bottle back over to Grace. Dipping the paintbrush into a circle of ochre on the palette, I examined my friend's face carefully while he examined mine. I felt uncomfortable at first, but as I moved the paint around my charcoal sketch I began to get a feel for the contours of his face. Heaven knows it should be imprinted on my mind forever after the makeover.

Arns finished way before me, but I had about five minutes' painting still to do. 'Can you wait a bit?' I asked Arns.

'Sure,' he said, and sighed, but I knew he didn't really

mind. He cleaned up quickly and sat back down, chatting quietly all the while. At 3.15 p.m. we heard the final bell of the day go, and Mr Tufton came striding back in. He was delighted with Grace and Delilah as usual. Arnold and I shot nervous glances at each other, but *he* had no need to be anxious. Tufty loved Arns's portrait of me.

'Good God, I'm good,' he proclaimed.

Arnold's eyes went a bit wide. 'Pardon?' he said.

'This portrait is the first step. Has resolved those issues, pretty much.'

'Issues?'

'Now you are free.' Tufty bowed to Arnold. 'Free to be an *artist*.'

What a pretentious creep, I thought.

Tufty came round to my side. He stood behind me and stared at my portrait of Arns. It was mostly done – I was just increasing contrast between light and dark around the jaw and background. My teacher was silent. I stopped painting.

'You're finished now,' he told me. 'Always, you paint too much. Put it to dry over there.' He gestured to a far table against the back wall. I saw my canvas from Monday propped up on it, and walked my tabletop easel over there carefully, and left it to dry, facing the wall.

'The next few weeks,' yelled Tufty, making us all jump, and Arns swear quietly, 'are going to be vital. I'll be choosing the best work from this art school to show at the Port Albert

Regatta celebrations. Our pieces will be hung on the main marquee walls for all to see.'

No pieces of mine, I thought, picking up my bag to go. Arnold's portrait of me was already dry, and tucked away in his portfolio case though he was supposed to leave it in the studio. He swung his backpack to his shoulder and carried the case carefully under his arm as we headed out of Art House. I was suddenly desperate to see it. 'Can I take a look?' I asked him.

'No,' he replied.

'Please?'

'Tatty.'

Heavy sigh. 'Then your sketchbook? I can see that?'

'Never.'

'Oh you *are* a little turd,' I muttered.

We reached the end of the path to see hordes of girls exiting the school gates just up the road. 'Hey, there's Helen Cluny. Let's ask her about the bird flu.'

Helen Cluny wasn't in the mood to talk, but she answered our questions. 'The Parks guy came round yesterday afternoon,' she sighed. 'Said they'd had an anonymous tip-off about bird flu killing all the ducks and swans up at Frey's.'

'All the birds are dead?' asked Arnold. 'Seriously?'

'Wow,' I murmured. 'Mr K was maybe right about the note . . .'

'Yes,' said Helen. 'The Parks guy had Dad burn his shoes, clothes, everything from going up there. He had weird overalls on, and put them in a big bag.'

'So have they, like, roped the area off?' I asked. 'We can't go up there?'

'The crime-scene tape has come down, but now the whole hillside is blockaded. No one's allowed in,' said Helen. 'Not even Parcel Brewster.'

'Geez!' I said. 'I'd forgotten all about him!'

'Who's Parcel Brewster?' asked Arns.

'Homeless guy who camps up at Frey's,' said Helen. 'But he's not there now.'

'Where is he?' I asked.

Helen shrugged. 'I don't know,' she said. 'Dad's a little freaked out. He's worried we'll have to foot the bill for a massive bio-hazard clean-up.'

'Oh no,' I said, my forehead creasing in concern. 'Seriously?'

'Seriously,' Helen ground out. 'See, Tatty, some of us have real problems to think about, not stupid things like imaginary jinxes just to get attention.'

My eyes went wide at her vehemence, and I was aware that my jaw had dropped a little.

She stalked off and I could feel I had a frozen *where the hell did that come from?* face on, but somehow I couldn't hide the dull stab of anguish I felt.

My cheeks burned and I was uncomfortably aware of Arns uncomfortably at my side. He bumped me amiably, nudging me a little way out of my embarrassment.

'She's not peed off at you,' he said. 'She must be really stressed. She's probably feeling bad right now for taking it out on the loveliest person at Hambledon Girls' High.'

I nodded and swallowed. 'I love it that you say things like "lovely", Arns,' I said in a small voice.

'I am pretty lovely myself,' Arns agreed, and I laughed. He put his arm round my shoulders and matched my steps back towards school, talking about the human condition all the way. Something about universal consciousnesses and how we as people pulled things out of the atmosphere and blah blah. All his scientific analysis was making me feel better.

Even though I was actually on the way to Dance Club. Groan. *Just* what I needed.

And suddenly I was telling Arnold how I hadn't seen much of Jack, and I told him all about Jazz, at which point Arns said, 'Yeah, I noticed she had a thing for Jack. She's pretty creepy.'

'Totally,' I said. 'But Jack doesn't see that.'

'No,' he agreed. 'And neither does Mona.'

'She doesn't?'

'No way. Think about it. Every time Jazz is with them she's sweet as pie to everyone, and all over them like a bad rash.' He shivered.

I smiled up at him. 'Thanks,' I said. 'I feel better now.'

'Wonder if Jazz knows about the bird flu yet,' said Arns. 'From what Mum said, it all sounds hush-hush till they get the results back. Would be great if you got Jack the inside edge yourself so he's ready with another local news piece the second an announcement is made.'

'So great!' I shouted, suddenly buoyed up. 'So, *so* great! *You* are great, Arns!' I planted a smacker on his cheek, bade him farewell and jived all the way to dance class.

Yes!

Nothing was going to keep this girl down. Tatty Bird was Back In The Game.

Chapter Twelve

Thursday afternoon. Sordid salsa

Having Mrs Baldacci demand hip rotations and pelvic thrusts with vigorous demonstrations was a shock to the system. She popped not a bead of perspiration the entire time, while we felt like a herd of stomping, sweating, heaving cattle. After twenty minutes, Mrs Baldacci clapped her hands to say well done and swung out for a cuppa, leaving a panting line of girls slumped against the wall.

'You see?' I hissed to Alex, pulling my tights off to let my legs breathe, even though we were in the hall and not the changing rooms. 'You see why I didn't want to do this?'

'It's pretty scary,' admitted Alex. 'Salsa is more complicated than I thought.'

'So we can chuck this in?'

'No,' she said.

'Everyone's telling me no,' I moaned. 'I want someone to do as I say, just once.'

'Stop whining, Tatty.' Alex sounded ratty. 'Your life is pretty much perfect.'

'A perfect life would have no salsa dancing.'

Alex sighed heavily. 'You *are* really bad at the salsa.'

I flushed. 'Am I terribly, awfully bad?' I looked at

Alex pleadingly. 'Or just *quite* bad?'

Alex was about to reply when Mrs Baldacci came swanning back in, a cup of tea in one hand and an ice pack in the other. She tossed it elegantly at Alex. 'For your foot, Alexi,' she said, with a hard look at me.

'I said I was sorry,' I mumbled.

Mrs Baldacci bent her head in acknowledgement, taking a delicate sip of tea. 'Don't worry, dear. Next week we have the boys, and the boys have tougher feet. You can stomp on big hairy toes instead of poor Alexi.'

'Eep!' I said, my eyes wide. I whirled to face Alex. 'Alex! Did you know about this? Did you? *Did you?*'

'Er . . .' said Alex, concentrating on the ice pack. 'I hope this toe's not broken . . .'

'But for now,' continued Mrs Baldacci, 'we do the hula. Hula is a lot more gentle. Even Tallulah can do the Coconut Tree motion. Maybe some kaholo with the legs. We have no time to lose. Everybody up!' She set her empty teacup down on a windowsill. 'We make most of every minute. Just two and a half weeks till we dance hula at the Port Albert Regatta!'

'OH NO!' I cried.

'I beg pardon?' said Mrs Baldacci, turning slowly, her eyes narrowing to scary slits. Any other teacher, and I would have been out of there, declaring myself unfit to continue, but Mrs Baldacci is a force to be reckoned with. I looked wildly at Alex. She had a grim stare of determination on her face. The expression of someone who was thinking *Leave me now and you die!*

'It's just that . . . I'd love to do the hula for . . . um . . . all of Hambledon and Port Albert, but my dad is performing, and I'll need to be helping him.' Mrs Baldacci continued to stare at me. With menace. 'I think. I think I'll need to be helping him.'

'Dance is five minutes. Your papa can spare you for five minutes, no?'

'Er, no, actually.' I went bright red at my audacity.

'I will speak to him,' said Mrs Baldacci. 'I need eight girls for hula dance and you . . . you are number eight.'

'Oh!' I blustered. 'Um, I'll talk to Dad. If it's a problem, then you can . . . you know . . . talk to him.'

Mrs Baldacci inclined her head in another imperious nod. 'Everyone standing like so. Hips ready for swaying like this . . .'

After another half hour we were slumped again against the hall wall.

'Dear God,' I whispered. 'What have you done, Alex? Was she serious about playing an instrument called the *ipu*? While *dancing*? The *IPU*? Frik. I don't feel well.'

'Put your tights back on,' commanded Alex, starting to gather her things together. 'Why you wore them I do not know. This is the summer term, Tallulah. *Summer.*'

'Errgh,' I moaned. 'I think I hurt my back. Can you put them on for me?'

Alex gave me the slow blink. 'You want me to touch your sweaty legs? Your sweaty *feet?*'

'If you were really my friend, you – nyafrikfrik! I think I really have hurt my back.'

'I'll get Mum to give you a lift home. Because I'm such a good friend.'

'Thank you,' I whispered gratefully, and began pulling the stupid tights back on myself.

Alex cleared her throat. 'So the bad news is . . .'

I was instantly alert. 'Bad news? There's bad news?' My thoughts flew first to Emily Saunders. No, I'd have heard. Then to Jack. Had something happened? I'd trusted Mr K to make sure he was all right!

'Don't panic,' said Alex, pulling her hair into a high ponytail. 'It's just that Jack can't make the movies tomorrow night. He's tried calling you, but your phone's off. Again.'

'Nooo!' I wailed, yanking the tights smooth and stepping into my shoes with little mews of pain. 'Why?'

'Because you keep forgetting to charge it.'

'No! I mean why can't he make it to the movies?'

'Work, of course,' said Alex. 'I offered to help, but he said he had it covered with that Jazz.' She looked huffy. 'You ready to go?'

'Mm.' *Jazz, AGAIN?* I wanted to vent right then and there, but actually, if I'd leaked even a little of the raging emotions and bottled-up anger I felt towards Jazz Delaney, Alex might have had to seek medical assistance.

We staggered out of the hall, up the stairs and through the front doors. Alex's mum was waiting in the car outside.

'Hey,' said Alex. 'You okay, Tatty Lula?'

I sighed and, like a deflating balloon, all the fury I felt just drifted away. 'I'm irritated with Jack,' I admitted. 'But what makes it worse is that he's doing nothing wrong . . . I shouldn't really be irritated with him . . . you know?'

'*Nothing wrong?*' Alex's face was startled. 'He's spending every waking moment with a girl who openly wants him just for herself.'

'He doesn't get that.'

Alex shook her head. 'I know. Stupid boy.' She pulled me into a hug. 'I can see he's making you sad.'

'He is, but he doesn't mean to.'

'You'll still come to the cinema with us, though, tomorrow, yeah?'

'I guess,' I sighed, my face glum. 'What's showing?'

'*Love in the Time of Cholera*, with Javier Bardem.'

'*Great.*' I put on my best sarcastic voice. 'That's going to be cheery.'

'At least Jack won't have to see you after you've been

drizzing for an hour and a half. Your nose goes so *red*.'

'Alex,' I begged, 'please stop speaking. Please.'

Friday night, Hambledon cinema, lights down low

True to form, I howled away at the sad movie, but at least I had Carrie on my left and Alex and Tam on my right, instead of being all on my own. Thank goodness it was nearly the end. I blew my nose and turned to Alex. 'I don't think this is good PR,' I whispered. 'We're the only ones here without boys. *I'm back to square one*.'

Alex shook her head and popcorn landed all over my jeans. I brushed it off before the butter could grease-up my legs. 'You didn't see the way Tony Bufindle looked at you?' she asked, spraying more popcorn.

Tony Bufindle's dad owns Hambledon's ancient cinema. He is the pimpliest boy in Hambledon except for Jason Ferman. And he looks at everyone.

'Don't talk with your mouth full,' I hissed.

'Will you two be quiet!' hissed Tam. 'This is a meaningful moment.'

Alex and I considered the characters on screen.

'Losers,' was her verdict.

'You got any more Maltesers?' I asked hopefully.

'Quiet!' hushed Carrie. She was totally dry-eyed.

'I can't take any more of the grief!' moaned Tam.

I dissolved into giggles, and so did Alex, but at last the

credits rolled up. We sat for a minute, slumped in our seats, exhausted by the emotional toil.

'We've got to get Tatty out before anyone sees her nose,' decided Alex suddenly.

I sighed, but she was right. We pulled on our jackets and swung through the front entrance, being careful on the old, cracked marble steps.

'Let's go for hot chocolate,' suggested Tam. 'I need to recover from that film.'

'Let's,' I agreed. 'I have a cunning plan to reel Jack back in.'

We got to Big Mama's, which is a deli/café/tearoom kind of place, just before eleven. It stays open for a couple of hours after the cinema is done for the night so people can have a slice of something calorific and a cup of something calorific too.

I got to the front of the queue and promptly went as red as my nose. Which was still, like, really red. 'Chocolate cake and hot chocolate, please,' I asked the boy behind the counter.

'Ha! No surprises there-a,' said Gianni Caruso, pulling out the cake and a large knife.

I watched Gianni wield the knife aggressively, and swallowed.

'You got lemon cake, Gianni?' asked Alex. 'Where's Big Mama?'

'Big Mama probably knew this girl was a-coming,' said Gianni, pointing at me with the knife. He put the cake on a plate and spun it on to the counter in front of me before turning to the coffee machine.

'Probably,' agreed Carrie. 'Is there any Victoria sponge left?'

'For you, Alexi, there is the lemon cake. For Tamara' – he gave her a sexy grin, and she blushed – 'melt in the mouth mousse! You must have it! My treat-a.' He kissed his fingertips to her. 'For Carrie, no Victoria sponge. Sorry-a.'

'What? But I can see –'

'Instead, vanilla cream cake. Look here-a.' He produced an amazing confection that made me a little weak at the knees, and there wasn't even a crumb of chocolate on it.

'Ooooooh,' we all said. Gianni spun and whirled behind the counter, producing plates for all of us, and foamy mugs of hot chocolate. The girls saw the leather sofa at the back was finally free and went to claim it. I was the last to pay.

'Thanks, Gianni,' I said, pocketing my change.

'Tallulah,' he said, and winked. 'This new boy of yours okay with the jinx, huh?'

'Oh,' I said. 'There was never a jinx, Gianni. Just a bit of bad luck.'

'You still carrying that around, though.'

I raised my eyebrows. 'Why'd you say that?'

His forehead creased. 'You no see in-a window?'

'Pardon?'

Gianni nodded towards a small table for two tucked into the front window, behind the counter and away from the door.

My heart stopped.

Jack de Souza enjoying a frikking night out with bumly bumly bum bum JAZZ.

She was laughing, and bowing her head intimately towards him while licking chocolate mousse off a long-handled spoon.

I took a deep breath, my pulse going three hundred and four.

Gianni was looking at me expectantly.

'Oh, that's Jazz,' I said airily. 'She and Jack are running the news story on Emily Saunders. Can you believe it?' I smiled proudly.

'What,' said Gianni, unimpressed. 'Every night-a they go on-a and say no news.'

'Pretty much,' I admitted.

'Why no one is freaking out-a?' asked Gianni. 'Huh? No offence-a, but they put students' – he gestured with his head at Jack and Jazz – 'on a beeg news story?'

I blew on my hot chocolate and took a sip. 'To be honest,' I said, 'I think it's because Emily has taken off before. You know? She generally turns up at her grandparents' place over in Jersey, and her parents seem convinced that's where she's headed. At least that's what all her friends at school are saying to everyone now. And she took her phone, her purse, a bag, clothes with her. She must still have it otherwise it would have been found. Even so, the police are looking, apparently.' I took another sip. 'And Jack is a good news reporter,' I said quietly. 'If there was anything worth knowing, he'd find it out.'

We both turned and looked at the couple in the window.

'Okay,' said Gianni. He grabbed a bag of foil-wrapped chocolate coins from a bowl on the counter and tossed them to me. 'Take-a these. You're gonna need 'em. She's a hot babe.'

I laughed, and it came out okay – just a *touch* hysterical. 'Thanks, Gianni.' He gave me a sympathetic look that made me want to do terrible violence. I picked up my hot chocolate, chocolate cake and chocolate coins and staggered over to the couch.

'What's wrong?' asked Tam straight away.

I looked at Alex. '*Your* cousin,' I said with venom, 'is enjoying a cosy soirée with *Jazz*! Over there in the corner!'

'No!' she said. 'They didn't see us come in?'

'Too wrapped up in each other!' I snapped, stabbing at my cake with my fork.

'You've got to do something, Alex,' said Carrie. 'Right now.'

'*Right* now!' echoed Tam. Her mouth was so full I was surprised she could speak.

'Okay, okay!' huffed Alex. 'Gimme a minute.' She took an elegant sip from her mug. 'Mmm, this is *ve-ery* good.'

'Alex!' we all hissed.

She took another sip. 'Don't rush me!'

'I can see I'm going to have to take matters into my own hands,' I said, standing up quickly. 'Do I have chocolate anywhere?'

'Top lip,' said Carrie, showing me where.

I cleaned my face and strode to the front of the deli. I knew the girls would be listening to every word I said, and I felt a little disconcerted.

Jack was saying, 'What about that old lady, Esme someone . . .' when I approached their table.

'Hi, guys!' I said brightly.

'Lula!' said Jack with a delighted grin. 'I hoped you'd come here after your movie! Sit down, sit down!' He sprang up and looked around for another chair.

'No, no, you carry on,' I said breezily. 'I'm with the girls. We saw your car outside, Jazz, and I thought it such a shame it got keyed all down the front.'

'Keyed?' Jazz looked stricken. 'I don't think so.'

'I could be mistaken,' I said with a thoughtful look on my face. 'Only there was a bunch of kids out there –'

Jazz was already out of her chair. I'd never seen her move

so fast. She snatched her tiny bag up off the table. 'Back in a minute,' she said, and dashed out the door.

Jack sighed, still smiling at me.

'What?' I asked.

'You're so beautiful,' he said, 'even with your sobbing nose on.'

'Omigod,' I said, and covered my schnoz. 'Is it still red?'

'I'd better kiss you better,' said Jack, pulling me into a hug.

'You're good at that,' I said, lifting my face to his, feeling better already.

Chapter Thirteen

Alex, to put it simply, went nuts.

First of all Jazz came back and went on and on about how her car was absolutely fine, before I'd even got a peck on the lips. Jack made polite 'oh, yeah?' and 'oh, good' noises, but he was mostly staring at me and not letting me move away. I wasn't complaining because my legs were so wobbly I was sure I'd fall down if he let go of me, and then when Jazz went to get an espresso refill and Jack finally put his beautiful lips to mine, then *theeere* was Alex.

'What do you two think you're doing?' she whispered in a shrieky way. 'Are you out of your minds? Why are you snogging in a *shop window*? Tatty? Tatty! I thought you didn't want people talking about you any more! This will give them *something else* to talk about. Is that what you want? Hmm? Answer me!'

There was a rap on the window and I broke away from Jack. Pen and Fat Angus both stood on the pavement, arms crossed, heads on one side.

'At least people can see he's alive!' I bleated. 'That . . .' My voice went small as I leaned to whisper in Alex's ear. 'That he's still my boyfriend!'

'What?' asked Jack, still holding me to his chest. 'Wha–'

'Not good enough!' replied Alex, her arms also crossed now.

I heaved a sigh, and looked regretfully at the boy in my arms. The romance was over. 'Okay, Jack,' I said. 'You need to know about the latest outbreak of bird flu. It's not official, but lots of people know –'

'Wait!' said Alex. 'First things first.' She looked round to see where Jazz was and spotted her still at the counter talking to Gianni. He was having to redo her espresso for some reason. 'Cuz! What's the story? Why are you spending all this time with Jazz?'

'Alex . . .' I warned.

'No! No!' said Alex, flapping her hand at me. 'I don't like the way you and Jazz are so insular with your work, Jack. You've been very offhand lately. We can all help, PLUS I'm a published journo too, you know!'

'Hey!' said Jack, looking worriedly at Alex. 'I know you are! I'm not being offhand! You need to understand that Jazz – quite apart from being a great reporter – is sharing all her sources with me. She has connections everywhere.'

'We've got better connections,' said Alex. 'Ditch her. I don't like her.'

'Now hang on a minute,' said Jack, starting to look angry.

Pen was still outside, gesturing to Alex in a commanding way, so Alex gave Jack a last inscrutable look, turned on her heel and went outside to talk to my sister.

'Geez,' said Jack. 'She does not get Jazz at all.'

Okaaaay, I thought. Clearly the up-front approach was not going to work with Jack on the Jazz issue. Not one little bit.

'Listen,' I said desperately. 'Alex is right about us knowing a lot of people around here. We've lived here sixteen years, you know!' I laughed. Jack didn't look convinced and my heart fell. No matter what he said, obviously some part of him really did see me and Alex and our friends as school kids, girls just playing at being grown-up.

I cleared my throat. 'Did you know about the bird flu that's hit the ducks and swans up on Cluny's land?' I asked.

'Ohh,' drawled Jazz's voice behind me.

I turned to look at her.

'You shouldn't dabble in journalism, Talluley. I think we got it covered.'

'Jazz,' said Jack with a small frown. 'I –'

Alex burst back into Big Mama's with an ecstatic grin on her face. 'Jack! Tatty! Fat Angus says Bludgeon's got the results on the bird-flu testing!'

'Well, I've got one better,' lilted Jazz, one eyebrow raised. She took a tiny sip from her tiny cup. 'The lab technician is meeting us at the Guilty Felon in five minutes.'

'Yesss!' said Jack. He pulled his jacket off the back of his chair and grinned at Alex. 'Come on! Jazz'll drive us!' and he dived out of the deli like Boodle the Poodle after a bone on a string.

Tam looked confused. 'So . . . what, like, no one's interested in covering the Emily Saunders story now?'

'Tam, you *know* Emily's parents think she's en route to her grandparents,' declared Alex. 'She packed a bag and everything. End of! New story – let's go!'

'I'll be driving *Jack*, not you lot,' sneered Jazz as the deli door slammed shut behind Jack. 'The Felon is strictly eighteens and over after 10 p.m. Juveniles are hardly welcome.' She followed Jack and we watched her bleep her car open, but Jack didn't get in.

'Ha!' said Alex. 'He loves you more.'

We hurried outside. 'If they can't come in, then let's just give the girls a lift home first, Jazz,' Jack was saying in reply to Jazz. We joined him on the pavement, Alex beaming up at him. Carrie and Tam had followed us out to see what was going on.

'I'd really love to, Jack,' said Jazz, 'but if we don't meet the guy right now, we're going to lose this lead. Do you want the story or not?'

Jack blew out a sigh.

'Call me tomorrow,' I said, and reached up to kiss him on the cheek, but he was already ducking down to get in the car. My cheeks flushed and I bit my lip.

Jazz laughed at me. Not breaking eye contact, she flicked

her luxuriant hair over her shoulder and got in the driver's seat, smirking all the while.

Alex says Jack was trying to find the button to wind the window down. I dunno. What hurt was that he'd not thought to say goodbye before he'd left my side. A pulse of loud music burst from the stereo and Jazz pulled out with a squeal of her mag-wheeled tyres.

'Well!' exclaimed Tam, staring after them.

Carrie put her arm round me, and I squeezed her back, my breath all bottled with an emotion I didn't want to think about.

'She is such a b—' started Alex.

'Come on,' I interrupted, my cheeks hot and prickly. 'Let's go eat cake. Lots of.'

Chapter Fourteen

Sunday morning, chilling on the green outside Sassy's Salon

Aunt Sassy's not my aunt, she's Tam's, but that doesn't matter. We all call her Aunt Sassy just the same. Her salon: buttery walls, big ornate mirrors in gold gilt, black marble counters, black leather seats. So the seats have their stuffing kind of coming out and the flagstone floor is totally beaten up – it doesn't really matter. It does the business. If it weren't for Aunt Sassy, Mum would still be making me have short back and sides instead of letting me look like a girl.

Aunt Sassy does Seniors' Sunday, a sneaky hour just before church. There's no better place in town for information-gathering. Tam works there part-time and I was waiting for her to emerge.

But it was Mr K bowling towards me now, looking freshly shorn and very pink about the ears.

'You untrusting bastard!' screeched Esme Trooter from inside the salon.

'Whoa,' I said as Mr K collapsed on the bench beside me. 'What have you done to incite wrath on the Lord's Day? Is she gonna have to confess to that?'

'I don't think Esme is a churchgoer,' muttered Mr K grimly.

'Kadinski!' came Esme's voice again, and seconds later she followed after, slamming through the glass door and coming straight over, thwacking her stick down on the tarmac with every step. 'Why don't you believe me about Parcel Brewster?' she shrilled, bending slightly to eyeball Mr K.

Before he could answer, a Russian-accented voice cut through the still morning air and yet another figure emerged from the salon.

'Oh, leave him alone,' called Madame Polanikov. 'Find another private detective, Esme. My lover's wrists are wrecked after the last escapade.' My eyebrows shot up into my scalp, and mine weren't the only ones, but Madame was not finished: 'I have told him vitamin E oil is the way to go, but he won't listen to me. And I'm so good at massage. He needs rubbing three times a day.'

Mr K had gone bright red. I'd never seen him this disconcerted.

'*Rubbing?*' I asked quietly.

'Rubbing,' he confirmed bitterly. 'She makes me.'

'Wow. You two are a match made in heaven.'

Mr Kadinski growled, but that did not deter Esme, who sat down beside him.

'Three's a crowd,' he said to her clearly, looking straight

ahead at Madame Polanikov making her slow and heavy way across the road.

'Did you go talk to Parcel Brewster, Alfred?' persisted Esme.

'I can't get up there now, can I?' he replied. 'They've cordoned off the whole area to contain the bird flu.' He twitched at his fedora irritably.

'Bird flu . . .' I mused, my brain whirring. 'Hmm. Is Parcel Brewster still living in his shack?' I asked.

'That is precisely the question!' chirped Esme. 'Did you know, Tallulah, how close he was to your grandmother? Did she ever talk of the bird man? Always tending to the geese and the ducks up at Frey's Dam?'

'Yep,' I said, 'of course.'

'Well,' said Esme, 'no one's seen Parcel for days. Add Emily Saunders's disappearance and I bet there's no bird flu there at all! I bet something else is going on!'

'Ooh!' I said. A memory flashed across my mind. Esme on the telly at the appeal on Monday. Jack pressing Jazz for a chat with Esme. And something else . . . 'Mr K, the note. Could it have been Parcel? He called the police, didn't he? Asked them to go up there. Was he worried about bird flu there? Did he leave the note for Grandma Bird?'

'What note?' asked Esme. 'What's going on?'

I was about to explain when Madame Polanikov finally

staggered to a halt at our bench. 'Whooof!' she huffed, and I got up hurriedly so she could sit down.

Madame fell gratefully back on to the bench, wedged in tightly next to Esme. She nudged my ankle with her umbrella. 'What is this note you speak of?' she enquired. 'My love pudding is not investigating anything, *da*? *Nyet, nyet!*'

'Don't tell us *nyet*!' said Esme hotly, clearly feeling crowded by Madame.

There was a jangle of keys at the salon door. Aunt Sassy was locking up while Tam came over to our overpopulated bench.

'*Nyet*, nothing!' continued Esme, wriggling for more room. 'There's a man's life at stake here!'

'Whose life?' asked Tam. She looked at me accusingly. 'What now?'

I held up my hands, not involved, totally not involved. 'Don't look in this direction, Tam. I was just siiiiitting on the bench. Miiiinding my own business.'

'Oh, please,' said Esme. 'No one sits on this bench on a Seniors' Sunday not looking for info. Now what note are you talking about?'

'It was just Parcel telling Grandma Bird about the bird flu –'

'Grandma Bird is dead, though,' said Tam.

'Parcel may not have known or remembered that,' mused Mr K.

'Alfred!' barked Madame Polanikov. 'You do not become involved! *Da?*'

'Oi!' shrieked Esme. 'There's been traffic up the mountain! All hours of the night! Something's going on! Talk to Parcel, Alfred! Talk to him!'

'Alfred is not going to put himself in any danger,' said Madame Polanikov. She waved her bejewelled fingers about dramatically. '*I'm* looking after this fine figure of a man now.'

'Maria Polony-baloney!' yelled Esme Trooter. 'You're going to turn this man into a namby-pamby! He needs to get back in the game. Things keep happening in this town, and no one takes any notice! If it wasn't for me, the whole place would be cemented over with property developers living in Barbados all year round off the proceeds and we'd have no one left here at all! People disappearing willy-nilly! Birds dying!'

I shot a look over at Mr K. He was watching me out of the corner of his eye.

The birds will die! I mouthed at him. He nodded.

'Parcel Brewster . . .' I murmured.

'Yes,' said Mr K. 'Your house is the closest to the mountain from his shack, and he knew all about you lot from your grandma. He probably felt he could trust you to do something, left the note and took off until everything dies down. He would have noticed the birds starting to get ill before anybody else realised anything was amiss at all.'

It all made sense. Though I hadn't felt particularly worried about the note, I still had a wave of relief wash over me. I hoped Parcel was okay being a hermit somewhere else for a bit.

Mr K was chewing his lip, thinking, but didn't get a chance. Esme was already elbowing him and squeaking, 'Alfred? Alfred? Don't ignore me, old man!'

I tried to placate our town campaigner. 'Mr K has other things on his plate right now, Esme,' I said, thinking guiltily of Jack. 'Maybe he could check on Parcel when this whole bird flu thing is over.'

'No!' said Esme. 'No! No! No!' She looked feistier than ever. 'Someone's got to go up to Frey's, see what's actually going on up there. See if Parcel's okay. Must I do it myself?'

Mr K sighed heavily and the general Sunday morning buzz around the green seemed suddenly to still. The chairs outside Big Mama's were empty, the cinema doors still firmly closed, the salon clients all disappearing into the cathedral. For a minute there was total silence.

But there wasn't silence in my head. A part of me couldn't help feeling she was right. What if Parcel *was* still around, being freaked out by the authorities crawling all over the place? Esme had turned her attention from Mr K to me. She arched an eyebrow and I nodded, very slightly. I leaned forward to help her up off the bench and murmured, 'I'll go up there tonight, Esme, okay?'

I was sure I'd spoken too softly for Mr K to hear, but he gave me a certain kind of look, regardless. Previous experience had taught my old and wrinkly friend that I had a tendency to *get involved*. If there was something going on, I'd be in it up to my neck, that's for sure. *Tallulah Bird, supersleuthy supersleuth!* . . .

Or, um, not.

Yet even if Mr K had wanted to say something to me he had no chance. Madame Polanikov had her ringed fingers on him, and he was going to have to behave himself.

Unlike me.

Chapter Fifteen

Sunday afternoon, back on the bench at the green

Tam and I had spent a day catching up, mooching about town, lunch at hers, over to Carrie's, and now we were back on the bench at the small green outside the cathedral. The sun was already sinking, and the breeze was chilly. Jack surely should have been back in town by now, but I'd heard nothing from him, and I couldn't bear to leave more than one voicemail for him. (Okay, two . . . but that's *all*, I promise.)

'How did we end up back here?' I asked.

'Ohh,' sighed Tam, 'dunno.' But her eyes slid sideways across the grass to that small coffee shop called Big Mama's.

'Hn,' I said, trying not to smile.

'What you doing tonight?' asked Tam.

'Depends.'

Tam groaned. 'You're going to turn into one of those creatures that dumps her mates when she's got a boyfriend. Like Alex with that Gavin. We haven't seen her all day.'

'As if!' I took a breath to argue furiously, but Tam just laughed.

'I'm only winding you up. I've got supper tonight with Mum and the Carusos.' She blushed a little.

'Really?' I was surprised. 'I didn't know your mum was matey with the Carusos.'

'Not so much,' said Tam. 'They got talking a couple of weeks ago about polenta pizza bases and next thing you know . . .' She shrugged.

'Next thing you know' – I made my voice dark and forboding – 'arranged marriage between Tam and Gianni. Tam becomes Italian mama like no other. Bearing twelve children and making the best gnocchi in town.'

'Lula!' yelped Tam. She punched me in the shoulder. It didn't hurt.

'It is what it is,' I said. 'You thinking about kids and all.'

'Like, *not*. Don't be ridiculous, Lula Bird!'

She sat back and fiddled with the strap on her bag, muttering insults at me.

'If you and Gianni –' I started.

'Never!'

'Well, if you did, I wouldn't mind. I swear.'

'Really?'

'Really. I was never into him, you know. Just wanted that kiss to be done and dusted.'

'You *were* desperate,' remembered Tam.

'So desperate.'

We sighed in sync, then grinned and hugged. I stood and stretched, ready to head home. 'I wouldn't have made it through half-term without you guys.'

Her hazel eyes grinned back at me. 'We love you, Lula, even though you're a little unhinged.' She stood too and after another glance at Big Mama's swung off in the other direction. 'Ring Arns,' she called over her shoulder. 'He can find out from Mona where Jack is.'

'Genius!' I muttered. I blew her a kiss and pulled my phone out.

Sunday evening, my love shack

Thump! Thump! Thump!

'Hey!' yelled Pen from outside. 'Let me in!'

'Not by the hair on my chinny chin chin!' I yelled back. I was reading a Silhouette Romance and Petronella was about to be ravished by Baron von Sturenhopf. Some things cannot be interrupted.

Then I heard Boodle whining and relented. Tucking the book under my pillow, I got up and opened the door. 'What do you want?' I asked Pen. 'Hey, Boodleyboo.'

Pen looked like she had to ask me something she didn't want to.

'What?' I said again.

She sighed. 'Can you walk Boodle tonight? Angus is coming over here to watch England play Pakistan, and we won't have time.'

'Sure,' I said. 'But can't Mum and Dad do it? They've been big into their romantic strolls.'

Pen came in uninvited and looked for chocolate in my usual hiding place under the quilt on my chair. No chocolate. She sighed again. 'They're going to an AA meeting tonight.'

'Oh.' I felt instantly uncomfortable. I was glad Dad was still off the booze, and getting better, but it still felt strange thinking of him as having a real-life drinking problem.

Boodle the Poodle came up to me and sat down. She whined.

'We'll go walking, Boodle, no problem. In a minute, okay? Jack will be here at eight.'

'He's coming round?'

'Yep.' My smile stretched over all my face.

'Where's he been? I haven't seen him since Friday night. And really, Lula, you're going to be called a slut if you carry on like you were in Big Mama's.'

'Yeah, yeah. That's for Alex to deal with.' Pen rolled her eyes. I pulled out a bag of Maltesers from a cupboard in the tiny kitchen and threw one to her and one to Boodle. 'Jack's been away at his granny's with Mona. He's coming here as soon as he's back.' I crammed five chocolate balls in my mouth at once.

'You are such a pig,' announced Pen.

'Who'smgwrshafter you?'

'Great-aunt Phoebe is staying in, not actually *looking after me*. I'm old enough to look after myself.'

I flicked my eyebrows up and shrugged, throwing her and Boodle another ball each.

'Who were you talking to for so long this afternoon?' asked Pen. 'Angus couldn't get through for, like, hours.'

I swallowed, considered how much I'd eaten and put the bag away. 'Forest,' I replied. 'And Arns. Mostly Arns.'

'Huh. I could hear you laughing from the house.'

'Yeah, well, he's a funny guy.'

Pen gave me a look. 'Seems to me like you spend more time with Arnold than your own boyfriend.'

I got a prickly feeling all over that I didn't like. 'I'll walk Boodle, okay, Pen? We might be quite a while. I'll see you later.' I held the door open.

'Fine, fine,' she said, and got out of the armchair. 'But don't go too far with her. Her back gets sore.'

'Mine too,' I said, and rubbed it. Damn that hula dancing. 'Laters.'

I was waiting so anxiously that I heard the gate squeak before Boodle did, and flew out with her lead and my jacket tucked under my arm, and my backpack over a shoulder. Jack hadn't even made it round the side of the main house by the time I'd got to him.

'Hello!' I said, breathless.

'Mm,' he said, and I could see a whisper of a smile in the moonlight. 'You smell good.'

'Maltesers,' I said.

'You don't have to tell me.'

'You want one?'

He grinned and pushed his hair behind an ear before pulling me towards him by the belt loops on my jeans. 'I want a lot.'

'Oh.' I gulped. 'You talking about chocolate?'

Jack laughed. 'Sure I am. I take it we're not staying in? Your phone message was very mysterious.' He let go of my jeans and turned back towards the gate. He was wearing sturdy boots, dark jeans and a long-sleeved black T, like I asked. The T hung just right. I wished he wasn't walking away.

'I said we'd walk Boodle the Poodle for Pen, so we'll take her with us, okay?'

'Cool,' said Jack. He held the gate open. I clipped the lead on Boodle and walked out first. 'So what's this about new info on the Cluny land?' He shut the gate.

'Before we talk about that' – my chest suddenly got tight – 'did you come over tonight because you wanted to see me, or because I lured you here saying I had news-story information?'

'What?' Jack stopped dead in the road ahead of me, looking over at my worried face.

I stopped too. 'It's no big deal either way,' I added hastily. 'It's just that –'

Jack stepped up to me and tugged me against him. 'Hey,

Lula. I'm sorry. I feel like a jerk not letting you know we were away this weekend. Gran was ill, Mum called, everything was last minute and then I left my bloody phone, and – Look. This is so messy. I've got no excuse. I'm not used to thinking about another person all the time.'

'Stop,' I said. 'Just stop. You're making me feel like a needy girlfriend. I don't want you to *have* to think about me. I'd like it if you just *did* think about me. Okay?'

'Everything I say is coming out wrong,' groaned Jack. He stepped away, dropped his head and pinched the bridge of his nose. His hair fell across his face and suddenly I felt like I didn't know anything about him at all. It left a strange sensation in the pit of my stomach that I wanted to go away.

'Forget I said that,' I murmured. 'Okay? Let's just have fun tonight.'

Jack opened his eyes and stared into mine. He put his arms round my shoulders and hugged me gently, and I tilted my head back. I had a glimpse of night sky and stars and a crescent moon before his lips were on mine.

It felt so good I got a little trembly.

'Are you cold?' asked Jack, pulling away.

'No,' I said, stepping closer.

Boodle whined and snuffled round our feet, but we kissed again anyway.

And, again, WOW. With Jack even a kiss was never just a kiss. He brushed his lips gently against mine, teasing, his warm hands circling my waist beneath my shirt. I felt my heart flutter and my breath grow uneven as he tugged me closer, running his fingers up my spine.

'Shall we go back to your room?' asked Jack.

'TALLULAH BIRD! ARE YOU UP TO YOUR SHENANIGANS AGAIN?' shrilled a voice from over the road.

I peeked over Jack's shoulder at the thick foliage of the Setting Sun's new residence across the way.

'Esme?' I asked.

'DOES YOUR MOTHER KNOW YOU'RE CARRYING ON IN THE STREETS WITH THAT BOY?' Esme Trooter came into view, wearing a stripy seventies pantsuit and dragging Jeremiah Coldstock behind her by the hand.

Jack grinned, but did not pull away.

'Yes, thanks, Esme,' I called back, my cheeks on fire. 'Just going to check up on what we spoke about earlier.'

'Oh! Okay, then. Good girl! See you tomorrow!' and she clipped down the road with Jeremiah hustling alongside.

'All still very mysterious,' said Jack.

'It is,' I answered, reluctantly letting him go. 'You should know I've been on the phone to Forest this afternoon. You and I are heading up to Frey's Dam to find dead birds and a man called Parcel Brewster.'

Chapter Sixteen

Sunday 8.30 p.m. Breaking the law

'So you don't mind being an unconvicted criminal,' hissed Jack, hunkered down on the south ridge overlooking the still water of Frey's Dam.

'Not for a good cause,' I whispered back. 'If Esme is right, and there's something going on that's not actually bird flu, then we've got to fix things. Why's it taking so long to hear back from that lab technician?'

'He'd left by the time we got to the pub, and now he won't talk to us. Jazz keeps ringing, but . . .'

I bet she does, I thought unkindly. 'Never mind,' I said, 'we'll do our own samples.'

'What?' Jack was surprised, but not horrified. 'How?'

'Forest.'

Jack grinned at me. 'Ohh, you are so clever, Lula-lu.'

'That's why you love me,' I grinned back. Doh! I just did it again! Is it too dark for him to see me go reddest red *red*? Any other boy would have come back with: 'I do?', but Jack's grin just got wider and he leaned in close.

Ooh. Moonlight. Beautiful boy. What's not to like . . . He kissed me on my cheek, then my lips.

'Mmm,' he murmured.

I don't know how I heard that. My heart was pounding so hard I don't know how anything could make it to my ears, all that blood rushing about, my brain in serious shutdown . . .

We would have got totally distracted then, but bliddy Boodlington pulled on the lead, unbalancing me, so I ended up flat on my back.

'Whoa!' said Jack. 'You're keen!'

'Ha!' I retorted, cheeks aflame. 'Come on. Let's get down there.'

At the water's edge it was obvious that all the dead birds had been cleared away. Footprints and drag marks littered the shore, and I couldn't see a trace of birdlife anywhere. I wondered whether we were wasting our time here, whether every last feather had been found and burned by the Parks guys. Taking my backpack off, I opened it and crouched down to rummage inside. I hauled out a glass jar, some old ice-cream containers and a big plastic bag.

Boodle nosed around my stash, and sniffed appreciatively where ice-cream smell lingered.

'Nothing in here for you, lady friend,' I said to her. I held the jar out to Jack. 'This is for the water sample,' I said to him. 'You fill that while I get sand and look for birds. If you see any bird food, or bread, or anything like that, bag it too.'

I was about to move off, anxious to get out of here as fast

as possible, when Jack grabbed my arm.

'Hey,' he said slowly. 'I'm seriously impressed, Tallulah.'

I felt my cheeks flare, even in the icy moonlight.

'Why didn't I think of this?' he continued.

'It's probably nothing,' I said hastily. 'Mr K thinks Esme's totally overreacting.' I paused. 'But I spoke to Arns this afternoon and he says his mum isn't very happy with the lab results. She won't tell him why, though. I guess she's not supposed to tell him every single thing that goes on. Unprofessional, you know?'

'You like Arns,' observed Jack. He was looking at me intently, as if he were searching for something that wasn't there.

'Sure,' I said. 'He's a good friend.'

'Sure,' he said, echoing me, and still staring into my eyes intently. He smiled suddenly and my stomach flipped. 'Okay, let's do it,' he said, and with a quick kiss on the lips we headed off in different directions, moving quickly and quietly. Boodle was walking obediently at my side, so I unclipped her lead and she found a big rocky shelf to flop down on to. There were bushes on each side of her and in the moonlight she looked like an ornamental stone lion guarding a palace. I stepped up to the outcrop and rubbed her forehead. 'Your back hurting?' I asked her. She gave a little whine and dropped her head on her paws, huffing out a sandy breath.

'Wait here for me, then, Boodle, okay? Wait.'

Boodle flicked her eyes open in a yes, and I set off again.

Jack and I each had a torch and I could see his light bobbing not too far away. I felt vaguely terrified in the dark on my own, but swallowed it down and swung my torchlight carefully back and forth all the way round the water's edge looking for a bird. I was just about to give up and go back over to Jack when I saw something white in the water and a tiny movement on a mound of sticks under a bush just ahead.

I looked back across the dam, and could just make out Jack putting the jar back in the bag and shouldering it. He began walking round towards me. I left the containers I had on the sand and tiptoed over to the pile of sticks.

Just as I'd thought.

It was a cleverly hidden nest, but my eyes teared over because in it was a female mallard and three ducklings, all dead. The tiny movement I'd seen had come from the smallest duckling of them all. Even without my torchlight I could see it was barely alive. Instinctively, I reached forward and picked it up. Its tiny heart thundered in the palm of my hand.

'You poor little thing!' I murmured. It was shivering uncontrollably and I'm sure it nestled closer to my skin, laying the side of its head against my thumb. 'Ohhh,' I breathed, 'I'll take care of you,' and before I could think anything sensible at all I'd placed that newly hatched duckling in the fuzzy warmth of my jacket pocket.

I walked back over to the bag and containers I'd left on the ground to find that Jack had reached my pile of stuff. 'Jack,' I said, about to show him the tiny duckling.

But then he said, 'Wait till Jazz hears about us coming up here tonight. I *bet* she can get some stats out of that lab guy. I'm going to call her the second we get back.'

And the moment was gone. There was no doubt in my mind that my brand-new boyfriend would go nuts at the idea of me nursing a bird that I'd removed illegally from a bird-flu zone, but I felt too deflated by Jazz being here when she wasn't really here to have an argument with Jack. I don't know what I was thinking, except that I had a weird sense that Esme was right – there was no bird flu; something else was going on – and I hoped our samples would prove it. I bent down and picked up the plastic bag.

'Could you go back there and put the female and a little one in this bag, Jack?'

He took the bag. 'Sure,' he said, and I heard him curse softly when he got to the nest. I felt for the duckling, murmuring reassurances. It felt less shaky now, though the heartbeat was still pattering too fast.

Jack returned.

'Now for Parcel Brewster,' I said.

*

We scoured the area around Frey's as best we could with our torches and by moonlight, calling quietly all across the north ridge, but could find no sign of anyone living in the area.

'I think we should go, Lula,' said Jack. 'It's nearly ten o'clock now and I don't want your folks getting worried about you.'

'Their meeting ends at eleven,' I said, distracted, 'but they might go for coffee after. Let me think.'

Jack was quiet while I tried to remember everything Esme had told me. Nothing new came to mind. I thought back to when Grandma Bird was alive and often came up into the hills around here with her witchy friends. There was a movement in my pocket and I reached in to stroke the soft feathers. I turned slowly on the spot, searching the skyline while keeping the dam in my peripheral vision.

'The bird man,' I muttered.

'Hmm?'

'Esme called him the bird man, and Grandma used to bring grain up here sometimes. He would have wanted to be able to see the birds from his camp, surely.'

'You said Esme suggested the north ridge.'

I sighed. 'She did, but we've searched those slopes . . .' I looked over at the ridge again. Trees lined the horizon, some rocks, gaps in the woods here and there. 'Maybe higher,' I wondered out loud.

'Wait,' said Jack. 'What's that?'

He pointed ahead and then I saw what he'd spotted, right at the top of the ridge. A sharp angle tucked to the side of an enormous pile of boulders. 'A tree branch?' I suggested.

'Let's check it out.'

It was a serious hike to get up there. We had to scramble over a lot of rock and stone, and I had to keep checking the duckling was okay in my coat pocket. It was very still now and I hoped it was still alive. I made sure it could breathe, put my torch in my mouth and hurried after Jack.

Boodle was still slumped on that rocky ledge, way below us now. It looked like she was power napping, and I worried that I'd walked her too far.

Jack and I got to the top at the same time.

My jaw dropped. 'Frik!'

'Holy moley,' said Jack.

'Mr Brewster?' I called, but there was no answer from inside the crashed and smashed shack. Bits and pieces of broken wood were strewn about the tiny area, the roof had fallen in and it didn't look like anyone could ever have lived there.

'Wait here,' said Jack, and he stepped forward carefully. As he went he snapped pictures with a tiny digital camera. He took a few of what was once the inside, standing just under the roof, then put his camera away and pulled out a palm-sized camcorder. He filmed all around the area, then called, 'Mr Brewster?' to the surrounding area.

Nothing stirred.

He walked back over to me. 'We need to let the police know about this.' He gestured to the chaos behind us. 'It must have happened today, yesterday maybe, otherwise they would have seen it when they were searching for Emily Saunders.'

'That means getting into trouble. We're not allowed up here, Jack.'

'Yeah, but we are wearing overshoes.' Jack pointed to the showercap-like plastic bags on our feet.

I gave him a look.

'Yep. We're going to have to get into trouble,' he sighed.

'Unless we do the anonymous tip-off thing,' I suggested.

Jack nodded thoughtfully. 'The anonymous tip-off thing is good. That'll give us time to get this stuff analysed. You said Forest will help?'

'He said it's good I asked him for help – he's the best in his class. I just can *not* imagine him being a biotechnician. Someone so big doing something so microscopic.'

'Hey, he's second-year now and they've been doing soil analysis for two terms already. If I have to hear one more time about how Richard Murphy put his poo under the 'scope, I –'

Suddenly I heard something. 'Jack! What was that?'

He listened. 'What?'

'Do you hear a truck? A big car or something?'

Jack listened again. 'Sounds far away.'

I listened. The noise had stopped. 'So, once Forest's results come back, and if it *is* bird flu?'

'Everything gets incinerated.'

I thought with a pang of something small and fluffy in my pocket. It was time to tell Jack, even though I knew he'd try to make me leave it behind. I wondered if bird flu were treatable, if –

'IT'S JUST UP HERE.'

Jack and I were shocked into instant action. We scrambled up the boulders to the west of the shack and squeezed behind a bush overlooking Parcel Brewster's destroyed home.

'Keep your voice down!' The words were fiercely whispered. It sent goosebumps shivering across my skin and made my hands turn to ice.

'Who is that?' I mouthed to Jack.

He shrugged and put his finger to his lips, then pulled out the camcorder.

Oh boy. Boodle was still at the dam. Please, please let her just stay still and quiet.

'There's no need to whisper now,' came the first voice, someone young.

'Just keep it down!'

'The old man is dead. Dead as dead. And no one's going

to come here for weeks because of the bird-flu story. Our problems are over.'

I shot a look at Jack, and his eyes, though glued to the camcorder, were as wide as mine.

'My problems will be over when you've cleared away this mess,' said the second voice, a much older man. He cleared his throat and spat. 'It's bad enough we've had to wait an entire day to sort this out. I knew I should have done the whole job on my own. Were you even sober last night? We said take him out *quietly*, yeah, but you end up tearing down his house to get to him?'

'Sometimes plans don't go according to plan.'

'And then I end up having to finish it off, don't I?'

'But –'

'Shut up, you idiot.'

Two silhouettes came into view against the night sky. They grunted their way up to the level ground where the shack was and dropped some empty bags at their feet. Soon both of them were piling things into the bags. As soon as one was full, they'd hurl it over the edge where it landed far below on the sandy beach of Frey's Dam.

When the first one hit the ground, there was a sharp bark that cut the air.

'What the hell was that?' asked the older man.

'Just a fox, probably,' said his companion, but he kept just as still as the old guy. There was a rustling in the undergrowth and another bark.

Boodle, I thought desperately, tingling with dread all over, *please stay still! Please, please don't move!*

'You hear anything else?' whispered the old man at last.

'It was a fox,' said his companion. 'For sure. I know the wild.'

The older guy snorted and they both began filling bags again. 'Don't take too much stuff,' he said to his partner. 'It needs to look like he lived here peacefully, but left peacefully.'

The other man laughed. A high-pitched giggle that made my hair stand up on end.

'And how long are you going to keep the bird-flu scare going?'

'As long as it takes for us to clear the evidence.'

The men were only another few minutes – Parcel Brewster hadn't had much, it seemed – and then the older man shunted the shack's structures this way and that until it looked vaguely habitable again.

'Let's go,' he said. 'We'll take the bags to the truck, get rid of them, and then you need to get back to keep watch again. I don't want anyone round here poking their noses in where they shouldn't.'

The two men scuffed and rattled and tramped their way back down the ridge. My heart stopped when I heard another familiar bark, but the men were going round the other way and it was coming from the bank on the far side. My legs screamed at me to stand up, and the base of my spine sent a persistent dull ache into the rest of my body. Jack looked similarly cramped, but he'd gripped that camcorder like a vice the entire time and hadn't moved a muscle.

It took a long time for the night-time stillness to settle in. A long time before we couldn't hear the voices, the rustling of bags being taken away, the thudding of our own hearts.

'Frikking frikly frik,' I said.

'We've got to move,' said Jack quietly. 'Fast.'

Boodle had trotted back round and was waiting exactly where I'd left her.

'You clever, clever girl!' I whispered, and pulled her lead out of my jeans pocket. She bounded down from the rock and licked my hand. 'Just wait a minute,' I said. 'This clip is tricky,' but she danced away, staring over at Jack. He was dithering near the water's edge.

'Come on, Jack!' I said, knowing he'd hear me clearly. He held up his hand, still looking around at the shore. 'You heard that old man!' I called quietly. 'The young guy is coming back here to keep watch! Let's go!'

'It's definitely not bird flu,' said Jack stubbornly. 'They must have poisoned something.'

'We've got water samples,' I said.

Jack frowned. 'What if the poison has worked its way out of the water? It's a hot spring that feeds Frey's.'

'They could have poisoned the whole dam,' I suggested.

Jack shook his head. 'The evidence would stay for too long. It's got to be in the food the birds ate.'

I remembered something. 'There might have been bread in the water on the other side,' I said. 'I saw something floating near the rocky bit where we found the ducks' nest. Could just be feathers.' Jack was already moving in that direction. 'But be careful round that edge! It's a sheer drop and it's really deep there.'

'I can swim,' said Jack.

'I'd rather you didn't,' I sniped, then bit my lip. I was scared and it was making me ratty. Jack jogged carefully round the shore by moonlight, too nervous to use a torch. He got to the spot where I'd seen stuff floating and I saw him get an empty container out and scoop at the surface. He'd just put the lid on and shoved the container back in the bag when I saw him suddenly jump with fright and stumble.

'Jack!' I called, in horror.

His feet slipped, and he fell, the incline of the slippery rock sending him down to the water.

'Omigodomigod!' I sobbed, sprinting across the shore towards him, Boodle hot on my heels.

Somehow Jack stopped the slide, and pulled himself up, handhold by handhold, then loped across to the safer sandy area. He came fast then, sprinting almost, and I wondered suddenly about tracks and whether anyone would notice fresh footprints. I was already moving by the time he got to my side.

And then we heard the truck.

The engine chuntering fast, then stopping. The sound of a vehicle door slamming. The beep of an alarm setting.

Frik!

The guard was back!

Chapter Seventeen

Sunday 10 p.m. On the run

'This way!' I hissed to Jack. 'Come, Boodle!' and we bounded out of the clearing round the dam and into the trees. Luckily the ground was soft and quiet with winter mulch, new ferns and bracken silent underfoot. We ran like deer, dodging fallen branches and closely packed trunks, rocks and boulders. Now and again we'd pause to listen, crouched down low behind banks of last year's bracken, but we didn't stop more than a few seconds, the adrenalin pushing us on.

It wasn't long before I began to recognise the familiar treescape of the area around Coven's Quarter. It was much darker now under thick firs, and we had to go slower. At last I saw the paler shapes of beech trees coming into view and found a path I knew.

'Not far to go,' I whispered to Jack.

'Stop!' he said in a low voice, and grabbed my arm. 'Where's Boodle?'

'She was just behind you,' I replied, my chest heaving from the run. 'She'll be a little slower because of her sore back maybe.'

Jack did not let go of my arm, and together we retraced

our steps on tiptoe, ears pricked for any sound at all.

Nothing but our breathing. Nothing whatsoever.

'I should have put her lead on!' I agonised. 'You stay here in case she's done a loop or got lost – I'll creep up to the high ground over there, okay?'

'No! Not okay! We need to go, Lula! If that man heard us, or saw our tracks or anything, he's going to be right behind us. We can't risk being found! He'll have a gun for sure. Parcel Brewster! Lula, they got rid of Parcel Brewster.'

'And they would get rid of us,' I said, finishing his thought process.

'Exactly.'

'Well, I'm not leaving here without Boodle,' I said, my throat starting to tense up.

'Lula –'

But I didn't wait to hear what Jack had to say. I felt suddenly angry with him and even a bad man with a gun wasn't going to stop me looking after my – Pen's – dog. I scrambled up the steep slope as fast as I could, trying to remember the way we'd hurtled down. Was I just going to get hopelessly lost? No, I remembered that tree, all leaning to the side like that, and there was that big bank of bracken. I picked up the pace, darting from one recognisable thing to the next, until at last I was back on high ground. I stopped, breathing hard, and crouched behind a tree.

A hand on my shoulder made me jump and cry out.

'Sorry!' whispered Jack in my ear.

'Quiet!' I hissed back, furious with him.

He ignored me, staring over at thick vegetation before us. 'I don't see or hear her anywhere,' he muttered. 'Where on earth could she have got to?'

And then we heard her bark. Another sound, a jangling noise, and in the distance, moving closer, an angry voice. 'Get back here! Get back here now!'

'Frikking frik!' I hissed. 'Boodle's got something of his!'

'No way,' whispered Jack. 'No bloody way.'

'Yes way! And she's coming towards us!'

'So's that man.'

'Run!'

We ran. We ran faster than we'd run before, but still Boodle overtook us. As we leapt through a clearing on the path to Coven's Quarter, Pen's dog flew through the air beside me and I saw that in her mouth she had a set of keys. Vehicle keys.

She sailed into the Coven's Quarter clearing in triumph and stood waiting for us, her tail waving gently. I dropped to my haunches to face her and snapped her lead on without a word. Jack was beside me then, and said, 'You know the way back to yours?' though we both knew that was a silly question. Only last month Jack had filmed this clearing, with its huge stone seats made of immense slabs of rock, and we'd walked in and walked out together. I ignored him.

'Boodle,' I said. 'Drop the keys!'

'Oh no!' said Jack, whirling down and checking Boodle's mouth. 'She's got that man's keys.'

And that's when torchlight strobed from the higher ground and began spooling out across the stone chairs, examining each seat one by one.

Frikking frik frik!

We darted behind the widest of the seats, and I kept my arms firmly round Boodle's neck, while Jack held her waving tail down. I dropped down with my back to the stone of the seat, staring in horror at Boodle, and Jack staring at me in horror, and watching the torchlight flashing closer and closer across the tree trunks around the clearing.

We could hear the soft sounds of someone walking carefully.

Closer and closer.

We could hear him breathing.

Then – too, too close – a young man's voice lilted through the night air:

'Heeere doggy doggy doggy dog! Heeeere! I've got a treeeaat for you!' Then that creepy giggle.

I swallowed, and closed my eyes. Boodle sensed how completely terrified I was and licked my face. My eyes flew open and I glared at her. *This is all your fault!* I shouted in my head, and there's no doubt she heard me. She blinked an apology and I bit my lip.

The crunch of another step closer. 'Heeere doggy doggy doggy dog! Where aaaare you?' The singsong call chilled me to the bone. Boodle didn't like it either. Her nostrils flared and a low growl rumbled in her throat. My grip on the scruff of her neck tightened into a fist straight away. I made big eyes at her and shook my head, mouthing, 'NO!'

The torchlight stopped instantly and bounced in our direction, searching all around the seat we were hiding behind. Jack reached over to me and just as I was thinking he really was being careless and stupid and irresponsible and and and –

he flicked a stone high over our heads at a low gliding angle.

The torchlight bounced quickly away as stone clicked against stone in the opposite direction.

'Oh, doooggy,' sang the man. 'I've got you now.' He hurried away, and didn't stop, crashing heedlessly right out of the clearing, through the bracken and up on to the slopes.

We stayed frozen in our hiding place until not a flicker of torchlight could be seen.

When I felt it was safe, I nodded. Jack took the keys from Boodle's mouth and shoved them in his pocket.

'I think you should leave those here,' I said. 'Most definitely. You're going to make things complicated.'

Jack smiled at me, but it was strained. 'Lula, I'm so sorry I said to leave Boodle. I just wanted to get you out of here.'

I shot a glance over my shoulder. 'Just drop the keys. It's time to go.' And I was off, with Boodle on a tight leash. And we didn't stop, not even at my front gate. Just kept going till we were all the way inside.

Jack didn't stay for longer than five minutes when we got home. He could barely look me in the eye as he asked if I was really okay. Then he took off for his digs with my backpack full of dead bird, sand, water, bits of sodden bread, after checking that I'd locked the door behind him, and that my phone was working.

He called me when he got back home, but the conversation was stilted and left me feeling upset enough to cry. How could the perfect plan to win Jack back from Jazz have gone so horribly wrong?

'You sure you okay?' he'd asked.

'I'm *fine*!' I said testily, then felt bad straight away. He was just worrying about me, and I shouldn't snap just because I was freaked out by the fact that we'd stumbled upon a murder scene. 'Is Forest still okay to test that stuff?'

'He is. And I called the cops from a payphone on the corner of Aston and Freeman. Said Parcel Brewster is presumed dead.'

I swallowed. 'The anonymous tip-off. Good. No camera

at that callbox. Jason and Jessica are always snogging in it. Hey, I'll ask Arns to ring me when his mum has news about it. Our inside line to the police force. See? Alex and I do know people.'

'Mm,' he said. 'You sure you're okay?'

'Oh, for goodness' sake!' I cried before I could stop myself. 'Stop treating me like a child!'

'I'm not, Lula! That's the last thing I –'

'I'm sorry,' I interrupted. 'I . . . I just can't believe Parcel . . .' My throat clenched shut and I couldn't speak for a moment. 'I'm being a total b–'

'No, you're not,' comforted Jack. 'I get it. You're upset.'

'It's not just that. Jack, I'm worried we won't be able to do anything because I was so stupid, making us trespass . . . Did you check your camera? Can you send the police an mpg file?'

Jack took a deep breath. 'You're not going to like this.'

'Oh no. What?'

'There's no sound. And it was so dark it's impossible to make out anything at all.'

'*No!*'

'I'm sorry.'

I sighed. 'Don't apologise. You were brilliant to think of it in the first place. All that came to my mind was hiding. Will you phone me when Forest has some answers?'

He was silent on the other side, as if he were thinking

about something, and then he said, 'Sure, and will you call me with information from the police department? To check that they're taking the tip-off seriously?'

'Yes. Of course. If I hear anything.'

We said goodbye, both of us feeling deflated and upset. Well, *I* felt upset. Difficult to know what goes through boys' minds. Like, did he think I was a total amateur after tonight's mess? What an idiot I was. I'd put myself on the same level as Jazz with the journo leads, and now look. How could I have hoped to compete? All I'd done was embarrass myself entirely and put us in terrible danger; I was still the silly schoolgirl, someone he had to worry about all the time, and Jazz was still the beautiful independent university student, her sparkling career and fantastic contacts all before her – a far more appealing girlfriend candidate.

I puffed out an exhausted breath, and would have collapsed on my bed, but Boodle pushed against me and went, 'Wrooarf,' at my pocket.

'Oh my goodness!' I said, my pulse thundering up to race pace again. I stood quickly and carefully, and cautiously eased the tiny duckling out of my jacket pocket into the light. Its eyes were closed and it was completely still, but I could feel its heart beating fast in its fragile chest. It didn't take long to make it a nest out of my fake Blahniks' shoebox. I put the carton on the floor next to my bed and went into the main house to make it some warm oats, Grandma Bird's cure-all for feathered creatures in need. When I got back to the annexe, I found Boodle curled round the box, huffing her warm breath on the duckling, which still hadn't moved.

At first it seemed I'd never get the little thing's bill open to get the oats in, but with patience I think some finally went down. I covered the bowl and put it in the kitchen. I'd try again in the morning.

Great-aunt Phoebe called across the courtyard at eleven to check that I was okay and ready for bed. 'Your young man has gone, Tallulah?'

'Yes, Aunt Phoebe,' I replied, opening the living-room window so she could hear me. 'He's gone.'

'Penelope says Boodle can stay over with you tonight.' Aunt Phoebe stepped closer, shading her eyes from the glare of my outside light. 'Lula? Are you all right? You sound tired.'

'I am.'

She came up to my window and bent down to look at my face. 'He didn't seem to stay after you got back from your walk. Did you two have a disagreement?'

'Kind of,' I answered, and felt suddenly teary.

Aunt Phoebe kissed me first on one cheek then the other. 'He'll see the light,' she assured me. 'You're one in a gazillion. Have a hot bath and get some sleep now, Tallulah.'

Monday – frikking early. On the run again

So the thing about pets is that they're a huge responsibility. I know this now because at some inhumane hour a little bird in a box in my room began *peep-peep*ing like there's no tomorrow. To be honest, the peeping didn't wake me, but Boodle thumping my head with her enormous paw did.

I rolled out of bed, staggered to the kitchen and picked up the bowl of oats. Back in bed, I sat cross-legged, bird box on lap, feeding. The duckling spread its wings with delight and gaped, putting its head right back. In went the oats. When it had had enough, it settled down again and Boodle curled round the box. I tried to go back to sleep, but box, Boodle and my body did not all fit comfortably and I was *not* king of the heap, that's for sure. When a faint glow finally seeped through the blinds, I threw on my running stuff and headed out.

Usually I run up the mountain road, but last night's experiences had me thinking I really didn't want to be anywhere near there, especially as it was still pretty dark and misty, so I turned down Darling Street, which runs past the side of our house, down a steep incline, into a welter of little roads and tightly packed houses. Not many lights were on, but the streetlamps were bright, the roads quiet and I felt safe. After about half an hour of hard running I was starting to feel better in my head – less angry and confused about my beautiful boyfriend – though my back was still plaguing me. Then suddenly I remembered I'd left Boodle inside and that she hadn't been out to do her business yet.

Frik! I thought. *That could be a biiig accident.* Nothing about Boodle was small, especially not her poos. I was in the centre of town now, and began pelting up Hill Street, the chimneys of Cluny's Crematorium dark against the skyline. Working hard up the incline, I heard the car before I saw its dark shadow, and I'm pretty sure whoever was driving wouldn't have seen me, though they were rumbling along at a strangely slow and furtive speed.

Something made me duck behind a tree, I don't know what. The car drifted to a halt outside the crematorium, and a figure emerged from the mist, carrying a heavy load that seemed to slip and slide in his arms. He staggered up the steps to Cluny's veranda, deposited the package and thumped the door loudly with his fist before dashing away.

The car door slammed and the vehicle was off. I couldn't see it, but I heard it take a hard right up Henderson Avenue a few houses up.

'Couriers,' I muttered in disgust. 'Don't even wait for a signature any more.' I shook my head at what a scaredy cat I'd become, and stepped out from behind the tree.

How it happened I don't quite know, but suddenly I was down on my knees on the pavement, bent over in agony.

Chapter Eighteen

Monday 5 a.m. In serious pain

'Nyeeep!' I squealed, clutching my back. The spasm of pain wracked my whole body, and I didn't think any human being had ever felt such suffering. 'Frik! Frik! Frik!' My spine had well and truly spasmed. Or pinched a nerve. Or slipped a disc. Or, actually, just *broken*, judging by the pain.

'Bumly poxly bum bum!' I whimpered.

I somehow managed to ride the spasm out, taking deep breaths, trying to relax.

There. That was better.

I looked up. Cluny's was just a few metres away, and my house two hundred from there. Maybe three.

Okay. I just had to get to a standing position, and then I could shuffle home.

Bit by bit, by gripping on to the trunk of the tree, I managed to haul myself up. I was hunched over like Quasimodo from Notre Dame, and didn't even have the guts to brush the gravel from my knees. Only essential movements would do right now. I took a step.

'Nyeeep!'

And another.

'Nyeeep!'

The pain sent tears coursing down my cheeks.

'You frikking useless girl!' I scolded, and took two more steps.

'Nyeeep frik! Nyeeep frik!'

I stopped and heaved more teary breaths.

'Bliddy Alex and her hula frikking hula class!'

It must have taken me twenty minutes to get the twenty metres to Cluny's. The mist was fading away. I looked down the road. I still couldn't see my home. The pain from my back was making my legs shudder and shake. I stopped and held on to the crematorium railing.

'Hello, dead people,' I whispered. 'So sorry to trespass.'

I took another step and my left leg buckled.

'Nyhee!' I gripped the railing with all my might and my leg steadied.

'Okay,' I muttered. 'Plan B.'

Inch by agonising inch I got myself up the two steps and on to the veranda. Finally I was at the front door, legs shaking badly now. I wasn't sure if it was from the exertion, the pain or the fright of a multitude of dead, past and present, within.

I rang the bell.

And waited.

I had been ringing and waiting for about fifteen minutes. Every time I was just about to give up, I'd try to turn away and make for home, but I couldn't move a muscle without my whole body spasming again.

I held my breath and rang again, leaving my forefinger on the buzzer so that the faraway ringing went on and on and on. Then I lifted my fist, and, though it nearly killed me, I whacked on that door like Bludgeon gaining entry to a perp's hideout.

At last, the sound of footsteps. The door clicked and vibrated as bolts were shot back and latches unlocked, and then there I was face to face with Helen Cluny's scary dad.

Mr Cluny was everything you'd expect from the town's undertaker: tall and thin and ghostly white. His hair was sparse to the point of baldness, just short drifts of white across a strong-shaped head. His eyes were the most lively part of him and right now the dark blue of them sparkled with anger. 'You have been banging on my door since the crack of dawn!' he bellowed at me. 'Not even bothering with the etiquette of the doorbell!'

'Uh, that wasn't me,' I said quickly, remembering the courier delivery.

'Banging and blasting then ringing and ringing! We were up for all hours last night incinerating birds! This family is exhausted! What do you want?' His thick silver eyebrows beetled together and I saw that the knucklebones of his hands gripping the door and frame were shining through his thin, papery skin.

'Sorry to bother you, Mr Cluny,' I said, white-faced and feeling sick and shaky, 'but I've hurt myself and I can't get home.' It came out suitably pathetic, and Mr Cluny's thunderous face looked a little less furious.

A shape shifted in the darkness behind him. 'Who is it, Arthur dear?'

'Helen's friend,' he barked over his shoulder. 'Sally Bird's granddaughter. The witchy one. The one with the boy trouble.'

I did not correct the man. I needed his help and, besides, he was right on a few points there. 'Tallulah,' I said, stooping a little further to ease the ache. 'Tallulah Bird.'

Helen's mum bustled into the doorway. 'Hello, Tatty! Helen's still sleeping.'

'She's hurt herself,' announced Arthur Cluny.

'Well, let her in, dear! What are you doing keeping her out on the veranda! What's wrong, Tatty?' She shouldered her husband aside and grabbed my forearms. Just that little nudge had me falling to my knees with a ridiculous yelping scream.

'My back!' I managed.

'Looks bad,' observed Arthur without compassion. 'No wonder you were beating the door down.'

'Wasn't me,' I gasped. 'Not the first time, anyway. You had a delivery.'

I gestured with a look to the side of the door and that's

164

when I screamed for real and even Mrs Cluny's muscly arms couldn't keep me from dropping to my knees. Again.

On the Cluny's front veranda was a body wrapped up in clear plastic. A puddle of dark liquid oozed from its folds and I could make out tufts of grey hair, an open eye staring up at me and a slightly parted mouth, the lips very blue. The worst was the hand that had fallen out from the plastic wrapping. It was old and clawed and it looked like it was beckoning to me.

It freaked me out.

Totally.

When I'd stopped screaming I realised dully that I could move again. That my body, while in pain, wasn't in a total rictus any more. And that was lucky because the Clunys had forgotten all about me. They'd moved into overdrive and were calling to Helen, running for the telephone, phoning the police, phoning my parents.

'*This* was the delivery?' asked Arthur Cluny. '*This?*'

I nodded, still in shock.

'Did you see who made the delivery?'

'I – I –' I stopped and took a breath. 'I thought it was a courier,' I said. 'Couldn't really see. The mist . . .'

Helen came running down the stairs in her pyjamas. 'Tatty? What are you doing here? Mum? What's going on?'

'Someone dropped a body on the veranda,' said her mum.

'Oh,' said Helen, yawning and rubbing her eyes.

'Anyone want tea? Tatty, why are you here?'

'She saw the guy who dropped the body,' said Mr Cluny. 'Police will want to talk to her.'

'Oh,' said Helen again. 'Geez. Only with you around, T. Come get a hot drink.' She shuffled away down the corridor in her slippers. I followed her cautiously, looking left to right as I went. The Cluny home did not look like I expected it to. It was totally normal.

Helen glanced back over her shoulder and gave me a look. 'Stuff for doing the bodies is down in the basement and out back,' she explained.

'I wasn't –'

'Sure you weren't, Tatty,' said Helen, smiling wryly. 'Sure you weren't.'

'Doesn't it creep you out?' I asked tentatively.

'Just the fluids from the embalming,' she said, putting the kettle on. 'Not the stuff that goes *in*, you know, the stuff that comes *out*.'

'Right,' I whispered, but before I could slump into a chair and put ten sugars in my tea for the shock of everything I'd suffered so far, I heard my mum at the door. She was talking urgently to Mrs Cluny, but Mrs C was obviously calming her down, because by the time she got to the kitchen she was laughing at something Helen's mum was saying.

'Lu?' said Mum. '*Whatever next?* Are you hurt?'

I stood up and she came over and held me gently.

'Martha said something about your back?'

I nodded. 'I was running this morning and I hurt it coming up this last hill. Just after the man dropped the . . . the –'

'The body off,' said Helen. 'Hi, Dr Bird.'

'Hello, Helen. Did my daughter wake you?' Mum had a twinkle in her eye even though she still looked worried.

Helen grinned. 'Tatty is totally weird,' she said.

'Ohh no!' I replied. 'No no no! Don't pin this on me! I was just running by. Nothing to do with me. At All. Nothing To Do With Me At All!'

'Uh-huh,' said Helen.

I felt like I was going to burst into tears suddenly.

'Let's get you home,' said Mum. 'And I'll call the surgery to see if Dr McCabe can take a look at your back –'

'No!' I said again, vehemently this time. I had seen the look on Helen's face and I knew that if I stayed away from school today there'd be too much damage for even Alex to control. 'I'm fine now!' I said.

'I don't think –' started Mum.

'Let's go!' I said.

'What about the police?' asked Arthur Cluny, coming into the kitchen.

'We're only down the road,' said Mum. 'Can you point them in the right direction? I'd like to get Tallulah home now.'

'No problem, Anne,' said Mr Cluny. He opened the

front door and blinked in surprise. Parked outside was a police vehicle, lights flashing. And Sergeant Trenchard was standing on the veranda, her hands on her hips, staring down at the plastic-wrapped body while a man in a white coat stepped around it taking pictures.

'Hi, Hilda,' I said.

'Hello, Tallulah,' she replied, and smiled. 'I see you found Parcel Brewster.'

'What?' My eyes slid to the body. '*That's Parcel Brewster?*' Sweat slicked out across my body.

Had he been *drowned* at Frey's Dam?

Frik!

Who the hell had brought him here? Surely the old man and his partner would have made sure he stayed at the bottom of the dam?

'Yes, there's no doubt it's Parcel Brewster,' said Sergeant T, while Mum and the Clunys exclaimed in shock. 'Matches a picture Esme Trooter brought in last week. And apparently the boys at the station had a call last night to say they needed to check for him up at the dam, but they thought the tip-off was a hoax. Laughed out loud, apparently.' Sergeant T pursed her lips disapprovingly.

'Oh,' I said, my thoughts whirling and jumbling and settling on nothing helpful. 'Did your policemen call you about it last night?'

'Well . . .' I could see Sergeant T was choosing her words

carefully. 'No. The officers felt that the anonymous tip-off was not worth investigating.'

'Right,' I said. 'And now the body turns up here.' My thoughts skittered to a few places, and I reined them back in pronto. *Don't go there, Tallulah.*

Sergeant T ran a hand through her wild and curly redhead afro and looked over at the man in the white coat. He had stopped taking pictures now and was on his haunches, examining the body's exposed hand. 'Donald,' she said, 'can you hazard a guess as to when this man died?'

He glanced up at her sympathetically. 'Nothing you could have done for Parcel Brewster, Hilda. Been dead thirty-six hours at least.'

Sergeant T nodded, and it was obvious that made her feel better. 'Can you answer a few questions, Tatty?' she asked.

'Sure,' I said, 'but I'm not much help, I'm afraid.' I explained to her exactly what I'd seen and heard that morning, feeling useless. Because what I really wanted to tell her was to do with last night's visit to Frey's Dam. Handcuffs on Sergeant T's belt glinted in the early morning sunlight, and I swallowed. I couldn't tell anyone I'd been up to Frey's – not until we had evidence to prove there was no bird flu. Until it wasn't a big deal that we'd been up there, treading through infected territory.

Sergeant Trenchard made notes on what I said, and asked me things I hadn't really thought about, like the direction the drop-off vehicle came from and went away to. I thought carefully about everything and gave her as much detail as I could. 'Good work, Tallulah,' she said.

But it didn't feel like good work to me. Guilt at the things I hadn't said twisted in my gut. My back began to throb.

Chapter Nineteen

Home again – busy doing a spot of self-medicating

I'd contemplated taking my little duckling to school, but Blue had blown my cover first thing in the morning by charging in unannounced as I was reading the side-effects of Nurofen, and how much a person could take in one go. (Not enough when experiencing this kind of agony.)

'Blue! You should knock!'

'Aunt Phoebe is knocking,' she replied, racing over to see what I was doing.

'Hi, Aunt Phoebe. How're you?' I asked, trying to hide the duckling on the kitchen counter.

'Excellent condition, dear. I came to see how you are after all the drama this morning.'

Blue squealed loudly. 'Aunt Phoebe! Lula has a pet chicken!'

'It's a duckling, Blue. And you'll scare him if you shriek so loudly.'

'He's so likkle! Can we call him Big?'

'Are you sure you should be looking after an orphan bird with avian flu on the loose?' asked Aunt Phoebe, coming to my side to investigate.

'Big is not a name, Blue,' I replied. 'Besides, he's not.' I turned to Great-aunt Phoebe. 'I couldn't leave him to fend for himself!'

'Where did you find him?' Aunt Phoebe had lowered her stylish spectacles and was looking at me intently over the top. 'Frey's Dam, no doubt. Really, Lula. Really and truly, I don't –'

'Biggins, then,' announced Blue. 'Just like Boodle not a poodle, so Biggins not big. Okay, Lula? Okay? Please? Please, please, please!'

Biggins opened his bill and began bleating in unison with Blue.

'Fine! Fine!' I exclaimed, punctuating with the spoon I held for emphasis. Cold oats splatted on Blue's forehead.

She promptly licked it. 'Yuk,' she decided.

'Yegads. You've just given your sister bird flu!' said Aunt Phoebe in a rare, rare panic. 'Bird flu! For the Birds! It's not even funny! Blue, open your mouth! Spit! Spit!'

'Aunt Phoebe,' I said wearily, spooning oats into Biggins as fast as they would go. 'Humans don't get bird flu. Besides, there *isn't* any bird flu. It's something else.' I stopped abruptly.

Aunt Phoebe exhaled loudly. 'Oh, God. What have you done. What do you know.' She didn't ask, she just *said*, like statements of insider knowledge: clearly I had been up to something terrible.

'I'll explain later,' I said, hurriedly scooping up the last of the oats. 'I've got to get dressed now. Could you two take care of Biggins today while I'm at school?'

Monday morning, PE with Mr van der Merwe

'Please, sir,' I begged. 'My back is in agony.'

'Rubbish!' retorted VfrikkingD. 'I don't know what it is with you girls. Always trying to get out of exercise.' He left our class at the changing-room door and marched up the corridor towards the hall. 'Get dressed quickly, you lot. Volleyball today.'

'What we want to know, Tatty,' said Jessica, coming alongside me and throwing her arm round my shoulders, 'is how you got the sore back. What kind of *energetic exercise*, huh?'

There was a lot of giggling.

Alex sighed melodramatically. 'It's always sex with you, Jess,' she said. Jess winked back, taking this as a compliment. 'But not so with Tatty,' continued Alex. 'She was running.'

'Got to run to keep the chocolate gut under control,' added Carrie, her eyebrows raised in disapproval at my cocoa addiction. She pushed open the changing-room door. 'Where's Helen?'

'The police are interviewing her and her parents,' I said quickly. 'A body was dumped on their veranda.'

'Well, it *is* a crematorium,' said Tam, who I hadn't had a chance to speak to before school. 'That's where bodies go.'

'Yeah, well,' I said, very casually, 'I saw it, actually. On my run this morning. Big guy dropped it off.'

'Lucky Helen missing PE,' said Alex, changing the subject with masterful speed.

'Come on, girls. Let's get it over with,' added Carrie, with a wink at me.

'This is going to hurt,' I grumbled.

'I dislocated my finger the last time I played volleyball with you guys,' huffed Alex. 'And I've still got a fat knuckle.'

'*Oh noooo*, not the *fat knuckle*,' moaned Matilda McCabe. 'No one's going to hold your hand *ever*.'

'Oh, shut up,' said Alex, getting undressed. 'No one's going to hold your hand for sure, you big jock. Not with all those weeping blisters and callouses and cracked skin from rowing. Does your dad, like, get you special plasters and stuff?'

'Nah,' said Matilda, pulling on a terrible pair of shorts and lacing up her trainers. 'He likes me being all strong and tough. Says all girls should row. Good for posture, good for physique.'

'But not good for the lungs,' said Tam. She stood up and smoothed down her PE kit. 'You'd think it would be, but no. Not with those smelly boys.' Even Matilda had to agree. 'Let's go kick some volleyball ass.'

So I got picked last, and my team wasn't happy to have me

174

on their side. It was no secret I was the clumsiest person around, useless at ball sports and now to top it all off had a gammy back.

'Pity it wasn't from sex –' started Jessica, smacking the ball to the other side of the net.

'*Rampant* sex,' added Matilda, bracing to volley back.

'Because then the back pain would be worth it,' finished Delilah Goldsmith, choosing *now* to speak. 'Right, Jessica?'

'You're the only one who would know, Jess,' I muttered. 'Because the rest of us are pure and undefiled.'

The ball came punching over the net and hit me in the ear.

My team howled as it ricocheted to the floor.

'Sorry, sorry!' I said, holding my ear.

'Concentrate!' bellowed Carrie.

I flinched. Carrie is seriously competitive and seriously good at ball sports. She is frightening with a hockey stick and I know for a fact she's drawn blood – an accident, apparently – in a basketball game against the PSG first team.

When the next ball came my way, I got right underneath it, hands gripped together, thumbs at the ready to take the thwack. It was further left than I expected and I had to lunge, but I got to it. I gave it my best shot, though Jessica still had to help it over the net. She got a great volley in and the ball thudded to the ground on the other side.

'Yesss!' we all cried, and I punched the air.

'NYEEEP!'

I dropped like a stone.

'Tallulah! Get up!' bellowed Mr VDM. 'Everyone's ready for the next point.'

'Can't move!' I gasped. 'Help! Help!'

'Don't be pathetic!' VD came over and yanked me up by the arm.

My body convulsed as the spasm hit again, and I saw my teacher's eyes widen in sudden remorse. 'Oh, Tallulah!' he said, lowering me to the floor. 'Your back is sore?'

'Yes,' I ground out. '*Like I said.*'

'You should have told me you had an injury!' he lamented, his accent getting thicker with the outrage of withheld information.

'I DID!' I yelled, and winced at the stabbing pain.

'Don't get cheeky. I meant to say you should have described your ailment to me in detail.'

'It's from sex,' said Jessica helpfully.

'Rampant sex,' added Delilah.

'Stop saying that!' I shouted. 'It's not true!'

VD went very red. 'Er . . .' he said.

'NO!' I yelled. 'Alex! C'mon!'

'I don't know if I can help you here, Tatty,' said Alex. 'Really, you're impossible to micro-manage.'

'It was the hula dancing,' I pleaded. 'Then the running.'

'So there *was* pelvic thrusting involved,' said Jessica.

'See, I know the human body. I think I should be a doctor.'

The whole class erupted in dissuading her from this folly. Jessica in charge of a person's life was a frightening thought.

'Who were you hula dancing with?' she demanded. 'You sure it wasn't salsa? Salsa is way sexier.'

'Get me out of here,' I begged.

It was clear to me that, if Alex didn't step in, another rumour would be doing the rounds faster than Jessica Hartley could blow a kiss.

Frik.

And could I even stand up for myself? Ha ha. I could not.

Monday 4 p.m., agony in the annexe

A knock at my door. I was flat on my back in my bed. I couldn't yell to come in because yelling hurt, so I just lay there. I wasn't interested in talking to anyone. Great-aunt Phoebe had already been in, cosseting me and updating me on Biggins's welfare.

Another knock. A polite wait and then my door creaked open.

'Tallulah? Are you decent? Dr McCabe is here to see you.'

'Yes,' I whispered.

Mum appeared in the doorway. 'Tallulah! Why aren't you answering me? I thought you were asleep.'

'Hurts.'

A polite male cough. 'Hello, Tallulah.'

'Hi, Dr McCabe.'

He laughed. 'I never thought I'd see the day.'

Mum came over and stroked my forehead. 'What do you mean, Edward?'

'The witch girl hurt and everyone else all right. I mean, what are the chances?'

I rolled my eyes.

'Tallulah! That's terribly rude!' scolded Mum. She turned to Dr McCabe. 'Though, actually, I see Lu's point. Those boys and their medical emergencies around Tallulah were all coincidences, and it's not particularly kind of you to bring it up now.'

Dr McCabe looked at me for a beat too long. 'Where does it hurt?' he asked.

'Lower back,' I answered.

He put his bag down, rummaged around and then snapped gloves on. 'Roll over.'

'Can't,' I whispered.

Dr McCabe sighed and grabbed me by the left shoulder and hip, flipping me expertly.

'AAAAARGH!' I yelled. 'OMIGOD GET OFF ME, YOU BUTCHER!'

'Tallulah!' gasped Mum. I couldn't see her because I was face down in my pillow, struggling to breathe, but I could hear she was trying not to laugh.

Dr McCabe muttered something about lax parenting and ordered Mum to help me get undressed for an examination.

Lovely.

Getting nudey for the rubber gloves.

Just what every girl dreams of.

'Can you sit back up, Tallulah?' asked Mum.

'Mum,' I whimpered, 'just cut my clothes off. I can't. I honestly can't.'

'Oh, for goodness' sake!' said Dr McCabe. 'Anne, I'm going to pop out to my car for a bigger Voltaren shot. Back in five, okay?'

He left the annexe and Mum got to work, pulling my clothes off gently.

'Did he say a bigger shot?' I asked Mum, my voice going a little high and stressy. 'Does he mean like a more powerful drug, or a bigger needle?'

'Relax, Lu,' said Mum. 'He hasn't even examined you yet. Maybe you just need a bit of physio.'

'Yeah, right,' I replied. 'Don't you get that the man hates me? There's going to be a needle. Huge. Maybe two.'

Mum laughed. 'He does not hate you, Lula! I'll go and make him a cup of tea, though, shall I? Just to sweeten him up?'

'Don't leave me!' I begged. 'Don't go!'

'Oh, Lu,' said Mum, stroking the back of my head.

'I'll be back before Dr McCabe. I can hear him talking to Dad outside.'

She bustled out, leaving me butt naked on the bed.

After five minutes my eyes began to droop. *Don't fall asleep!* I urged myself. Waking up to a shot in the ass would be no fun at all.

But the sun was on its way down, angling rays through my window and across my bed. I would have sighed at how wonderful it was just lying there in the warmth, not frantically scribbling homework or rushing around or doing chores, but sighing hurt too.

I closed my eyes.

There was knocking at the door again. I must have fallen asleep. I drew breath to call come in, but my muscles locked down and I gritted my teeth against the pain, squeezing my eyes shut. 'Mum!' I whispered hoarsely. 'Please stop with the knocking. Just come in. How many times must I tell you: it hurts to yell out to you?'

'Uhhh . . .'

My eyes flew open. There, in my bedroom doorway, stood Arnold Trenchard, while here on my bed was me NAKED, my ass in the air for all to see.

NO!

THIS COULD NOT BE!

'AAARGH!' I yelled, and tried to pull a throw over myself.

'Don't move!' shouted Arnold. 'I can see your – I can see – JUST LIE BACK DOWN!'

The worst spasm yet wracked my body and I buried my head in the pillow, willing myself not to scream, the throw clutched ineffectually in my hand, providing maximum coverage for all of my bed and none for me.

'Do you want me to –? Should I cover your –? Lula –'

'Go!' I shrieked, still face down in the pillow.

'Pardon?' he asked, coming closer.

I tried to raise my head, tried to flap my arm at him to keep back, but the minute I tensed to lift my face from the pillow a stab of pain jolted my body again and I slumped back down, immobile.

'So I'm guessing something's wrong with you? I'm guessing this isn't like, um, a seduction plan that I've stumbled in on? Oh, geez, I bet it is. Is Jack coming round?'

I turned my head very slowly and carefully. I could just about see him through the hair that had scraped across my face.

'Hurt. My. Back.'

Arnold continued to stand frozen at my bedside.

I was overwhelmed. Incredulous. Suddenly CROSS. 'Arnold. You are witnessing a person in pain. I cannot move to cover myself and you are *standing there, STARING AT MY ASS* for, like, *the second time* in, what, *three weeks*? My mother is going to come in here and *go into orbit!*'

I took a shuddering breath.

And then he was reaching over me for the throw, and covering my body.

'Um,' he said.

There was a very long silence.

I think my entire body had gone scarlet with embarrassment. I wondered if it were possible for toenails to blush. Then I wondered if my butt looked big. Then I wondered what the frik Arnold was thinking right now.

'Uh,' he said. 'So . . .'

'So what the hell is this?' Bludgeon loomed large behind Arnold, who stepped aside hurriedly, going bright red.

'Bludgeon?' I whispered. 'What the hell are you doing here?'

'Whoa,' he said. 'Put your kit on, babe. I tell ya, if this were, like, a 'undred years ago, I'd be, like, ooh I can see yer ankles! Naked ankles! Ooh! Ooh!'

'I don't want to live any more,' I whispered. 'Someone cut off my head.'

'Oh,' said Bludgeon, looking from me to Arnold to me. 'Am I disturbin' somethin' 'ere? Yeesh, Tatty, sorry, babe. I'll go now.'

'Wait.' But my voice didn't work. I swallowed.

'I'll come back another time, yeah? Maybe I phone you. Jus' wannid to talk about that thing you wannid Mr K to keep an eye on for ya.'

'Wait!' I whispered. 'Is Jack okay?'

'Well . . .' said Bludgeon, and he looked uncomfortably at my ankles. 'Let me ring ya, yeah?'

'Tell me!' I hissed. 'Tell me now – what's happened?'

Suddenly the door to my annexe banged open. Who now? Who else in this town would like to gather round while I was naked?

'ARNOLD!' shrieked Mum from the doorway. 'This is not a good time! And who are you?'

'Uh,' said Arnold again. I sensed that he wished he'd never met the Bird family.

Bludgeon stepped forward, holding out his hand. 'Hi, Mrs B. I'm Bludgeon, Fat Angus's brother. We met the night of the fire, yeah?'

'Yes,' said Mum. 'Lovely, lovely. Please leave. You too, Arnold.'

'Wait!' I whispered.

'Dr McCabe is on his way, dear,' added Mum. 'Out, boys.'

Bludgeon and Arnold left, murmuring to each other, while my mind whirled. Was Jack okay? No, he couldn't be. Not if Bludgeon had come here to talk to me about him.

What the frik had happened now?

Chapter Twenty

Monday evening, the diagnosis

'If you want to carry on running, missy,' intoned Dr McCabe, packing away his vile hypodermics and sundry drugs, 'you're going to have to start rowing.'

'Excuse me?' I whispered. The Voltaren shot had been seriously painful, but my body was feeling decidedly ecstatic. Maybe I was hallucinating right now.

'What a good idea!' exclaimed Mum, carefully pulling pyjama trousers up my legs. 'To strengthen the back, Edward?'

'Exactly!' proclaimed Dr McCabe. 'You've seen my Matilda?'

'I have!' said Mum. 'I bet she's never had a moment's trouble with anything like the pain Lula's feeling. She looks really strong.'

'Quite!'

Even with my face squished against the pillow, I could see how this was not going to go my way.

'Erm,' I said. 'I don't really have time for rowing.'

'Nonsense!' said Mum.

'Mr van der Merwe said no newbies on the squad.'

'Nonsense!' said Dr McCabe. 'Vanessa Ohlssen was just at the surgery with a stress fracture in her shin, and

Matilda was fretting about replacing the bow.'

'The bow? Stress fracture? No. No. I'm not strong enough to be a rower, Dr McCabe. Not like your Matilda.' A prickle of panic was starting to lap at my consciousness. It made me speak a little too fast.

'But that is precisely my point,' said Dr McCabe, clipping his bag shut and standing up tall. 'Do you want to have that core of deep muscular strength? A muscle tone that will keep you hale and hearty all your days? Or are you content to be ringing me every five minutes so I can come round with my big needles?'

'Oh,' said Mum. 'Oh, goodness, Lu.' She grabbed at Dr McCabe's forearm. 'When is the next session, Edward? Will Tallulah be fit for that?'

'You should aim to get her on the bus for Wednesday's session,' said Dr McCabe. 'Tallulah will be right as rain in a couple of hours, but she'll need bed rest tomorrow. Definitely no running for quite some time.'

I thought of how much chocolate I consumed in any one day. How many calories I had to burn. 'I *must* run,' I moaned. 'I *need* to run.'

'First the rowing,' said Dr McCabe. 'It'll strengthen that weak back of yours. Then you can start running again. In maybe six months.'

'*Six months!*' I squeaked. I was going to look like Kung Fu Panda after *six days*.

'Ha ha ha.' Pen had appeared at my bedside, rustling a paper. 'Weak back, eh? Maybe if you did some bending over backwards for me you wouldn't be in this condition. Ha ha.'

I had a brief flash of hatred. 'I'm always bending over backwards for you!'

Mum was murmuring assurances to the evil man who called himself a doctor. He said his goodbyes and left. Pen turned to go too.

'Pen! You get back here!' I whispered. 'I need you!'

She glanced over her shoulder, an eyebrow raised. 'Hmm. Could cost you.'

Oh, how my life sucked. How it sucked!

'Look,' I said desperately. 'Something's up with Jack. Bludgeon knows something. Could you call him for me? His number's on my phone in my bag.'

Pen said nothing, but she sat down on the bed next to me and began to read from the afternoon edition of the *Guardian*. It was a short piece questioning the evidence of an outbreak of bird flu at Frey's Dam and noting that a man was presumed dead. A short piece by Jack de Souza and Jazz Delaney.

'Jack de Souza and Jazz Delaney,' I murmured, my eyes filling with tears.

Pen was staring at the paper. 'Mm,' she observed. 'Jack de Souza and Jazz Delaney. They sound like a celebrity couple.'

Next day, Tuesday, in bed, going out of my mind

'You finished your breakfast?' called Mum, slamming into the annexe. 'I've got to hurry scurry today, Lula – you would not believe how much I've got to get through before Friday. Next week is stocktaking –'

I groaned in sympathy. 'I'm so glad I'm not helping out with that. So so glad.'

'– and the whole historical division is locking down to go over and help the main library count books. We're going to lose a week's work. A week's work!'

'What's the stress?' I asked. 'It's not like any material is going out of date, or you have any massive deadlines or anything. Everything in your department is already ancient.'

'You say that like it's a bad thing. *We're* not ancient. Where's your plate?' she asked. 'Oh, there it is. Right, I'm taking these pillows out and you need to be flat on your back till lunch.'

'Please, no,' I begged. 'Leave a pillow. Just so I can read comfortably, or eat some more.'

'Your spine needs to stay straight,' said Mum.

'I'm so bored! And hungry!'

'Boredom is the sign of a simple mind.' Mum sniffed imperiously and picked up my plate. 'And you can't possibly be hungry after all that toast.'

'Maybe it's a chocolate craving,' I suggested. 'Maybe just one little Malteser ball will keep me going till lunch.'

'Tallulah! It's eight in the morning! You are not having chocolate at eight in the morning. Your teeth will rot in your head!'

'Cup of hot chocolate?' I begged. 'Pain au chocolat?' Mum was shaking her head. 'Please! Something! Give me something!'

'This family is a bunch of addicts,' proclaimed Mum. 'Time for you to go cold turkey, young lady. And as for that duckling of yours . . . You're jolly lucky it doesn't have bird flu! I can't believe Phoebe called the vet – the vet! – and let me tell you, Lula, if it had been up to me, I wouldn't have bothered with vet's fees!' She pulled my pillow away, leaving me staring at the ceiling, and hustled out with my plate, slamming the door of the annexe behind her.

I blew my fringe out of my eyes.

It was going to be a long day.

9.15 a.m., officially out of my mind

'T-Bird!' yelled Dad, bashing the door to the annexe open. 'You need to hear some lyrics!'

Now, usually I protest. Usually I say no way, because what generally ends up happening is I laugh out loud at him, he gets offended and we all get cranky with each other.

This time, desperate with boredom and my arms aching from holding my Silhouette Romance in the air so I could read it, I said: 'Bring it on, Dad.'

188

He bounced up the steps to my bedroom and flung his arms wide, his chest all swelled up.

'Oh no,' I said. 'Another ballad.'

He ignored me and gave it full throttle.

Oh whoa whoa whoa baby
You're my kind la-la-lady
Don't leeeeeeave me in this turmoil
Don't go swiiiiiiitching me on to boil

At which point I shrieked with laughter. Dad ignored me and his left leg started jumping to a beat that was all in his head.

Oh whoa whoa whoa baby
You're seeming kinda shady

I shrieked again.

Oh whoa whoa whoa baby
Don't leave me here in your fire
Wracked with unfulfilled desire –

'Stop!' I yelled. 'You've got to stop! It's so bad!'

Dad ground to a halt, his leg gradually slowing down till he was standing with arms crossed, legs astride and a stern expression on his face.

There was something cherubic about my father. All that wavy brown hair, maybe, or the clear complexion, the pot belly definitely, even though he was a big strong figure of a man. All that big bulkiness with the cherub thing going on made Dad's poetry students like him straight away because he was the easy professor to read. His vulnerable side was out there for all to see. And he was getting better at telling people how he felt about things.

'You are not being very nice, Tallulah,' he said, sounding a bit sulky. 'I'm not pretending this is poetry. Song lyrics these days need to be punchy and catchy and easy for the youth of today to remember.'

'The youth of today,' I pointed out, 'are not brain dead.'

Dad glowered at me.

'But the youth of today,' I continued, '*could* be brain dead. If they listened to those lyrics long enough.'

He gasped dramatically. I could see a part of him wasn't so thrilled by my reaction, but mostly he knew it for himself and his outrage at my brutality was funny.

'I've had six number-one hits! Countless top tens! I'm the best independent songwriter there is in this country!'

'Go on,' I said, relenting. 'Gimme some more about the boiling la-ay-ay-dy.'

Dad laughed. 'Don't mock me. You'll drive me to drink.' He turned and headed outside.

'Well, we definitely don't want that!' I yelled.

190

12.18 p.m. *Now I'm out of my mind.* TOTALLY Out Of My Mind

Baron von Sturenhopf and Petronella were all a-quiver, but not as all a-quiver as my arms. My arms could not hold the book up above my head an instant longer. I dropped the book, stared at the ceiling and groaned.

With no Baron and Petronella to occupy my mind Jack was there in my head. I didn't want him in my head. Jack in my head hurt my heart. I sighed and closed my eyes. Maybe now was time for a siesta, though Mum had promised me lunch. The sound of a car stopping outside the front of the main house had me wide awake. It wasn't Mum's car, but it sounded familiar. I heard the front gate open and shut, and a heavy tread come down the path.

By the time a dark shadow crossed the living-room window, reaching right up the steps to my room, I'd worked out where I'd heard that vehicle before, and I was frozen in fright.

It was the car that had dropped Parcel Brewster's dead body at Cluny's Crematorium.

Frik!

And whoever had driven the car was now knocking on my door!

Prickly frik!

I lay motionless, barely breathing, watching the shadow

just to the left of the living-room window that I could see through the bedroom doorway.

Another knock.

My eyes shot to the phone and I reached out to pick up the receiver. I punched in Mum's work number, wincing at the tiny click each button made.

Come on, Mum! I remembered my door was unlocked. *Pick up! Pick up!*

The handle turned. The door creaked open.

I was about to disconnect and hit 999 when Jack de Souza appeared.

I was so relieved and astonished and angry that I got seriously shouty.

'You!' I yelled, hanging up. 'You dropped the body!'

His jaw dropped. 'Wha–? Wh–How? No! No –' But one look at my savage outraged face had him admitting: 'We-ell, not me exactly.'

'You drove the vehicle!' I continued. 'I just heard it! Don't try to deny it! I just nearly died of fright! I thought that a bad man was about to walk into my room.'

'I've brought you lunch,' said Jack, holding up a sandwich. 'But it seems to me you need something to settle you down.' He came in and put the sandwich on my bedside table.

'Where did you find the body? Why did you drop it at Cluny's? Are you nuts? Are you seriously deranged?

I have been answering questions from the police!'

'A lot of settling down.' Jack looked down at the length of me under the thin coverlet. 'Is your back still sore?'

'Yes! No! What do you care?' I bellowed. 'Tell me what's going on!'

Jack's floppy fringe fell forward over his eyes. It looked like he was trying not to laugh at me. He bent over me, leaning a hand on either side of my shoulders.

'What are you doing?' I squeaked. 'Just what the frik do you think you're doing?'

'Settling you down,' he said, and lowered his body over mine. His face was close, so close, and his lips kissed my lips very lightly and very carefully. 'You look way too tense.'

Chapter Twenty-one

'Oh boy,' I whispered. 'I do not feel settled.'

'Okay, so here's the thing,' he said, leaning back to trace my collarbone with his forefinger. 'On Sunday night when I went back for the bird-food sample, I thought I saw a body in the water.'

'*What*? Why didn't you *tell* me?'

'We were running away from that old guy's henchman, remember?'

I nodded. My heart was not thundering so much, though I still felt shaky all over.

Jack's finger traced my lips. 'And I wasn't sure that's what I'd seen, so I didn't want to freak you out for nothing. I went back later with Forest.'

'But what about the henchman?'

Jack grimaced and shifted so he was lying alongside me. 'You're not going to like this bit.'

'I'm not?'

'I had his keys –'

'You didn't leave them? Like I asked you? *Jack!*'

'So we drove in as far as we could, then I hid while Forest went and started his truck. That got him out of his hiding place in a flash.'

'Frik!' I said. 'You . . . you . . .'

'Forest drove the vehicle up the west dirt road, parked it in the top clearing and doubled back through the woods.'

'Frikking frik!'

'He drove slowly enough to lure the guy up there, but he took the keys with him when he jumped. By the time Forest made it back to the dam, I'd found what I was looking for.'

'Parcel Brewster.'

'Parcel Brewster,' Jack confirmed.

'*You disturbed a crime scene,*' I said hotly. 'You are in a whole mess of trouble, Jack!'

Jack shook his head. 'No,' he said. 'Well, yes, but the police wouldn't take me seriously, would they? They were *laughing* at me on the phone. I had to make them see for themselves! The longer a body is left in the water, the less evidence is available for a coroner to determine cause of death. I've done the police department a favour. If they'd left it till the bird-flu scare was over, or until someone was willing to take things seriously, there'd have been nothing left of Parcel Brewster.'

I closed my eyes. 'I don't want to know this,' I said. 'I just don't want to know.'

'It doesn't matter now.'

'Excuse me?'

'Sergeant Trenchard has already questioned you, hasn't

she? You've given your statement, not knowing anything. It's all good.'

I studied his face. Could he be right? Could it all be okay? 'What about the evidence we collected?' I asked. 'Has Forest tested it yet?'

'Yesterday,' said Jack. 'No bird flu.'

'Wow. So the birds *were* poisoned?'

Jack nodded. 'Lots of chemicals in the water. Parabens, ethanol, mercury. Forest has everything bagged and labelled and witnessed by Professor Conyngham.'

'Geez!' I blurted. 'Someone *else* knows about this?'

'We had to. Otherwise the evidence wouldn't be allowed. Jazz knows too, of course.'

'Of course,' I said, and wanted to scream. Really loudly.

Jack continued, oblivious. 'Prof. Conyngham says he'll stand by us. He'll say we went up there to collect samples for an eco-viability study, and we'll get a slapped wrist for continuing with our research without due regard for the bird-flu restrictions.' He smiled and kissed me lightly again, but I was feeling hot and cross about Jazz and didn't kiss him back.

Jack smiled tentatively. 'Not many mums would allow a boy into their daughter's bedroom all alone. She's very trusting.'

'I can be trusted,' I said tightly.

He looked at me, and his smile faded. 'Here, let me

196

help you sit a little,' he said, and eased me forward while he tucked pillows in behind me.

'Maybe you should go,' I said, not looking at Jack, feeling all crowded and irritated and strange.

'Lula . . .' Jack stopped pulling pillows around and sat on the edge of the bed, looking at me over his shoulder. 'I'm getting mixed signals from you. Sometimes you're all happy and warm; sometimes I feel like you don't want me around. What's going on?'

I wanted to say I did like him, that I liked him desperately, but I couldn't think how to explain that I didn't like him *with Jazz.* I didn't want to say that and feel mean-minded and jealous. I didn't want him to think I was mean-minded and jealous, because I was pretty sure I wasn't. Jazz was just souring what I had with Jack. She was everywhere, it seemed, while I was nowhere.

'Lula?' asked Jack. 'Will you answer me?'

There was a loud bang on the door. 'Tatty! You here? Tatty?'

'That's Bludgeon,' I said to Jack.

He continued looking at me. 'Are we not going to talk about this, Lu?'

I stared back at him. 'Please could you let Bludgeon in?'

'Bludgeon. On my way out. Sure.' Jack nodded curtly, got up from the bed and ducked out of my room. I heard the door open and Bludgeon come in, a few words, hello, goodbye, and then Bludgeon was peering round my doorway.

'Hey,' he said. 'What you wearing?'

'Clothes,' I said, not looking at him, staring at the skylight and trying not to cry. Frik. It felt like I'd spent every day since I'd first kissed Jack trying not to cry.

'Pity,' said Bludgeon. He kicked his boots off and lay down on the bed beside me. 'You gonna have this sarnie?'

I glared at him. 'I am, Mr Bludgeon. Pass it over. And what are you doing lazing around on my bed?'

Bludgeon passed my sandwich. 'Do you see any chairs? Any place to sit besides the bed? You're not bein' very polite like.' He paused and looked at the sandwich. 'I'm starvin'.' I handed him a triangle. 'Thanks, babe.' He bit into it happily. 'And my feet hurt. Cos of all the legwork I bin doin' for you. Y'know?'

'Un?' I went, my mouth full.

'That's why I gotta take the weight off.' He eyed my triangle. I ate hastily. 'Starvin',' he said again, then, 'Oh! Yer man said to give you these,' and he pulled a bag of Maltesers out of a capacious jacket pocket. 'Shall I open 'em?'

I swallowed the last of my sandwich, and handed the empty box to Bludgeon. 'You can have some only when you've told me what's going on with Jack. You've been keeping an eye on him?'

'Surely 'ave, babe. 'E's a nice bloke, but 'e should watch 'is back.'

I took the bag of Maltesers from Bludgeon and prepared to open them. 'Carry on.'

'Well, that trick 'e pulled with Parcel Brewster was dumb.'

I stiffened. 'Pardon?'

'Don't tell me 'e didn't tell you about pulling Parcel out the water and dumping him on the veranda. You saw for yerself.'

'HOW?' I yelped. 'How on earth do you know all this?'

Bludgeon tapped the side of his nose with his forefinger and nodded wisely in a way that made me want to hit him. 'I'm the best there is. Now 'e's got 'is mate all tied up in it –'

'*And* Jazz Delaney,' I said bitterly.

'Yeah, she's a nasty piece o' work.'

Ha! Exactly. I passed Bludgeon a Malteser because he deserved it. He crunched happily. 'A *real* nasty piece o' work.' I passed him another Malteser and he crunched that too. 'A *real, real* nasty piece o' work,' he said, and we both burst out laughing when I handed him another two.

'Oh, all right,' I said, holding out the bag. 'Tuck in, skinny. And tell me what you came to say yesterday.'

'When I found you with yer arse in the air,' he said, face dead straight. I closed my eyes. 'Sorry, babes. Lucky you got a good arse.'

I went red. 'Enough with the arse,' I said. 'What do you know that I don't?'

'All the original test results that came up positive for bird flu?'

'Mm?' Crunch, crunch.

'Gone.'

'No!'

'Mm-hm. And can't retest cos all the birds were incinerated.'

'At Cluny's.'

''S right. I went to go lean on the lab techie, but he said he'd said enough.'

'To Jack and Jazz?'

Bludgeon laughed. 'Them two sound like a backing band. Yeah, them.' He shook his head. 'By the sounds of it, though, he just told 'em the bird flu had been confirmed. Nuthin else.'

'What a waste of a Friday night,' I muttered.

'The meetin' in the Felon?'

I nodded.

'Yeah,' agreed Bludgeon. 'That Jazz ain't friendly like with the right people, know what I mean?'

I offered him the last Malteser. 'Like *you*, you mean.'

Bludgeon gallantly let me have it. 'Yeah, like me.' He shook his head and sighed. 'Poor Bing.'

'Bingley Clarendon?'

''E's been droppin' gluten-free vegan pizzas round there most nights just so's 'e can see 'er.'

'Poor Bing,' I agreed. 'I'd quite like her to like him too.'

'Sure you want Mr K and me lookin' out fer Jack?' asked Bludgeon. 'Maybe one of yer jinxy accidents is just what the boy needs. Get 'is priorities straight like.'

I pushed myself up urgently by the elbows, and pointed a finger at Bludgeon. 'If something happened to Jack, I'd be a goner in this town,' I said, my voice starting to go an octave higher. 'I've only got to run past Cluny's and *someone drops a dead body*! I've gone from being with the *damaged* people, to being with the *dead* people!'

'Sure, sure!' said Bludgeon hastily.

I flopped back down and heaved a sigh. 'Plus,' I said quietly, 'I want you to keep him safe, you know?'

I opened my eyes. Bludgeon was looking at me.

'What?' I asked.

'Um . . . need a massage 'fore I go?'

I looked at Bludgeon in horror. 'No thanks, Mr B!'

'Don't be so hasty, Tatty Bird. I hear you're signed up for Hambledon Girls' rowing squad, and your first go is tomorrow. You'll need to be all limbered up for that.'

I gaped. 'You *do* know everything.'

'I do.' He grinned. 'Get ready to blister, babes.'

Wednesday after school, the motor running

'Please Mr VDM! Remember what happened last time you didn't believe me about my back? Stretchers! Crisis! House call from doctor! I had to have an *injection*!'

'It's because of that injection that you are fine now,' said Mr VDM, one hand on the bus door. 'Get in.'

'Stop your fussin', Bird,' said Matilda McCabe. She was sitting right up front with her feet on the dashboard, her eyes closed. Her quads were all bulgy and she looked hardcore.

'Frik,' I said, and got in. The rest of the girls were up front too, just behind Matilda, and they were talking about stuff like bowside upsetting the balance, and ratings and pulse ratios and stuff I'd never ever understand.

'Come sit up here with us,' said Jessica Hartley.

'Thanks, Jess, but I just need some space,' I said, feeling stressed, and scooted to the back of the minibus.

'You're not going to get any space there,' she said. 'Believe me.'

'Where do you guys row, anyway?' I asked, though I really didn't care.

'Saddler's Pond, up in the safari park.'

'FRIK!' I yelled. The other girls turned and looked at me curiously, except for Matilda, who looked like she was asleep. 'There are wild animals in that park! It's not safe for us to be out of a vehicle! I'm going home right now.'

I hefted myself out of my seat just as Mr van der Merwe jumped behind the wheel and slammed his door. He took off at such a speed I fell back where I'd been sitting.

'The boat *is* a vehicle,' intoned Matilda. 'And the lake in the park is the only stretch of water big enough in fifty miles.'

The safari park. They've got to be joking, I thought. *They have just got to be joking.*

But they weren't joking. And Jessica hadn't been joking about no space in the back either, because instead of heading out to the boathouse Mr VDM swung by Hambledon Boys' High. I'd been slumped in denial in the back seat with my eyes closed, but when the door shunted open and nine smelly boys climbed in I nearly peed in my pants.

Firstly, because they were mostly strangers, huge ones, who thought nothing of squashing in happily around me, burping and belching and making nasty odours.

Secondly, because guess who was first on the bus? No, not Fat Angus. He was second.

It was Arnold Trenchard.

'What is going on?' I yelped.

'I know,' sighed Jessica. 'Thank goodness I've got Jason in my life. Since sharing our rowing sessions with these losers I've lost the will to flirt.'

The boys erupted into manly assertions of their wondrous masculinity.

'There's no space back here!' I yelled as I got rammed into the corner.

'Told you,' said Jessica, rolling her eyes and facing forward. 'Wait till they start with the farting.'

'Let me up front!' I begged.

'Too late, little lady,' said a huge creature with an astonishing amount of chest hair, serious five o'clock shadow and a massive mop of dark curls. 'What's your name?'

The bus fell silent, and the girls turned round. All of them were smiling, waiting for the moment.

'Tallulah Bird,' I said.

He blinked once, then jerked away from me. 'Don't touch me!' he yelped.

'The feeling is soooo mutual,' I drawled, and caught Arns's eye. 'How long have you rowed?' I asked the friend *I thought I knew*.

'Forever,' said Jessica Hartley. 'He's the saddest of them all. Even after the makeover.'

While everyone else had got the boats in the water, with a lot of banter and sparring, Mr VDM had me in the training tank, showing me how to move up and down the runners on my seat, and how to move the oar at the same time. After I'd been in the tank twenty minutes, both boats were in the water, their long narrow bodies resting gently either side of the jetty.

The boys went off in theirs and did their own training, their cox Billy Diggle squeaking orders through a tiny microphone the whole time. Meanwhile, Mr VDM cruised alongside the girls' boat yelling at me.

'Sit up straight! Don't race up the slide! Don't lean out when you come in for the catch!'

On and on it went. I didn't understand anything he said.

At last he stopped so we could have a rest. The blisters I'd got in the tank had burst and my hands were raw and bleeding.

'Frik!' I said. 'This really sucks.'

Hilary St John turned round in her seat. 'You know what the slide is?'

'No!'

'That's the runners under your seat. You got to match my rhythm exactly. You move when I move, got it?'

'Sure,' I said, uncertain. 'What's the catch?'

'That's when your blade goes into the water.'

'Oh.'

'Don't call it an oar. You sound like a newbie if you call it an oar.'

'Blade,' I said. 'Got it.'

Hilary turned back round as Michelle Wong gave orders for us to get ready for another paddle.

'You're not bad, Tatty Bird,' she said over her shoulder. 'I think we're all a little impressed.'

'You are? Seriously?'

'Stop talking.' Hilary was already gliding forward, following Michelle's orders, and I copied her carefully. 'Here come the boys, so for God's sake don't mess up now.'

I didn't dare look out of the boat to where the *smack-whoosh-thwack* rhythm came ever closer over the water. The sound of VD's voice came blaring through his loudhailer: 'Yes! Really good, guys! Good pace, Ivor, and, Boris, you're gonna be worth the money, my man. You've taken thirty seconds off the thousand-metre time! *Unbelievable!*'

I caught a flash of movement in my peripheral vision as nine boys in sodden shirts shunted past in perfect rhythm. Their faces were focused, intense, and they moved as one creature with eight legs, Billy Diggle at the stern bent over, rasping into the cox's mike, sounding a world older than his twelve years.

Then they were gone.

Michelle's voice crackled from the speaker next to Hilary. 'Whoa, Tilda. Did you see Ivor?' She squeaked something incomprehensible, then Matilda's voice replied, and Michelle cleared her throat. 'Sorry, lovers, didn't realise the mike was on. Okay, last piece of the day, yeah? Holding it steady at twenty-five, this will be a ten-minute piece, then we're going in.'

I understood the ten-minute bit, and I really didn't think my hands were gonna make *that* grand plan, but . . . 'Twenty-five?' I gasped to Hilary. 'What the hell is twenty-five?'

'The rating – how many strokes we take in a minute. Focus, VD's on his way over.'

As she said that, I heard VD's boat engine coming towards us and gripped the handle of my blade as hard as I could. Last time he'd roared up like that, the wake of his boat had slapped across us and I'd nearly lost my grip. If you lose control of your blade and it starts flailing around, it's called 'catching crabs' and I sure as hell didn't want to be doing that.

I flinched as the motorboat drew up alongside me.

'Tallulah!' yelled VD.

Was I supposed to answer him? Presumably I just kept going? Isn't it rude to ignore someone like this? Oh, man, what was he going to say?

The loudhailer crackled and shrieked, then VD's voice boomed out again. 'Tallulah! This is magnificent! Fantastic!'

Frik! Had I just heard right? Was he talking to me?

'Good rhythm, wonderful, wonderful, perfect timing! Just try a little more power at the catch, yes? Remember, *bunch* and *driiiive, bunch* and *driiiive . . .*'

He moved on to examine Hilary's stroke, commenting on the size of her puddle, whatever that meant – weren't we on a billion-cubic-litre puddle, all of us together? – but I wasn't really listening. I couldn't wipe the smile off my face, and even though my hands hurt like hell I felt *really, really* good. Wow. Who would have thought.

The boys had got back to the jetty before us, so we pulled up on the other side of it and I paid close attention to how they got the boat out of the water. Before I'd seen it for myself I'd have said probably Boris did it single-handedly, but it was definitely a teamwork thing, involving leaning out dangerously far and putting strain on bits I didn't know I had.

'Frik!' I said to Kelly Sheridan as we marched up the incline with a sixty-two-foot boat on our shoulders. 'I can't believe we plucked this beast from the water like that!'

'Yeah, we're awesome,' droned Kelly. She threw me a look over her free shoulder. 'Something you should know.'

'Yeah?'

'If you thought the boys stank before, you'd better brace your nostrils for the trip back. The trip home is the hardest test of all, and you don't want to be ruining VD's good impression of you.'

Half an hour later pretty much everyone was confirming that I'd just failed this test.

'Tallulah!' yelled VD from the driver's seat, where he was obviously doing his best to ramp my nausea levels with some crazy driving. 'You're *brave* in the boat, now be *brave* in the bus!'

'I can't!' I wailed, my eyes watering. 'Zac just spat out

the window and the phlegm has stuck to the glass! And I can't breathe! I —' and then, to my shame, I retched AGAIN.

'Stop the bus, please, sir!' wailed Boris. 'She's gonna be sick on me!'

'It's you, you know, Boris,' remarked Arns. 'You smell worse than any of us. It's all that garlic sausage you keep bingeing on.'

'He sweats it out of his pores,' added Fat Angus. 'Even I can smell it, and I reckon I'm pretty ripe myself.' He lifted an arm and took a deep appreciative breath from his hairy armpit.

I gagged and retched, my hand clamped firmly over my mouth, while Mr VD screeched to a halt on the side of the dirt road.

'Out!' he yelled.

I didn't give the wild animals even a passing thought. Not a one. I elbowed my way out past nine smelly boys to the door and fell out on the road where I staggered to a halt on the grassy verge and retched some more before throwing up the McCoy's and Maltesers combo I'd had for a 3 p.m. snack.

'Nice,' I heard from the bus window behind me, but I couldn't even whirl round and point my witchy finger threateningly.

Oh, *why* hadn't I staggered into the bushes for a bit of privacy?

Another heave assaulted me.

'Do you think we worked her too hard?' Matilda's voice floated out from the passenger window. 'She is *actually* being sick now.'

'Maybe,' came VD's reply, 'but she'll man up, no problem. She's a natural, that one.'

Another heave threatened, but I forced it down, my face flushed with the shame of all this. There was the rattle of trainers on gravel, and my eyes slid past my own red-Conversed feet to see some familiar black-Conversed feet.

Arns came no closer, but held out a handipack of Kleenex. 'Here,' he said. I would have thanked him gratefully, but then he added, 'not so much for your runny nose, more for the post-puke drool,' and laughed. After I'd pulled out a tissue with shaking hands and cleaned my sorry self up I followed him back to the bus and, just as he was climbing back in, I kicked him in the ass. Hard.

Dinner at home – for once we're eating it instead of feeding Boodle under the table

'Thankoo, Daddy,' said Bluebird. 'Yumyum in my tum.' And she swirled her spaghetti vigorously.

I sighed heavily. Holding a fork hurt. I wondered if anyone would mind if I just kind of slurped it up with my lips and teeth.

'Oh, Lula-lu!' said Mum. 'I'm so sorry your hands are sore. How's your back feeling?'

'Will you stop pandering to her pathetic whimpering and moaning!' Pen had fixed her eyes on me and they were all narrow and cross-looking. She pointed her fork at Mum. 'She got herself into this mess. Everyone knows you have to warm up before you go running. It's Tallulah's own fault.'

'You're just miffed because you're getting no attention,' I said.

'Giiirls.'

We both ignored Mum's warning tone.

'I don't need attention,' said Pen. 'You're the attention-seeker. Helen Cluny was saying that to Matilda McCabe today when Tilda told her about your public vomiting.'

My cheeks flamed and I had no response to that.

'Well, really!' exclaimed Mum. 'That's not very kind!'

'No, hollible 'len 'luny,' said Blue, and she shoved her chair closer to mine. 'You are lovely, Luli, and I'm sowwy your hands hurt.'

'Well, exactly, Bluebird,' said Mum. 'That's very mean of Helen . . . Maybe I should tell you . . .'

'What?' said Pen, stabbing her creamy prawn pasta viciously. 'What's there to tell? She's only saying what everyone's thinking. I mean . . . *vomiting in public*?' Her face was pure scorn. 'There's always some drama with Tallulah.'

'And thank heavens for that!' exclaimed Mum.

'Otherwise we'd all die of boredom in this village. Eat your pasta, Penelope.' She got up from the table and cleared some plates. Dad raised his eyebrows at me and winked. I tried to smile, but the lump in my throat was all big and spiky and I could hardly swallow. Blue passed me a square of kitchen roll and I swiped at my nose while pretending to dab at pasta sauce on my mouth.

'You should know, and this goes no further, mind, the Clunys are under a lot of pressure,' continued Mum. 'They've had some financial tangles, and there's nothing like money stress to bring out the worst in a person. Try not to take it personally, Tallulah.'

She put a bowl of Ben&Jerry's Phish Food ice cream in front of me and took away my plate. Blue jumped up and came back with a hot handful of Maltesers, which she tipped on top, and Dad reached over and squeezed my shoulder.

'Your hands look bloody awful,' he said. 'I'll get you some Micropore tape to protect them next time you go out, okay?'

I nodded and bit my lip, staring fixedly at the ice cream. No way on this earth was Pen going to see me cry.

'Oh, FINE!' yelled Pen suddenly. 'Sorry, okay? Sorry, sorry, SORREEEE! Helen is a cow and I did actually stand up for you, you know, and money pressure is no excuse for being a bitch.'

'Pen!' squawked Mum. 'Blue is sitting right here!'

'Bitch,' said Blue clearly.

'OH!' shouted Mum. 'Now look –'

'Who's a bitch?' asked Great-aunt Phoebe appearing in the doorway.

'OH! OH!' Mum flapped her tea towel at all of us, and we started to laugh. '*Don't say that word!*' said Mum to Blue, and she turned back to the dishwasher.

'Hi, Aunt Phoebe,' said Dad, trying not to laugh as he waved a warning fork at Pen and Blue. 'Where've you been? Pasta's getting cold.'

'I'll bung it in the microwave for you, Phoebe,' said Mum. 'It's delicious. Lula is a genius.'

'I've been consulting recipes too,' said Great-aunt Phoebe, throwing me a conspiratorial wink. She sat down and handed Dad a bottle of something clear and fizzy. 'Your mother's remedy for stress, Spenser.'

Pen perked up. 'Did you get that from her spell book?'

Great-aunt Phoebe sighed. 'For the last time, it's not a *spell book*. It's natural remedies, Penelope. I thought your father might be under a lot of stress with the luau coming up and we'd like him to hit *this* bottle, if at all, rather than any other.' She threw him a pointed look.

'Yes, yes . . .' muttered Dad. 'I'm off the booze, I promise.'

'Are you that stressed about performing at the regatta luau, Spenser?' asked Mum, handing Great-aunt Phoebe a plate of piping-hot pasta. 'I thought you were looking forward to it.'

'I am, I am . . .' said Dad hastily. He pulled the anti-stress bottle closer and scrutinised the label.

'Well, I don't know why you should be looking forward to it,' said Pen baldly, 'with Lula up on stage alongside you, hula hularing in a bikini for all to see.'

The tissue in my hand clenched instantly into a ball, and the lump in my throat vanished. *A bikini?* 'WHAT?'

'Yeah,' continued Pen. 'If ever there was going to be anything to make a person drink heavily, it's got to be Lula half naked in public.'

'Penelope!' scolded Mum. 'Stop that!' She turned to me. 'Don't worry, Lula. You're going to look lovely. You're perfectly proportioned.'

'Yes,' I wailed. 'Big butt, big stomach –'

'Oh, you have *not*,' snapped Great-aunt Phoebe. 'Just stop it now, girls.'

'– big knockers,' added Pen, and I let out a squeal of outrage.

'What's knockers?' asked Blue.

'NOW,' said Dad, waving the bottle around with a dramatic expression of anguish, 'now I'm feeling stressed! Stressed and thirsty!'

'We help you be unthirstly,' said Blue, slurping up a wiggly spaghetti, then licking the sauce off her chin.

She looked round at us all like an old and wise woman, a person we could trust in our darkest hour. 'I am Daddy's favouwitest water spwite and I get him fizzy water allatime.'

Chapter Twenty-two

Thursday afternoon, dance class

'Stop moaning,' hissed Alex. 'Moan, moan, whine, whine! These steps are not hard! This dance is frikking easy! I can't wait to take Gavin salsifying.'

'My hands hurt,' I bleated. 'No one told me rowing is a contact sport!'

'What's the problem back there?' shouted Mrs Baldacci.

I flinched. 'Er . . . my hands,' I admitted. 'I can't even wave them.'

Mrs Baldacci threw her own beautifully manicured pair in the air. 'You! You cannot even wave now?' She muttered something darkly and I flushed. 'Concentrate, girls! We must perfect our steps before the boys get here. And I think we must have some music that is live. We cannot just have the recordings, no?'

'Yes, just the recordings,' I begged under my breath. 'Don't make us play instruments too. And no, no boys!'

'Back in a minute!' proclaimed Mrs Baldacci, and she hurried out of the hall.

'Oh, thank frik,' I exclaimed, falling to my knees. 'A break!'

But a break it was not. It couldn't be, with Alex

haranguing me, and especially not when Mrs B returned with not only a sorry-assed troop of dewy-eyed boys, but ALSO, my FATHER.

PLUS his shiny Chanel handbag!

Dear God! *Whyyyyyy?*

'Dad! What are you doing here at school?' I hissed to him once he'd been triumphantly introduced by Mrs Baldacci as our talented tunes man. 'You should be faaar away! At home! On campus!'

Dad raised his eyebrows and rumpled his rumpled hair. 'I was just chilling in the staffroom after my Year Ten tutorials. Why are you looking all cross and frantic?'

'What? You teach *here* now? *Dad?*' Frik! No one in my family ever tells me anything!

'I started this week. Don't worry, it's just on Thursdays, just to help out. The school's got no funds – they need all the help they can get . . .' He sat down at the piano and tried a plinky plinky island-stylie riff with a beatific smile at me. 'La la la-la-la!' he trilled.

'No singing!' I hissed. 'Please, Dad.'

He sighed in a deeply wounded way that was supposed to make me feel guilty, but so did not. 'Ohhhkaaaaay, T-Bird.'

Truly. Pathetic.

It was a terrible afternoon. I could tell that Alex was deeply regretting asking me to do dance with her. I was so bad at it.

217

I stepped on all those boys' toes. *Stomped*, even. It was just about bearable until Mrs Baldacci yelled my full name at me – 'TALLULAH BIRD! WILL YOU *NOT*! PLEASE!' – there was a little whisper around the room and I could hear the words 'witch girl' and 'dead boyfriend' and 'A&E', and then that was it. No one would dance with me. Not even when Mrs B shook weird instruments at them, like the upi. Not even with upi shaking going on.

Dad was a bit taken aback by all of this. I could tell. I could feel waves of sympathy rolling across the hall from the piano, and it made everything much worse. If I was tense before, now I was past tense. I couldn't think straight, couldn't dance straight, was in dire straits.

I was about to publicly resign from the whole debacle, in front of my father, and face the wrath of Mrs B and all that it would entail, but then there was a little miracle.

Jack.

Yep, that's right.

He just appeared. Like some kind of knight in shining armour, or a cinematic hero, or, let's face it, drop-dead gorgeous Greek god.

There was a crash of the hall doors opening and there he was. A uni student on school premises. It had never been done before.

'Hey!' he called, catching sight of my misery-stricken face before I could change my expression.

Dad's hands stayed on the keys, and the music ebbed away.

'Who are you, tall boy?' yelled Mrs Baldacci.

Jack was about to say something, anything, but she was already issuing orders. 'Get over here and dance with the rhythmless one. You are late, you must suffer.'

'Nice,' breathed Jack, coming straight over to stand in front of me. 'But look! This is fate! We were meant to be together!'

'*What are you doing here?*' I whispered, my cheeks all fiery. 'Are uni students even *allowed* on school premises?'

'I have information that could not wait,' he twinkled back. 'Is that your dad at the piano?'

'Yes.' Unfortunately, no time for conversation. Step one two, step one two and twiiirl – 'Hey!' I exclaimed in delight.

'Aha! We have breakthrough!' announced Mrs B. 'At last the girl can dance. Maybe . . . maybe is the beautiful partner.' She swept Jack a deep curtsey and he swung into a graceful bow.

'Oh, don't,' I said, but I was trying not to laugh.

'Quiet down,' said Jack, still smiling at Mrs B, 'or I won't kiss you later.'

'Frik!' No laughing now. 'Did we not *discuss*' – I could hear my own voice getting shrill – 'that my father is *right here*? In this room? Playing the piano and listening to you get flirty?'

'I am brave,' consoled Jack. 'And you're paranoid. I'm speaking incredibly quietly.'

'Still,' rumbled my father, his back to us as he picked out a pretty tune, 'your incredibly quiet voice is not quite quiet enough, Jack de Souza.'

But I could tell Dad didn't mind, and that actually he was pleased I was getting the hang of the hula. I could also tell he liked Jack, and, frankly, who wouldn't.

'Thank you,' I whispered as we did a tricky move to the front and then to the back.

'For what?'

'For turning up just at the right time. I wish you could hula with me at the luau too.'

'Mmm.' Jack smiled across at me, then his face turned serious. 'I'm probably going to be filming the race, and doing interviews, and . . .'

'Okay,' I sighed.

'I know, not great, but you won't dump me, right?' He was grinning at me, the perfect smile, and though his fringe had flopped over most of his eyes I could still see he was gazing at my lips. My stomach flipped and I lost count of the moves, turning left instead of right so that my arm spun out and caught a Hambledon boy in the sternum.

'Oof!' went the boy, winded, his eyes rolling.

'I'm so sorry!' I gasped, making a grab for him, but to no avail. He fell back hard, tumbling Alex in the process, though she had a soft landing – only because she fell on him, obviously.

'Raymond's down!' someone near the back shouted out.

Alex rolled off the boy and we both crouched over him, Dad's music still lilting away in the background.

'He's not breathing,' announced Alex, leaning close.

'Wha–?' gasped everyone onstage, immediately looking at me with scared and staring eyes.

Oh no. Not this again. 'He's not breathing because he's *winded*,' I said, giving Alex a slitty-eyed look. 'Geez. Anyone would think I'd killed him.'

Immediately, of course, a whispering started up and I just know I heard *witch girl* and *no good can come of this* and similar stuff all echoing around the hall.

Mrs Baldacci came hurrying over. 'Raymond? Raymond? Get up. This is not a football pitch. We dancers arc tough stuff.'

Raymond's eyes flickered, he hauled in a juddery breath and I leaned back abruptly. 'He's coming round. Give him space, Alex. Otherwise next thing you know he'll be needing the kiss of life and Gavin wouldn't be happy with that.'

Alex stood hurriedly, dusting her knees and turning towards our dancing teacher. 'He's all right, Mrs Baldacci. He's okay!'

'Good! Good!' she replied, changing course for the piano. 'Could we take it from the beginning, please, Professor Bird?'

Professor Bird gave a her genial nod, and winked at me as I took up position next to Jack who, I have to say, had been having a fit of the giggles.

'Oi,' I said. 'Stop that. You're laughing like a girl.'

'And you hit like a boy,' he replied, adding, 'Raymond's never going to take a full breath again,' as the two of us dissolved into silent laughter.

'Maybe it's for the best that you're working at the regatta,' I whispered. 'You distracting me is no good for anyone.'

Thursday evening at Big Mama's: me, Tam, Alex, Carrie, Arns and Mona

After hula hell, we headed straight for the Carusos' café, though Jack had to head back to campus. The information that could not wait was only that he couldn't see me this weekend. Siiiigh.

Tam, Arns and Mona were already there, waiting for us. Gianni came over to our table with his pen and paper at the ready, all swagger, though his smile at Tam was shy. When he saw me, he burst into song: 'Are you lonesooooome toniiiiight! Do you –'

'You should be ashamed!' I retorted. 'People our age are not supposed to know Elvis.'

'Where is Jack?' asked Tam.

'Working,' I said, 'and he's away again this weekend.'

'We've got to go to our gran's,' explained Mona. 'She's not very well.'

We were about to commiserate, but Gianni bounced up, bearing one small plate only with an exquisite piece of something vanilla-ish on it.

'I bring-a you most beautiful cake-a,' said Gianni to Tam, his eyes going all soft and shiny.

'Pukerama,' said Alex. 'Really.'

But she winked at Gianni as we all ordered, to make sure he didn't spit on her cake.

'So what's the deal behind Parcel Brewster's demise?' asked Tam. 'Who could possibly want him dead? What possible motive?'

'Oh, pick one,' I said. 'Maybe Parcel saw someone abducting Emily, so he had to be taken care of. I reckon that's it.'

'No,' said Alex. 'Gav had a call from Sergeant T saying he's definitely off the hook. That Emily is with her grandparents.'

'Yes?' I asked, interested. This news had not reached school.

'Yes,' said Alex firmly. 'Julie Saunders found a message on voicemail last week already saying she was okay, that she was at Tide's Up, her grandparents' cottage.'

Mona shook her head. 'Wow. Mum would kill me if I ever worried her like that.'

'Well,' replied Carrie, 'it turns out Emily is apparently always going off somewhere.'

'Now Parcel,' said Alex. 'Maybe he saw the poisoning. Maybe that's why he was done away with.'

'We don't know there was poisoning up there,' said Tam.

We all looked at our friend in stunned amazement.

Alex was the first to speak. 'Tam! Where have you *been*? It must have been poisoning because now the labs are saying the bird flu verdict was all a "mistake".' She made quote marks in the air with her fingers. 'They can't find any trace of bird-flu there now, and they can't retest old samples because they've all disappeared.'

'Again you keep me out of the loop!' wailed Tam. 'Again!'

Carrie patted her kindly. 'Why pretend there's bird flu, though?' she asked the rest of us.

'To give them time to get rid of the evidence,' I said, before I could think not to.

'What evidence?' asked Tam.

'The evidence of the poisoning,' said Arns.

'What's the motive for the poisoning?' I asked.

A gravelly voice came from doorway. 'You lot are talking in circles. I've only heard the last part of this complicated conversation, and already my head is spinning.'

'Mr K!' I raised my hand in a salute and he winked back, hanging up his coat and fedora and coming over.

'So what came first,' he asked, 'the poisoning or the murder?'

'The poisoning, then the murder,' said Alex decisively. 'It was all plotted out before. The area would be declared a no-go zone while the body rotted away.'

'Why kill Parcel?' asked Mona.

'Well,' said Alex grimly, 'Cluny would not have been able to sell the land if there'd been a squatter on it.'

'He wants to sell?' asked Tam. 'How do you know this? Why don't I know this?'

'Because you're too busy kissing me-a,' proclaimed Gianni, back with more plates.

'EEEEEE!' I shrilled in scandalised delight.

To be honest, I don't think Gianni would have said anything if he'd known how we'd all go on – there was SQUEAKING and SQUAWKING and entirely too much noise for a coffee shop in Hambledon.

Tam, totally cerise, said, 'Well, I had to get in with someone who'll tell me what's going on in Hambledon!'

'That's not-a why you love me,' said Gianni, serving hot drinks with a flourish. 'It's a-cos I'm –'

'Italian stallion?' finished Carrie, and we all dissolved into snorty laughter. We were giggling so hard at Gianni's discomfit that we couldn't hear his retort as he turned on his heel and left.

'He won't come back now,' mourned Tam.

'Just eat your cake,' I advised. 'Before I do.' Tam lifted her fork hurriedly. 'So, squatters' rights. That's a biggie. Is it really true?'

'Indeed,' said Mr Kadinski. 'Brewster would have had legal right to remain, so Cluny would have had great difficulty selling that area. And he does need to release capital, doesn't he? Hmm. Squatters' rights. Didn't even think of that. Was all caught up in the witness theory.' He tipped back in his seat, staring thoughtfully at the ceiling.

'Well, there you go,' said Alex triumphantly. 'Now we just have to prove it.'

'What, that Mr Cluny is a murderer?' Tam was outraged. 'No way!'

'Maybe it wasn't Cluny, as such,' I wondered out loud, thinking of my previous misadventures. 'Maybe it's someone who knows Cluny will sell to them if he could . . .'

'You're making my head hurt,' said Mona.

'Leave it to Lula,' suggested Tam. 'And eat the cake. It takes you to a happy place.'

But it seems cake does not take Mona to a happy place. She picked at it delicately, and I wondered what the point of having a fantabulous bodacious body was, if you couldn't EAT.

The high point of the evening was definitely the arrival of Jack. The best kind of surprise . . .

'Hey,' he drawled, pulling me out of my seat, and then

hugging me back on to his lap. 'Any cake left?' I couldn't speak: my lips were smiling too widely to move.

Alex lifted an eyebrow. 'Do you not *know* Tallulah Bird?' she asked with heavy irony. 'Her cake was gone the second we all lifted our forks.'

'It's true,' I admitted, still grinning like a crazy person. 'Sorry. I didn't know you were coming. I thought –'

At that moment the bell on the door jangled and in came someone small and gorgeous and beautifully dressed in clothes too skimpy for this time of year. For any time of year. For anyone. ANYWHERE.

'Hi, Jack,' she trilled. 'I see Talluley's got my spot.'

My jaw clenched and I'm afraid my nostrils flared of their own free will. I couldn't help it. But Jack didn't notice. He just laughed good-naturedly and said, 'So, what's the news, Jazz?'

'Ohh, you'll need to come with me to hear all that,' twinkled Jazz.

'Come on, Jazz,' said Jack, still smiling. 'This lot probably know more than you do. Spill the beans.'

I felt all warm and cosy inside, and on the outside too, with Jack's arm round me, but Jazz clearly did not. Her eyes narrowed for just a second before she said, with defiance: 'I've got the coroner's report.'

Alex gasped. 'No way!'

'The police don't even have that yet,' said Arns.

'I know,' smirked Jazz. 'Bruising on the neck and head –'

'Oooh!' went Mona.

'But no clear trauma to indicate a homicide.'

'Ahhh,' went Jack.

'Death by drowning,' concluded Jazz.

'Hmmm,' was the reply, from all of us, even though us girls didn't want to give Jazz the satisfaction, and then everyone was quiet. Parcel Brewster had kept to himself, but even those that hadn't known him didn't like to think of him dying like that, all alone and helpless. I was thinking about the autopsy, and adding it to the conversation Jack and I had overheard up at Frey's Dam in the dead of night. There must have been a scuffle, and Parcel either fell, hurting himself badly before rolling into the water and drowning, or they held him under . . . It didn't bear thinking about.

'May he rest in peace,' said Tam with a sigh.

'I'll be a whole lot more peaceful if I know how he went,' said Carrie.

'Well, because things are so inconclusive, they're going to get a second opinion on the autopsy,' said Jazz. 'Plus they're going to re-examine the crime scene.'

'When will that be?' asked Jack, meeting my eye.

Jazz shrugged, unwilling to admit there was something she didn't know.

Mr K was still staring at the ceiling, his hands behind his head, a toe tapping quietly. 'Interesting,' he murmured.

He would have said more, I'm sure, but the bell on the door jangled wildly and we all turned to look. There stood Pen, with Boodle pushing ahead of her on a short leash. Behind her was Fat Angus and he was carrying a box.

'Hi, everyone,' said Pen, smiling sweetly at my friends. Me, she did not smile at. Me, she glared at. Over she stomped.

I sensed this was not going to go well. 'Hi, Pen!' I said.

'Hi, yourself,' she hissed, coming round the back of my chair.

I kept a wary eye on her.

'What's up?' I asked.

'My bliddy dog won't go anywhere without your bliddy duck! It's pathetic! Everywhere I go I have to carry the dumbass box. With the dumbass duck. I'm not doing it any more. Today you have duck and dog. Angus and I need time alone!'

'You have a duck?' asked Jack, astonished. 'Lula, is that –'

'Uh . . .' I said, thinking furiously. 'Just give me a few minutes, Pen! You can't leave household pets in a café!'

'I can and I will!' she muttered, dropping Boodle's lead right there on the floor. 'Put the box down, Angus,' she commanded.

Angus put the box down gingerly on the table. Biggins stretched his neck over the edge of the box and went 'cheeep' longingly at the condensation on Jack's smoothie.

'Oh no, you don't,' I said to Pen. 'Oh no no no no, you don't!'

'Sayonara!' said Pen, drawing a Z-shape in the air, with a waggle of her head and hips. 'Angus, come!' Out she strutted, Angus shrugging and mouthing 'sorry!' behind her. The bell jangled, and all was quiet. I half-stood to make a grab for Boodle's lead and saw Mrs Caruso hurrying over.

'Did your sister just leave her big hairy dog here in my café?' asked Mrs Caruso.

'She did,' I said, with a look across at Tam. Tam's eyes went very big.

'And the duck in a box?' asked Mrs Caruso. 'She left that too?'

'Yes,' I ground out.

'Oh, boy,' said Arns. 'You about done, Mona?'

'Don't rush me, love-love,' she replied, taking another tiny mouthful of cake.

'The dog and the duck are here to stay,' said Arns with meaning. 'Here in the café. There's going to be a disaster.'

'I'm done,' announced Mona, hurriedly leaping from her chair, snatching up her bag.

'What dog and duck?' asked Gianni, struggling under a tray of glasses and the biggest jug of water I've ever seen.

Boodle turned towards him and skipped up to *whump* both her enormous paws square in Gianni's Italian-stallion bits.

'WHOA!' went Gianni. He went down like a tonne of bricks, his arms shooting up, the tray flying out of his hands. It was one of those slow-motion moments, and all I could see was the enormous jug of water hurtling my way. Not even my lightning-fast reflexes could prevent it sploshing its full load all over me and Tam but I was quick enough to snatch it up a hair's breadth from the floor.

The glass tumblers hit the wooden boards, bouncing and rolling in all directions, while I shouted, 'Frik! Stay! Oh no! Stay, Boodle!'

Gianni lay clutching his bits on the floor, moaning something that sounded suspiciously like 'witch girl! *Her* dog, *her*, again-a,' whimper, whimper, etc.

Tam was at his side in an instant, going, 'Are you all right? Gio? Gi? Are you okay?'

'No,' said Gianni. He raised his head to shoot me a venomous look from his watering eyes, but his gaze stopped short at Tam's chest.

'Whoa,' he said for a second time.

I gasped at what he was staring at – Tam's crisp white top was drenched and perfectly see-through, leaving absolutely nothing to the imagination.

'Tam!' I squeaked.

She looked up at me, and her jaw dropped. 'Tatty! Your shir–!' she began, just as the hairy hound tugged against the lead. I was about to rein Boodle in, but she was only picking Biggins up from the table with her massive drooly jaws. She dropped him gently into the puddle of water on the floor at my feet.

'Chee-ack,' said the duck, splatting his tiny feet happily.

I ignored them and threw my cardi over to Tam. 'You'd better put that on,' I said. 'Before Gianni has a heart attack.'

Tam looked down at her drenched shirt. 'Eek!' She slapped Gianni – still gaping like a loon – on the head as she snatched at my cardi, and held it to her chest, spluttering with indignation, before putting it on at the speed of light.

'Very generous of you, Lula,' said Arns, standing and trying to urge Mona towards the door. 'Seeing as you need that far more than Tam.'

I glanced down at myself and discovered that black chiffon, even if it is quite crinkly, is also totally see-through when wet.

'Frik!' I yelped, scrabbling for my coat. Damn the tangly sleeves!

Jack, behind me, was going, 'What? What? Are you going, Lula?'

Mrs Caruso had not noticed the breasts on display. 'Tam-a, you okay? Gio? Stop being such a wimp-a. Towels! We need towels! Someone could fall-a.'

'I'm so sorry!' I huffed. 'So, so sorry!'

'Don' worry, darling,' soothed Mrs Caruso. 'I'll put the dog and the duck over in the window. Outta the way.'

I nodded gratefully and helped Tam to her feet while still struggling to get my arms in the sleeves of my stupid, stupid coat. Jack was trying to help, but just getting in the way, and all the time he was going, 'Did you get that duckling from Frey's Dam?' and various variations of the same question over and over again in a confused undertone until at last I said, 'Kind of,' and then I couldn't read his expression.

Mrs Caruso settled Boodle and Biggins to the left of the counter in the window. They were both looking out through the glass. Boodle's plumed tail was waving happily, which was okay because it was only a fake grapevine that was taking a beating. Arns and Mona still hadn't left, mainly because Arns was still pointing at my chest and laughing a particularly nerdy laugh that made me want to harm him. Mona was staring too, her hand over her mouth and her eyes terribly wide.

Mrs Caruso was hurrying towards Gianni who was now staggering back from the kitchen with a load of tea towels. 'Put them on the floor here-a,' she commanded, but her sandalled foot hit the puddle and with a 'WEY-A!' she fell hard, taking Gianni down with her. All that could be seen of Tam's latest flame was his right leg, which was jerking reflexively beneath his enormous mother. She was like a bug on its back, waving her arms and legs with no chance of getting up on her own.

I reached over, still only half my coat on, and grabbed one of her hands. 'Jack! Mr K!' I shouted. 'Help!'

Tam was at my side in an instant and we were both tugging on Mrs Caruso's arm, while her other flailed like a rodeo cowboy's. She was utterly speechless.

Mr K had stopped staring at the ceiling. He was leaning forward, elbows on his knees, his fedora tilted back so he had a good view of the chaos before him. Jack had to step right round him to get to my side.

'Mr K!' I pleaded, pulling as hard as I could.

'Sure, Tallulah,' said Mr K, getting to his feet with a devilish look in his eye. 'But you know how feeble I am.'

'Stop kicking your legs, please, Mrs Caruso,' said Jack. 'Someone could get hurt.'

'Mrwmee,' squeaked Gianni, whose head had emerged. His purple complexion suggested he wasn't getting quite enough air.

'Indeed,' said Mr K. 'Everybody ready? One, two, three!'

He, Jack, Tam and I pulled at Mrs Caruso's hands, while Carrie and Alex got behind and pushed her upright. She stood dizzily and looked so wobbly I momentarily forgot about my see-through top. I braced my legs and held both her hands. 'You okay, Mrs Caruso?'

She let go of me and clutched the back of a chair.

I stooped to help Gianni up.

His legs seemed a little shaky too, so I held him by the

elbows for a moment before letting go carefully.

'Whoa!' he said, his hands clutching his heart while he gaped at my wet shirt.

I was distracted by Boodle stepping out from the window area. 'Boodle!' I said warningly. 'Stay!' I held my hand out in the stop position and looked at her sternly.

'Can I stay too?' asked Bludgeon from the doorway, looking at me, then my chest, then back at me. 'Looks like there's good viewing in this café.'

Chapter Twenty-three

Friday afternoon, rattling to the safari park on the rowing bus

Arnold was sitting right behind me, but I couldn't look him in the eye.

'So,' he said. 'How come you wouldn't talk to me in art this morning?'

'I did talk to you,' I muttered.

'You said, "Get away from me, Arnold Trenchard." That's what you said.'

I murmured something under my breath.

'Pardon?' asked Arnold politely. 'What was that? Did you just call me a rude name?'

'Arns!' said the big burly rower with the German accent. 'Back off, man. Don't get her riled.'

I saw Arnold shoot him a cursory glance. 'What are you afraid of, Boris?'

'Ah,' I said softly. 'I remember you from last time. The sausage-eater slash German exchange student slash rowing champ. Nice to meet you, Boris Weinstührer.'

Boris made a high-pitched sound in the back of his throat and shifted in his seat. 'I'm not afraid of anything, man. Nothing at all.'

I faced forward and a few seconds later a burp of epic proportions thundered forth. A pungent odour of bratwurst filled the bus.

I turned slowly till I was facing the boys at the back. (How come all the girls got on the bus before me so I was left with the last seat before the boys? *Again?*)

'Who burped?' I asked quietly, staring directly at Boris. 'Who did that?'

'Er,' said Arns. 'Wasn't me.'

'You!' I stabbed a finger at Arns. 'You be quiet!'

'Hey!' said Arns. 'It's not my fault that every time I see you you're getting naked! That's got nothing to do with me! Don't take it out on me!'

'Ooooh!' said Jessica Hartley, fully swivelled in her seat for a view of the proceedings. 'Doing what naked, Arnold?'

'Now that would be telling,' said Arnold with a wink.

Something inside me snapped. 'I WAS NOT NAKED!' I yelled.

Mr VDM slowed the bus to take the corner up to the safari park gates. 'You kids have your own change rooms now!' he called back. 'No more towels dropping *by mistake* so we can all see everything.' He pulled up at the gates and glared at Jessica. 'Understood?'

There was general muttering while the game guard came out and got VD to sign into the park.

'You still scared of this place, Tatty Bird?' drawled

Matilda McCabe from the front seat.

'You are having a laugh,' I said bitterly. 'This wildlife habitat is old hat to me. It feels like I've been rowing for years instead of just Wednesday, Thursday, now *Friday*! Who does sport on a *Friday*? I've been here *every* morning and *every* night since I first went out in that *old* and *stinky* boat' – I dropped my voice to a hiss – 'thanks to VD getting the dumbass idea that I might have to row in the regatta! Me! A total novice!'

'Well,' said Jessica. 'He has taken quite a shine to you. That speech he made in assembly about your incredible talent, blah blah, being a crew member at the last minute, blah blah. Pukerama.'

I went red. The boys in the back stifled giggles. Jessica's narky tone sounded a wee bit jealous and I wanted it fixed, but I didn't know how.

'Anyone would get the hang of rowing if they had to do tank sessions twice a day as well as rowing with you lot,' drawled Arns. 'She's not that good. VD just likes her tight Ts.'

'I do not wear tight Ts!' I protested. 'That is a total lie, you lying liar!'

'You do and you make me wear them too.'

'Oh, please.' I shot him a withering look, though actually I was quite grateful to him. That look had left Jessica's face. 'You love wearing your new clothes. I should have got you more camo gear so you could hide away from the animals out here.'

A smile stretched across Arnold's face. 'I'm not scared of the animals,' he replied.

I rolled my eyes. 'I was never *scared*,' I countered. 'Just a little concerned about our safety, that's all.'

More snarfy laughter from the back.

'This place, pffft!' said Mr VDM with a dismissive wave of his hand. 'They call this a safari park? What's a park without the big cats, hey? They got one rhino and they call it a safari park. Pffft!' Another wave of the hand.

'There is a leopard too, sir,' said Boris.

'And the rhino is a black one,' said a big blond boy. 'Those guys are nasty. Nasty tempers.'

'Just like me,' I said warningly to the fellows in the back.

Someone farted and I shifted to look at them with my eyebrows raised while the girls all yelled abuse and rolled the windows down as fast as they could.

'Pardon me,' said Boris in small voice. 'Pardon me, please.'

I gave him a cursory nod and turned back, concentrating hard on not throwing up.

We tumbled into the boathouse with relief. The changing room used to be big enough for a whole crew to get dressed in, but since the boys started tagging along it had been divided by a piece of plasterboard into separate girls and boys. So now only four of us could get changed at any one time. It was an unwritten rule that the first four: Matilda McCabe, Jessica Hartley, Dionysia Demas and Kelly Sheridan went first, while I went with the O'Connelly sisters and Hilary St John. Dionysia, Kelly and the Irish O'Connelly sisters were all big girls, oh, and Matilda McCabe too, but you knew that. They weren't fat, they were *big*. Mr VDM said they were the best girl powerhouse on the water he'd ever seen.

The boys I was only just getting to know. Boris was rowing six in the Hambledon Boys' powerhouse, behind Arnold who was seven and Ivor at eight. At five was Zac Rutter who was quieter than Arnold, but the smelliest of them all (silent but violent, I was reliably informed), then came Fat Angus, a guy called Skinny Jenks (though he wasn't), then Llewellyn Scott and finally Thor T. Birtley. Thor I reckoned was okay, though we hadn't said two words to each other. He was as cocky and smelly as the rest of them, but he was respectful of us girls and kept his distance.

Mr VDM locked the minibus and went on to the jetty to check the speedboat engine. 'Ten minutes!' he bellowed. 'Both boats on the water in ten minutes!'

'He's tetchier than usual,' I observed, sinking on to an old crate outside the changing room.

'Worried about the regatta a week on Sunday,' said Matilda, crashing the corrugated-iron changing-room door closed behind her and the others.

'Has Vanessa been signed off by your dad?' I asked.

Michelle Wong, our cox, dropped her bag next to mine. 'Course not. A stress fracture takes forever. You'll be rowing in the Port Albert Regatta – your first race. Not bad going.'

'No!' I yelped. 'I run; I don't row! I'm just doing this for a bit to fix my back, you know?'

'Oh, please,' said Michelle. 'Get ready to race. And don't say you didn't know. That's why you've been worked so hard.'

I *had* been worked hard. That light paddle on Wednesday had been, strangely, really quite wonderful and, although I'd never admit it, I was beginning to see the appeal of the whole malarkey – but the thought of the regatta was terrifying. No way did I feel ready for that.

'Oh. Frik,' I breathed. 'I thought Vanessa would be better by now.'

'That was dumb,' said Kelly Sheridan.

'What's dumb is me racing! With you guys! In the Port Albert Regatta!'

'Where have you *been*?' asked Michelle with a weary widening of her eyes. 'What did you think all of these extra training sessions have been about?'

'I just . . . I just . . .' Distant memories of previous years' events chimed into place. 'Frik!' I said. 'We're racing in the Port Albert Regatta next *weekend*?'

'Let's hope she's quicker off the mark at the start of the

race,' said Matilda, coming out of the changing room. She threw an oily rag at me as she walked over to the boat racks. 'Get with the programme, Bird, because if we lose that race I'm holding you personally responsible.'

Down on the water Mr VDM left us girls to get on with it as he sped alongside the boys, bellowing at them through a rusty loudhailer. The 'Pond' as it was called was really a long twisty stretch of dammed water that flowed from hills and mountains even further up than Hambledon all the way down to the coast. The Pond was about fifty miles from the ocean, and the stretch of river where we would be racing, five minutes before it hit the sea at Port Albert, was salty and rough and a challenge to race on.

After three sessions out on the water thus far I knew enough to be afraid of rough, salty challenges.

'Aaand . . . take it down,' came Michelle's voice through a speaker just up the boat. 'Watch your speed, Tatty – you're rushing.'

'Sorry,' I mumbled, concentrating on following Hilary's speed up the slide.

Our boat glided to a stop, the water hissing gently beneath our feet, blades resting lightly on the water. Everyone reached for their water bottles between their runners and I did the same.

I heard Matilda say something to Michelle, then

Michelle's voice came over the speaker again. 'Pull hard, bow, the boys are coming down.'

I dropped my water and moved into position to take a stroke. Bow was me, and I did what I was told.

Only just in time.

The boys' boat came hissing to a halt alongside ours.

'What the hell,' shrieked Michelle. She still had her mike on. We all winced as her voice echoed across the water. 'Could you not see us resting here, Billy, you dumbass?'

'Er, actually no,' said Billy, cowed. 'Sorry.'

There was general muttering. The boys' boat had slipped further down, and now Arns was beside me.

'Hello,' he said, taking a pull on his water bottle.

I sighed. 'Hello, Arnold,' I said, and also had a drink. 'Where's VD?'

'Gone to get more petrol for his boat,' said Boris. 'Told us to wait down here for him.'

'He'd better hurry the hell up,' said Sinead O'Connelly. 'It's getting dark.'

'Maybe we should turn round,' said Thor from the water behind me. 'Be ready to race back to the jetty.'

'He wants to race back?' asked Dionysia. 'That's not safe. It's too narrow round these bends, especially in the dark. Someone's going to get whacked.'

A low laugh came from the guy sitting in front of Arns: Ivor Markman, one of Hambledon's studliest studmuffins.

'No one's going to get whacked,' he murmured. 'No way.'

'Excuse me?' said Matilda, twisting round in her seat. 'What do you mean by that, Ivor Markman?'

'Ivor,' warned Arns.

'Like, you girls really think you can keep up with us round the bends?' Ivor laughed out loud. 'We're gonna leave you lot bleating at the start. You and your puny bow!'

Matilda whacked her blade hard into the water. It splashed up a whale of water all over Ivor. Arns ducked down and to the side, rocking the boat madly, but he also got wet.

'Bloody hell,' complained Arns. 'You asked for that, Ive. And, just for the record, that bow is not so puny.'

'Not so puny at all,' confirmed Boris. 'Watch it, man.'

Ivor slid alongside me as the coxes got us turning the boats. 'Hmm,' said Ivor, tugging gently at his blade as he looked across at me in the twilight. 'I'm watching all right.'

I saw the glint of his teeth as he smiled, and it made me shudder.

Mr VDM took ages to refill his tank. By then Arns and I had had a good yak. The girls were mostly talking amongst themselves, and Ivor was talking strategy with Billy Diggle.

'You wanna hear what I came to tell you in the café?' asked Arns. I flushed. 'And what I was trying to tell you at art?'

'Go on, then.'

Arns stared at me for a beat, then grinned. His curly hair was still short and tufty, the way I'd cut it, but water had darkened it past auburn. I wasn't close enough to see the flecks of green in his hazel eyes, but I knew they were sparkling at me right now. He'd be teasing me mercilessly if it weren't for everyone else out here on the water.

'You're gonna owe me,' he said.

I sighed, and raised my eyebrows.

He laughed. 'Okay, so Mum says the lab came back about trace from Parcel Brewster's body.'

'Oh, yeah?' I sat up and leaned out towards him.

'In the boat, Tatty!' yelled Michelle. 'Otherwise we're all in the water!'

'Sorry!' I called back.

'They found hairs, but they're synthetic, like a wig. So no DNA.'

'That's it?' I said to Arns, incredulous.

'Well, yes,' said Arns uncertainly.

'That's pathetic. Synthetic hairs could be anything. I owe you nothing.'

'You do so!' said Arns. He dropped his voice. 'Who helped you with your coat last night at the café, huh? Who?'

'I could have helped myself!' I hissed back.

'Yeah, yeah,' said Arns, and I could hear him smiling. Then he said, suddenly serious, talking quickly before the others stopped their banter about Ivor's latest conquest, 'One other thing that you're not going to like.' I kept quiet. 'Arthur Cluny. Mum's looking into that angle.'

'Right,' I said. I shifted uncomfortably and the boat wobbled again, causing outrage from my crewmates. I didn't like to think of Helen's dad implicated in something like this. He was a scary man, but not that kind of scary. Not bad scary. But the sale of that land would mean money, and money was always a powerful motivator, especially if you were desperate.

The sound of a boat engine cut into my thoughts.

'Who's ready to race?' called Mr van der Merwe, revving the throttle. 'Boys against girls! *On your marks . . .!*'

Chapter Twenty-four

Friday night at the boathouse, boys jubilant, girls cranky

VD surged up to the jetty with a roar, and cut his engine, leaping out nimbly to tie his boat to a pole at the shore. 'Good racing, boys and girls,' he shouted. 'Boys out first, please, and in the bus after changing.'

'Can't we just go straight home?' asked Michelle, steering carefully to the right of the jetty.

'Nuh-uh,' said Ivor, holding on to his rigging, his blade held high. 'Us athletes have got to get warm.'

'Athletes, my butt,' said Matilda. 'We would have had you at the western bend if it wasn't for Boris. Without him you lot are just –'

'Oi-oi!' interrupted Arns. 'Steady on! We won the regatta last year against six other crews!'

'Whatever,' muttered Matilda.

Michelle climbed out of the boat and held it against the jetty while the rest of us unclipped our blades from the rigging and untied our feet from the footboards. She shot a look up at Ivor, but I noticed it was an *I'll keep you warm* kind of look and not an *oh go to hell, you arrogant pig* kind of look.

Interesting.

By the time we'd finally got our boat on the rack, it seemed the boys were mostly in the bus already. The O'Connellys, Hilary and I stood shivering outside the changing room.

'Where's Michelle?' I asked.

'She stayed dry,' said Siobhan. 'Probably already on the bus.'

'Hurry up, you guys!' called Sinead to the girls in the changing room. 'We're gonna catch our death out here!'

'Specially if there are wild animals in this park,' called Kelly Sheridan from safely inside. She did a hollow laugh, then Matilda did a leopard noise while Jessica asked what rhinos sounded like.

I got to my feet and paced up and down, my eyes staring into the shadows. 'Our parents are going to be worried!' I fretted. 'It's really late!'

'You can call your mum from my mobile,' suggested Hilary. 'Go to the far door for better reception. Don't worry about the leopard, Tatty. Leopards are shy, solitary creatures and are hardly going to come down to a noisy boathouse, yeah?'

'Yeah,' I said uncertainly. I knew I should believe her because they wouldn't let us roam around if it wasn't safe but still . . . I took the phone from her with a thank you and felt my way down the boathouse in the dark. 'They need lights in here,' I grumbled to myself. On the other side of the building it seemed darker than ever, an old rowboat only just visible in the shadows. I looked around nervously for vicious animals, though I wouldn't have been able to see an elephant in this light.

I pressed a button on the phone and it made a little *blip* noise in the night air. Then suddenly the boat beneath me was rocking wildly. I spun in fright, dropping the phone to the ground and saw two pairs of eyes staring back at me in the pitch black night.

'AAAAAAAAAAARGH!' I yelled, frozen to the spot. 'AAAAAAAAAAARGH!'

The two pairs of eyes winked back and went, 'AAAARGH!' and, 'EEEEE!' in total terror.

The sound of thundering feet came from all directions.

'Oh, geez!' I squeaked, staring into the boat. '*Who is that?* You scared the crap out of me!'

'*WHAT IS GOING ON OUT HERE?*' roared Mr VDW, skidding to a halt beside me.

He had a powerful torch in his hand, and swung the beam into the rowboat.

I gasped.

He gasped.

Michelle Wong (virtually naked) gasped.

Ivor Markman (like, totally naked) gasped.

The whole girls' crew now at our sides gasped.

'Oh, frik!' I said.

Mr van der Merwe was apoplectic with rage. We were in the minibus and he was yelling about the youth of today, trust, teamwork and the evils of the pleasures of the flesh. He was threatening to report Michelle Wong and Ivor Markman to their respective principals for lascivious behaviour.

'Why the hell did you have to go yelling your head off?' hissed Kelly Sheridan to me. 'Are any of us having a good time now, huh? *Any of us?*'

'You think I did this for a *good time*?' I hissed back, outraged. 'I was genuinely terrified out there! You didn't see their eyes! Staring at me in the dark like wild animals!'

'Wild animals,' mused Fat Angus. 'Michelle Wong and Ivor Markman. Who would have thought.'

'Did anyone see that coming?' I asked. 'Is this, like, a rowing thing?'

'*No one* saw that coming,' whispered Hilary. 'She's the smallest girl in our school and he's got to be the biggest in theirs.'

'We rowers have standards,' said Jessica primly. 'And boy rowers do NOT come up to scratch.'

'Hn,' said Arns.

I looked over at him. He looked back at me. Nobody said anything. Nobody said anything the whole way home.

Five days later – five days of total physical agony – Thursday morning at school

'What's wrong, Lu?' asked Carrie, bumping me with her hip as we walked down the corridor. 'We've got a free period right now! An hour to chat in the library!'

'She's bummed because the whole rowing squad hates her, and the Port Albert Regatta is on Sunday and they have no cox,' explained Alex.

'Are you being rude?' asked Tam.

'Rude how?' Alex looked confused.

'Cox, Tam. C O X,' I spelled out. 'The person who yells instructions and steers the boat.'

'Ohhh!' said Tam. 'I thought little Shelli Wong was your steerer.'

'*Was*,' I said.

'Till Lu bust her and Studly Ivor making out after dark at the boathouse last Friday,' chipped in Alex.

Carrie sighed. 'Didn't know he was a rower. So fit . . . Tatty, you sure none of those rowers is boyfriend material for, like, me, yes?'

'Extra specially doubly sure,' I said, my eyes big with the emphasis. 'Don't go there, Carrie. Don't go there, anyone.'

'Easy for you to say,' sighed Tam. 'You with big handsome Jack.'

'I don't feel like I am *with* him,' I replied.

'Nooo!' said the girls in unison as we swung into the library.

'Find yourselves a desk, please, girls, and I want to see you doing your book reports, not chatting,' called Miss Fitzroy.

'Back corner,' said Alex out of the corner of her mouth. 'But don't run.'

We hustled and got the best desk for nattering.

'How's it going with Gavin Healey?' I asked Alex. 'You never talk about him.'

'Huh,' said Carrie. 'They probably never talk to each other. What *have* you two got in common?'

'An interest in crime scenes, for one,' said Alex, arching an eyebrow and pulling out her pencil case. 'He has to wear this kind of special suit if he's doing crime-scene clean-ups, just like in the movies, and –'

'I get it,' said Carrie. 'No one can resist a man in uniform.'

We snorted with laughter, even Alex, at a boiler suit being even remotely attractive.

'I like the fact that he goes sailing,' said Alex, twinkling, 'even though that's totally pretentious of me.'

'It is,' said Carrie definitely. 'Does he go down to Port Albert?'

'No, actually,' said Alex, thinking. 'Though that's weird. They've got a boathouse down at Saddler's Pond . . .'

'Prime property,' I noted. 'And I should know.'

'Hmm,' said Tam, eyeing Alex. 'I bet the real attraction is that your mum would rather you were dating a boy from St Alban's instead of someone who does crime-scene clean-ups.'

Alex squirmed and we laughed at her discomfit.

'And what's with Jack?' Tam asked me. 'You don't sound convinced, but you two are perfect together.'

'Except we hardly ever are,' I said. 'Together I mean. I haven't seen him since Thursday, and then he was away at his granny's for the weekend, which I totally understand, but when am I going to see him again? Not tonight, because he's working with *Jazz* . . .'

The girls pulled sympathetic faces and Tam put her arm round my shoulders in a sideways hug.

'Oh, Tatty,' said Carrie. 'He doesn't like her, you know. He likes you.'

'If he liked me, he'd be spending time with me,' I replied. 'It's that simple.'

'Yeah, but life's not simple,' said Alex.

'What, you're *defending* him now?' I pulled some books out of my bag. 'I thought you didn't approve of him doing so much with Jazz.'

'He phoned and said sorry,' said Alex. 'He's lucky to have a forgiving relative like me.'

'Huh,' I said. 'I wish I had forgiving crew members.'

'None of that was your fault, Lula,' said Carrie firmly. 'They'll come round.'

'It's Thursday,' I wailed quietly. 'The race is on Sunday!

I'm not going to be forgiven in the space of two days, plus we have to find another cox!'

'One of us could help out,' suggested Tam. 'Do you want us to turn up for tryouts this afternoon?'

I smiled happily. 'You guys would do that for me?'

'Reluctantly,' sighed Alex. 'What time does the bus leave?'

Miss Fitzroy loomed in front of our desk. 'I thought I could hear the murmur of gossiping voices back here,' she snapped. 'Split up, the four of you. Tallulah, please take this note to the office for me.'

I took the note and hurried to the office. Having one of the girls with me in the boat would be brilliant! I tried to squash a smile at the thought of gentle Tam yelling instructions to eight sweaty girls, or Carrie steering a fine line through the bridge ramparts, or Alex keeping her eyes off the boys. One of them could be an excellent cox, and an excellent cox was one step closer to me being forgiven by the crew. Being forgiven was important to me. I'd never been any good at team sports, mainly because they all involve a ball of some sort, and it had felt great being a valued part of this crew, even though I was the newest in the boat. I sighed hopefully.

Everything was going to be okay.

But, then, as I rounded the corner of the corridor to the office, my hopes were dashed:

I love you a go go go
Oohooo you're my big man man
Never tell me no no no
I saw you and – aha – ran ran

I froze. That was Dad! Singing some terrible chart topper.

Everything was NOT going to be okay!

I peered round the corner. In front of the school office was Dad, thankfully not in his *chest-swelled-out* ballad mode, but regrettably in his *down-with-the-kids* bopping mode (shoulders hunched, a lot of swaggering).

At the office window I could see Mrs Fergusson, her hands clasped in rapture before her, her tightly curled head nodding in time to Dad's tuneless rhythm. To the left stood three Year Eights, bopping away too.

It had to stop. Before anyone else gathered at the scene.

'Dad!' I cried, loping over. 'What are you doing here? Aren't your tutorials in the music rooms?'

'T-Bird,' he called happily, arms outstretched. 'Just dropping off Pen's bag.'

'Oh, sir,' simpered the blondest of the Year Eights. 'I love your lyrics! I can see why they call you Song Bird!'

Dad swept them a bow and they ran off giggling. I handed Miss Fitzroy's note to Mrs Fergusson and she disappeared into her office after giving Dad a flirty little wave.

'Frik!' I said, rounding on my father. 'I absolutely *hate* that song.'

'Those lyrics are making us a lot of money,' said Dad, with only a hint of shame. 'Most of which is being saved up to pay for your uni-tuition fund and –'

'I have nothing to say to that right now,' I scorned, my hand up to stop him from speaking. 'What I do want to know, however, is what Pen needs with – is that a – yes, it is! With a gym bag?'

'She's trying out for the boat crew this afternoon,' said Dad. 'Very excited. Could hardly make out what she was saying on the phone.'

'I'll make sure it gets to Penelope right away, Professor Bird,' trilled Mrs Fergusson, back at her window. 'Don't you worry about a thing.'

Oh, who is Mrs Fergusson to talk about worry? I knew aaaaall about worry, and the thought of Pen, the most obnoxious human being on the planet, telling me what to do from the front of the boat, made me feel far more than worry. It was time for Panic Stations and Desperate Measures.

Still Thursday, but I've sprinted to the uni library, after dancing before rowing – I tell you my life is full
'Please, Mum, say Pen can't try out this afternoon! Please, Mum!'

Mum stopped leafing through an old leather-bound book and looked up at me sternly. 'Tallulah Bird, your sister does no sport at all, and I'm certainly not going to discourage her from this now.'

'Being a cox isn't sporty!' I wailed.

'Oh? Just because they *drive* the boat and don't row it? Are you calling Jenson Button unsporty? Or Lewis Hamilton? As far as I can recall, that Lewis boy was up for sportsman of the year two summers ago! Pen may just surprise you, Lu.' She turned back to her ancient document. 'Well, will you look at this! Elias Brownfield met Queen Victoria in 1842!'

I tried very hard not to scream. 'Mum! The only reason Pen wants to be part of the crew is because Fat Angus –'

'Also rows. Do you think I don't know my girls, Tallulah?' Mum shifted her glasses down her nose and gave me another look. 'I knew you'd be good at rowing, and I just know Pen is going to be a little star at coxing. What's really going on here is that you don't want your little sister on your turf.'

'Is that so terrible?' I asked. 'Is that really so terrible? C'mon, Mum!'

'I'll give you a lift to the bus,' said Mum, putting the ancient diary into a desk drawer and locking it. 'Otherwise you'll be late. I wonder how Elias Brownfield came to meet Queen Victoria. Right here in Hambledon!'

I sighed. I was a victim. In more ways than one.

On the road, on the water, on a hiding to nothing

I didn't get much conversation from the crew in the bus on the way to the afternoon's session. Good thing Carrie, Alex and Tam came along to try out for the cox position, along with other hopefuls who clearly hadn't heard how traumatic a bus ride with boy rowers could be. The girls and I laughed about Alex and Gavin's date last night at the cinema where Alex had sat in blueberry bubblegum in white jeans. Disaster. Except that Gav had the perfect cleaning agent in the back of his van.

'You kept the jeans on, right?' asked Tam, worried.

'Ta-am!' we yelped in unison.

'Left butt cheek . . . more outer thigh, really,' Alex hastened to add. 'Jeans stayed on, *definitely*, though I have to say that Gavin –'

But we'd arrived. The crew piled out of the bus and got ready to row.

An hour later we'd had our toughest session in the boat yet, and Mr VDM was ecstatic with the efforts of the one and only Penelope Bird, who'd been the first to try out for the cox position. No one else had even had a go. They'd be fuming up there at the boathouse. Or maybe not. They'd probably all be deeply relieved. VD pulled up alongside our boat, keeping the loudhailer to his lips at full volume.

'BRILLIANT!' he bawled, while we all squeezed our eyes shut at the noise.

'Sorry!' he continued, dropping the loudhailer. 'You!' He pointed a finger at Pen. 'You are a natural!' Turning to the rest of us with a beatific grin he shouted, 'All agreed? No need to try the others? Great! Let's have a sprint, rating thirty-two, all the way back!' He gunned his engine, yelled, 'Whoo-hooo!' and was away.

A small but triumphant voice echoed through the speaker further up the boat.

'Bow. Bow, do you hear me? We need a little more oomph from you on the home straight, please. Your puddle is smaller than all the rest.'

'Frikking frikking frik frik!' I ground out quietly. 'I frikking hate her.'

Hilary looked back over her shoulder. 'She's your own flesh and blood, T! I think she's great.'

'Flesh, yes,' I muttered back, 'and I'll *definitely* be drawing blood.'

Chapter Twenty-five

Friday afternoon, outside Hambledon Girls' High School

'So this is what I don't like about rowing,' said Pen, coming up to me and the O'Connelly sisters. 'Friday afternoon training. And in the misty freezingness. What's with that?'

I expected the O'Connellys to brush off my pipsqueak sister, but they didn't.

'It sucks,' agreed Sinead, 'but it's only been for the last few weeks while we get ready for the Port Albert Regatta. Is it true you go out with Fat Angus?'

Pen nodded and went red. I saw her look less confident suddenly and something made me say, 'He's brilliant in the boat.'

'He's the only one who doesn't burp or fart,' added Siobhan.

'No, he burps,' said Hilary, joining us. 'But we like him anyway.'

'Arnold Trenchard doesn't burp or fart,' I said.

The girls looked at me, looked at each other and then burst out laughing.

'What?' I asked. 'What did I say?'

'Forget it,' said Hilary. 'Here comes Jessica, and she is *riled*.'

'Oh.' I nodded. 'Did she hear about Jason and Daisy Nantley-Brown?'

'She did,' said Siobhan. 'And she's going to make him pay.'

'Uh-oh,' said Pen. 'Isn't Jason in the boys' boat?'

'Yep,' I said. 'He's usually in the B side, but with Ivor suspended from rowing he gets a shot at the first-eight crew. Please let me sit with the girls this time!'

'Pen,' said the O'Connellys in unison, 'you're with us!' And as the school bus pulled in, they tugged the door open and grabbed the first seat behind the driver, wedging Pen in between them. I got shouldered out of the way, as per usual, and ended up on my ownsome in the middle of the bus, where I'd soon be joined by the boys.

'This is not fair!' I said, and hated how that sounded.

Hilary looked back sympathetically. 'It's just because you're the only one who can keep them in line, Tatty. Smells and phlegm have gone down seventy-five per cent since you started riding with us.'

'Fear of the witch,' added Pen sagely.

'You are my sister!' I cried. 'Also grandchild of the witch!'

'But boys near me don't end up in hospital,' she countered, and there was general agreement from the rest of the girls, and wailing and gnashing of teeth from me until Jessica turned round and looked at me thoughtfully.

She shook a silver flask and smiled. 'I'll sit with you today, Tatty Bird. You and me both against the boys.'

Oh, frik. Frikly frakly frok. I knew how this looked. Witch Girl and Psycho Slut. Where was Alex when I needed micro-management?

By the time we'd pulled up to Hambledon Boys' Jessica's eyes were glittering dangerously, and the rest of the crew were darting glances at each other. The boys piled on and Jason plonked down right next to Jess.

'Hey, babe,' he crooned. 'Now this is motivation for being in the first eight!'

He stroked her forearm and kissed her on the cheek.

'NO KISSING!' yelled Mr VDM, pulling the minibus round in a U-turn to get back on the road. He examined his rear-view mirror and slammed the bus into a kerb. 'NO KISSING AT ALL!'

Jason saluted him. 'Sorry, sir!' he called, but I saw his hand move up Jessica's thigh. I swallowed and looked out the window.

'Hi!' said Arns brightly in the seat behind me. 'What's going on?'

'Later,' I said out of the corner of my mouth.

'Would you like a drink, Jase?' asked Jessica, opening her flask. 'Nothing like a shot of hot Horlicks on a dark and stormy afternoon.'

Jason took the flask with a wink and a swagger and a leer. Jessica maintained a frosty smile that the rest of us knew meant bad news, but Billy Diggle, who didn't know much, seeing as how he was *twelve*, thirteen if he were lucky, had a few swigs from the flask too.

Arns leaned forward and whispered, 'Wasn't Billy Diggle on your kissing list?' Then snorted with laughter. 'He's got hiccups from the Horlicks!' And ha-ha-ha-ed some more.

At 5 p.m. when Mr VDM pulled up at the game gate, Jason Ferman had stopped his swaggering. He had stopped speaking too. By the time we drew up to the boathouse, Jason was as white as a sheet. When the door slung open he was the first out, sprinting through the mist for the outhouse just to the side of the boathouse.

The rest of us got changed, and carried the boats down to the water. I noticed that Pen looked like she'd coxed her whole life long, and, weirdly, I didn't feel any jealousy at how the crew was so inclusive of her – if anything, I was a leeeetle bit proud of her. Even though she was giving me a hard time.

'I'll go easy on you today,' she said in passing, but I just rolled my eyes and let it go. She and Angus were sweetly ignoring each other, being very professional and rowing focused, which I thought was adorable. I was about to climb into my seat when Skinny Jenks came sprinting on to the jetty. He grabbed my shoulder and started stuttering, 'W-w-what did you d-do t-to Jason Ferman?'

'Me?' I squeaked, genuinely astonished. '*Me?*'

'J-J-Jase has exploded!' cried Skinny, shaking my shoulder. 'All over the out-h-h-ouse!'

Mr VDM was busy with his engine, checking the oil, and didn't hear.

Boris came lumbering down the slope. 'Skinny! Get back! Don't touch her!'

Everyone was staring at me with big eyes. There was absolutely no doubt in anyone's heads that whatever had gone on with Jason Ferman's insides was totally down to me and the dark arts.

'Oh for frik's sake!' I yelled, unlacing myself from the footboard. 'That's it! I've had it!'

'Uh-oh,' said Hilary.

Pen's voice came over the speakers. 'Bow, calm down and get in the boat.'

'In a minute!' I yelled. And charged up the slope.

I stomped all the way up to the corrugated-iron outhouse and hammered on the door. 'You stupid boy, Jason Ferman!' I yelled. 'Daisy Nantley-Brown has been going on about you and her all week! You thought Jess wouldn't find out? I hope you've learned your frikking lesson.' And turned to stomp back to the jetty.

'What does that mean?' asked Boris, open-mouthed.

'Dude,' said Arns, leaning up against the boathouse watching me with a lazy smile. 'Take a look at Billy Diggle.'

I shot a look across the dirt road at Billy Diggle hunkered

down by the side of the bus. With Jason hogging the only toilet on the premises he'd been forced to squirt his insides out with minimum privacy.

'Ohhh,' breathed Boris. 'The Horlicks.'

'Right,' said Arns. 'I think you guys' – he gestured with his eyes – 'owe the witch girl an apology. And it looks like we're going out in a coxed four.'

Going out at all was madness, to my mind, and it seemed the rest of the crew shared my opinion. The mist was thick on the water now despite the wind picking up, but it was barely two days to race day, and this was going to be our last training session. So Mr VDM was determined.

The clouds were boiling blackly overhead and we were about to push off from the jetty when the boys came down carrying a four boat – just Boris Weinstührer, Arnold, Fat Angus and Skinny Jenks, with Thor T. Birtley coxing.

Thor was moaning like crazy. 'Mr VDM,' he bleated. 'It's going to be storming any minute! This is a bad idea! If lightning strikes, it's gonna hit us out on the water.'

'When I hear thunder, then we turn back,' growled Mr VDM. 'And not before. Why are you boys not in the eight?'

They explained about Billy and Jason, while Mr VDM went purple with fury, and we were off. With the wind whipping the water, and limited visibility, these were perfect training conditions, bellowed Mr VDM through the loudhailer. He set us four pieces to work through, told us to take pulses after each and went off to find the boys.

'Get us to a straight, flat stretch!' I heard Kelly Sheridan yell to Pen.

'Round the west corner!' agreed Matilda.

We struggled on, battling to balance the boat in the easterly wind. I was concentrating on everything at once, and praying Pen wouldn't pull me up on any bad technique. So far today Mr VDM had only given us general comments, and I liked the fact that I wasn't being picked on for a change. Especially in front of my sister.

Once we got round the west corner, the vicious wind dulled to an occasional gusting, though it was darker here in the shadows.

'Here okay?' asked Pen. A murmur from Matilda. 'Right. We're going to do these pieces with racing starts like we practised yesterday. Everyone ready? Come up!'

We slid to the front of our slides, arms angled left or right, depending on whether we were bowside or strokeside. Pen dropped her voice to a whisper, and I sensed she'd moved her mouth closer to the mike. It sounded like she was in our ears, and then she was calling the start strokes and we were away. I kept my body straight and true, focusing on Hilary in front of me: moving when she moved, turning when she turned, keeping my eyes on the bowside blade ahead of me to make sure mine went in at exactly the same moment.

Our rhythm was perfect, and even in the gusting, choppy water, I felt the pull and surge of the boat beneath me, the hiss of water skating fast beneath that. When Pen called an end to the piece, we were all heaving for breath, but grinning with exhilaration as she counted the pulse time.

By the end of the fourth piece we were exhausted, and I could feel the protective Micropore tape Dad had given me coming away from my hands. I grimaced, wishing I'd brought some in the boat.

We rested, breathing hard and staring into the mist that was starting to drift up from the water. The thunderclouds above were so black and heavy it felt like night.

'Right,' said Pen. 'I can't see much now, so I need you all to be eyes and ears for me.'

I smiled. Pen sounded so grown up. How could she be so confident around girls two to four years older than her? I felt another surge of pride.

'Anyone know where the boys' boat went?'

We all muttered that we hadn't seen or heard anything for a while.

'I'm sure they wouldn't follow us down here, though,' said Sinead O'Connelly. 'Not when it's so dark. And Mr VDM has a light on his boat so we'd be able to see them.'

'Let's go back in,' said Pen.

'Get ready for the wind,' shouted Matilda, turning the boat. Ten strokes later we were back in the full force of it, struggling through sloppy waves that smacked in and over the boat, greasing the grips of our blades and unbalancing every one of us.

'Keep it together,' yelled Pen into her mike. 'Keep it slow! Short strokes in the bad weather, people!' I was concentrating hard on Hilary in front of me, guessing when she went for the catch because I couldn't see Siobhan's blade in the water up ahead any more, when I felt something in that buffeting air, heard a discordant splash, a shout maybe.

'PEN!' I yelled. 'PEN!'

And then the boys' boat hit us.

Chapter Twenty-six

When a boat of eight are all rowing together, strokes perfectly timed, water smooth and still, a crew can get up to 24kph. When an eight is struggling through stormy water, struggling to keep a rhythm, it's not so fast. But when two boats collide, one of them a crew of four strapping lads with the wind in their favour and the mighty Boris in stroke position, it's going to be ugly, whichever way you look at it.

At the first shattering of wood, I heard Thor yell, 'Pull up! Pull up!' and heard blades whir through the riggings. In that instant Matilda cried out, then Dionysia, as the impact rattled right down the boat. There was chaos and shouting and surges of wave and wind and wake. Mr van der Merwe pulled up alongside, yelling at everyone to stay where they were. He played his torchlight quickly over all of us.

I was holding on to my blade for dear life as the wind buffeted us every which way, but trying to sit up straight and tall for a glimpse of Pen. I could only think that if Matilda had been the first to shout, then my sister had to have been hit before her. Then Pen's voice crackled over the mike, and she sounded okay. From what I could see in the dancing torchlight and swirling mist, the boats were fine, just one or two riggers smashed, but then Mr VD's torch halted and he called out, his voice blown away in the gale and the fast slapping of waves.

I leaned out of the boat as much as I dared, scarcely able to believe what I could see. Someone in the boys' boat was slumped back over his crewman's footboard, white, unmoving and covered in blood.

'*Arnold!*' I screamed. '*Arns!* Are you okay?'

Boris was in the seat in front of Arns. He was twisted round, desperately trying to untie the laces of the shoes on Arnold's footboard to get my friend free. His fingers fumbled, his eyes squinted closed against the rain and wind and spraying waves. Mr VDM had pulled alongside now and was hauling out a first-aid kit. As he stood up to get closer, his boat tipped and the first-aid kit landed in the water next to me with a splash.

Before I could think I'd pulled my feet from my shoes, shucked my blade right across the boat and jumped into the water. I struck out for the first-aid kit and got it as it began to sink below the surface. It was heavy, but not too heavy to throw. I tossed it to Boris, who heaved it across to Mr van der Merwe. Then I kicked hard to get to the boys' boat. I was there in an instant, yanking at the laces holding Arnold's feet in.

'Brace!' I yelled at Thor and he signalled for the girls' boat to come alongside the boys' to provide balance. Before they got too close, I pulled myself up into the boys' boat, legs astride Arnold's and looked over his broken head at Fat Angus.

'You out of your shoes?' I cried.

He nodded yes and I looked over at our coach. He was standing at the edge of the motor boat and nodded that he was ready. 'Come!' he yelled.

What am I doing? I thought suddenly. *I'm the puny bow! How did I get here?*

But there was no time to make way for Boris to help now. On the count of three, echoing across the waves from Pen's mike, I got my left foot up on Mr VDM's boat, linked my hands under Arnold's hips and Fat Angus and I heaved Arnold into the motor boat.

'*Take the extra blades,*' yelled Skinny Jenks and he passed across my blade and Arnold's. I found myself in the boat with our coach, Arnold's head in my lap, scrabbling in the first-aid kit for swabs, bandages, anything. Mr VDM swept both boats again with his torchlight to make sure they'd get to shore okay, and we took off for the jetty.

In the bright beam, even through the mist and spray, I saw that Arnold had a deep slice through the left side of his head, from front to back, but it was clean and the blood was already starting to thicken and slow. I pressed the edges together and found a thick gauze pad in the first-aid kit, which I held in place.

By the time we got to the jetty we found Zac and Llewellyn, five and two from the boys' eight, waiting there, ready to rant about how long we'd been out on the water. They were silenced immediately by the amount of blood that met them.

'Help Tallulah!' commanded VD as he tied up his boat and began shining his torch for the other boats to get in.

Zac and Llewellyn struggled up the slope towards the bus with Arns, me cradling his head, explaining quickly what had happened. When we got to the bus, Zac threw the door open and stepped up and in.

'Back seat, so we can lie him down,' gasped Llewellyn.

I had the first-aid kit still clasped in my left hand. I flung it on the floor and pulled out reams of gauze bandage. 'Call Dr McCabe,' I ordered, and Zac pulled out his mobile. I rattled off the number and Zac held it to my ear when it connected.

No silly comments from Dr McCabe this time. He said he'd meet us at the hospital and told me how to apply pressure, and asked questions about whether there was any clear fluid coming from the wound.

'I can't see any clear fluid,' I gasped, 'because there's so much *red* fluid!'

'You're doing well, Tallulah,' said Dr McCabe. 'Don't panic. Just tell your coach to get to the hospital stat. I'll have X-ray and MRI facilities ready. Is the blood stopping?'

'I think so,' I said, too afraid to relieve pressure on the wound.

'Well done, Tallulah,' said Dr McCabe again. I passed the phone back to Zac, and then I began to cry, bent over my friend, his blood smeared all over me.

The two crews got to the bus so fast that I figured they must have abandoned their boats on the shore. They threw themselves in and we took off with a rattle of gravel. Mr VDM drove like a man possessed, but at the top of the last rise near the game gate he came to a screeching halt. 'What the —?'

There in front of us was the rear end of the biggest black rhino I've ever seen in my life, and that includes viewing of the Discovery Channel. It was lumbering slowly down the road. At the sound of us screeching to a halt it turned slowly and blinked a small and malevolent eye at us. Then it lowered its horn.

'Oh, sh—' said Mr VDM.

Pen, next to him in the driver's seat, leaned over and honked the horn. It came out all wheezy and soft.

Parp.

'Oh, puhlease!' yelled Jessica Hartley. 'I can tell without even seeing its sorry-assed goolies that this thing is a male!'

She reached over and pulled on the door handle hard, and before Mr VDM could open his mouth to tell her to get her suspended butt back on the bus, she was rocketing down the road, yelling, her arms spread wide.

'*Oh my God!*' squealed the twins at exactly the same time as Thor T. Birtley leaned out of the window yelling at the top of his lungs and pausing only to vent piercing whistles at the scary beast.

The black rhino ran. Mr VDM gunned the engine and drew up alongside Jessica, who was still sprinting down the road.

'Get in!' yelled Hilary, stretching her arm out.

Jessica grabbed hold of Hilary and jumped, landing back in her seat. Thor slammed the door shut again and we were off.

'Hey!' cried Thor. Everyone on the bus turned to look at him. 'Where are Jase and Billy?' he asked.

Mr VDM nearly slammed on the brakes again, but Jessica was already leaning over the seats to bellow in his ear. 'Tell the game guard to get them!' she yelled. 'And I'll send my dad up to bring them back to town!'

Mr VDM did as instructed, with startling speed, and we were at Hambledon Hospital in twenty-five minutes flat. A stretcher was waiting outside, along with Sergeant Trenchard, Arnold's sister Elsa and Mona.

Only Sergeant T got to go in with the stretcher, which left two boat crews, Elsa and Mona in the waiting room, all slightly out of breath, most of us much the worse for wear.

274

Elsa grabbed me by the forearms. 'Is he gonna be all right, Tatty?'

'Sure,' I said, my eyes wide. 'Sure he is. Looked like the bleeding had pretty much stopped.'

Mona had stepped up to us. She looked at me, her eyes narrowed, and choked out, 'Yes, but how did the bleeding *start*? You and your stupid dog, again, huh, or just *you* this time, Tallulah Bird?'

She whirled away before I could answer, striding off to the nurses' station.

I bit my lip hard, willing back the tears that swam in my eyes.

'She's just upset,' said Elsa. 'Forget it. From what Dr McCabe said, it sounded like you were a serious paramedic out there, Tatty!' She laughed, but it was tight and strained.

'Thanks,' I whispered.

'Mum will come out and tell us what's going on,' continued Elsa. 'She won't want us to worry.'

'Good,' I said. 'Did she bring Mona?'

Elsa nodded. 'She was over at ours waiting for Arns to get home. They were going to dinner in town.' Elsa's eyes slid over to mine. 'Jack is supposedly on his way over.'

At the sound of his name I felt a surge of something – relief, it felt like, that he might be coming – but that brief high plummeted when I heard Jazz Delaney's strident tones echoing through the waiting room. 'Can someone tell us about the boating accident that took place up at Saddler's Pond this evening?' I turned to see her small, neat figure smiling up at Boris. He looked a little shellshocked as she confronted him with a small camcorder and a separate mike. 'Speak clearly, please.'

And then I spotted Jack. Wasn't he supposed to be picking me up from home to go out tonight? Wait. Maybe he'd heard about me being in an accident, and rushed over. But . . . it really didn't look like it. It looked like he wasn't thinking about me at all. There he was, standing near the nurses' station, asking questions, scribbling answers in a reporter's notebook. He got an answer to something, nodded and set off towards us. When he saw me, he stopped and stared.

'Lula?'

I walked over to him. 'Aren't you supposed to be over at my house, picking me up to go and see a movie?' I asked tightly.

'Your mum said you were still out –'

'So you turned tail and scurried back to Jazz and yet another news story,' I finished for him. 'Hope you get some great details, Jack.'

'No! Lula, I –'

'Oh, Jack!' laughed Jazz, appearing at his side. 'Please let's get a shot of this girl! She's *covered* in blood!' She paused, putting her hand to her mouth in that fake expression of surprise. 'Oh, it's you, Talluley. Do you mind?'

'Yes, actually,' I replied, swallowing the lump in my throat, and turning away.

'Wait! Lula! Are you okay?' Jack reached out and grabbed my shoulder, his eyes wide.

No, I thought. *No, I'm not okay, but probably not because of tonight. Probably just because of YOU, you always with JAZZ.* It felt silly being jealous now, when my friend was badly hurt, when so much other stuff was going on. I looked down at my body. The blood that had coated me so redly just minutes ago was already turning rusty and brown. The metal smell of it blocked my nose, and I itched to scrape it away from under my nails. I wanted to be alone under a hot shower, washing it all away, washing every single thing away.

'Lula?' asked Jack again. 'Please?'

'What is it they say to journos in the movies?' I returned, raising my eyes tiredly to his. 'No comment?'

I saw his face freeze in surprised hurt as I walked away down the corridor to Mr VDM, who was explaining everything to a very big and very dishevelled person at the other end. I recognised the bright red patent leather Chanel bag before I recognised the man.

Dad.

Our eyes met and suddenly I felt about four years old. I needed a hug, from my father, even if his accessories were

277

totally shaming. The truth is I was too shaken by everything that had happened tonight to be embarrassed by the bag. Too upset by Jack. Too scared about Arns in this hospital somewhere with his bleeding head.

'T-Bird!' cried Dad, as I walked quickly towards him. 'Are you okay?' The bag clobbered me in the back as he pulled me into a huge hug. Mr VDM gave my dad an embarrassed slap on the shoulder and moved off.

'I was so worried about you!' said Dad. 'Look at you! Your coach says you aren't hurt, but all this blood! Is this from Arnold?'

I nodded my head, pressed deep into his shoulder, and said, 'Sorry you had to come, Dad. Aren't you supposed to be at your AA meeting?'

'Oh, Lula-lu,' whispered Dad into the top of my head. 'Who cares about that when you girls need me?'

'I don't want you going off the rails,' I said, hugging him back.

'*You* keep me on the rails, my love, more than any silly meetings,' replied my dad, squeezing me so tight I could hardly breathe.

I began to cry.

'Oh, my gorgeous girl,' he said, kissing the top of my head, still hugging me. 'It's okay, it's okay. Let's get you home.'

'Me too,' said a small voice at my shoulder. I pulled away from Dad and saw Pen standing there.

278

'Sorry, Pen,' I said, Helen Cluny's words about me always getting attention suddenly bouncing around in my head, 'shall we go find the car?'

'No,' said my sister, 'I meant me too for the hug.'

Dad pulled us together and we stood there rammed into his burly chest until Pen said, 'Okay, enough with the family bonding,' and pulled away. But I could see she'd had a little driz too, and I grinned at her through watery eyes.

'You were great, Lula,' she said.

'You really were,' came a voice behind me. I spun round, and there was Jack, alone, his hands empty at his sides.

Dad and Pen both murmured hello to Jack and began walking back towards the waiting area. 'I'll bring Tallulah back later,' called Jack after them, and Dad turned to look at me with a question in his eyes. I nodded a hesitant yes, and he slung an arm over Pen's shoulders and continued down the corridor.

Silence. Even though the chaos of the hospital was ebbing and flowing just metres away.

Jack cleared his throat. 'I'm not stupid,' he began. 'I know how it looks. You know . . . me and Jazz everywhere with cameras. She said to me her contact up at the hospital called to say there'd been an accident, that we'd bag a story, be back in time for the movies. I didn't know it was you up here in all this mess.'

'Oh,' I said. 'I thought . . .'

'I know,' said Jack. He stepped forward and reached for my forearms. 'I'm sorry.'

I looked down at his big strong hands holding my arms, pulling me closer, and sighed.

'I don't like feeling jealous,' I admitted, 'but I do.'

'Jealous?' Jack sounded confused.

'Yes,' I said, biting my lip. 'You'd rather be with Jazz than with me.'

Jack gripped my forearms more tightly. 'You can't be serious,' he said.

I met his eyes.

'No,' he said. 'No way.'

'Jazz really likes you, Jack,' I said. 'She really does. And she doesn't like me or my friends, because, well, because we take your time away from her.'

'No,' said Jack. 'That's not how it is, Lula.' I gave him a look, but he carried on: 'She's just really ambitious, Lula. I am too – that's why I spend time with her. She wants the same things I do, and together we can get them. You know, slots on real-life TV news, inches in paper columns, magazine features . . .'

As he began listing the rungs on the ladder to superstardom I began to smile. My boyfriend's face had lit up; he took no notice of the crusty blood under his fingers as he held on to me – he was totally focused on sharing his dreams with me.

'I understand,' I ventured. 'And I always will. I'm not

going to get in the way of your ambitions. I just need you to tell me things, that's all.'

'You feel I push you out?' His face was anxious, his eyes puzzled. A frown line had creased up just above his nose.

'You do push me out,' I said. 'And there's no need because I'm not going to crowd you, okay?'

'Wait a minute, Lu! I do *not* push you out.' Jack looked startled. 'That's so not how it is.' I raised my eyebrows. 'You,' said Jack, that smile beginning to tweak at his lips again, 'You, Tallulah Bird, are a temptation that I have to resist until after the day job.'

He lowered his gaze to my lips and pulled me closer, but, 'Huh,' I interrupted.

He drew back. 'You still cross with me?' He tried on his best hangdog look and I laughed.

'Noo,' I replied. 'Just . . . you don't have to resist all the time . . .' Jack laughed, and I could feel it in his chest under my hands. My stomach did that flippy thing again.

'Oh, Tatty Lu,' he answered, lowering his lips, 'you'll be sorry you said that.'

So I had blood on my hands but a song in my heart as I came out of the A&E bathroom. Well, strictly speaking I'd got most of the blood off my hands, though there was still plenty under my fingernails. A pretty nurse was coming down the corridor towards me.

'Tallulah Bird?' she asked.

I nodded a wary yes.

'Come with me, please,' she said. 'Arnold Trenchard is asking for you.'

I thought about returning to the waiting room to tell Jack and Mona where I was going, but reckoned they were probably already at Arns's bedside, so I hurried quickly after the nurse.

'Is he all right?'

The nurse smiled. 'He's fine. This way.' I scrambled after her up two flights of stairs and down another long corridor till she pushed open a door into a small room with two beds. Arns was lying back comfortably, talking quietly to his mother while Dr McCabe wrote stuff down on a chart.

'Thanks,' I said to the nurse. She smiled and left, while I walked over to Arnold's bedside. He was as white as a sheet. Where was his sister? And Mona? And Jack?

'Ah, Tallulah,' said Dr McCabe.

'Hi, Dr McCabe,' I said. 'Thanks for being so great on the phone. You know, on the way over here.'

Dr McCabe nodded, not saying anything. 'Did you see Matilda?' I asked. 'She was at the front of the boat with my sister. I'm so glad no one else besides Arns got hurt.'

Dr McCabe shot a look at me. 'What is it about you, Tallulah Bird?'

'Pardon?' I said.

'Luckily I'm a scientific man. If I were remotely superstitious, I'd be frightened by the kind of chaos you attract.'

I felt my face fall. Oh, no. Not this again.

'Dr McCabe?' called Sergeant T from the other side of Arnold's bed. 'Is everything all right? Tatty? You look upset.'

Dr McCabe blinked and pulled himself together. 'Oh, God,' he said. 'What am I saying? I'm sorry, dear.' He patted my arm awkwardly, shaking his head. 'I-it's just the thought that my Matilda could have . . . I'm sorry. I-I'm feeling . . . I'll be back in a bit,' he concluded, and left the room, the double doors whoomphing closed behind him.

Heat rushed to my face and I felt tears smart at my eyes, while my legs wouldn't move me anywhere at all. Sergeant T came quickly over to me. 'Well!' she said. 'What's got into him? Come say hello to Arnold, dear, over here.'

She steered me towards Arnold, who was staring at me with bright eyes.

'Thanks, Tallulah,' he said, his voice quiet. 'You could have told me you wanted a scar added to complete the cool-guy look.'

'Ha,' I said. 'Ha ha. Don't pin this on me!' I reached out and grabbed his arm, swallowing down tears at the sight of him there stretched out in the bed, his head all bandaged up, his eyes so huge and bruised-looking.

He didn't reply. His eyes were closing and he just sighed out a shaky breath and looked away.

'Hey,' I ventured. 'I'm glad you're all right.' He may have nodded. I'm not sure. 'People are going to start calling me jinxed again. You're going to prove them wrong, yes?'

Arns looked back at me and swallowed, before turning his head away.

I wondered why he'd asked for me if he didn't want to see me. Did he blame me for the accident? My eyes flew to his mother.

'Arnold?' said his mother. 'Don't be rude, son.'

The nurse was back, checking a drip. 'I think maybe he's just very tired, Sergeant Trenchard,' she said. 'Maybe no more visitors tonight?'

'Oh. Okay,' said Sergeant Trenchard. 'Is it all right for me to stay a little longer?'

'Of course,' said the nurse. 'I'll just take Tallulah back down the hall.'

I waved at Sergeant T, my throat too thick with unshed tears to speak, and followed the nurse back to the waiting room.

Still seated there were Jack, Mona and Elsa. At the sight of the nurse they all shot to their feet.

'Is he okay?' demanded Mona. 'Can we see him?'

'He's fine,' said the nurse gently. 'But we're going to keep visits to tomorrow, if that's all right? He's very tired. Can barely keep his eyes open.' She smiled at me. 'Don't take it personally,' she said.

'You've seen him?' Mona was outraged.

'Well,' I said nervously, 'not really. He was kind of passing out.'

'*Passing out?*' spat Mona. Jack put a hand on her shoulder, but she shrugged him off. 'So he's not okay, then, is he?' she asked the nurse. 'He's in hospital, for heaven's sake. This is the second time in a matter of weeks that Arnold has needed medical attention, and Tatty has been there on both occasions! Maybe that whole jinx thing was never about *kissing*!' Her eyes flashed. 'Maybe it was really about people *getting hurt*.'

Jack shook his sister firmly. 'Stop it, Mona! That's ridiculous. If it weren't for Lula tonight, Arnold would be a lot worse off. He *is* all okay, and that's what's important.'

'I need to go now,' said Mona abruptly. 'Take me home, Jack.'

I shot a glance at Elsa. She'd been standing stock still, her gaze frozen on the nurse's face. 'I'm sorry I saw Arns before you,' I said. 'And I'm sorry you're not going to see him tonight. I think it's just because the nurse here saw me first, and probably just one visitor at a time . . .?'

'It doesn't matter, Tatty,' said Elsa. She reached for my hand. 'Here comes Mum now. She wouldn't be leaving him if he weren't totally fine.' I gave her a grateful look and she grinned back. 'You look terrible,' she said. 'And you smell really bad.'

Before I could reply, and insist that Jack take Mona home, Sergeant T huffed tiredly up to us. 'Well,' she said. 'What a night. And it's' – she consulted her watch – 'not even seven thirty. I'm sorry you didn't get a chance to see him, Mona, but he really is all right. Secretly pleased about the scar, probably.'

'There'll be a scar?' Mona's voice wobbled, and Sergeant T laughed.

'His hair will grow. No one will ever see it, probably, unless he goes all skinhead to show it off. Let me take you back to school, dear. Your matron will be worrying. And I've got to get back to work.' A cloud crossed her face.

'Has something happened?' asked Elsa.

'Well . . . you'll all know soon enough anyway,' said Sergeant T with a glance in Jack's direction. 'I've had my team searching the Frey's Dam area for evidence relating to Parcel Brewster's drowning, and Emily Saunders's bag has been found. With her mobile phone, her purse, her change of clothes.'

'She didn't run away,' gasped Mona, her anger at me forgotten. 'She . . .'

'She was taken,' finished Jack grimly.

Chapter Twenty-seven

Saturday, last day before the regatta

Tam called me at 7 a.m.

'Tatty!' she chirped.

'Tam? Smfrikkingearly.'

'Usually you'd be up by now, T.'

'That's when I lived with the yodeller. Now I get to sleep in. *Unless my friends call really really early.*'

Pause while Tam laughs heartlessly.

'How's Gianni Caruso?'

Tam: 'What? What have you heard?'

My turn to laugh heartlessly. 'Nothing, nothing. Don't worry. But I have news for you that you get to hear before Alex and Carrie. Emily Saunders really has gone missing.'

'No!'

'Yep.'

'But what about the voice message?' asked Tam. 'The one about her being at her grandparents' place, their Tide's Up beach shack or whatever.'

'Sergeant T had Mrs Saunders bring in her phone, and they downloaded the voice message again. Turns out Emily was saying something like "I'm not okay, they say my *time's up*" and then it ended. Maybe they found the phone or the battery died or . . .'

'Omigod. Is there anything we can do?'

I shrugged, even though Tam couldn't see me. 'We'll find out soon enough, I guess. I don't want to interfere. Maybe . . . maybe Emily just *lost* that bag . . .'

We were both silent for a bit, considering this, but it sounded implausible even to me, the eternal optimist.

'Gavin . . .' said Tam eventually.

'I know,' I said. 'But he did have alibis. I don't think they're considering him at all.'

'Oh yeah,' agreed Tam.

I chewed my lip. 'I wonder if Mr K has any thoughts.'

'Probably. But Sergeant T will get to the bottom of it all, with or without his help. Alex will probably be scouting around too, so remember you've got quite enough going on without worrying about all this. The regatta tomorrow, for starters. You ready to row, Lula? Ready to hula? Ready to have your artworks on display for all to see?'

Maybe I was just tired and a little freaked out about Emily, but having Tam listing the potential humiliations, one after the other, just like that, made me want to vomit.

'Oh, frik . . .' I breathed.

'Tatty Lula? You okay?'

I didn't feel okay. I felt like I'd been hit by a rhino. My mind danced over the events of last night. Had I been hit by a rhino? No. That hadn't been it.

'Frik,' I said again.

'Pardon?' Pause. 'T?' Pause. 'Hey, talk to me.'

I pulled myself together. 'I am, I am. What do you want to know?' Yawning, I sat up in bed, holding the phone receiver to my ear. My reflection in the dressing-table mirror swam into view, but I looked away quickly. My face was puffy from crying for hours and my hair was standing up in all directions from going to bed with it wet. Sheesh! Jack had come back here with me from the hospital, and I looked like *this*? I was impressed. What a honey! What a total –

'Tatty?' Tam sounded impatient now. 'Are you listening? Answer me. What will you be wearing? To row? Crop top and leggings?'

I flopped back on the bed. 'A frikking trisuit.'

'What's a trisuit?'

'A frikking leotard thingy with, like, legs.'

'*Legs?*'

'You know, like, cycling short legs.'

'What, with the *padding* and stuff?'

'No! No! They're bad, but not that bad.'

'Okay, well I can see that the trisuit's not gonna be so bad on you. You've got a cute bum, no stomach. The other girls . . . I mean, Matilda for starters.'

'Matilda might not be rowing. Actually, maybe our race

will be called off.' I explained to Tam what had happened last night.

She was quiet on the other end of the line for a long time. 'Tam? Hello?'

'I'm still here. Look, that was mean of Mona, and Dr McCabe. But it sounded like the people who were actually there, who saw everything, those people don't blame you one little bit, right?'

'They didn't last night,' I said grimly.

'Come on, Tatty! Don't get all paranoid. Everything's going to be fine.'

'I bet you a bag of Maltesers, cinema size, that if you ring up Gianni Caruso this morning, he'll have a different story mainlined from Billy Diggle next door at the DVD store.'

'You're on. Call you back in five.'

We hung up and I rolled out of bed.

There was panting and scratching at my annexe door. I staggered over and opened up. Boodle and Biggins were sitting outside in puddles. 'Hi, guys. How's it going?'

'Mrwourfweh,' said Boodle.

'Yeah, well, you shouldn't have sat your hairy butt down in that puddle. Just because your little duck friend likes the damp, doesn't mean it's so good for you, okay?'

The kitchen window across the way slammed open. '*I'll* do the parenting for Boodle, Tallulah! Stop trying to mother her! I know your game, and you're not getting my dog!'

'No offence, Boodle,' I said quietly, 'but I DON'T WANT YOUR DOG!' I yelled back to Pen.

'And you need to take that duck back to Frey's Dam,' added Pen. 'I do big poo, not green poo!'

'Just leave the green poo!' I called back. 'It's good for the garden!'

'We don't want *any* poo around here!' yelled Pen. 'Get rid of the duck before I take it down to Hoisin's!'

I gasped. Hoisin's did good Chinese, and crispy duck was a speciality.

Another window opened, high above the annexe roof. Uh-oh.

'The poo,' came a gravelly voice from the heavens. 'The poo, the green, the big, the duck, the dog, PLEASE, please . . . enough.' I ventured out of the annexe into the courtyard and looked up. Next-Door Dan was leaning out of his window, chest bare, bed-head on, all blond and rumpled and unshaved. I swallowed. Some things could make a depressed girl feel alive again.

'Hi, D-Dan,' I stuttered.

'Hey,' he said. 'It's early. Again.'

'Sorry.'

'No problem.' He was about to get back inside, but paused. 'Tatty, how's your car doing?'

I frowned. 'Not so good. I've still got to lift the engine block back in, and Dad's been busy with songwriting.'

'When's Darcy back?'

I sighed. Next-Door Dan and Darcy had serious chemistry, but with her away at music school Dan had to do a lot of pining. Even though he knew her term dates better than we did he still asked every five minutes if she'd be home soon. Still, I shouldn't be irritated. If it wasn't for Dan, I'd never have got the gasket to fix Oscar, the Morris Minor 1976 that I'm secretly rebuilding in our cellar. He was lovely, really.

'Dunno. About four weeks?'

The kitchen window slammed shut. Even with a half-naked boy in sight, Pen had lost interest.

Dan examined me. I shifted uncomfortably and pulled my PJ trousers a little higher.

'Have you been crying?' he asked bluntly.

'No!' I replied, and rubbed my nose.

'Are you frustrated about the car?'

'No!'

'I can help you with the car. I'm available today. Shout if you need me.' He withdrew from the window, shutting it firmly against the Bird household noise as Blue began her morning yodelling.

Dad's hoarse voice came floating out of the kitchen too, even though the window was closed: ballad mode – very loud. I was about to go back into the annexe when the back door opened and there he was, resplendent in leopard-print boxer shorts and a T-shirt saying I'M THE DADDY.

'Flirting with the boy next door, T-Bird?' he bellowed.

'Dad!' My face was bright red. I shot a look at Dan's window. The curtains twitched. I dropped my voice to a hiss. '*He likes Darcy!*'

'Oh, that's right,' said Dad, retreating into the kitchen while scratching his behind.

'*Flirting with the boy next door,*' he sang quietly, '*leavin' mah heart bleeeedin' on the floooor.*'

'I have no hope,' I muttered, 'no frikking hope,' and went to get dressed.

At breakfast Blue was shoving milk-sodden Cheerios on each finger, and I could hear Dad still working *the boy next door* concept upstairs somewhere.

'*Blee-heeeee-heeediiiing –*'

'What you doing, Bluebird?' I asked, ruffling her hair as I reached for the Weetabix.

'Making big twoll fingers,' she said, flexing them into claws to demonstrate. 'It's my turn to dwink blood today. Aunt Phoebe pomised.'

'Cool.' I sat down and poured milk over my cereal. 'Mum going to play too?'

'Mum's working,' said Mum, hurrying into the kitchen with the portable telly.

'On a Saturday? Sheesh.'

She plugged the telly in and turned it on. 'Stocktake at the main library all next week, remember?' said Mum, zapping away with the remote and grabbing a hot-cross bun from the breadbin at the same time. 'And I wanted to finish cataloguing Elias Brownfield's stuff before I forget where I am. There's some jolly interesting material about Queen Victoria visiting Hambledon.'

The telly burst into life as Pen shuffled into the kitchen. 'Why would the Queen come to this hellhole?' she muttered, putting the kettle on and slumping at the table. 'What's with the telly?' she asked Mum. 'You hate telly.'

'I'm trying to keep up with the Emily Saunders case,' said Mum. 'It's all over the news. That Jazz girl sent in a clip, obviously, but I didn't see anything from your Jack, Lula.'

I blushed. My Jack had left Jazz to her own devices last night and given into temptation. I.E. ME! We'd snuck into the annexe, I'd got into something less bloody and we'd cosied up on the enormous armchair, eating Maltesers and talking till 2 a.m. Eating, talking, kissing.

'Oh, puke,' said Pen. 'Look, Mum, Lula's gone all red.' She dropped a cereal box back down, attention caught by the telly. 'Hey! There's Jazz.'

'Jazz? This time of day?' said Dad coming in, looking smart for once. 'Rock or pop for me in the a.m.,' he said.

'Jazz that *girl*,' explained Blue through squidgy Weetabix. 'She not like Lula.'

Dad raised his eyebrows and was about to demand more info, but Mum waved an arm for us all to quiet down as Jazz's dulcet tones flowed into our kitchen.

I reached up and grabbed the chicken claw, focusing on Jazz's face with narrowed eyes.

'Let. It. Go,' said Pen. 'You're scaring Blue.'

I sank back down to my chair, releasing Grandma Bird's witchy good-luck charm and dropping a wink in Blue's direction, but she too was riveted by the telly.

'Emily Saunders has been missing for three weeks,' crooned Jazz, her eyelids batting dramatically. 'Her parents, used to her unexpected absences, were unconcerned about her latest expedition, until this' – she held up a backpack – 'Emily's weekend bag turned up.'

Pen gave a startled shout. '*She's missing?* Like, *really* missing?'

'Shush, shush,' said Mum, gesturing frantically.

'It seems Hambledon is a nest of intrigue right now,' continued Jazz. 'A homeless man is dead, we still await the coroner's findings, and with the bird-flu scare now truly refuted the question still hangs over what really killed the birdlife, and indeed most of the creatures that depend on the Frey's Dam water' – she paused dramatically – 'Frey's Dam . . . Emily Saunders's last known whereabouts. Are the three incidents connected?'

'Whoa,' said Dad. 'And there you were worrying about

whether I'd be okay in London tonight, Anne. Looks like a safe haven compared to our village.'

'Shush, shush!' said Mum again, gesturing more frantically than ever. 'There's Hilda!'

Arnold's mother appeared on the screen, her Sergeant Trenchard badge glinting authoritatively in the lights of the cameras last night. You couldn't tell, even if you knew her, that she'd just kissed her injured son goodnight in the hospital and started a nationwide search for a girl who'd been missing for twenty-two days.

'. . . important thing is not to panic,' she was saying. 'We need residents to think back carefully to the night of Friday the thirtieth of April –'

'Luckily not the *thirteenth*!' interrupted Jazz with an inappropriate smile.

Sergeant T did not return the smile. 'Any unusual occurrence on that night would be worth reporting,' she said, and, turning to the camera: 'Please. We need everyone's help. If Emily is somewhere, without food or water, every hour counts. Call the number on your screen with anything you feel may help us in the search for her.'

Jazz went on to push Sergeant T for the family's reactions, but Arns's mum was not about to comment on that, and emphasised again the importance of the community's support.

'Maybe I should cancel my meeting,' frowned Dad.

'No, Spenser,' urged Mum, clicking the telly off as Jazz did an eye-batty sign-off. 'Hilda will find that child, and Hambledon is perfectly safe. Plus you're really buzzing with ideas right now, and I think your boily heart song has something.'

Dad grinned and kissed Mum on the cheek. 'Really?'

'Really,' said Mum, smiling back at him and planting one on his lips. 'I'm always right. Go wow the musos.' Another kiss.

'Ew,' groaned Pen. 'Get a room.'

'She *is* always right,' said Dad, still beaming. 'She's spotted every hit so far.'

'Yes, yes,' said Mum, dismissing him with a flapping hand. 'Be off with you. Back by tomorrow morning, soon as, Spenser. We've got to get Pen and Lu to the regatta, and you all set up in the party tent. Will you need your pirate shirt?'

'No!' yelled Pen and I in unison. 'Nooooo!'

Great-aunt Phoebe swanned into the kitchen, smelling of J'adore and looking sensational as always. 'No pirate shirt, Spenser,' she added. 'Please.'

'And no handbag!' I added.

Dad ducked his chin and narrowed his eyes. 'Do not leemit my creaaativiteee,' he said in a heavy French accent.

We all rolled our eyes and finished off our breakfasts, thoughts in turmoil about Emily Saunders and poisoned birds and murdered people and what on earth was going on. Dad and Great-aunt Phoebe wandered into the sitting room, both of them eating toast, and Pen grabbed Boodle's lead, ready to head out for a run with her. 'I might stride past Elsa's,' she announced. 'See if Sergeant T's dug up anything else since last night.'

Mum winced at Pen's unfortunate phrasing and grabbed for the chicken claw.

'Did you just mutter something?' I demanded. 'Something spellish?'

Pen, standing in the doorway, looking out, suddenly gasped. 'Tatty, your duck has crapped all over Boodle. When I get back, you're going to have to wash my dog.'

'Yay!' yelped Blue, clapping her hands. Fake knuckles flew everywhere. 'Can I help?'

'No,' yelled Pen, and, 'Yes,' I said at the same time.

'Yay! Yay!' said Blue. 'Mum, where Dad's gogs? I get them!' She bounced down from the table and set off at a run.

'Dad has goggles?' I asked. 'He *swims*?'

Mum sighed. 'Welding goggles. There was a time in your father's life when he could do useful things around here.'

'Ooh! Could he be useful before he heads off to London?' I asked. 'I've only got to lift the engine block in and Oscar could be ready to rumba!'

'Don't delay him, Lula, please. It would be so great for

his self-esteem to get another contract, and that won't be happening if he turns up late all covered in grease. His reputation is shot as it is.'

'Hmm.' Alone in the kitchen, I looked my mum in the eye. 'How's Dad feeling? Is he okay about performing at the regatta, or is he stressed? Is he . . . I mean . . . He's been going to all his meetings?' I flushed. 'Apart from last night, of course.'

'Oh, darling, your dad is doing so well. I'm proud of him. And we caught the end of last night's meeting, Lu, don't worry. Went out after you got back. Glad to see Jack brought you home safe and sound. You should have brought him in here so you two could have spent some time together.'

My face went scarlet.

'Right,' said Mum. 'I'm off to the library. 'Are you busy today, Lu? Do you want to earn a bit doing photocopying for me?'

'Hm.' I thought for a minute. 'Actually, I promised to help Alex with her Cleo Cosmetics feature this afternoon. Maybe next weekend?'

'What about this morning?' asked Mum.

'Lula's going to lure Dan over with her broken-down heap of a car,' scorned Pen, still hovering in the doorway.

'I am not!' I was outraged. 'I'll take any help I can get! I was going to ask Dad, but –'

Pen grinned and stuck out her tongue at me. 'Don't lie! I heard you going all' – she made a coy, flirty face – '*Oh, okaaay, Daaan!* Don't you think you should finish with Jack before you start making moves on the neighbours?'

'Your dog can stay crusty,' I growled. 'Crusty with poo.'

'Finish with Jack?' Mum was hoisting an assembly of plastic bags up her arms. She threw her handbag over her shoulder, ready to go. 'What do you mean *finish with Jack*? He was just here last night! What's going on?'

'He prefers his sexy student journo flatmate Jazz,' said Pen bluntly.

I bit my lip. Though I'd never admit it, I kind of liked the banter between me and Pen, but sometimes she could go a bit too far.

'Oh, I'm sure that's not true,' cried Mum, coming over and squeezing me into a hug. 'That Jazz is so small and dark and mean-looking!'

A wobbly smile crept over my face. 'She is, isn't she.'

Mum left just as the phone burst to life. I snatched it up. 'Hello?'

'Lula, it's Tam.'

I sighed. 'Has the rumour-mill been working?'

Tam groaned. 'I was so sure you'd be the hero in all this!'

'Please.' I glanced at Pen, who was leaving her bowl and

spoon on the counter to go all hard and horrible instead of putting it in the dishwasher. 'I'm always going to be the bad-lucked, jinxed-to-hell, weirdy witch girl.' My eyes flew to the chicken claw, dangling above me. 'What's Billy Diggle saying?'

Pen was about to leave, Boodle's lead firmly in her hand, but she stopped and turned, her arms crossed over her chest.

Tam laughed. 'Okay, this bit you *are* going to like!'

'I'm listening,' I said.

'Put it on speaker!' hissed Pen.

'Only if you help with Boodle!' I whispered back.

'Lula?' asked Tam. 'You want me to ring back?'

'No, Pen wants to hear too.'

'Well, this is good, and we're the first to hear, so get a favour.'

I looked at Pen and narrowed my eyes. 'I'll put it on speaker if you let me ride up front with you on the bus to the regatta tomorrow,' I said. Oh man. That was pathetic. Why couldn't I get my own prime spot on the bus? I was SO pathetic.

Pen held my gaze. 'Fine,' she said. 'But that's not a permanent arrangement.'

I hit speaker before she could change her mind. 'Okay, Tam,' I said.

Tam laughed. 'So the game guard goes back to get Jason

Ferman and Billy Diggle and finds the two of them up the tree at the boathouse door, freaked out about the leopard. Well, the *thought* of the leopard.'

'Like a leopard can't climb trees,' scoffed Pen.

'Exactly, so the guard goes up close on his motorbike with the sidecar and tells the two of them to get down, that he's taking them to the gate – only Jason has his pants down, his butt hanging out over a branch, still doing toilet business because of Jessica's brew, and it goes all over the game guard!'

'Nooooo!' howled Pen and I, horrified, but totally delighted too.

Tam was laughing now, and it was hard to hear what she was saying. 'The game guard has to go for a swim in the dam to clean up and he makes Billy and Jason sit in the sidecar, Jason piled on top of Billy' – Tam wheezed for breath – 'and by the time they get to the gate' – more wheezing – 'Billy Diggle is *covered*' – wheeze, wheeze – 'Billy Diggle is a potty!'

Pen and I shrieked and laughed and guffawed until the tears ran. I felt all the strings of tension that laced me up slowly start to loosen.

'But how has that got anything to do with Lula?' asked Pen at last.

'Jason is saying Jessica got the brew from Tatty,' said Tam, sobering up.

302

'Well, that's just not true!' I said. 'No way is that true!'

'We'll stick up for you,' said Tam stoutly. 'Won't we, Pen? And Jess will fess up.'

'Better get Alex micro-managing,' replied Pen. 'But this really isn't a big deal.'

'Okay, well, that's not all,' muttered Tam. 'The boys are saying there's never, ever, been a collision on the Pond; Tallulah Bird starts rowing and within a fortnight there's a fractured skull.'

Pen and I were silent.

'It doesn't help that last night was full moon,' added Tam.

'The moon wasn't up yet, and if it had been we wouldn't have seen it,' argued Pen. 'That's the whole point! That's why we had the accident in the first place! We couldn't see a thing!'

'Well, I'll say that to any rumour-mongers that cross my path,' said Tam. 'Now don't worry, Tatty Lula, it's all going to be okay, yeah?'

'Yeah . . .' I said, but I really didn't believe it.

'I'll call the girls right now so we can start nipping stories in the bud. First person I'm ringing is Alex – I can't believe I'm going to be telling her *something she doesn't know already*!'

I grinned at Tam's glee. 'So glad I could have been of some use,' I said drily, and after several *mwah-mwah*s and optimistic promises that everything was going to be all right, I hung up.

'You are so screwed,' said Pen, leaving me alone in the kitchen. 'I'd help to distract you from your terrible fate, but I've got calories to burn . . .'

I wasn't totally freaked out by the rumours that would soon start to fly around Hambledon, mainly because the distraction I settled on was my not-so-secret interest in motor mechanics. I was up to my armpits in engine oil. Dad had taken the family snotmobile so the drive at the back was free, and Dan came over to push Oscar out of the cellar.

Pen got back from her run just in time, and even she was impressed by how my car was looking.

'Wow, Lula!' she exclaimed, poking her head into the driver's seat window. 'It's gorgeous in here!'

'Where did you get the interior leather?' asked Dan, propping the bonnet of the car up.

'Rukshana found a supplier for me, from a lady that makes her bags.'

'Who's Rukshana?'

'She owns the dress shop on the high street that does loud stripes for old people. Are you saying you've never been in there?'

'Ha!' scoffed Dan in an *as if* tone of voice. 'Are you

saying I'd look great in a zigzaggy pants suit?' He ducked into the cellar and began wheeling out the trolley with the engine block on.

'Don't joke,' I replied. 'Esme Trooter made Jeremiah Coldstock, the oldest man in Hambledon, get a white Lycra Elvis-stylie shirt from in there, and Aunt Sassy saw him in it at bingo last week. Are we going to need a winch or something for the engine? How're we going to get it in?'

Dan explained what we had to do, and even Pen helped. At 10.30 a.m. Dan held out two ancient-looking bolt nuts. 'Don't be alarmed,' he said, 'but I can't see where these go back.'

'You're joking, right?' I said, my eyebrows well into my hairline. 'I'll just be driving along and next thing you know my engine will drop out!'

Dan laughed. 'Your engine's going nowhere,' he said, in a way that made me wonder what kind of engine he was talking about. 'In the old days they often put two nuts on to a bolt for extra strength, but there's really no need. Hang on to them in case, though.'

I took the nuts from him. They were heavy and clinked comfortably in the palm of my hand. I unhooked the plain silver chain from round my neck and looped them on.

'Hey,' said Dan. 'That's a good look for you. Though people may find out you like to fix cars. You might get called grease monkey or something.'

'Believe me,' I said. 'There are worse things.'

'Like witch girl,' said Pen.

Dan held out the key to my car. 'Got your driver's licence?' he teased.

I heaved a deep breath and took the key. 'Dad should be here for this historic moment,' I said. 'He helped me with most of this.' I patted Oscar on the fender.

'Go on!' laughed Dan. 'Just rev her up!'

'Him,' corrected Pen, as I slid into the driver's seat and put the key in the ignition. In went the clutch, my right foot hovering over the accelerator. I turned the key.

Clunk-a-chunk-a-clunk-a-chunk.

'Give it just a little juice,' suggested Dan, coming over to my side of the car and bending down.

I did as he said, less hesitant this time, and after a few goes the engine roared to life.

Pen laughed and clapped, while I squealed like a child.

'Let it run for a minute,' called Dan over the noise of the motor, grinning at me.

I eased off the accelerator and Oscar continued mumbling along, whereupon I leapt out of the car with a shriek of triumph.

'*Yeeehaaaa!*'

Dan threw his arms wide and I jumped in for a triumphant hug. He whirled me round and round till I was dizzy, Oscar still throttling away happily behind us. I planted a big kiss on his gorgeous lips, about to say thank you, when a figure appeared at the back gate.

Oscar puttered and died, the whisper of petrol in his tank probably gone.

Chapter Twenty-eight

'Hi, everyone,' said Jack, his face stony. 'No answer at the front so I came round here, but I see you're a little wrapped up in something else right now, Tallulah.' He levelled a cool look at Dan, who lowered me quickly to the ground.

I flushed and would have blathered like an idiot, but Pen danced over and grabbed Jack by the hand.

'Jack, this is Next-Door Dan – he's just helped Tatty lift Oscar's engine in' – Jack stepped forward, his hand outstretched – 'and, Dan, this is Jack, Tatty's um –'

'Boyfriend,' finished Jack, shaking Dan's hand firmly.

'Ha! Jack de Souza,' said Dan, holding on to Jack's hand and pumping away, a big grin on his face. 'So good to meet you! Heard so much, you know! You're a survivor! You're –' One look at me silenced that train of thought. He stopped abruptly, then said, with an embarrassed cough, 'Okay, well, thanks for letting me in on the big moment with your car, T. Better get going. You need me to roll her into the cellar again?'

'No thanks, Dan. Dad's back tomorrow and I'm thinking he'll want to see Oscar spring to life too.'

'Well, shout if you need any more help, okay?'

Dan took off and Pen sighed deeply.

'He can roll me anywhere,' she said, and sighed again.

'Pen!' I said. 'How can you *think* like that? You're *fourteen!*'

'Did seem like he was more into Lula,' said Jack. He put his hands in the back pockets of his black jeans and scuffed his high-tops against a weed growing up through the drive.

'Oh, please!' said Pen. 'Dan is into Darcy, Jack. Not Lula. And I bet if I hadn't just come out and said that, you two would have been all *um this er that um you er me . . .*'

She rolled her eyes.

'Hey!' I said. 'That's not true!'

'So true,' said Pen. 'You two are a bit pathetic. Is it so hard? To *communicate?*'

'I do communicate!' I insisted.

'Badly,' said Jack.

'Very badly,' said Pen, stomping off once again. 'Wash my dog, Tatty! Or the duck is roast!'

Jack looked at me, trying not to laugh. 'We never actually talked about the duck.'

I bit my lip, smiling back. 'Yeah. So . . .?'

Jack stepped closer, till we were nearly touching, but didn't reach out to hold me. 'So . . .' he said.

'So,' I said. *Oh, what the hell,* I thought, and put my arms round his waist. I looked up at him, relieved to see his smile widen. 'So, it's good to hear you call yourself my boyfriend . . .'

He lowered his lips to mine. 'Delighted to be of service,' he murmured.

'LULA!'

I jumped, and narrowly avoided bashing Jack's nose. Blue was standing at the top of the steps wearing enormous goggles, a snorkel and her swimsuit. She had the hosepipe in one hand and was dragging a large plastic tub in the other. 'What Boodle liking today? Barf or shower?' she asked, coming slowly down the stairs, the tub bumping down behind her.

Jack loped over to help her down. 'Hi, Blue. Isn't it a little chilly to be in your swimsuit?'

'I'm hot,' she said. 'And so is Boodle.'

I took the hose and the plastic tub from her hands and put them down in the drive behind Oscar. 'Where's Aunt Phoebe?' I asked.

'Talking to Mr Splinkyninky.'

'Splinkyninky?' repeated Jack.

'Mr Kadinski,' I translated. 'What are they talking about?' I asked Blue, twisting the nozzle so the tub began to fill.

'How package man drowned,' she said, and squirted dog shampoo into the water with great satisfaction.

'Whoa, Blue,' I said. 'We've got to put that on Boodle's fur, okay?'

'Boodle and Biggins need bubble bath,' she replied, and began swirling the water like crazy.

310

Jack stepped back, away from the splashing. 'Who is Biggins? What are they saying about the package man?'

'Biggins Lula's duck,' explained Blue, standing up to survey the bubbly bath. 'He poos lots, but Boodle still loves him.'

Jack looked at me with a question on his face.

I shrugged. 'Where are Boodle and Biggins, Blue?'

Blue looked back at the steps. She took a deep breath. 'BOODLE! BIGGINS!'

There was a skittering noise from the courtyard above, and then Biggins appeared on the top step. He splatted over on his tiny webbed feet and stared sadly down at the impossible jump to the next step. Slowly, he lifted his little wing stubs and flexed them.

'Quack,' he said, defeated.

'Biggins!' I cried happily. 'You can quack! What a clever boy!'

Boodle appeared behind Biggins.

'Wrooarfhim.'

'You're teaching him well,' I replied, going over to the steps, but Boodle had already scooped the tiny duckling up in her enormous mouth and was bringing him gently down the stairs. She got to the bubble bath, Jack staring in amazement, and lowered Biggins into the water. Biggins splashed about for a minute or two, sneezed at the bubbles and then quacked twice, quite crossly. Boodle dropped her head to the tub, and Biggins flapped and splashed his way to the edge. He sneezed twice again, and clambered out on to Boodle's nose. I scooped him up. 'You two are such a great team!' I enthused. 'You don't like the bubbles, Biggleyboo?'

'No,' said Blue mournfully. She brightened. 'Boodle in!'

I stepped back while she tugged on the huge dog's collar. Boodle got into the tub quite happily and a wave of water went over the side. I turned on the hose and began gently drenching Boodle from the head down.

Biggins was skating around in the soapy water on the drive, and Boodle made a huffing sound like she was laughing.

Jack came round to where Biggins was playing, looked at the duckling closely and shook his head.

'Lula, you definitely took this duck from Frey's, didn't you.'

'Biggins!' I laughed hastily. 'Where've you been pooing on Boodle? I don't see anything.'

'Penly lies,' announced Blue, handing me a towel for Biggins. 'Penly wanted you to wash Boodlepoodle.'

Pen poked her head out of a window above us. 'Well, yeah,' she said.

'You owe me,' I said, totally unsurprised. 'Blue, will you hold the hose like this?'

Blue held the hose while I squirted shampoo into

Boodle's coat and began to lather her all over.

'You took a duck from Frey's Dam when there could have been bird flu . . .' persisted Jack, his eyebrows raised.

'He needed us!' I defended myself. 'He could have *died*!'

'Yes, he could have *died*! Of *bird flu*!' answered Jack. 'And infected the rest of the nation's birdlife! Not to mention poultry!'

'But we knew that was pretty impossible, especially after hearing those men up at the dam!' I argued.

'*Shh!*' hissed Jack. '*That's between you and me only.*' He nodded at Blue who was carefully hosing the bubbles from Boodle's fur. Boodle was sitting very happily in the water, her head tilted back, enjoying the trickles through her coat.

'Blue won't say anything, will you, Blue?'

''Bout package man?' asked Blue.

'Probably,' came Pen's dry voice from above us again.

Jack's eyes went panicky and he started mouthing something to me.

'Come here, Pen,' I commanded.

'No.'

I sighed. 'Come here, *please*.'

'Quiet.' Pen dropped her voice to a whisper. 'I'm eavesdropping on Aunt Phoebe and Mr Kadinski. They're talking about the Frey's crime scene.'

Jack and I exchanged glances. He took the hose from

Blue and began pushing the last of the suds from Boodle's coat with long, strong strokes. I got her out of the tub and she stood patiently on the drive while Jack did a final rinse with Blue's help.

'Tatty,' said Jack seriously in my ear. 'Promise me you won't say anything to anyone about going up to Frey's that night with me. Or about the body drop at Cluny's.'

I looked at him, wounded. 'What do you take me for? You think I'd *blab*? That I'd *snitch* on you?'

Jack shook his head irritably and twisted the hose nozzle to the off position. 'No! I just want to make sure you understand how serious this is!'

I glared at him. 'I *know* how serious this is! In fact, I'm *so* aware of how serious this is that I'd never *dare* – my voice dropped to a hiss – '*to move murdered bodies around*!'

Jack was about to retaliate, but Aunt Phoebe's voice came drifting down to us from the courtyard. 'Do you think it could be to do with getting Parcel Brewster off the land? So Cluny could sell it? Maybe the poisoned water was for him? And maybe the girl was just in the wrong place at the wrong time and had to be taken care of?'

Mr Kadinski said something about Aunt Phoebe being terribly clever as well as Aunt Phoebe being terribly beautiful and Aunt Phoebe giggled.

I raised my eyebrows. Aunt Phoebe never giggled.

'Auntie Phoebe likes Mr Splinkyninky more than me,'

said Blue, pressing her wet feet on to dry bits of the drive and watching the wet prints fade in the sunshine.

'Mr Splinkyninky is a great guy,' I replied, leaning over and giving her a hug. 'But not nearly as much fun as you, Bluebird. Can you get us a towel from Pen?'

Blue nodded and ran back up the steps inside.

'Am I a great guy too?' asked Jack. He smiled a slow, lazy grin that made my insides melt.

'Great at kissing,' I said. 'But you'll have to get quicker at it. We're always being interrupted.'

Jack dropped the hose and had my face cupped in his hands before I even saw him move. His lips whispered across my cheek and found my lips. 'Fast enough for you?' he murmured.

'OH, GET A ROOM, LULA!' yelled Pen from above.

'Ew . . .' added Blue to the chorus. A towel got dropped from the window and landed on Boodle's head.

'Mwrwlyy,' she whined, trying to paw it off.

Biggins hopped from one webbed foot to the other, going *quack, quack, quack* in his little voice. It looked like he was worried Boodle couldn't watch out for him.

'Tallulah?' came Aunt Phoebe's voice from the courtyard. She came over and looked down the drive, shading her eyes in the sunlight that was dancing through the apple tree at the gate. 'Are you behaving yourself out here?'

'Yes, Aunt Phoebe,' I said, hastily stepping away from

Jack, my cheeks guiltily flushed. 'Jack just came round to walk me to Alex's.' I went over to Boodle and began drying her with the towel.

'Good,' said Aunt Phoebe. She looked at Jack. 'Why haven't you written anything for the papers about the autopsy proving inconclusive?'

Jack glanced from Aunt Phoebe, to me, then at Mr K who had joined Aunt Phoebe on the top step. 'Uh . . .' he said. 'I didn't know it was inconclusive.'

'Tatty didn't tell you?' said Aunt Phoebe.

'I forgot,' I mumbled. 'It's not like it was big news, anyway.'

'Not without vital information from the crime scene itself, but news is news,' said Mr K. He pulled at the brim of his fedora so it shaded his eyes. 'I hope the crime scene gives police what they need. Right, Jack?'

'I'll call the coroner's before I go,' said Jack. 'Maybe Jazz could follow it up.'

'Go where?' I asked, giving Boodle a final head rub and stooping to brush some water off Biggins's back.

'Mum's coming to get me this afternoon. Gran's going in to the hospital for a check-up and she needs moral support.'

Pen appeared between Aunt Phoebe and Mr Kadinski. 'Is Mona still cross with Tatty?' she asked.

Jack frowned. 'About the accident?'

She paused, then grinned. 'Sure,' she said. 'The accident.'

'No,' replied Jack. 'I don't think so.'

Pen's grin stretched wider. 'Thanks for helping with Boodle,' she said. 'See you guys later.'

Everyone started going back inside. I scooped Biggins up and brought up the rear, leaving Oscar gleaming in the dappled sunlight.

We'd been standing outside Alex's front door, ringing the bell for ages. No one was opening up. Not even when I knocked. They were probably upstairs and couldn't hear my puny knuckles rapping away down here.

'Phone her,' said Jack.

'My phone's dead,' I confessed. 'Could I borrow yours?'

'For a supersleuth superagent, that's not good,' scolded Jack. 'Be prepared.'

'I thought that was for superscouts.'

'Yeah,' he said, hunting about his person for his phone.

I reached round him and fished it out of his back pocket. Our bodies were very close together.

'Hm,' he said. 'The supersleuth is good at finding things.'

I smiled up at him. 'Will the knight in shining armour be offering his phone services for the desperate maiden?'

'And lip service,' he murmured, bringing his face down to mine.

The door to Alex's house clicked open. Jack and I shot apart at the sight of her mum standing in the entrance with her arms crossed.

'Jack,' she said. 'Tallulah.'

'Hi, Aunt Sarah! Is your doorbell not working?' asked Jack. His fingers touched my forearm. 'I'd better go, Lu.'

'Hmm,' said Mrs Thompson. 'I hope you teens are playing it safe.'

My eyes went big and my cheeks flushed. 'Er . . .' I said.

Jack had twinkly eyes and was not flushed at all. It looked to me like he was trying his best not to laugh. 'Bye, Aunt Sarah!' He raised his eyebrows at me. 'I'll call you later? I'll try Alex's number.'

I smiled back, my cheeks still bright red. I handed his phone back to him and he loped away.

'So,' I said, following Alex's mother inside.

'Don't *So* me, young lady. Goodness gracious. Next thing I'll have the neighbours complaining.'

I kept my mouth shut. Mrs Thompson had a point there. She and Alex lived alone in a huge white house on a big quiet street with pretentious neighbours who sent their children to the fancy public schools in town. They were the type to complain to the council about the grass not being green enough.

'Tatty!' Alex came running down the marble stairs. 'Did I hear my cousin? Did Jack drop you off?'

'Yep.' I smiled up at my friend. She was wearing white jeans, a bright red halter-neck top and red spotty wedges. Her long dark hair was tied up in a high ponytail and she had make-up on. 'Wow. You look great, Alex.'

'Hn,' sniffed her mother. 'Alex is smitten with the idea of Flavia Ames at the minute.'

'Quite cool having such a big celebrity endorse cosmetics that are produced on our doorstep,' I observed.

Mrs Thompson's eyes narrowed at me. 'Alex should chase bigger, more serious stories, don't you think? Like the missing girl. This silly celebrity kind of thing just leads to paltry inches in the rag mags. If she's lucky.'

I bit my lip and glanced at Alex. Her cheeks were flushed, but she spoke lightly, and hardly paused as she came down the stairs. 'Got to start somewhere, Mum.'

'*Mother*,' ground out Mrs Thompson. 'How many times must I tell you to call me *mother*? What time is that ridiculous muttonhead coming to pick you up?'

'Should be here right now,' replied Alex blithely. 'We'll wait for him outside. Can you carry the camera bag, Tatty?'

'You'll do no such thing,' spat Mrs Thompson.

I paused, my hand held out for the camera bag, wondering why I was denied the option of carrying it.

'No daughter of mine waits outside for a boy – it looks *so* cheap.'

I gulped. Yowzer.

Alex had her two angry spots blazing at the top of her cheeks, but before she could get into anything there was a loud knocking from the front door.

Mrs Thompson eyed her daughter sternly while sashaying to answer it. She was wearing ridiculous heels and a floaty dress that looked very designer. I wondered if she ever let Alex wear any of her stuff, and then nearly laughed out loud at the possibility. This woman wouldn't share a thing, not even with her own daughter.

'Gavin,' she announced at the door.

'Mrs Thompson,' came a voice on the threshold. 'Looking spectacular, as always.'

'Bye, Mother,' said Alex, walking forward. 'Come on, Lula.'

I said my farewells as politely as possible and hurried after Alex and Gavin. Mrs Thompson watched us go, leaning against the side of her doorway with a strange expression on her face.

'I bet she never thought she'd see the day when her Alexandra loaded herself up into a waste-disposal van,' whispered Alex to me when she caught sight of my face.

I gave her a look. 'Oh. So that's how it is, Alex. Huh. Things are making a lot of sense to me now.' I spoke quietly, slamming the door shut as I got in next to Alex, watching Gavin walk round the van to his side. He was a big, blond, beautiful boy, with green eyes that glazed a little every time he looked at Alex.

'Just give my mother the happy smiley face,' she said through gritted teeth as we pulled off, watching Mrs Thompson disappear back into her luxurious interior.

Chapter Twenty-nine

Heading up to Cleo Cosmetics in the crime-scene clean-up van

'So, Gavin,' I said once Alex was done with all the introductions, 'it must be fun doing the crime-scene clean-ups?'

Gavin smiled over at me, shifting gears and rumbling along up North Road out of town. 'Haven't had any of those yet. Good thing, really, seeing as how we've been so busy out at Cleo's.'

'Oh, yeah?'

'Yep, remember the discontinued line I was telling you about, Lu?' said Alex. 'Nail polishes, body creams, cleansing products, all of it had to be disposed of.'

'Wow,' I said. 'Good for you guys. Must be great having such a high-profile contract. Where do you have to take it? Do you have to drive miles?'

'Miles and then some. Got to put it all in special containers,' said Gavin. 'Expensive to get rid of that stuff, you know?'

'Sure.'

'You've got to pay through the nose for decent disposal.'

The gates to Saddler's Pond whizzed by and I pushed

thoughts of the regatta and the hula and my dad out of my head.

'Sure,' I said again, and then didn't know what else to say, really. Except that clearly Healey's Expert Disposal was not short-changing itself. The van was brand new, and Alex boasted that Gavin liked to go sailing on Saddler's Pond, that his grandfather owned a boathouse there, a rare piece of private property within the reserve.

'You look hot,' said Gavin to Alex, who was sitting between us on the front seat of the van.

'Thanks, Gav,' she simpered back at him.

'Hotter than Flavia Ames. She's gonna feel all inferior to you, babes. What are you gonna ask her?'

Alex explained the thinking behind her interview questions as the van climbed higher, and I was impressed. It would be a good piece.

'What will you do, Gavin, while we're busy with that?' I asked.

Gavin made a face. 'Got to pick up the last of the rejected product, load it up and then hang around for you two.'

'You don't mind waiting for me, do you, Gav?' asked Alex.

I closed my eyes. Pukerama. Shoot me on sight if I ever sounded like that with Jack.

'Oh, babes. You're worth the wait.'

I groaned.

'You all right, Tatty?' asked Alex.

'Just a little carsick. So, Gavin, you're not tempted to flog all the nail polishes and stuff on the black market? Save yourselves a few trips to the dump? Just because Flavia Ames doesn't like the colour or whatever doesn't mean it's no good, right?'

Gavin threw me a startled look and slammed on the brakes going round a corner on the mountain pass out of Hambledon. Below us I caught a glimmer of Saddler's Pond curving in the foothills, and squeaked in alarm.

'Sorry,' said Gavin. 'That corner's always a nightmare.' He seemed flustered and I wasn't surprised. It was a long way down and I wouldn't want to be responsible for that kind of accident. If the hundred-metre fall didn't kill you, that leopard would, for sure.

'Oh, frik,' I said, breathing fast. 'I think a load of Maltesers just fast-tracked to my lower intestine.'

Alex's death grip on my knee loosened. 'Sushi to the duodenum,' she said.

'Huh?' said Gavin.

Alex swallowed. 'What were we talking about?'

'Nail polishes,' I said, my heart still thundering.

'All that stuff was never packaged,' said Gavin shortly. 'It's still in vats. Saves us a job, because it's got to be contained in our special barrels, anyway. That's the first thing I've got to do when we get there, start syphoning all that stuff off.'

'Did you always want to do this?' I asked.

'Waste disposal?' Gavin shot a grin at me. 'Nah, but I'd do anything to make a bit of money. My granddad and I got that in common. I've always been his boy. I reckon Healey's Expert Disposal is mine when he kicks it.'

Alex stiffened, and I knew then Gavin would be getting the boot pretty pronto. He'd just revealed a leeetle too much. Alex didn't like a materialistic attitude. She got enough of that at home.

Ten minutes later we were pulling up at Cleo Cosmetics and getting out of Gavin's van. He roared off round the back while Alex and I took stock of our surroundings.

'Wow,' I said. 'Nice offices.' The front of the building was all sheer plate glass and the gardens expertly landscaped. It was modern and clean and stylish.

Alex took a deep breath and we walked towards the automatic doors.

Inside it was plush but restrained, and before I knew it we were being shown into a light and airy boardroom. Alex began setting up the camera while I stared out of the windows.

'I've just got to point and shoot, right? Nothing complicated?' Alex murmured an affirmative while I wittered on. 'Wow, what a view, even if it is the loading bay. I think I could live here. No chicken claws, no dog hair, no weeds, no crazy people . . . Hey, I can see Gavin.'

'Gavin,' said Alex bitterly. 'What a numpty.'

'Who knew?'

Alex sighed. 'I hate it when my mum is right.'

'Your *moth-err*,' I teased.

'Shut up,' she said with a grin. 'She's not that bad, actually, deep down. She has to love me really.'

Deep down, very deep down, I thought to myself. 'I wonder what's happened with Emily Saunders,' I said, watching Gavin wheel out an enormous black drum with HAZARDOUS WASTE stamped on the top of it. 'I wonder if Jack minds that he's got to go to see his grandma instead of being on the case. I didn't even ask him if he'd be back for the regatta tomorrow.'

'Tatty!' Alex stopped what she was doing and stood up, her hands on her hips. 'Of course he'll be back! And Jack's priority is always the people he loves, not the story. He tries to be this hardbitten journo guy, but actually? Mushy mush mush. He'd drop anything for his friends, his family. You know that.'

'Hmm. He cares about his career too.'

'Don't we all?'

I made a face. 'I don't, Alex.'

I had no idea what I wanted to do with my life, let alone a career. My life currently consisted of doing a load of stuff that I was terrible at, like dancing and painting, and then messing up stuff I might be slightly good at, like rowing and running and motor mechanics . . . actually, the motor mechanics had gone well today. I shouldn't do myself down.

'Even with the mask and the rubber gloves and the overalls Gavin looks good,' I observed. 'Maybe you could just keep him quiet somehow. The perfect boyfriend.'

A low laugh came from the door. Alex and I whipped round to find Flavia Ames entering the boardroom. She was the tallest woman I've ever seen, perfectly proportioned, with incredible long blonde hair, pitch-black eyebrows, dark brown eyes and a body to die for. This was one pop star that deserved a double-page spread.

'Wow,' I said before I could think.

'You talking about me or the boy outside?' asked the singer, joining us at the window.

'Please ignore my friend,' said Alex with a smile. She held out her hand, her expression perfectly relaxed and natural in the face of all this fabulous celebness. 'I'm Alex Thompson. It's wonderful to meet you.'

'Flavia,' said Flavia, returning the handshake and offering her hand out to me. 'And you are?'

'Tallulah Bird. I'm not going to say another thing,' I said, my cheeks on fire.

'No,' laughed Flavia. 'Don't stop! I sense you know a great many truths.'

I bit my lip, trying not to giggle like a child.

'So, Alex,' she continued, 'that's your boyfriend?'

'Yes,' said Alex, and she blushed.

'She's blushing because she gets shy about personal stuff, not because her boyfriend is a bin man,' I said immediately.

'Hey!' said Alex. 'I thought you were going to be totally silent. And there's nothing wrong with a bin man!'

'Nothing at all,' agreed Flavia. 'My brother's a bin man.'

'He is?' Alex's eyes widened.

'Oh yeah. I keep offering him his own business, but he's not interested. Likes his life.' She shrugged. 'I'm sorry I've made so much work for your man, though. But those lines just weren't right.'

'He's not sorry,' I said. 'He's delighted. Rolling in dineros.'

'Tatty!'

'So the colours weren't right?' I asked, then bit my lip as Alex widened her eyes and shot me her *what the frik?* look.

'Nooo!' Flavia flapped her hand at me, and laughed again. 'I'm not that kind of person, honestly.' She sat down at the table and flicked her hair back over her shoulder. 'I wasn't happy with the ingredients. Here at Cleo there's been a lot of hype about natural products, incredible recipes for things, and the samples I was sent were fantastic. But some of the products that came out of our discussions were not up to the same standard. I don't want to be the face of a line full of parabens and ethanols and a load of other toxins. It had to go.' Again with the dismissive flap of the hand, this time no smile.

Parabens, ethanols . . . Something clicked in my mind, but wouldn't reveal itself . . .

I started the camera and Alex began her questions.

It was a great interview. Flavia was interesting and interested, and the best was she had a goody bag for both of us.

'These aren't in production yet,' she said. 'But they will be soon. And nothing in here is detrimental to the environment or your gorgeous selves.'

'I think I love her,' I breathed, standing back outside, clutching the goody bag to my chest.

'Not as much as me,' replied Alex, also clutching and staring and looking starstruck. 'Ohh, she's lovely. Look! Flavoured water! A smoothie too! And chocolate! I bet these are her favourites!'

We compared our stash, resisting the foodie treats to ooh and ahh over nail polishes, eyeshadows, lipglosses, while we waited for Gavin.

Alex checked her watch for the zillionth time. 'Where *is* he?' It had been a while, the sun already halfway down the horizon. 'Any longer and Flavia's going to see us hanging around on her way out.'

'That would be embarrassing,' I agreed. 'Let's go round the back and find your hunk o' love.'

We set off and found the van parked right up against the loading bay. It was all locked up, no Gavin, but the doors were open and I could hear someone laughing.

'Come on,' I said to Alex.

'I don't know. Are we allowed in there?'

I sighed and shook my head, walking down the ramp, but something stopped me dead in my tracks. More laughter, and an answering giggle.

Loud and high-pitched and totally creepy.

I'd heard it before.

At Frey's Dam. The night Jack pulled Parcel Brewster's lifeless body from the water.

The night we ran for our lives.

Chapter Thirty

I was about to back up when the giggling got suddenly louder and a figure walked out of the shadows and up the loading-bay ramp.

Alex drew up to my side and called, 'Hello,' nervously down to him.

The man stopped, surprised. 'Oi! You're not supposed to be back here!'

'Oh, sorry,' replied Alex. 'We're just looking for Gavin?'

'Oh,' said the man, and he walked a little closer, squinting in the afternoon sunlight. 'Are you Alex?'

I recognised his voice now, too, and every hair on my body was raised in prickly goosebumps. *We're gonna die, we're gonna die, we're gonna die.*

'Come on down,' he invited, gesturing with his arm. 'Come into my lurve shack.'

'Oh,' I said. 'Oh. No. No thanks. Come on, Alex. Time to get going.'

Alex laughed, swinging easily down the ramp. 'I'm not walking five miles in these wedges, Tatty Lula. Come on.'

She stopped when she reached the man on the ramp and said, 'Ah. You must be Gavin's cousin Michael?'

'Yeah,' he said, and I saw a glint of gold on a front tooth.

'Call me Mickey.'

'Good to meet you, Mickey. We need to be getting back. Is Gavin ready to go?'

Mickey was already turning and going back down the ramp. 'Let's go get him, shall we?' He giggled again, and my mouth went dry.

'Alex,' I said, 'hold on just a minute.'

'Come on, Lula,' she said, waving me down impatiently. 'I want to get back and edit all this. Let's go grab Gavin.'

'Let's not!' I hissed.

'What?' Alex turned and looked back up at me. I realised she couldn't see my face, silhouetted against the sunlight outside, so I made mad *come here* gestures.

She started uncertainly back up the ramp. Slowly, carefully, in her silly wedges. 'Hurry!' I hissed, my gestures getting wilder.

'What is it?' she whispered.

'We have to get out of here!'

Mickey suddenly appeared at the bottom of the ramp. 'Oi!' he called. 'You girls comin' or not?'

'Just a minute,' I called back, my voice wobbly. 'Gotta borrow Alex's phone.'

'Oh, sure,' she said, and stepped towards me, rummaging in her bag. She pulled it out and handed it over. As soon as she was close enough I said, 'Alex, these are bad people. Dangerous people. We've got to go. Now.'

She opened her mouth to protest, her brow creased in confusion, but I kept talking. 'Alex, you don't know this, but Jack and I went up to Frey's Dam after Emily Saunders went missing, and we overheard two guys talking about killing Parcel Brewster. One of them was Mickey.'

Alex didn't say a word. Her eyes bugged nearly all the way out of her head, and she grabbed my hand. 'Just got to make a call, Mickey,' she shouted down. 'We'll wait out here, okay?'

But just as we turned to leave someone stepped into the loading-bay entrance, like a cowboy western villain, long thin legs astride and voice all old and raspy.

'You girls won't be calling anyone.'

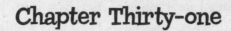

Chapter Thirty-one

The old man I'd heard at Frey's Dam held out his hand for Alex's mobile. I'd already shoved it into a pocket of my cargo pants, but I reached into the pocket of my other leg and handed over my own dead phone.

He walked over to Alex, his hand outstretched for her phone too.

'M-Mr Healey?' she stammered. I swallowed. *This was Gavin's granddad?* 'What are you doing?'

'Covering my tracks,' he said grimly. 'Wasn't aware I'd left any. Phone, please, Alex darlin'.'

'I-I don't have mine on me. Battery died at home, so I left it charging.'

'Hn,' grunted Mr Healey. 'Arms up and turn round. Hand me your bag.' He searched through Alex's bag, the goody bags and the camera bag I was holding. He took the battery out of the camera and handed it back. I felt sick thinking that he'd pat Alex down, but her close-fitting clothing left no room for a phone to hide, no matter how small. Then he examined the phone I'd given him, and laughed, a short harsh bark. 'And this one's dead as a doornail too. You girls . . .' He shook his head at our stupidity. 'Come with me.'

We would have made a run for it – I could see the question

in Alex's eyes when she glanced at me – but when Healey pulled a brushed-steel handgun from his jacket pocket, we walked ahead of him, slowly, back down the ramp. The last of the natural light seeped away, turning my brown boots to black. I remembered with a stab of guilt that this was the footwear I'd worn up to Frey's the night we'd found out about Parcel Brewster, the night I'd rescued Biggins. The night Jack and I had gathered evidence, tampered with an official crime scene . . .

At the bottom of the ramp, Healey urged us through a curtain of plastic strips and into a huge basement area. Massive vats were ranged in rows along the floor, labelled with various things, but each had the DANGER! FLAMMABLE symbol, and I got the feeling they certainly were.

Slouching in a fold-up chair was Gavin, his back to us, laughing at something Mickey was saying.

'There you are!' he said, turning as he heard us approach. 'Sorry, girls, I got to playing poker, and –' Then, 'Hey! Hello, Granddad.'

'Hello yourself,' said his grandfather. 'We're going to have to take care of these two.'

I shot Alex a warning glance. Her angry spots had flared up and her eyes had gone all flashy. She returned my glance and I knew she could hear what I was thinking.

We have a phone. We'll be okay. Let's keep quiet and get out of here alive.

'What?' said Gavin, still smiling. 'What do you mean, Gramps?'

'They know about us and Frey's Dam. Get 'em in the van.'

Gavin's smile vanished. 'No, Gramps. Seriously. They don't.' He put a grin on his face again and jutted his chin. 'My Gramps,' he laughed, winking at Alex. 'Always taking the mick.'

'In the van. Now.'

Gavin stood hurriedly.

Oh boy. No arguing with Gramps.

Alex and I were bundled into the back of Gavin's van, though there wasn't much room in there amid ten huge barrels of hazardous materials. I flinched as the doors slammed shut and our world went dark.

'Don't worry,' I whispered, at exactly the same time as Alex hissed, 'The phone!'

I pulled it out of my pocket and hit the contacts menu. A pale glow lit up my friend's face, pinched and scared, but I concentrated on one name only:

Jack de Souza.

I found it, hit call, then held it to my ear. 'You wanna speak to him?' I asked suddenly, holding the phone out to my friend.

She shook her head vehemently. 'I have no idea

what's going on!' she hissed. 'Get Jack to get us out of here, then we're going to have a talk, Tatty Lula!'

Uh-oh, I thought, just as the van rumbled to life and Jack answered the phone.

'Hey, cuz,' he said. I could barely hear his voice over the roar of the engine.

'Jack!' I bleated. 'It's me, Lula. Alex and I have been locked in a van heading towards the North Road by those men we saw that night at Frey's.'

There was cursing and a loud squealing sound. Could have been Mona, could have been tyres on tarmac – difficult to say with all the engine noise on my side.

'Lula? Lula?'

'Calm down, Jack! What are you doing? Who's screaming?'

'Forget that. Where are you?'

'I only know we're moving out from Cleo Cosmetics. We'll hit North Road for sure, but then I don't know which way we'll go.' My voice wobbled a little and Alex grabbed my knees in both her hands and squeezed reassuringly. I couldn't meet her eyes. What had I got us into?

'How? Where? Who? Who, Lula? Who are they?'

'Michael Healey and Granddad Healey,' I said clearly.

'Granddad Healey? *Granddad Healey?* Come on, Lula!' urged Jack.

Alex, pressed close to me, murmured, 'James. James Healey.'

I relayed the information, explaining these guys were related to Gavin, Alex's hot new boyfriend, and part of Healey's Expert Disposal, Gavin's granddad's company.

'Sheesh!' It fell into place for Jack as quickly as it had for me. 'The parabens and ethanols Forest found in the water samples! They're from *cosmetics*! They've been dumping Cleo's toxic waste at Frey's and I bet Parcel saw them!'

Alex gasped and snatched the phone from me. 'Emily Saunders!' she cried into the phone. 'She was up there that night too! Do you think they –'

My mouth went dry. 'No . . .'

Before Alex could comment the van rumbled to a halt, then turned left.

'We're heading back towards Hambledon.' Alex's voice was calm, but her grip on my knee had reached painful proportions.

Jack's voice was small and tinny. 'Tell me everything you know about the Healeys, Al.'

'We don't have time for this!' Alex hiccupped and a tear slipped down her cheek. 'You've got to get on to Sergeant T, Jack! Please!'

'I'm not letting you go till you've got some idea of where you are!'

'But you're wasting time! Sergeant T could be sending people back up North Road towards us as we speak!'

'Just tell me where their premises are. Where they live.

I'm on my way back to you right now. I'll get there faster than any police.'

Alex sobbed, and I took the phone from her.

'Gavin Healey lives up near Stone's Hill, but the only other place I know of is a boathouse his grandfather owns at Saddler's Pond. We're heading in that direction, but I'm sure they can't be –'

'Thanks, Lula. You don't know where James Healey lives? The other guy? What about business premises?'

Alex took a deep breath and explained that the warehouse for Healey's Expert Disposal was about ten miles west on the coast road, but other than that, she knew nothing.

'We can't be going to their warehouse,' I said to Jack.

'Because you're going south on the North Road,' agreed Jack.

'So that leaves Gavin's house or –'

'Saddler's Pond.'

'Get Sergeant T,' I begged. 'Quickly.' Thoughts of leopards and drownings and toxic-waste spillage were crowding my already crowded head, and I felt myself close to tears.

We hung up. I turned the phone to silent and clicked through to Google Maps.

'Alex,' I said urgently. 'How does this thing work exactly?'

Chapter Thirty-two

Trapped

Having something to do calmed my friend. She pushed the tears from her face with the backs of her hands and blew her nose on a patchouli-scented tissue from a handipack she'd found in her goody bag. But by the time she'd loaded up our exact location, I already knew where we were.

'How can you be sure?' whispered Alex, staring intently at the screen of her phone. 'Hurry up, hurry up . . .' she murmured.

How could I *not* know? We were travelling a route I'd been enduring twice a day for the last ten days.

From North Road we took another turn, about fifteen minutes out, this time to the right, on to dirt. A pause. A familiar voice asking for a sign-in, and we were off again.

'That was the checkpoint at Saddler's Pond,' I hissed to Alex.

'Oh, God,' she whispered back. 'They are! They're taking us to the boathouse! They're going to drown us!' She made a little sound at the back of her mouth, like, 'eemph' and it made those digesting Maltesers want to head straight for the nearest exit, because, even though she'd been crying, Alex was a much braver girl than me.

'Jack will send Sergeant T,' I whispered. 'He will. He really, really will!'

Alex nodded, and we both knew we just had to think about that and nothing else, or we'd be doing a Diggle.

A few minutes later the van came to a stop and the back doors crashed open. Mickey grabbed Alex, and Gavin got hold of my arm. It was dark now, the night cool and clear. It was obvious Gavin thought I was the cause of all this, because he yanked me out with more force than necessary. I reckoned he'd been given a bollocking of epic proportions for being the reason two girls had stumbled upon their dirty little secret. I was glad I was wearing my boots, and no silly wedges, or I'd have broken my ankle. You could drop Alex Thompson from the moon in stilettos and she'd still land elegantly upright.

'Here's hoping neither of you are claustrophobic,' said Healey Senior, and he dropped his cigarette butt on the ground, and started heading for a huge, sleek building on the shores of the lake. This was no boathouse. Half hidden behind dense foliage, the building looked like something from the future. It seemed to be made of a strange composite metal and hugged the ground, just three metres in height, and I had no idea how long. Painted a dark matt slate colour, it was pretty much invisible at night, and I imagined was perfectly camouflaged in the day. The structure of it was entirely seemless. No windows as far as I could see, and no doors.

Then Healey Senior pressed a button on a remote in his pocket and an entire area just slid away.

Once the doors were completely open, Healey gestured us all inside. I caught a glimpse of a powerboat in the shadows before we were shuffled towards a hole in the floor.

No, not a hole. A stairwell. Going down. Just as I was about to panic, lights fizzed on, and Healey barked at Gavin to move out of the way of the sensor so he could shut the doors.

'Don't need any nosy neighbours spotting activity out here tonight, do we, boyo?' he asked. 'You stay here. We'll be back in a sec.'

'Er,' started Gavin. 'Granddad, just because they know about the dumping doesn't mea–'

'Quiet, boy!' barked Mickey. 'Who said anything about the dumping?'

'But you said they knew about the barrel leaking into Frey's Dam! I think we should . . . What are you –'

'That's enough, that's enough,' said Healey hastily, his eyes flicking to us and then away.

I was frozen in place. *So it's true. They've been dumping toxins, and there'd been a leak, and Parcel had seen it, and maybe Emily too, and now here we are . . .*

My heart began to pound, and sweat prickled across my skin.

'Don't worry, Gav,' continued Healey. 'Leave it to us, eh? Everything's going to be fine.'

'Fine,' said Gavin warily. 'Okay, Granddad.'

Okay? I thought wildly. *Are you out of your mind? Your gramps is taking two girls down into the bowels of the earth, a gun to their heads, and you think this is OKAY?*

My body tensed, and I would have done something stupid for sure, but Alex nudged me gently in the small of my back, quietly saying, 'Lula . . .'

Mickey giggled, making goosebumps scatter across my skin. 'Come on, Lula,' he crooned. 'We just want a little chat, like.' He grabbed my forearm in a painful grip and pulled me towards the gaping stairwell.

A little chat. Sure.

I resisted and Mickey's mouth curved into a yellow-toothed grin of delight. He glanced back at Healey and cocked an eyebrow. I tried to move along quietly, I really did, but my heart was drumming like mad, and my blood was up. Way up. Then an image of Jack flashed into my head. Him racing along the roads towards us, Mona on the phone to Sergeant T beside him, squealing occasionally at the twists and turns taken at high speed. The wild panicked urge to kick the bad people in their groins passed, and I took a hesitant step forward.

Mickey's grin faded.

Down we went, a good way below the surface of the

earth, with spotlights overhead casting deep shadows at our feet. The stairwell seemed to narrow the further we descended, and our footsteps echoed eerily.

'It smells down here,' I whispered to Alex. 'Like when the birds died at Frey's.'

'Quiet!' barked Healey. 'You can talk all you like in the fuse room.'

At the bottom we came to a metal door, snug in its solid concrete surround. Healey slipped a key-lock access card into a rectangle on the wall. It winked at us and bleeped. He punched in a code and leaned on a huge steel bar handle. It grated in protest and then the door swung open into total darkness.

While Mickey pushed us forward, Healey reached for the light switch on the outside, and clicked it on. A glass box on the wall inside above the door whirred to life and a green glow fizzed into the room. Along the left was a steel workbench, with wires and tools and bits and pieces on it. On the other side was a single mattress, and curled up on it the still figure of a young girl.

Chapter Thirty-three

How do you describe a feeling of fear and anger and horror so intense that it renders you motionless? If I thought I'd been afraid before, I'd been wrong. Mickey stepped over to the girl and felt her neck for a pulse.

'Geez,' he said to Healey. 'Still going. Faster than ever.'

'Fast is good. Not long now,' said Healey. 'Let's lock 'em in. They got their bags? We don't want any more mistakes. Everything together.'

Without another word, he'd shoved us both right the way in, flicked the light switch off and slammed the door.

'WAIT!' I yelled. 'You can't just leave us here!'

Mickey's voice came lilting through the air grille at the bottom. 'It's for the best, girlies. You get a peaceful departure, and we get to dump your sorry dead asses in Morgan's Bay.'

'Quiet, Michael,' ordered Healey. 'That's enough. Less said, understand?'

Alex grabbed my arm, and I didn't need to see her face to know the expression on it. Dropping to our knees, ears to the air grille, we heard Gavin call from the top of the stairs, 'Granddad?' His voice was quavery. 'I-I . . .'

'I-I nothing, son,' replied his grandfather. 'These

girls just need a little quiet time.' His voice faded as they clomped up the stairs. 'Don't worry, they just need to realise that nosing about where they're not wanted leads to . . .'

The faint light coming through the grille at the bottom was extinguished and Alex grabbed my arm again. 'We're gonna die!' she hissed.

'No,' I said firmly, 'but it looks like Emily Saunders might.'

Morgan's Bay was the stuff of legend in the halls of Hambledon High. You could only get to it by sea, surrounded as it was by sheer cliffs that reached high on all three sides. It was a big stretch of sand, beautiful, but those clifftops were treacherous and locals had long lobbied to get it fenced off. Every now and again a silly nutter would try to climb down. If they made it to the sand by some miracle, there was no getting out, unless by boat. Two people had died there in recent history, of dehydration mainly, trapped by the high sandy cliffs and the undrinkable salty water.

The corpse of a runaway girl found in Morgan's Bay, dead of dehydration, would arouse no suspicion, though plenty publicity. But three of us? Surely that was pushing it a bit far.

I reached for the phone in my trouser pocket and pressed a button. The screen light came on – no reception, obviously – and we could see the girl curled up in the corner. Yes. Emily, definitely. Alex hurried over, rummaging in her goody bag.

'Emily,' she said quietly, 'Emily. You okay?'

There was no response from Emily. Looking around the room by the light from the phone it was obvious there were no regular meals going on here.

'Maybe . . . Maybe they just left her here. Literally,' I ventured.

Alex's voice was uncertain. 'To . . . to die?'

I didn't say anything.

'No,' whispered my friend. 'No way. Gavin's ridiculous, but he's not *bad* . . . is he?'

'I don't know. I don't think Gavin knows about Parcel Brewster. I think Gavin has just been aiding and abetting his grandfather in dumping hazmat at Frey's Dam. Y'know, from what he was saying up there? What do you think? Forest found parabens, ethanol and mercury in the water. Those are all used in cosmetic products. No one would know, because the barrels would stay hidden underwater, but if one of them leaked . . . If Parcel saw them damage a barrel . . .'

Alex's brow cleared. 'Oh, geez.'

She took a shaky breath, and nodded towards Emily, lowering her voice: 'We can't wait for Jack. We need to get her to hospital, like, *now*.'

I went closer with the phone and we stared at the face of a girl we hardly recognised. 'Emily, can you hear me? We've got water here.'

'She's got so thin,' observed Alex.

Emily moaned and we both jumped, startled, then we went, 'Emily? Emily? Emily?' in crazy high-pitched whispers, even though no one could possibly hear us down here.

Alex got beneath her and eased her head and shoulders into her lap. The girl moaned again and Alex looked up at me, her gaze hopeful. 'Come on,' she said urgently, uncapping the sports-top of her drinks bottle. 'Drink.' She drizzled a little water across her lips, and Emily sighed.

Alex talked and talked, dribbling water across Emily's mouth, and it sounded as if she was getting somewhere. I held the phone up high and looked towards the table. On the back corner of it was something that looked familiar. An old car battery. I moved closer to the bench. There were wires and screws and tape and a whole bunch of engine-fixing things. Nothing weaponish, like a mallet or a hammer, but there were long-nosed pliers . . .

'I've got an idea,' I said to Alex.

'Yeah?'

'You know when you bunk in and out of your house and last summer you lost your card over at Barry Bruce's house?'

'Don't go there,' said Alex, concentrating on Emily.

'I'm serious. You jimmied the entry device, didn't you? How did you do that?'

'Easy,' said Alex. 'You've got to short it out, with the . . .'

I tuned out. Mechanics I could do. *Really* basic electricity. But this was sounding a little techy. 'Leave Emily for just a sec,' I begged, 'and come and look here. Before this phone battery gives out.'

Alex was at my side in an instant and we both stared at a panel just below the light at the door.

'Ed's Electrics. Same company that did our house.'

'And all of Hambledon, probably,' I added, barely daring to hope. 'Can you do it?'

'It's different . . . I don't know . . .' she said. 'I'm not that good. Last week when I did the entry pad, I messed up the doorbell, and I still haven't got that working again.'

'You've got to try, Al.' I handed her the long-nosed pliers.

She sighed and hefted the tool in her right hand. 'I'll need your boots.'

I grinned and began unlacing. 'Got to have some rubber soles,' I agreed.

'Who are you?' We barely heard the whisper from the mattress, and Alex only glanced over there, already intent on the keypad. I gave her the phone and went over into the darkness. I could hardly see Emily.

'Alex Thompson and Tallulah Bird,' I said. 'Can you drink something?'

I got down next to her and helped her with the bottle. She spluttered and choked, and I leaned closer to hear what she was rasping out.

'Pardon?' I asked politely.

Emily coughed and cleared her throat. I bent closer still. 'I said, *fantastic*. I get locked away to die and then they throw in the witch girl, just to finish me off.'

'Ha! SOH still intact,' I said, sounding like a surgeon. 'How are you still so chirpy?'

Emily retched a little, her skin clammy under my hand. 'Okay,' I murmured. 'Maybe not so chirpy.'

Suddenly there was a fizz and a spark from the keypad and Alex lunged for the door handle before the lock could reset.

'Yessss!' she whispered, one hand on the handle, the other punching the air.

We were free!

Sort of . . .

Chapter Thirty-four

'Oh my God!' I hissed, jumping up. 'Alex! You're frikking BRILLIANT!'

'Let's get going,' she murmured. 'Do you think the Healey clan will all have left?'

There was a sudden movement from the mattress.

'Don't leave me,' whimpered Emily.

I glanced at Alex in mutual outrage. '*Sheesh*, Emily Saunders!' I said, bending down to pull her to my chest, then struggling to stand. 'What do you take us for? And what are you *doing* here?'

'I left a message,' whispered Emily. 'But nobody came.'

'They thought you were saying you were at your grandparents' place,' said Alex. 'Tide's Up.'

'Then they worked out what you were really saying,' I added, 'but in all that time no one was looking for you at all. And the trail obviously went cold. You could have d–'

'Can you carry her?' interrupted Alex.

'I'm worried about my dodgy back,' I admitted. 'Can you take her arms?'

'Wait,' said Alex. 'Swap shoes.'

'Don't worry – keep my boots. You won't be able to run in the wedges.'

'You can't go barefoot! We're in the wilds out here. Thorns! Snakes! Sharp rocks!'

I grinned, despite myself. 'Sharp rock or gun to the head,' I muttered. 'Forget the footsies. Let's just get going!'

'Take mine,' whispered Emily. 'Size six. I'm not going to be running anywhere.'

We lowered the girl back to the mattress. 'I can't believe you're still alive,' I said. 'A person is only supposed to last ten or eleven days without water. In the shade. Not moving.'

'There was distilled water in the supply cupboard,' said Emily. 'I tried to drink as little as possible, but it ran out a while back. How long have I been in here?'

'Three weeks,' said Alex shortly, finishing with the last lace of Emily's boots. 'And, just for the record, I am bloody amazingly fast in wedges.'

'Good to know,' I said, unpacking the goodybag stuff into the camera bag before slinging it across my body. My boots were back on – we were ready to move.

Alex hoisted Emily in a piggyback and moved up the stairs at speed. I followed. Small spotlights overhead winked on as we approached and after a few minutes winked off again. I hadn't noticed them doing their own thing on the way down.

'The lights know we're here,' I said. 'And I'm not sure I like it.'

Alex shot me a look over her shoulder, still walking.

'Quiet. We don't know if the Healeys are gone.'

A few steps up and she froze. 'What was that?'

I'd heard it too. 'Was that the door?'

Alex waved at me to be quiet. We stood perfectly still for a while longer and the stair lights went off. It was very, very dark.

Another click, then nothing.

At last Alex took another step, and we both winced as the spotlights went on again. Higher and higher we climbed, until at last Alex disappeared up and out. I followed her into the dark cavernous space of the boathouse.

'Don't turn any lights on,' she warned.

'What do you take me for?' I asked. 'This isn't the first time I've saved the day, you know.'

'What's the plan?' asked Emily.

'I hack the keypad,' said Alex, 'and we head up to that security point on the main road and get the guard to call your mum, Lula.'

'Firstly,' I said, 'you forget the leopard. I'm not walking around in the wilds with a half-dead person. He'll smell us and we'll be the hors d'oeuvres.'

'I'm half dead,' whimpered Emily. 'Not deaf.'

'Secondly, there is no keypad.'

Alex still had her phone. She fumbled in her pocket and shone the screen around. 'Bummer. Can you pick locks?'

'No need.'

'Huh?'

I gestured with my head to the far end of the boathouse. 'The good ship awaits, m'lady.'

'Oh no.'

'What?' asked Emily wearily. 'What now? Why don't you guys just call someone with that mobile?' She began mumbling a number, and her head drooped to Alex's shoulder.

'The only reception in this park is on the top exit road,' I replied, though I wasn't sure she could hear me. We had to get her to the hospital, and fast. 'But there's a sat phone at the Hambledon High boathouse.'

'I've never been in a speedboat,' announced Alex, moving into the boathouse by the light of her phone. I kept close, squinting in the darkness. 'To be honest, I'm a little afraid.'

'*Now* you're afraid?' I squeaked. '*Now?* Geez.'

Alex cursed the heavens, and her luck and mainly me for landing her in this crappy situation while I helped to get Emily in the boat. It was positioned at the top of the slip – all I had to do was untie it, and we'd be away, gliding into the water. But first I had to open the slipway door. I scouted around with the phone light and found a bog-standard activation switch for the massive roll-up garage door.

'Our luck has turned,' I called to Alex, pressing the button.

'Hurry!' she urged. 'If the Healeys are out there, they'll

hear that for sure! Do you know how to start a boat?'

'Just like a lawnmower,' I said confidently, and got it going in a trice.

In minutes we were out on the water, the engine throbbing quietly behind us, and the roll-up door rolled decorously down as we exited.

'Now,' I murmured, 'which way to the school boathouse?'

Alex was giving Emily more water, and had got chocolate out of the camera bag. 'Try this,' she was saying, but Emily had started to shake and wasn't making much sense. I took off my press-photographer-stylie jacket and threw it over her, opening up the throttle on the boat to accelerate further into the lake as fast as I dared. I looked back at the shore, dreading what I might see.

Whew.

No bad men with guns.

But up on the ridge, close to the gatehouse, there was something moving.

Car lights!

I was just about to warn Alex when a shot went off, cracking across the water. Oh! My! God! I don't know how I didn't scream out loud, but instead the adrenalin whooshed in and I went for the throttle again.

'Sheesh!' squeaked Alex. 'Tatty!'

'I'm on it,' I muttered, and went up to full speed, hanging on to the wheel like a woman possessed. Thank goodness the Hambledon boathouse was out of sight of the road. I careered round the lake at top speed and came up to the final straight in no time. The engine was roaring at full throttle, but even with that massive volume we all heard another two shots ring out.

'Tatty!' screamed Alex. 'Get down!'

'I've got to drive the frikking boat!' I yelled back, but even so I crouched as low as possible, keeping the westernmost peninsula in view. If we could just get to that corner, we'd be out of view of the top road and minutes from the Hambledon boathouse jetty.

Another bang cracked out just as we cleared the corner.

Ha haaa! I thought. *You're too late, bad men! We've made it!*

But then a pained 'OOF!' came from the back of the boat.

'*What . . .?*' I yelled, looking round wildly. '*What happened?*'

'Just saying that was close,' murmured Emily, saying, 'oof,' once more, quietly, before her stricken face lolled back into Alex's lap.

'You're telling me,' I murmured. 'You okay, Al?'

'Yeah, but Emily's passed out again.'

I eased the throttle back, and slowly, carefully, stared into the darkness. Thank goodness it wasn't like last night, all thick mist and wild waves. Thank goodness for still water and moonlight. I made out silhouettes of trees I recognised, familiar rocky outcrops, and in no time I was pulling up to the Hambledon jetty with a pounding heart and shaky knees.

'Wait here in the boat,' I commanded, leaving the boat idling quietly, and took off for the boathouse, blocking all thoughts of leopards and rhinos from my mind.

'I'm so brave, I'm so brave, I'm so brave,' I muttered, as, fingers shaking, I fiddled the combination lock open and reached for the satellite phone just inside the door. I snatched it up and raced back down to the jetty. The sound of car tyres on the road somewhere drifted on a breeze down to us, and then there was another shot. Throwing myself into the boat, I threw the phone to Alex. 'Call Mum!' I said. '999! Anything!'

'Wait!' said Alex, staying my hand from the pull cord. 'Don't we have to keep still to pick up a signal?'

'Don't know!'

'I think we do! Just hang on!'

'Someone is shooting at us from up there! There's no time to hang on! Let me get to the other shore. You can't get there without a boat – we'll be safe! All the time in the world to call whoever we want!'

'What about Emily?' asked Alex, her thumbs dancing over the keys of the phone. 'She's . . . she's . . .'

I looked down at Emily Saunders, shaking like a leaf in Alex's lap. By the light of the moon I could see her eyes had rolled back in her head and her tongue was protruding from her mouth in a totally frightening person-on-the-brink-of-death kind of way.

'Okay,' I said quickly. 'Here's what we do.'

Chapter Thirty-five

Alex didn't like my plan. She didn't like it one little bit. We were having a heated discussion when Emily's eyes rolled the right way round and she jerked to attention.

'W-what?' she moaned. 'What are you talking about?'

'Quiet, Emily,' I whispered. 'That car is coming round the corner. Dammit, Alex! Now we really can't get away! If I try powering out of here, we'll be riddled with bulletholes like a ripe Swiss cheese! Why is no one answering their phone?' I turned off the engine for the best chance of staying unheard and unseen.

Alex ignored me, just calmly punching numbers in, then listening, then hanging up with a shake of her head and trying again. Her cool demeanour made me pull myself together. Taking a deep though shaky breath, I sat up a little in the boat and watched the headlights come ever closer. I could just about hear the engine now. Funny. It didn't sound like the Healeys' van. Maybe Healey Senior wanted to finish me and Alex off neatly and cleanly without his family getting all squeamish, and he'd come alone in his own vehicle. I reached out for an overhanging branch near the jetty and pulled us away along the bank so we'd be a little more obscured by the bushes growing there.

No, definitely not a truck, not a van either, but familiar . . .

Another gunshot had me ducking down low, and Emily whimpered. Alex was crouched down, furiously tap tapping at the phone, her face set in grim determination.

Very familiar . . .

The car pulled right down to the jetty, sending gravel skittering across the boards and into the water. Alex shoved the phone with its telltale light under her jumper and crouched even lower. I held on to the branch we were hiding beneath, my eyes glued to the car, staring at the driver.

Then just as another shot rang out across the water, I sprang up from the boat and shouted, 'ALOHA!'

Alex's face was a study in total shock. I could see a thousand thoughts whipping through her head, none of them good, but when a dark figure hurtled from the car to the jetty and shouted, 'ALOHA!' back, her face creased up into a grin.

'Oh, thank God!' she breathed.

I hugged her tightly, both of us sobbing shamelessly in relief.

'My legs feel like they're going to give way,' I admitted, clutching at her. 'I was so frikking scared!'

'You were brilliant.' Alex pushed me away, holding on to my shoulders before swiping at her eyes with the backs of her hands. 'Bloody brilliant, Tatty Lula.' She took a shaky breath and called, 'How did you know we were here, Jack? And why are you just standing there? Were you shooting at the Healeys? Where are they? Can you get us out of here? Emily's in a bad way.'

'Not gunshots,' I said to Alex. 'Jack's rubbish car backfiring all through the safari park. I'm thinking that leopard has headed for the hills.'

'Leopard?' said Jack. 'Like a *leopard* leopard?' And jumped straight into the water.

'What are you doing, you maniac?' I laughed, my nose all prickly and tears still streaming.

'Bringing you to shore, fair maidens,' he replied, shooting me a look over his shoulder as he pulled the boat towards the jetty. 'I heard you say Emily. I'm guessing Emily Saunders?'

'Yep,' said Alex. 'We've got to hurry.'

'Mona,' called Jack. 'Bring the picnic blanket!'

There was a skitter of gravel as Mona – I hadn't even seen her standing there; did she still hate me? – ran to the car and back at the speed of light. I tied up the boat while the other three whisked Emily off into the car, cocooned in Jack's picnic blanket. I felt a rush of love for Jack and his picnic blanket, and regretted that I'd be squashed in the back seat with the girls instead of canoodling in joyous freedom and victory in the front with him.

'Will we all fit in there?' asked Alex, poking her head into the car's tiny interior.

'We won't have to.' Jack was standing, half in the car, half out, looking up the road. I followed his gaze to see a pair of headlights making its way steadily down to us. The rush of the engine was only just audible in the still air.

'Oh, frik! Who's that?' I asked, clutching my boyfriend. 'Is it them? Is it the Healeys?'

'Geez, don't say that,' murmured Jack, looking hard as the vehicle came closer. 'No . . .' He shook his fringe from his eyes, then nodded, now certain. 'I know that car – it's not the Healeys. I rang Sergeant T, like you asked. Couldn't get hold of her directly, though I told the duty officer everything. Rang Jazz to get her to keep calling – better if Sergeant T herself is on the case, y'know?'

I nodded. I did know. The last time Jack had called the station, even if it were under the guise of an anonymous tip-off, no one had taken him seriously. But, still, it stung a bit that he'd called *Jazz*. Like she was his rescuer, and no one else.

'You could have called Forest . . . or Arns,' I said.

'Arns, Arns, always Arns,' said Jack, his eyes finally leaving the approaching headlights to stare at me directly.

'Jack?' I said, startled.

Then Mona piped up, '*I* called Arns,' as if that were her right, and *her* right only.

And suddenly there was an unpleasant atmosphere in the air where there should only have been selfless urgency in getting our medical emergency to the hospital.

'Hey,' I said, swallowing down a lump in my throat. 'I'm sorry. I don't want to step on anyone's toes.' I looked at Mona. 'I only said Arns because he's a direct line, pretty much, to the best of Hambledon's police, really, and because he's a *good friend*.'

Mona blinked, a little taken aback. 'S-sure, Lula, I –'

'But a good friend is all he is, okay?' She blinked and nodded, but I was looking at Jack.

'I know,' he sighed. 'Sorry, Lu. I've spent the last hour driving like a maniac, thinking you're probably at the end of a knife or a gun or . . .' He swallowed and stepped over to me, pulling me into the biggest hug imaginable. 'Oh, God,' he whispered.

I wrapped my arms around Jack and hugged him back, tears coming to my eyes.

'Hey,' hissed Alex, rolling down Jack's car window. 'There's a car coming!'

'It's Jazz,' replied Jack, releasing me. 'But we'd better hurry, anyway.'

Jack was right. There was no telling what the Healeys would do next. I ran for the boathouse, replaced the satellite phone, locked the doors and by the time I returned a black Golf GTI was pulling up.

Forest shot out of the driver's seat and squeezed me up into an enormous hug, before running over to Jack. 'You okay, man?' he blurted. 'Jazz said you sounded crazy on the phone.'

'Jack *was* driving like a madman,' murmured Mona. 'I think I've aged, like, a hundred years.'

'Well, I'm gonna have to drive like a madman again,' replied Jack, 'to get Emily to the hospital.'

A lazy laugh came from the side of the GTI. I might have known. Jazz wouldn't let anyone drive her car unless she was in it herself. She stepped out of the vehicle, her long hair swinging beautifully free, and said, 'Emily? Tell me you've found Emily Saunders, Jack.' She lifted a camera to her shoulder and a red light winked on.

'Unbelievable,' breathed Alex, just at my shoulder.

'Unfrikkingbelievable,' I replied.

Jack, oblivious, shrugged and shot the camera a wry grin. Or was he grinning at Jazz? Which was worse?

'We'd better get going,' he said. 'She's in a really bad way. Can we use your car, J? We'd get to the hospital in half the time.'

J? *J?*

'I'll drive your car, Jack,' offered Forest, 'if you want to take the girl to hospital. Is she the missing person?' He leaned into Jack's beaten-up banger and I heard, 'Whoa,' before he emerged, holding Emily easily in his arms. Quickly, he made for the GTI and placed her in the back seat.

Alex turned to me. 'I'll go with them,' she said, 'to make sure Emily's okay and to explain how we found her. You go to the police station – Arns is probably already there, knowing him, freshly discharged from hospital to be at your s–'

'No!' Jack was poised at Jazz's car door. 'Tallulah comes with us, in the back seat with Emily, and you go to the police station with Forest and Mona.'

Alex's jaw dropped.

'No time to argue!' Jack finished, and slammed himself into the GTI, with Jazz sliding into the passenger seat beside him.

Mona seemed happy enough and got herself into Jack's car with Forest at the helm. Alex turned to me. 'Shouldn't have mentioned Arns,' she said. 'Seems Jack's got a stab of jealousy digging deep.' She punched me in the shoulder. 'Good luck with that.'

In the plush leather back seat of Jazz's GTI, however, all the petty jealousies bled away, much like Emily's life, shaking to pieces in my arms.

'Hurry,' I begged. 'Hurry, Jack. I think she's gone into shock. With dehydration . . .'

'Her heart just won't make it.' Jazz's voice was all documentary and fact, and her fabulous zoom lens was still filming.

'Shut. Up,' I replied, tucking Emily's ratty brown hair behind her ear so I could see her eyes. They were flickering quickly under closed lids and her pulse was too. 'Just shut up, Jazz. I need a phone,' I snapped. 'To call the hospital.'

'Ah yes.' Jazz was still hidden behind her camera. 'They know you well there. It's best *you* make contact.'

Jack handed me his phone wordlessly, concentrating on the winding dirt road. Why wasn't he saying anything to Jazz? Surely even he could see she was being a total cow?

I punched in the number for the hospital while Jazz laughed in my face. 'There's no reception in this park,' she drawled, as if I were some kind of cretinous idiot.

'There is once we get up to the top,' I retorted, and then the line went live and I found myself talking fast to A&E.

Again.

Dr McCabe was waiting outside when we arrived at the hospital. No clever comments, just a nod in the direction of swirling blue lights to the right of the emergency entrance.

'Sergeant T wants a word, Tallulah,' he said, his face tired and worried, wheeling a stretcher towards us. 'We'll take Emily from here.'

'Sergeant Trenchard?' asked Jack, exiting the car, his eyes on Dr McCabe and then on me.

Someone stepped across towards us, the blue lights silhouetting a strong, purposeful stride, but I was still watching Jack. I was sure we were both thinking the same thing. In order to explain everything, I was going to have to get two people in a whole world of trouble.

There was a question in Jack's eyes, but I couldn't answer it. My head was full of the last time we'd talked about that night on the mountain. Jack had said, '*Promise me you won't say anything to anyone about going up to Frey's that night with me. Or about the body drop at Cluny's.*'

My gaze dropped to my feet as Sergeant T came straight over to stand in front of me. Out of the corner of my eye I saw Jack walk away, following Jazz and the camera and the medical emergency, till all that was left to see were my boots.

'Tallulah Bird,' said Sergeant T heavily, 'will you come with me, please?'

Chapter Thirty-six

Police station: still Saturday, now 8.30 p.m.

Oh, WHAT a mess. Even if you've been missing a few hours, it doesn't mean your mother will welcome you back with open arms. Oh no. In my family it means your mother will go down to the police station and insist on riding around in a big van with the WHOLE of the rest of the family, dog and duck included, just in case any of THEM go missing, looking for her abducted daughter.

'I'm impressed, Anne,' said Sergeant T mildly, stirring her tea and looking at her crowded office. 'Most mothers wouldn't turn a hair if their daughters weren't home by eight.' She glanced at her watch. 'It's only eight thirty now.'

'And was I right?' demanded my mother. 'Was I?'

Sergeant T smiled and stirred, smiled and stirred.

Oh, frik, I thought. Here it comes. We now sentence Tallulah Bird to a gaschmillion years in a lesbian penitentiary for interfering with the course of justice.

'Is there anyone *left* at your house?' asked Forest. (Oh yes. Everyone was in the office with us. Maximum humiliation.) 'To let Lula in, in case you were wrong?'

Mum said, 'I. Am. Never. Wrong,' at the same time that Blue piped up with, 'Auntie Phoebe.'

Sergeant T's eyebrows shot up. 'Great-aunt Phoebe,' explained Pen. 'So will Lula need legal advice? I can provide legal advice. Also counsel. I'm great legal counsel. Will it all go to court or would you prefer to settle? Out? Out . . . of . . . you know . . . court . . .' she tailed off.

Sergeant T had put down her cup of tea and was looking at me with an odd expression on her face. 'This court,' she said, twinkling across at Pen, 'needs to hear Jack de Souza.'

'Oh boy,' breathed Forest, and Boodle shuffled over and put her big hairy head on my lap with a low 'Fwooarrphh' sound. Biggins climbed along Boodle's back and hopped into my lap from her nose.

Mum was not comforting or supportive. Mum was furious. A stoppered bottle of incandescent rage. She had made little popping noises when I told Sergeant T about that Friday night, when Jack and I had gone up to Frey's and what we'd overheard. I told her about Jack finding Parcel Brewster and taking him to Cluny's so he could be properly autopsied.

In front of everyone, she'd had a full-on rant: 'Tallulah,' she said, 'I trust you. I trust you not to do anything stupid. That is why your father and I do not tell you when to get up in the morning, why we don't tell you when to go to bed at night. We trust you on your own with boys. We have no bedroom ban –'

I was startled. 'You don't?'

'Tallulah! We don't tell you who to be friends with, who you can go out with or set limits on who you cannot see. I think, though, you've betrayed that trust! Bedroom ban starting now! And, so help me, I know one thing and that is you will not be seeing Jack de Souza again.'

'Mum!'

'Not only has he allowed you to make some very bad, very *irresponsible*, very CRIMINAL decisions, but he has acted in a reprehensible way himself.'

'Mum!'

'Do you realise that he could go to jail for what he did? That he made you party to his crime by telling you about it? That you were obligated to go to the police with this information?'

'He didn't tell me anything! I worked it out!'

'Well, I hope you've worked out that this boy is no good for you, Tallulah. I –'

'Well,' ventured Sergeant T. 'If I could add just a word or two.' *Oooh! Brave! Not many would interrupt my mother.* 'Not much goes on in this town without me knowing. I have my informants and, though I disapprove of Jack de Souza bringing Parcel Brewster's body back down, there is no denying he has done us all a favour. Which he knew at the time. There'll be no need for any investigations into that side of things and I understand completely that Tallulah believed she was acting in everybody's best interests, though you must never pull a stunt like that again, young lady!' she said, leaning into her desk towards me. 'And this goes no further!' she added, waving her hand across the room to everyone else, and everyone else assented most nervously indeed.

'Yes, Hilda,' I said too, red-faced and truly ashamed.

'I will talk to Jack,' continued Sergeant T. 'But I don't want to burn any bridges with that young man. Communication between us could be mutually beneficial, I feel. I'm lucky to have a good team in Hambledon.' She winked at me. 'I'd have you on my side any day, Tatty.'

I felt a wave of relief wash over me, though it was tempered slightly. 'Even if I do keep hurting your son?'

Sergeant T's jaw dropped. 'Are you serious? First you save him from a life of misery looking like his mother, then you get him the girl of his dreams, *then* you get him to safety at the hospital, reducing substantial blood loss to boot! Have people been talking again?'

I nodded. Mona shifted uncomfortably. Mum's rant about Jack couldn't have been easy on her sisterly ear, either.

Sergeant T heaved a sigh and shook her head. 'That's something you're always going to have to overcome, Tatty, I'm afraid. The whole witchy connection won't be forgotten. Small towns mean small talk that soon becomes talk of the town. Hmm?'

I nodded yes.

'I guess it is hard being you,' murmured Mum, reaching over and squeezing my arm.

'Oh, puhLEEZE!' yelled Pen.

'So hard,' I said, trying hard to keep a smile off my face, stroking Biggins, who nuzzled happily against my palm. 'Does this mean I'm forgiven?'

'No!' said Mum. 'I have not forgiven you.'

'No, Mum,' I said in my best servile voice. 'I shall do penance till the end of my days.'

'Terrible penance. Cleaning all toilets daily till you leave home.'

'Oh goody,' said Pen.

'Yes,' I said. 'With my tongue.'

Mum swatted me. 'Let's get you home, Tallulah. Can we use your big van again, Sergeant T?'

'Nope,' said Sergeant T. 'Sorry. I've got bad men to catch. My troops still haven't run them to ground, and I intend to do so asap.' (Only someone like Sergeant T can say *asap* without sounding like a moron.)

'We'll go in Jack's car,' rumbled Forest.

A dark look crossed Mum's face. 'I'd rather walk,' she muttered.

Saturday night: early to bed – 9.30 p.m. – to get sleep for race-day tomorrow, but sleep will not come
You'd think I couldn't sleep because the day had been

372

packed with mayhem and drama and near-death experiences. Oh nooo. I couldn't sleep because in my girl-sized bed there was a man-sized dog and a pocket-sized duck. And it was the pocket-sized duck that was the biggest problem.

'Biggins!' I moaned. 'Keep still.'

'Waaack, werk, haaack, k, k, k,' muttered Biggins.

'Well,' I said. 'That's what you get if you hang with Boodle. Smell and slobber and big poos.'

Boodle threw a huge hairy leg over my chest. 'And good hugs,' I added.

Now, I'd moan about the sleeplessness, but in the end, I think, it might have saved me. Because chatting with the creatures kept me up. And being up meant I could not be taken by surprise. At about 10 p.m. I heard our front gate open, and sat bolt upright in bed. Biggins hopped from my pillows to my shoulder to the top of my head in two stylish super-silent secret-agent moves, but I wasn't really paying attention. Boodle's ears perked up as high as their hairiness would allow them to go and she hopped off the bed to the annexe door – to *that* I paid attention. Boodle was an amazing bodyguard.

I followed her so soundlessly and stealthily that Biggins didn't need to claw to hold on. In one hand I had the requisite spiky hairbrush, in the other the requisite hairspray. (Pepper spray finito, as per chapter one.)

At my front door, I paused and pressed my ear to the keyhole. I could hear the usual night noises of frogs and insects, but I could also hear the *tac tac tac* sound of someone trying hard to walk quietly down the front steps of the garden.

Slowly, silently, I unlocked my front door. (Do not try this at home. At home dial 999 and wait for help. I don't know what I was thinking. A strange madness had taken me over.) Slowly, silently, I pulled the handle down and opened the door a crack. I expected to see, any minute now, the figure of a perpetrator rounding the corner. Instead I saw a figure slumped in a chair RIGHT OUTSIDE MY DOOR.

'AAAAARGH!' I yelled, squirting hairspray and beating the figure over the head with my hairbrush.

'AAAAARGH!' cried the figure, leaping to his full six feet and fending me off with huge hands and garlic-bread breath. 'Lula! Lula! Stop it!'

'Bludgeon?' I gasped, dropping hairbrush and hairspray with alacrity. 'I thought I heard someone at the front gate. What the frik are you doing here?'

We stared at each other in super-silent silence. Silent enough for us to hear the front gate closing. Someone *had* been coming down the garden steps!

'After him!' I yelled, and Boodle leapt past with a huge bark, me hot on her hairy heels and Bludgeon just behind.

But by the time we'd got up the front steps the intruder

was long gone. Boodle was going nutso at the shut gate, Biggins had slipped from my head to my shoulder and the front door of the main house had burst open.

'WHAT?' yelled my mother in her nightdress. 'WHAT'S GOING ON?'

Bludgeon caught my eye and I shook my head, once, a very subtle move. (This requires training.)

'Nothing, Mum,' I called. 'I got a fright seeing Bludgeon outside my front door, is all. You could have warned me I was getting a bodyguard.'

'Oh,' said Mum. 'Oh, okay. Well, yes, Sergeant T thought it best, but she said she didn't want to freak you out . . .'

'Nothing freaks Tallulah out,' grumbled Bludgeon, busy with his phone to call the police station.

'*You* freak me out, Bludgeon,' I muttered in reply, going down the steps. 'Your big villainous self outside my front door at the dead of night.'

I'm sure he would have had something to say about that, but his phone rang, and he slammed it to his ear, giving me a look. 'Bludgeon,' he barked. 'Yeah, sorry 'bout that.' He flushed, and scuffed his boot against the paving. 'Uhuh . . . yeah . . . You'll call the station? Orright. Laters.'

'What's up?' I asked.

'Mr K says Healey Senior just cruised down Hill Street from this direction. Must 'ave been 'im 'ere earlier.'

I shivered, my eyes wide. 'Seriously?'

'Don't worry, babes. Mr K's called it in, and 'e'll go after that no-good perp 'imself.'

'But Mr K is on his own! Who will . . .'

'Babes,' said Bludgeon settling himself back into the chair.

'Yeah, okay,' I said. It was no secret Mr K was good at secret stuff. The best. Even so, I should have been sleepless, but, unexpectedly, it was a strange comfort having big Bludgeon outside my door. Especially now that I'd given him my enormous Morris Minor Convention mug full of coffee.

I slept like a log with duck and dog.

Chapter Thirty-seven

'I feel nauseous,' said Pen emphatically. 'I can't believe Jack and Jazz are covering the regatta. No way is that cretin taking footage of me. I'll puke all over her sickening self.'

'You're such an angry person,' I observed. 'I think you need to see someone about that.'

'I'm angry because I got dragged around town in a POLICE VAN, a DRAUGHTY ONE, all night and then I had to spend hours down at the stinky old police station shivering my butt off with a noisy duck and a depressed dog. And later I'm going to have to watch your boyfriend getting flirty with his flatmate and you *just standing there!*'

'You were so great last night,' I said.

'I was,' said Pen. 'No trauma there.'

'You're good.'

'I am. I'm good.'

'Good at coxing too. It's a bonus that you didn't get supper yesterday. This way there's less for us crew to carry.'

Pen punched my arm. We ate toast half-heartedly, watching Bludgeon drink coffee outside. He said it wasn't professional, like, to hang around 'avin' brekkers wi' the clients. Our ears perked up when his did at the screech of tyres at our front gate.

Pen thundered out the front door and up the front path to smile at a car with claw marks across the bonnet.

'Hey!' I said, following at a more leisurely pace. 'Why are you driving Bludgeon's car, Mr K?'

Pen nudged me and hissed, 'Do I look pale and interesting?'

'So pale, so interesting.'

Angus, Pen's boyfriend, hopped out of the passenger seat and came over for a kiss. From Pen, not me. But still. Ew.

'Well, Tallulah,' said Mr K. 'It's all part of the service. I do drive exceptionally well.'

'I bet.' I grinned. 'Are you and the seniors looking forward to the regatta?'

Mr K shuddered. 'Not I.'

'You're not?' I was surprised. Pen and Angus were only surprised by how lovely each other tasted. Double ew.

'Madame Polanikov is insisting that I hula with her. At the luau.'

'Seriously? Come in, come in, tell all!'

'No, no thank you – just came to pick up Bludgeon. We've got a couple of people to talk to. Hello, Bludgeon.'

Bludgeon loomed behind me and I stepped aside so he could get by. He did a complicated handshake with Mr K, and I rolled my eyes.

'What's the latest?' I demanded.

'No one's been caught, if that's what you mean, but Parcel's autopsy results are finally available.'

Bludgeon grinned and clapped Mr K on the back. '"Available"! That's my man.'

Mr K winced. 'Well, the news is we're after a man with a wig.'

'We are?' That was unexpected.

'Lab results on the autopsy showed Parcel Brewster had advanced lymphatic cancer – should have died months ago. It may be that he fell into the dam in his weakened state and just drowned. Even a nasty bruise on his head and various other bumps and scratches are pretty inconclusive – *but* they found fibres in his mouth and gullet. Like he'd been eating *hair*. Though it wasn't hair, obviously . . .'

Oh yes! Arns had mentioned that. Maybe Parcel had bitten into his attacker's head in a struggle – ew! I wished I'd not thought that thought, though a struggle with an attacker would go some way to proving Parcel's death was not entirely accidental. But it hadn't seemed to me that any of the Healeys needed borrowed hair . . .

'Mr K,' I said, 'maybe we should go to Sassy's Salon. Wouldn't they supply wigs to certain customers?'

'No,' said Bludgeon, unconsciously stroking his bald head. 'There are special agencies for wig-fitting.' I raised my eyebrows and he hurried on: 'But Aunt Sassy will know for sure who in Hambledon has never been into the salon for a snip.'

'Exactly,' said Mr K. 'I've already left a message.'

Big Mama's, next door to Sassy's – source of all reliable info, 9 a.m.

It hadn't taken much to persuade Mum to go down to Big Mama's for a breakfast banquet. Mum is the worst cook in the world and we all agreed we needed something substantial to kick off the day of the Port Albert Regatta and Festive Luau!

Main topic of conversation? Yes: bad men with guns.

'So . . .' Pen thought for a second. 'Cluny wasn't involved?'

'No,' I said, adding, 'definitely not. Unless he wears a wig. But I heard those men talking that night and –'

'Yes, yes, so you don't know for sure.'

'Um . . . *Mr Cluny is Helen's dad.* He's not the scheming, murdering kind.'

'I heard Mr K tell Great-aunt Phoebe that Cluny owes five hundred thousand, and that the bank is threatening to take the crematorium away unless he starts repaying on a ten-year plan. He's got to be the scheming kind if he wants to keep everything okay for his family. Selling that land would be the perfect solution, and Parcel was the only obstacle to that.'

'*Five hundred thousand?* How did that happen?'

'Old Mrs Cluny had a thing for online poker.'

'*Helen's mum gambles?*'

'No! Her grandma!' Pen suddenly dropped her voice as Mum wandered off to find a menu and the Carusos. It was strangely quiet here at Big Mama's. 'You need to get the bedroom ban lifted,' she said urgently.

'Ohh,' I said, 'really? Seriously? Cos, I was thinking, maybe it's good! You know, no boys in bedrooms. Takes the pressure off. We don't have to worry about the whole do-I, don't-I sex thing.'

Pen flung her hands in the air. '*Thinking?* That's not *thinking*, you cretin! You are unbelievable! You don't think about anyone but yourself! Some of us don't have to worry about SEX, because it's just NOT AN ISSUE!'

'Shh! Keep your voice down!'

'Some of us have clear boundaries with our boyfriends! Some of us are just going to have fun! Getting to know each other! Without having to *make polite conversation in the living room*! IN FRONT OF EVERYONE!'

I winced. 'Okay, I get your point. I get your point. I'll talk to Mum.'

'You make this problem go away!' Pen got her stabbing finger out again. 'Otherwise Angus won't want to come around any more, I'll get really moody and make your life hell AND JACK WILL DROP YOU LIKE A SACK OF SPUDS!'

Suddenly I felt tense. My stomach flipped and all the weirdy feelings I had churning about – the nagging unease that bad people were still out there, that I had a regatta to row on camera, a hula to dance, a family to please, a father who could turn to drink on stage, a boyfriend who hadn't rung me since I'd snitched on him – it was all too much. The toast I'd had earlier didn't go well with the mix. I ran for Big Mama's toilet facilities, not caring that the stall door was shut, and threw up in the bathroom bin till the only thing coming up from my heaving body was stringy bile.

Pen followed me in, shutting the bathroom door behind us. She handed me a tissue. 'Okay,' she said. 'I'm sorry. I'm sorry, Lula.'

''S all right,' I whispered, blowing my nose. She handed me another tissue. I wiped my mouth, and straightened.

The toilet stall door opened. 'Babes,' said Bludgeon, barely a metre away, his hand on his fly, 'if you weren't so sick right there, I woulda thought you were after a sneaky peek at Mr Enormous.'

'Mr Enormous?' I croaked. I blinked at him. 'Seriously? *Seriously?*'

'Come on, Tatty,' said Pen, pulling on my arm again. 'Bludgeon needs to wash his hands.'

Gianni Caruso finally came over to our table and swept

us a low bow. 'So pleased you can celebrate being alive-a!' he declared.

Great-aunt Phoebe tapped a manicured finger on the menu and looked up at Gianni over her stylish glasses. 'Camomile tea for me, please,' she said.

Gianni went round the table taking orders. Pen made me get lasagne.

'This early in the morning?' I asked, appalled.

'Carbo-loading, Tatty! You want to be responsible for losing the race against PSG today?' she asked. 'For being the weak link in the chain? After all that's happened?' She shook her head sadly. 'Your friend Alex would be yelling at you right now, but I' – she looked lovingly at Angus (yes, of course he was there too, and the animals, if you must know) – 'I am calm and reasonable.' Her voice hardened. 'Get the pasta.'

'I'll have the lasagne,' I said. 'Thanks, Gianni.'

The bell on Big Mama's door jangled wildly and Tam came bursting in. 'You *are* here! Tatty, your life! I swear!' She shook her head and spun to leave. 'I'll be back in five with Carrie and we need all the details!'

'Wait!' I called. 'What about your shift at Aunt Sassy's?'

'Nearly done!' said Tam, halfway through the door. 'Alex will be here any minute. Don't start without me! Just got to finish Esme's toenails – they're not getting any shorter.' Out she slammed.

Mum shuddered. 'Esme Trooter's toenails?'

'You have NO idea what goes on in that salon,' I replied.

Aunt Phoebe raised her eyebrows. 'Thank heavens for small mercies,' she said, gratefully accepting her tea from Gianni. 'What happened to your finger, young man?'

'This, Aunt Phoebe,' said Pen, gesturing to Gianni, who was still looking at the space Tam had vacated with a glazed, lovestruck look on his face, 'is Gianni Caruso. He has *ice skated* in the past.'

'Oh yes,' said Great-aunt Phoebe. 'I remember.'

Big Mama brought over full English breakfasts for everyone, and a steaming plate of lasagne for me. Blue stabbed a sausage happily and gave Boodle a rasher of bacon.

'I have-a for the dog-a,' sang Big Mama, and she sailed off behind the counter and returned with a paper plate heaped with sausages, and broken-up bread for Biggins too.

'Even before this crisis, Mum,' I said, 'you have to admit that I've been through a lot.'

She sighed and speared a mushroom. 'And?'

'And I think it would be the final straw on my camel's back if you and Dad started saying we couldn't have *visitors* round to our rooms, or choose which *visitors* they were.'

Mum examined her plate, and speared a sausage. She held it up, bit it in half with one bite and chewed furiously, staring at Fat Angus.

He gulped.

'Don't look at us, Mum!' protested Pen. 'We have done nothing to earn distrust!'

I opened my mouth, thought better of it and closed it again. The less said here, the better. The lasagne was fantastic and while Pen put forward a very convincing case for judge and jury on the difficulties of getting to know a person within the confines of our nutso family living room, I ate ravenously.

'You don't want to encourage us to sneak off into the dark, dark woods, do you?' concluded Pen.

I shot a look at Mum. She was busy with the beans. Carrie, Alex and Tam had all arrived and were talking excitedly to Gianni.

'May I be excused?' I asked. 'To sit with my friends?'

Mum gestured with her fork. 'Go, go.'

I went.

First thing I wanted to know was whether Mr K had asked Aunt Sassy about wigs. Tam was smugly smug smug about having *that* inside info.

'I can't believe I know something you don't, girls.'

'Tam, don't make me hurt you. What's the deal with Healey's hair?' I thought I was being remarkably polite for a person who still hadn't had the required daily chocolate dose.

Tam sighed. 'I thought it would feel better, knowing stuff. Having the power of knowledge.'

Carrie laughed. 'You have the power of the muse – that's all you get in this lifetime, Tamtam. Now spit it out.'

'Fine, fine. It's like you thought, Lula – there's no doubt that Healey wears a wig – Aunt Sassy designed it herself.'

'Yessss!' I jumped up, punched the air and did a teeny dance of joy. Then something occurred to me and I stopped in mid-rumba. 'Hang on. I thought you had to go to wig agencies for wigs?'

'Aunt Sassy knows wigs. Look at this town! Most of the locals are well over sixty – how could she not do wigs? She's a middle-man, kind of, and works with a specialist in the city.'

'So . . .?' asked Alex. 'You're killing us here, Tam!'

'So Mr K took a sample of Mr Healey's wig hair down to the station first thing. Aunt Sassy always keeps them on file to save colour matching for the next one.' She clapped her hands. 'But we want to know about yesterday! And last night! Did Bludgeon really sleep outside your door? Does Mr K know where Healey is?'

The questions came ever faster. Alex was making me eat chocolate cake, and Tam was making me speak at the same time, but Gianni was getting all confused and the girls had to translate every sentence.

'Mff!' I said eventually, and clammed up.

Gianni threw his hands in the air. 'How you understan'?' he asked. 'How?'

'We've got a lot of experience listening to our friend when she's eating,' explained Carrie.

'She's always eating,' said Alex. 'Always. Bad carbs.'

'But today she did have good carbs,' said Carrie. 'Before the cake, I mean.'

'Good carbs for winning races,' said Alex. 'You win this race and people will love you again, Tatty.'

'People don't love her?' asked Gianni. 'What's not to love?'

He winked at me and I stuck out a chocolatey tongue at him, but I noticed to my satisfaction that as he was teasing me he was twirling some of Tam's twirly hair and she was getting girly and twirly herself.

'It's a temporary thing,' said Alex. 'I'm on it. Tatty, you've had lasagne?'

'Loads,' I assured her, patting my stomach. 'I had a lot of empty space to fill.'

'Where do you put it?' complained Carrie. 'It's a good thing you do occasional exercise, Lula. Otherwise you'd be enormous.'

'Oh no,' I said, grimacing. 'Don't say that word. Never again.'

'What – "enormous"?' asked Carrie, turning to Tam. 'What's wrong with "enormous"?'

'Stop!' I yelped, waving a fork threateningly at my friends. 'Stop or the lasagne's coming straight back up!'

Chapter Thirty-eight

When I got home Mum was talking nineteen to the dozen on the phone, and Pen was slumped in front of some cucumber slices at the kitchen table.

'Is Dad back with the car?' I asked Great-aunt Phoebe. 'I was hoping we could all squish in and go to Port Albert together.' I wanted to keep my eye on my father. I didn't want any relapses going down. The thought of him getting all anxious, then all red and sweaty and slurry, especially in front of my friends, made my stomach cramp.

Great-aunt Phoebe looked at me closely through her trendy specs. I swear that woman can read my mind. 'You don't want to go on the bus with the rest of the crew? And aren't there boys on the bus with you these days? You were fighting for rights with boys over breakfast with your mother. Seems a shame to waste the opportunities that come your way . . .'

'My crew hates me and the boys are terrified of me,' I said, getting more salad stuff out of the fridge. 'We got any feta?'

'Who's getting fatter?' asked Pen. 'You calling me fat?'

I looked at the cucumber slices and gave Pen my *what the frik?* face. 'Pen!' I said. 'Eat something! You're going to be hanging on to the rudder wires for a solid five kays, yelling yourself hoarse and steering the best line down the world's roughest river. You faint mid-race and I really am done for.'

'*All* the boys can't be afraid of you,' said Aunt Phoebe. She raised her voice. 'Blu-ue! Come and eat!' She put a piece of chicken on Pen's plate. 'What about Jack? And that boy Arnold?'

'Jack spends most of his time with his unbelievably gorgeous flatmate,' said Pen brutally, 'so we wouldn't know about him –'

'Hey!' I protested. 'I'm working on that! Besides, he came to rescue us from the Pond. A knight in shining armour.'

'– and Arns is only being released from hospital today.'

'How is Arns?' I asked quietly, sitting down at the table.

Pen pulled my plate of salad towards her and shoved some cold Pot Noodle in front of me. 'You don't know?'

'He hasn't returned any of my texts. And when I left him on Friday night he was ignoring me.'

'You're not allowed to have mobiles on in the hospital, Tatty,' said Aunt Phoebe.

'Yes, and maybe he was concentrating on his brains not spilling out all over the place, so wasn't his usual *having a laugh with Tatty* self.'

Blue came running in and sat down expectantly. 'Worms?' she asked.

'Worms,' confirmed Aunt Phoebe, pushing a Pot Noodle Blue's way.

'I eat them with fingers, like twolls do?'

'Today is a princess day,' said Pen. 'Princesses use their forks.'

'Trolls use forks also,' insisted Blue, picking up noodles in her fingers and dangling them into her mouth. 'For eyeballs, because eyeballs are slippery. When Daddy coming home?'

'He'll be home by three,' said Mum, hanging up. 'Blue, your fingernails are caked in dirt. Please go and wash your hands and come back and use your fork.'

'Three?' I stole a piece of cheese from Pen's plate and twirled it up in noodles. 'You mean we have to take the rowing bus?'

'You do,' said Mum firmly, 'so you'd better get your things together to go down there.'

I swallowed my cheesy noodles. 'Will you make it to Port Albert in time to see us race?'

'Course we will,' beamed Mum.

'What are you so happy about, Mum?' asked Pen. 'Glad to be alive-a?'

'Very,' said Mum, 'plus I've convinced the National Trust that they cannot do without Frey's Dam! They will, in all likelihood, buy it from the Clunys.'

There was silence while we all stared at Mum, open-mouthed.

'What?' I said, sounding and feeling stupid.

'While you were out getting nearly murdered, I discovered from Elias Brownfield's diaries that Queen Victoria took the waters of Frey's Dam way back when. They're warm and spa-ish and good for the insides and the outsides, apparently. A lot of history and a lot of potential for excavations. Roman ones, even.'

'Whoa!' I cried. 'Genius! Mum, you're a genius!'

'Frey's is perfect for them right now. They don't want any more expensive houses to maintain, and the spiritual history of Frey's, when linked to Coven's Quarter, is far older than anything else they've got on their books in the area. The Clunys will get the current value of the property, so their money worries will be over, and it will never be commercially developed. Excavated maybe . . .'

Great-aunt Phoebe sat back in her chair. Her eyes looked suspiciously misty. 'Well done, Anne,' she said. 'Sally would be so proud of you. We're all so proud of you. That place means a lot to this town.' She reached over and squeezed Mum's hand. 'The Clunys are going to be so very relieved.'

Mum smiled back at her and looked suspiciously misty too.

'Let's go rowing,' I said to Pen. 'Before they kill our vicious competitive spirit with their love and appreciation.'

On the banks of the Port Albert River. An hour before
we race. Feeling super carbo-loaded

'I have spent all of Saturday fixing this boat up at the
school workshops,' said Mr VDM. He stood in his usual
aggressive posture: legs astride, arms crossed over his chest,
chin tucked into his neck. 'I want us to put the accident
behind us, get out on the water and win this race. The PSG
squad is pathetic. Ridiculous dollies. I will be very angry if
you don't have them for breakfast. I will make your life hell.
Your hands will bleed. You will beg for mercy.'

The crew was standing in a circle, none of us looking
at VD. He was being loud and embarrassing. Most girls
had their arms crossed too, and were staring at their feet,
scuffing the sandy soil.

'Quite the motivational speaker,' I said quietly to Hilary.
She ignored me.

I saw Pen looking around, oblivious to VD's butt-kicking
pep talk. She saw Fat Angus tinkering with the four boat
they were going to race instead of the eight, and a smile
flitted across her face. She gave him a little finger wave and I
watched him blush. Pen flushed a little too, and I wondered
how it was that my fourteen-year-old sister always seemed
to be further on in the world than me. She and Angus gave
me the impression of twenty or thirty-somethings about to
be married.

I didn't bother looking for Jack. He'd be in the university

editing suite with Jazz back in Hambledon, the two of them working together intimately in the darkened room. Or he'd be back at the hospital with Jazz, garnering a few more gruesome facts. Or out in town with Jazz, taking a break at Big Mama's, maybe sampling that mousse off Jazz's long-handled spoon. Jazz, Jazz, frikking JAZZ!

It seemed to me that Jack now hated me for being a snitch. Why else would he not have called? Oh, frik. Was it time to face the fact that Jack and I were never going to work? The thought of it sent a pain shafting into my chest that made me want to sob aloud. I sighed instead. If I were him, I'd be distracted by Jazz too. I'd be cross with me, and happy with her. She'd never broken promises to him. I had. Big ones. And, forgetting all that, I'd also want to spend every waking minute with her. She was gorgeous; I was not. She had begun her life; I was still obeying the school bell. She had a kick-ass GTI; I was on the bus with boys who thought phlegmy bogies and stinky bums were funny.

Plus Jack was a busy guy. He had stuff going on with his sick grandmother, he had Mona to drive around whenever she needed to get places, he had his studies, he had the beginnings of a new career.

So I *understood*. I did. I could be grown-up and sensible about this.

But why didn't Jack have the guts to talk to me about it? Did he think that our relationship, if it had ever been that,

would just fizzle out painlessly? No need for him to deal
with a messy break-up? It looked like it would be up to me
to end it cleanly. Maybe it was a good thing that I'd been
through enough recently to know I'd be strong enough to
do what was necessary.

Even if it felt like my heart was going to shrivel up
and die.

VD had got to the punching-the-air stage, and his
voice was getting louder. The crew was looking even more
embarrassed, but I was beyond caring.

'Mr van der Merwe,' I piped up.

'Eh?' He stopped mid-rant, and looked at me,
eyebrows raised.

'I really need the bathroom.' His eyebrows came down
and met in the middle. 'Now,' I added. 'Before we get on
the water.'

'Good idea,' said Pen quickly. 'Let's go before there are
queues for the toilets.'

We all took off for the Port Albert sailing-club bathroom
before VD could say no. All around us last-minute preparations
were underway. Elegant white marquees surrounded the
sailing club, and caterers were setting out champagne glasses,
wine glasses, jugs of Pimm's and lemonade. Waiters rushed to
and fro finding things and losing things. I heard shouts and
instructions from parking areas a little way away, along with
the blast of a big bus's horn and revving engines.

Down at the riverbank the jetties were lined with crews getting in or out. The river sparkled in the sunlight and gulls swooped and yelled at the invaders. I spotted the PSG crew. A girl I'd met over the half-term break was tittering in the cox's seat. Her long golden hair was piled high on her head, her lips were perfectly glossed and her sunglasses were big and expensive.

'The blonde PSG cox is called Barbie,' I said to Matilda McCabe. 'For real.'

'Don't talk to me,' replied Matilda, walking into the clubhouse. 'My dad's all freaked out about my safety now because of you.'

My chest squeezed tight with hurt, but I kept my mouth shut and swallowed hard. I had that terrible feeling that comes sometimes when you hate where you are, or what's happening to you, but there's not a thing you can do about it.

Except maybe win a race . . . maybe that would work.

Back at the boat in a fashion no-no

I felt self-conscious in my Hambledon High trisuit. Like I told Tam, it was a leotard-type thing, but with legs, so that when you pulled the blade into your body, and pushed it away to come back up the slide, no clothing snagged on your hands, or on your seat runners, for that matter. There is nowhere to hide in the trisuit, though thankfully it was all black except for two pale blue lines running down the sides from under the arms to the bottom of the legs. Black is slimming, right?

Maybe it's a good thing I didn't eat much last night, I thought. Then I remembered the lasagne this morning. And the chocolate cake. And the Pot Noodle that nearly made me throw up. It was all probably still stuck up in a pipe behind my lungs. I worried about when it would make its way down to the stomach area. When that happened, I could stop worrying about people thinking I was jinxed, and start worrying about people thinking I was pregnant. Though, really, everyone knows Jack would rather sproink Jazz than me.

'Tallulah! Did you hear what I said?' snapped Mr VDM. We were all standing around the boat again, and our coach had calmed down a little, though he had a faint twitch below his left eye that unnerved me.

'Sorry, no,' I confessed.

Every one of the crew rolled their eyes and pulled a face, except for Pen, who just held my gaze without smiling.

'We're about to get on the water! Everyone to check their rigging – make sure you've got the right number of washers. Make sure everything works. Once you're out there, people, you're on your own. Tallulah, you'll row seven today. Jessica, you're down at bow.'

'*What?*' Jessica was apoplectic.

At the bow of the boat it gets really narrow, and the runners can slice you on the back of the calves if you're slamming down hard enough. Also, there was a feeling that bow was kind of reserved for the least experienced person in the crew, whereas seven helped eight, leader of the crew, to set up the rhythm. There wasn't much glory in bow.

'Oh, I'd prefer to be bow,' I said hastily. 'I'm comfortable there.'

'Are you saying *I* wouldn't be comfortable in bow?' asked Jessica, her voice going up an octave. 'Are you saying I'm *too big* for bow?'

'What?' I was horrified. Everyone was looking at me with squinty eyes. 'No!' I exclaimed. 'No no no! I –'

'Enough,' interrupted Mr VDM. 'Tallulah is up front because she holds the rhythm really well in the rougher water. She is very focused.'

'Single-minded, more like,' muttered Matilda.

'Jessica, you and Tallulah have the same number of washers on your rig, so there should be no need to adjust. Now, everyone, over to the shade for stretching, please. I need to check on the boys.'

Feeling my face burning, I checked that the bow rigger was all okay for Jess, then went over to check the seven spot. All was exactly as it should be. I turned round to find the crew staring at me, arms crossed.

'Let's go warm up,' said Pen abruptly.

We stretched in silence until Hilary said, 'Look there, guys. It's Tatty's boyfriend with his girlfriend.' I was sitting on the ground with my head on my knee, tugging at my toes, but I sat straight up and looked around. Through the trees we had a good view of the parking area, and sure enough there was Jack, getting out of Jazz's GTI. I bent quickly over my other knee, thankful that I could hide my face, thankful for the shadows of the shade.

Jack and Jazz's voices came closer and then stopped a little way off. They were talking to Mr VDM and it looked like he was explaining how rowing worked, where all the crew sat and what his hopes for the boys' and girls' teams were. After he'd finished talking to them, he came loping over. 'Everyone warm? Let's jog up the river, then back and we can get on the water. I want to talk through strategy for the final corner.'

I didn't hear much of what Mr VDM had to say upriver. I guess I was somewhere else. Thinking about my family on their way to watch me; wondering if Pen was being distant on purpose, if it was a self-preservation thing; remembering that night with Jack at Coven's Quarter when we'd kissed for the first time –

I stopped that train of thought. That hurt.

I thought about Arnold and his easy gangliness, then remembered how he'd blanked me in the hospital. I thought about my friends at school, but Helen Cluny swam into my head, all defensive and angry with me. Still.

I sighed. Thinking was doing me no good. I needed a serious workout to forget about all the people who no longer liked me. Right on cue, we began to jog back to the boat. When we got there, I saw a familiar figure through the trees at the boys' four.

'Hey, Arnold!' cried the O'Connelly sisters in unison.

He turned with a grin, his head patched on one side with a lot of white gauze. 'Hey, girls!' He said something to the guys he was with and came loping over.

Oh no. I cringed – I was about to be ignored again. I just wanted to heft the boat on to my shoulder and get to the water where all I could see was the back of Matilda McCabe.

Arnold walked straight up to me.

I held my breath.

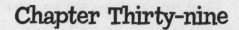

Chapter Thirty-nine

I darted a look at my best boy (pause) friend's face.

He was still grinning widely. 'So how do I say thank you to the girl who saved my life?' he asked easily.

A rush of tears prickled my eyes and nose, and Arns saw that before he pulled me into a close hug. I sniffed against his chest. This was weird, being hugged by Arnold.

'What's wrong?' he asked quietly, holding me at arm's length. My crew turned away, busying themselves around the boat.

'I'm going to check this crib from bow to stern,' announced Matilda, wagging a shifting spanner at everyone except me. 'This is our last chance to make adjustments.'

'Why did you ignore me at the hospital?' I asked Arnold.

He rolled his eyes. 'Dude. There's ignoring, and then there's passing out at the sight of blood. You weren't in the best outfit.'

An image of me on Friday night floated into my head. My shirt had been soaked with Arnold's plasma from neck to hem, my arms bloodied to the elbows, streaks of it across my face, in my hair, all over my legs.

'Oh, yeah,' I said.

'You look better now,' he said, staring at the trisuit.

'I don't *think* so!' I exclaimed. 'Too much Pot Noodle.'

'I can't see the Pot Noodle, but I'm hoping it's in there somewhere. Could win us the race. Jack and Jazz said you were rowing seven! Congratulations, Lula.'

'I wish,' I muttered.

'You're not rowing seven?'

'No, I wish it was congratulations. Everyone hates me.'

'The crew?' Arns turned to the girls. 'Why do you hate Tatty?' he called out.

'Arns!' I hissed.

'She's a walking disaster,' said Matilda bluntly. 'You should hate her too. If it wasn't for Tatty, you'd be rowing today and you'd have a whole head.'

'How do you work that out?' asked Arns, touching his gauze bandage gingerly.

'The recent past speaks for itself,' said Kelly Sheridan, shunting her seat up and down the runners and spraying more oil on it. 'Starting with Simon Smethy, Gianni Caruso, and ending with *you* – she's bad luck. Jinxed.'

'Interesting,' said Arns. He turned to face the crew, still holding one of my arms. 'But I think you'll find that crazy stuff happens when Tatty is around, because she *is always* around. She's never at home, like a normal person. Do you know anyone with more energy than Tallulah Bird? Whenever there's a movie on, or a dance to go to, or ice skating up at Frey's, Tatty's there. You guys don't talk about

401

the good stuff that happens when she's around, do you? You don't talk about how Tatty was the one who got Jason and Jessica together, how she saved this town from apartment blocks on every horizon, how she *saved my life*, actually, and Emily's too.'

There was an uncomfortable silence and I was so red I thought I might never return to a normal skin tone again.

Matilda tightened a bolt on her rigging, taking her time. 'You only say those things because you're in luuurve, Arnold Trenchard,' she said, but she looked at me quickly and I could see Arnold's words had hit home a little.

The rest of the crew giggled. Giggled, not sniggered.

'Mona's a good influence,' said Pen quickly. 'And I think you should all say sorry to my sister,' she added.

And – just like that, how? why? – everyone was murmuring apologies.

'Well, this is freaky,' I said. 'But thanks. And, Jess, I really don't mind rowing bow.'

'Oh, shut up,' said Jessica. 'I'm thinking if we lose this race, I can blame you. You're an easy target.'

I grinned uncomfortably.

'Hey, Tilda,' came a voice behind Matilda.

'Hey,' she said, turning to Helen Cluny.

'Hi, guys,' said Helen to all of us. Even me. I was startled. Had she forgiven me? We all murmured hello, and I was about to say thanks to Arnold, my cheeks still on fire, when Helen spoke up again.

'So the big news is my dad has sold Frey's. Anyone keen for a party up there next weekend before it's off limits?' Her eyes slid to to me. 'Tatty? Are you keen?'

My jaw dropped. 'Uh . . .' I said.

'We're there,' said Sinead. 'Will you get some boys to come, Arnold?'

'Who bought Frey's?' asked Hilary. 'I thought there was a whole squatters-slash-bird-flu thingy going on there.'

'All sorted. And it's the National Trust!' said Helen, her face glowing. 'Thanks to Tatty and her mum.'

My face flamed again, but I began to smile.

'Oh no,' said Pen gloomily. 'It's turning into a fan zone around here. I think I'm going to be sick.'

'Hold off on the fan-club scene,' said Matilda sternly. She rapped my seat with the shifting spanner. 'You didn't check your place, Tatty. Your seat wheels are jammed.' I saw her jaw flex. 'You see, Arnold? This is what I mean. If we'd gone out on the water and Tatty's seat wasn't right, she'd have been catching crabs, slowing us down . . .'

'Hang on just a minute!' I cried. 'I checked everything before we jogged upriver!'

'Sure,' said Matilda. She looked at Arns. 'Have you guys got a spare seat?'

'I reckon so,' said Arns. He gave my arm a squeeze

and went back to the boys to get it.

'I checked that seat!' I said again. 'How can the wheels be jammed half an hour later?' I went to my place in the boat and Matilda handed the seat to me. Turning it over, I ran my hands over the wheels. They didn't move. I peered at them closely while everyone else triple checked their places, the sound of seats whirring up and down runners filling the air. The car park was filling up now, and I was sure I could hear Esme Trooter's voice floating across the green grass under the trees towards us. I pushed the wheels back and forth and one of them began to turn. Peering closely at it, I noticed a strand of something caught in it. I tried to get at it with my fingers, but it was too short and too fine.

'What is that?' I murmured.

A familiar fedora landed in the boat. 'What's up?'

'Mr K!' I looked up, my face creased in a frown. 'Someone has laced up my wheels with something.' I held my seat out to him.

Mr K took the seat and examined it. 'Hmm,' he said. 'Fishing line.'

'Yes! It *is* fishing line,' I exclaimed.

'Try this out,' said Arns, handing me another seat.

I dropped the boys' boat seat on my runners and pushed it up and down. 'Perfect fit. Thanks, Arns. Do the guys need this for their race?'

'Nope, it's a spare.'

'Good, because with the witch girl in the boat we'll probably sink upriver,' said Siobhan O'Connelly, 'so there'd be little chance of returning it.'

'And then they couldn't row and that would be two events lost,' finished Sinead O'Connelly.

'Hey,' said Arns. 'What did I just say earlier? Huh?'

'Sorry,' said the twins to me.

I sighed. 'Look, everyone,' I said. 'If you'd rather not have me in the boat, then just say so.'

'We'd rather not have you in the boat,' said Dionysia.

'But we haven't got a choice,' said Kelly.

'And you will be a good seven,' said Jess. She walked over and put her arm round me. 'We're all just a little stressed and crabby. Right, girls? We love Tallulah, right?'

'We love her,' said the twins in unison. 'But it's fun making her squirm.'

Matilda was the only one who didn't nod and grin. I watched her tightening her rigging for the hundredth time and wondered if she'd jammed my seat up with fishing line.

No way.

She wouldn't have said anything about the seat if she'd wanted me to come a cropper. She'd have waited till we were on the water. Plus, what was the point of jamming my seat? I'd have realised the second we'd pulled off from the jetty. It would have taken a real moron to pull a stunt like that. A moron or someone who knew very little about rowing. Most likely the fishing line had just got in the boat somehow and got tangled up.

But I wasn't convincing myself. I looked over at Mr K, who had put his hat back on. He gestured to me and I stepped a little away from the crew.

'Be careful out there,' he said. 'I don't mean to scare you, but I lost Healey on the road between Hambledon and here. I'm sure he means you harm.'

I swallowed. 'Why? What would he have to gain?'

Mr K shrugged. 'He's just an ugly man, Tallulah. But I've informed Sergeant Trenchard and we're all looking out for you, all right?'

'Sure, thanks, Mr K. I guess he didn't mess with my seat.'

Mr K smiled. 'No. I've got a good idea who did, though. You've got nothing to worry about there either. Go and enjoy your race.' He patted my shoulder and loped away.

I rubbed my eyes, feeling stressed and relieved and bewildered all at once.

Come on. It's all sorted, and no harm done.

We took our places along the side of the boat, and on Pen's command reached over and pulled it overhead, bowside rowers stepping to one side and lowering the boat to our right-hand shoulder, strokeside doing the opposite. We walked down to the jetty, going slowly and carefully. Pen called the command, 'Above heads, *now*,' and we lifted the boat overhead, then swung it down to lower it into the river.

The birds were still wheeling and diving, and down on the water I noticed how the wind had picked up. People on the shore were staring at us, some even pointing and talking to each other about this crew from Hambledon. Mr VDM came shambling across the grass and on to the jetty.

'Girls!' he called, skidding on the slippery planks.

Pen stepped quickly up to him. 'We've got it from here, Mr van der Merwe,' she said politely. 'I'll look after them.'

He took a deep breath. 'You remember where to turn? After the warm-up? The hard right on the final bend? Tell me what you're going to call on the start.'

'You've done your cox coaching,' said Pen. 'I watched every DVD you gave me. I know my stuff. And Matilda is right in front of me. It's going to be fine.'

'The PSG cox is a crazy one,' said Mr VDM urgently, looking down at all of us, now lacing our feet into footboards and clipping our blades into the rigging. I felt strange where I was. I was used to seeing the backs of seven girls up ahead, plus the occasional glimpse of Pen. Now it was just Matilda, and Pen. I took a deep breath, noticing that my heart had kicked up a gear. 'Watch out for the line they take,' continued Mr VDM. 'They'll squeeze you on the bends. Get ahead fast, or there'll be crashes, and the umpires in the boats behind can only call for so much water.'

Just across from us was the PSG crew. They'd already been for their warm-up and were resting on the water. They looked fit and lithe and slightly flushed with the exertion.

'You're bigger than them,' hissed Mr VDM. 'Remember that!' He pushed us off, and Pen called for Jess to take a few pulls on her blade.

'We're doing our best to forget the size issue,' muttered Matilda, in a tone angrier than any I'd ever heard from her before. Which is saying something.

I raised my eyebrows. *Ha. So Matilda McCabe doesn't like being big. All she needs, really, is to stay out of the square-ass jeans and embrace a few different looks . . . Stop! Focus!*

Pen adjusted her microphone, and pulled her headgear on. Her voice came murmuring into our ears. 'Bow pair, together, *now*. Fall in, three and four.'

'Falling in is the issue I'm trying to forget,' I joked.

'No fooling around!' snapped Matilda, glancing over her shoulder. 'The whole of bowside needs to follow you, and Dion too for strokeside, so stay focused or you'll be responsible for another disaster!'

I gritted my teeth. 'Sorry.'

'Just shut up, Tallulah!' was Matilda's response. 'Shut up and row!'

The shock of her vehemence sent that tightness straight back into my chest. I tried to relax, following her up the slide, but everything felt wrong. My blade scraped across the water and at the catch it was hard to twist it up and in. At the end of the stroke I only just managed to get it out of the water and then rushed the slide back up to make it to the next catch in time. The boat jerked and flopped.

'What the hell is the matter with you?' hissed Matilda at me over her shoulder.

I took a deep breath and lifted my eyes from her slide to look straight ahead. Maybe my balance was off. As Matilda moved to the right, following her blade round for the catch, Pen came into view. She was frowning, but not in a cross way. *It's okay*, she mouthed, encouraging me on. My eyes filled with tears and this time at the catch of the next stroke I really duffed it.

The word *Frik!* had barely left my lips before the handle of my blade whacked into my body with such force that it sent me backwards. Though I was holding on for dear life it still caught me across my face.

'Hang on!' yelled Pen, and her voice echoed across the water.

Pulling with all my might, I managed to get my blade out of the river, while the rest of the crew slammed the brakes on by ramming the flat of their blades against the surface. There was a rushing of water and muffled swearing.

Slowly I struggled back up to sitting. On the shore I glimpsed Mr van der Merwe jumping up and down, waving his arms around like an orang-utan on an isotonic high. Arns had his hand on his hip, shading his eyes for a better view across the water with the other. I felt blood trickle from my nose to my chin, and my cheek was agony. The sound of laughter came from six metres away. Barbie sat straight and slim in her cox's seat, and her voice was clear, even though the wind was picking up.

'Rumours are true, crew. Hambledon Girls do catch crabs.'

'So original!' hissed Matilda sarcastically to herself, then whirled round to face me. 'What the –'

'Now *you* shut up,' I said. 'Just shut up and row.'

I was about to slide back up to the footboard, ready for the catch, when Dion's hand landed on my shoulder. I froze, waiting for more bitchy comments, but she said, 'You okay?'

I swallowed.

'Come on, Tatty,' said Sinead, from further down.

'We've all caught our share of crabs,' added Siobhan.

'You can do it, Tatty,' said Hilary.

'You can do it,' echoed Kelly. 'That's our disaster for today; now we can hustle the PSG sluts.'

I smiled tearily while the rest of the girls giggled, on my side at last. Pen called a slow start and we did warm-up exercises all the way upriver till at last we found a sheltered patch of calm, smooth water and Pen ordered a halt. Though I'd not had any more calamities, I wasn't feeling good. Nothing was working, and I couldn't find a rhythm at all.

The crew rested and drank water. The riverbanks went up steeply from this point, thickly wooded and verdant green. The lush foliage swallowed all sound, and here in the shelter only the calls of solitary water birds and our laboured breathing could be heard.

Matilda twisted round and stared at my rigging. She pointed at it accusingly. 'I thought so. I bloody thought so. What do you see, Tatty?' She was breathing hard, her chest heaving up and down, her short brown hair slicked with sweat behind her ears.

I stared across at my rig, not understanding. Then suddenly I saw it. 'My washers!' I gasped. 'They're gone!'

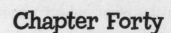

Chapter Forty

'How is that possible?' asked Kelly. 'Washers can't just drop off!' She paused. 'Can they?'

'No!' yelled Matilda. 'No! No! No! Tatty didn't check her rig and *this* is why she can't get her bloody blade out the water! It's just not high enough!'

I was gobsmacked. Speechless.

Jessica's voice came floating all the way up from bow. 'I saw Tatty check her rig, Matilda. I watched her. I watched her check my place and hers. And I checked my place and hers. Someone messed with Tatty's rigging, for sure.'

Matilda leaned out to look down the boat, and we all hastily raised or lowered our blades to keep from overturning. 'You sure?' she asked Jess.

'Positive, Tilda. Positive. Who would do that?'

I looked at Matilda McCabe's profile and narrowed my eyes.

'We can't worry about that now,' said Matilda. 'We've got to fix it.' She turned back to face Pen. 'You got the tool kit?' I heard her ask.

'Yes,' said Pen. 'But no extra washers.'

Matilda's shoulders hunched into a stressful posture that I didn't like the look of.

'Um . . .' I said, thinking desperately. I skated up on my seat, looking into the boat below me. Was there any extraneous washer I could extract from a nut and bolt in there? As I bent down, my necklace clinked out, the nuts from Oscar swinging forward. Of course! 'Hey!' I yelped.

Matilda had twisted round, a number ten spanner in her hand. She looked at my necklace that I was holding up for her to see. 'Perfect,' she said. Relief washed across her face and her shoulders dropped back down.

Hmm, I thought. *She didn't want this catastrophe.*

'What's going on?' called Kelly.

'Tatty's got some nuts that might work as washers,' called Matilda.

'Pass your blade back, Tatty,' said Dion.

I lay down and pulled the blade over my body. Dion grabbed it and I sat up, taking the spanner from Matilda. Within minutes, my rigging was back to normal.

'Let's practise the start,' said Pen, her voice echoing all down the boat. 'It's going to be windier than ever out there, and the forecast said gusts will hit round about now.' She paused. 'We're bigger than the PSGs, whether we like it or not, so we're going to sit more stably in the water.' Matilda said something to Pen. 'And we've got a solid stroke pair.' I flushed. Pen was talking about me and Matilda. 'Lastly, we had the roughest session ever on Friday night, and still managed to get this boat to shore – in the dark, with smashed blades and stern, with high waves, with strong winds, with a crew member in another boat entirely sorting out head wounds.'

I felt the smile that whispered up the boat and turned to see Dion giving me a thumbs up.

'I would rather not pee VD off,' said Pen. 'There's already been too much bleeding.' The O'Connelly girls laughed quietly. 'So let's go do this.'

We took off, and this time the boat pushed and shunted perfectly in time. The blade felt strong and comfortable for me at last, and I felt a gush of perspiration as relief flooded my body.

It was going to be okay.

We got to the start feeling seriously psyched, a sense of confidence and camaraderie buoying us up. It wasn't just the PSG crew waiting on the water. There was a crew in dark blue from a school down the coast, another in an unfortunate combo of burgundy and mustard from an inland town where I didn't even know they had water to row on and the last lot in Irish green. We were the closest crew to the west bank. The PSG crew was alongside on my right, and Barbie looked across at me. Her perfectly glossed lips curved into a smile and she gave me a mock salute. 'Need a doctor?' she called. 'For the crabs?'

'Loser,' muttered Matilda.

I wondered for a minute if she were referring to me, but

put it from my mind as she bunched up at the front of the slide for a power start. I followed suit, my arms stretched out far to the left, and felt the boat shift as everyone got into position. I glanced down at my legs, noticing quad muscles that I swear weren't there before, and triceps in my arms that ridged out alongside my biceps. They were smeared with blood from my nose, and my knees too, but I barely noticed. The umpire's boat had pulled up right in front of me, in line with Pen, and Dr Gordon, the university vice chancellor, was balanced at the helm, ready to call the start. Pen's arm was up, which meant we were ready to go. As soon as all the cox's arms were up, the umpire would call on your marks, get set, go and the race would begin. Five kilometres of windswept tidal river, bending round sandy shores to the finish under a high arched bridge in front of all of Hambledon, and more besides.

I blinked a drop of sweat from my lashes and concentrated on Dr Gordon, my gaze flicking back to Pen, then back to the umpire boat.

And that's when I saw him.

Jack, his arms tightly round Jazz, balancing in the umpire's boat and staring calmly downriver.

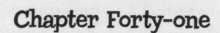

Chapter Forty-one

'Frikking *frik*!' I hissed. My eyes went crazed so suddenly that Pen dropped her arm and turned her head to see what I was looking at.

She whipped back round and met my eyes, switching off her microphone. 'Now, Lula,' she said, holding her hand out in a calming gesture. 'Clearly Jack is filming this event, and Jazz is holding the sound boom, okay? Looks to me like they're just hanging on to each other for, um, like, *balance*. Right? They're *balancing*. We need you to stay in the zone here. We've just got our rhythm right. Against all the odds. We can win this race. If you focus.'

'She looks like she's enjoying the *balancing*,' said Matilda.

I opened my mouth to get abusive, but Pen beat me to it. 'Shut up, Matilda McCabe,' she said. 'That cow's got nothing on my sister.'

Matilda's shoulders tensed up, but she didn't reply.

Pen glanced at me. 'Ready?' she asked.

I nodded. Pen clicked her mike back on and her arm went up again. I looked over at the umpire. He was lifting the loadhailer to his mouth. 'Here we go,' I murmured, and tension zinged through the boat.

'On your marks,' yelled Dr Gordon. 'Get set! Go!'

And we were off. Our blades danced in and out of the water in a high-speed chase. Tap, tap, tap, pull, pullll, puuullll, till we were slamming down a whole slide-length, then whizzing back up at a massive rating to lift the boat up out of the water and away.

Suddenly the umpire boat was gone. Jack and Jazz were gone. The seagulls were gone. It was just Pen, Matilda and a world of wind and water, with six bodies behind us, following our every move. I barely heard what Pen was shouting. She was leaning forward, her face flushed, her eyes sparkling, yelling in a hoarse voice that set goosebumps up all over my body and raised the hairs on the back of my neck. Up to the front of the slide I came, dashing the blade into the water at the exact instant Matilda did, bracing as she did, slamming down my legs as she did and leaning back at the finish at the perfect angle.

'*More power, more power! Get ready for a squeeze. NOW!*'

And then the water rushed beneath the boat as eight legs thumped hard at the finish, floated up the slide, smacked in at the catch.

Smack, thump, glide. Smack, thump, glide.

'*Take it up again!*'

'*Squeeze!*'

'*We're a nose ahead, girls! Hold it! Hold it!*'

I came floating up for another catch, my body staying straight and true in the boat even though my arms were reaching round for another dip of the blade. I saw Pen's knuckles whiten as her fists gripped and pulled on the rudder wires.

'*PSG is pushing us into the right bank!*' she screamed. 'I'm going to hold this line! Three, get ready to crash blades!'

I tensed and shunted down harder than ever as Siobhan's blade cracked against PSG's bow's blade. The umpire roared disapproval and yelled at PSG to move across so our boat would have more room. My eyes flicked to the motor boat and suddenly I was locked in a gaze with Jazz. She was smiling triumphantly, as usual, and had her forearm over Jack's, holding it against her ribs. Her left arm held the fuzzy sound boom in front of her. Jack's face was hidden behind a huge news camera, the lens zoomed out at the PSG crew.

If he wants you, he can have you, Jazz Delaney, I thought. *Just don't expect me to be a loser either way.*

'Another push!' I yelled at Pen. Her eyes widened. We were pulling in tight round the bend now, and a surge of power could unbalance the boat. PSG were nipping at our strokeside blades, despite the red-faced outrage of the umpire, and a push might not allow us the coordination to keep our heads in the midst of all the crashing and bashing.

'Do it!' yelled Matilda.

Pen screamed the instruction, and our boat lifted and surged again.

'We've got a foot!' yelled Pen in triumph.

Slam!
Slam!
Slam!

'Another foot!' called Pen. 'And they're coming off our line! We need half a boat length to move over for the next corner!'

We kept at it, squeezing away at a race pace that had our quads and hamstrings burning, our calloused hands feeling ripped and torn, our throats raw as we sucked for air. All the while Pen was at us, encouraging, begging, pleading, yelling, screaming. We went into the next corner with less water on the PSG boat than we would have liked and then all hell broke loose. The high riverbanks that had sheltered us before dipped suddenly to low sandy flats, and suddenly the wind roared and rocketed at us. It buffeted the water into high choppy swells that slopped over the sides of the boat and against our bodies, slicking our blade handles till they were difficult to control.

'Remember Friday night!' yelled Pen. 'Hold it together! Looking good! *We've got another foot!* Hold it!'

I snatched a glance across strokeside. Pen was right. We were pulling away from PSG, their boat beginning to flounder in the rough water.

'*Eyes in the boat!*' screamed Pen. 'The burgundy sluts are gaining!'

I looked to the right. They were too. One of their blades

clipped Matilda's, jolting the whole boat, and I held on like never before. The next stroke was going to be a clash for sure. I slammed my legs down for a hard finish and Pen yelled at the crew to ready themselves. My hands were clawed round my blade handle as I cruised up the slide. I cut my eyes over to the right again. The burgundy number two was looking across at Matilda, then at her blade and I watched as she jabbed at us, upsetting her crew's rhythm. I held steady and I swear it was just coincidence that Matilda caught the edge of her spoon. It cracked as Matilda's blade sliced through the air, and I heard her cry out at the impact. Another quick glance showed me that she was flat on her back in the boat, her blade fizzing out of control through the water.

We surged ahead, but it wasn't the end of the drama.

Oh no.

Not at all.

Pen opened her mouth to call the next command, but before she could there was a strange sound, then a *thock thock*, and Matilda exclaimed in fright. 'We've hit something!' I heard her yell.

Pen's forehead creased in confusion. She was looking down near the bottom of the boat, shaking her head in disbelief and pulling off her waterproof jacket and shoving it at the side of the boat.

She's plugging a hole, I thought. *What . . .?*

Then a realisation hit, and her gaze shot up and over to the west bank. Before she could react there was a plume of spray from the water near me that didn't fit with the crazy waves or the wind, then another and another, all of them *thock thock*ing closer and closer until finally – *thock!* – a ribbon of blood zipped across my forearm, and – *thock* – another across my right shoulder as I dipped into the next stroke.

No. Frikking. Way! Impossible!

Oh no you don't, I thought, searching the west bank for someone with a gun. *Oh no you don't, you miserable little man. Not now.*

'*Go!*' screamed Pen, her eyes wide and frantic and locked on to mine. Tears began streaming in that instant, the cords standing out in her neck, her face scarlet. '*Push for ten! Through the railway bridge! Now, now, NOW!*'

What? We were already at the railway bridge? We could do this. Just five hundred metres to go. Think about that. Don't think about who's out there. Don't think about the burning grazes across your skin. Make this the *fastest* moving target ever.

Pen was no help at all. She was not counting down the strokes; she had turned round in the boat, gesturing wildly at the umpire boat behind us. The one with Jack and Jazz on it. Through snatched glances I saw Jack suddenly handing the camera to Jazz to answer a call on his mobile, his face dropping as he listened. One look back at me, then at the west bank, and then it seemed as though he was about to dive into the water – but Jazz held him tight, holding on for all she was worth. He still had his mobile to his ear, then he stood tall, shading his eyes against the sun.

I tried to see what he was looking at . . . Was that a grey hat? A fedora? Someone sprinting through the bushes?

Looking back at Jack, I suddenly saw his arm fling up in a victory salute, a high thumb's up to Pen. Phone back in pocket, camera back at eyeball.

Pen looked from him to the west bank then to all of us. Tears were still streaming down her face as she ignored Matilda's yells for answers.

'Pen? Pen? What is it?'

Breath rasped in my throat, as much from fear as the effort of rowing this far, this fast. But no time to think – PSG were fighting back now, and had gained two feet on us.

Pen glanced across at them, her eyes streaming in the gale. A gust hit us and the boat flopped hard to strokeside. She yelled at us to adjust the height of our blades to compensate and we pulled together to get the balance right. Then at last we were round the corner, and through the railway bridge. The wind was coming at Pen's back, making it easier to balance. She yelled for the push, then to hold it, then screamed at us to up the rating.

I can't!

I blinked. That voice in my head was not helpful. Not

helpful at all, even though it said what I was feeling, and echoed the smears of blood across my body, the sting of salt water in the raw flesh of my hands. The push through the railway bridge had got my nose bleeding again, and hot blood spattered on my left knee every time I came up at the catch. *Attractive*, I thought, and winced as the umpire boat surged close to us, Jack and Jazz staring hard at us all.

Okay, seriously. I just can't.

I caught a glimpse of Jazz. She was throwing her head back against Jack's shoulder and laughing at something. Right, then. There were two minutes left of this torture and I was going to make them count. PSG were just to one side of us, the burgundy crew had dropped way back along with the others. Though the PSG crew looked scrappy and tired, they were still fighting back.

'*We've lost another foot!*' screamed Pen. '*Let's push for home!*'

A two-minute push? Was my little sister *nuts*? A two-minute push may not sound like a lot, but two minutes rating thirty-four strokes per minute is sixty-eight back-breaking slams that could burn a tray of millefeuille calories in a nanosecond.

But, just for today, my little sister was boss.

Matilda eased up the slide and we began to work.

Slam!

Slam!

Slam!

The PSG crew did their best, Barbie's voice growing more shrill with every stroke, but they were no match for our perfect rhythm, and the power it brought. I counted the strokes down, every surge of the boat bringing the sound of the finish line closer. Shouts from spectators on the riverbanks became more frequent, snatches of music from the hospitality tents were more audible now; out of the corner of my eye I saw three crazy figures on bicycles, pedalling madly along the river path to keep pace with our boat: Carrie, Tam and Alex, ringing their bells and shouting at the tops of their voices. I glimpsed the smug smile fade from Jazz's face and saw Jack's lens zoom for a shot of my friends.

I grinned. Three girls were better than one boy any day, even though my heart was not in the mood to agree at the minute.

'Ten strokes to the finish, with everything you've got, *now*,' came Pen's voice over the speakers as the long shadow of the final high arched bridge came chopping across the water.

Slam! Slam! Slam! Slam!

The noise from the banks was incredible. Shouting, chants, bicycle bells and hooters. I could see PSG pushing like never before. Were they gaining?

Slam! Slam! Slam! Slam!

A commentator's voice filtered through the roar of the

umpire's motorboat: '*Hambledon Girls in the lead! They're going to take it!*'

Slam! Slam!

The echoing honk of the hooter signalling the first boat over the line. A last glance at Jazz, the sound boom dropped down now, both her arms round Jack, laughing up at him again. Jack laughing too.

Hambledon Girls' High had won the race.

And I had lost my boyfriend.

Chapter Forty-two

There was no doubt in my mind as blood streamed from my nose, my shoulder, my arm, as my head grew fuzzy and dizzy, as the crew around me screamed with jubilation while I slumped over my blade handle, that I was the most disgusterous specimen on the river. I fully appreciated Jack's firm hold under the perfect breasts of Jazz Delaney.

'Hilary, two strokes, *now*,' came Pen's voice, quieting the excited chatter in the boat around me.

'No,' said Matilda. 'We're not going in just yet. We need to warm down.'

'*Now*, Hilary,' repeated Pen. 'Tatty needs a bit of first aid.'

Matilda twisted to look at me and I saw her eyes widen before the world swung this way and that before me. 'Blade up, Tatty,' commanded Matilda, doing the same. 'And drop your head on your knees, you moron.'

I obeyed, and began to retch into the boat beneath me, though nothing was coming up.

'Is she puking?' asked Kelly.

'Think so,' said Dion, 'but I'm not seeing the vomit.'

'Oh, this is totally gross,' moaned Kelly. 'Where's the

glory in tipping up our boat onshore and a billion litres of blood and sick spilling out?'

The O'Connelly sisters clamoured their horror, but in minutes Pen had steered us to the jetty and, though my nose was still gushing, I'd stopped heaving.

Mr VDM was doing a loony dance on the boards of the jetty. The whole platform was bouncing and splashing in the water. I tried to sit up straight, but the world spun again and I retched.

'Head *down*,' hissed Matilda. 'The camera's on you. Hide the blood.'

I heaved a shuddering sigh. Why the frik did nothing ever go my way? Stretching forward carefully, I unlaced my feet from the footboard and looked around for something to staunch the blood.

'You'd better have this,' said Pen, and she hauled off her sweatshirt, passing it down to Matilda, who shoved it under my nose.

''Ankoo,' I mumbled. 'Ayeeingothesoff.'

'What?' asked Matilda.

'She's whining about me taking my clothes off,' said Pen. She held on to the jetty and eased herself out of the cox's seat, then leapt nimbly on to the boards in her trisuit and nothing else. I saw her scanning the crowds, and then her face lit up and she raised her arm in a wide wave. She looked sensational.

And, clearly, Angus thought so too. He was beaming and hurrying over as fast as his muscle-bound legs could carry him.

Then a big hairy arm with a very bling red patent-leather Chanel handbag over the shoulder stretched out and held my rigger firmly against the jetty. 'Hop out, Tatty, but watch the shirt. I've got to go onstage in this later.'

'Dad? Whaoinghere?'

I staggered ashore, Pen helping too, leaving my crewmates and Arns to bring the boat in, while my father held me at arm's length all the way to the first-aid tent.

'Aren't you pleased to see me?' burbled Dad. 'I got such a welcome from the Setting Sun folks, and they're so proud of you. What a race! Jack was filming the whole time, with commentary! They're going to rerun it in the members' tent after the men's final. Car broke down, of course. Nearly didn't make it. But Dan said Oscar was ready for a drive?'

'He made it all the way here?' I smiled behind the wadding of Pen's shirt. 'Go, Oscar.'

Dad squeezed my shoulder. 'I'm sorry I got to drive him before you. I thought it would be better to do that than miss the race.'

'Definitely,' agreed Pen.

We came to a halt in front of the first-aid tent, and I found myself smiling at my father, though probably the only thing he could see of me was smiley eyes.

428

I didn't mind at all that Dad had driven Oscar – or that he had his crazy woman's bag with him. I was just so relieved to see he was entirely sober. And relieved that I was entirely alive.

'Lula,' said Dad, 'I see you looking at my bag. But just let it go, okay? See this?' He tugged at a bunch of gold clasps and pulled it open. 'The *most* convenient pocket for my iPhone. Right here.'

I groaned. 'Put it *away*!'

Pen hugged me even closer and suddenly burst into tears. 'Oh, Tallulah!'

'P-Pen?' I stammered.

'Do you have any idea what was going on out there?' she bleated. 'Any idea?'

'A very tough race, and you at the helm, brilliant girl,' I said firmly, squeezing her forearm more firmly still and sliding my eyes to the left, to my father, about to go onstage in a few minutes, and needing no high drama to tip him over the edge. 'Why don't you see if you can find Sergeant T, and then wander back later' – another eyeslide left to Dad – 'and tell me what's new.'

Pen was about to argue, but she saw someone in the crowd, nodded and hurried off with Angus in tow. Ah. Bludgeon. Ha. She'd post him as sentry for sure.

'Your nose is bleeding again,' said Dad. 'Thank goodness Dr McCabe is doing first aid today.' He stepped into the tent, bag neatly on his shoulder again. 'Hi, Doc. Could you take a look at Tallulah's nose? And her face?'

I nearly turned and ran. Then I remembered that we'd won the race and Dr McCabe's only child was safely ashore. I could deal with this man's anti-Tatty vibe no problem when I had no guilt to compound it. I stepped out from behind Dad and watched Dr McCabe do a double-take.

'Goodness!' he said. 'Goodness gracious!' And then he started rummaging in a small cardboard box of gauze and bottles and tape and vicious-looking syringes.

'Don't leave me,' I muttered to Dad, grabbing his arm in a vice-like grip.

'My shirt!' moaned Dad. 'Look what you've done!'

'Where's all your famous sensitivity?' I hissed. 'I'm probably going to faint from loss of blood!'

'Yes, but did you have to lose it *all over my shirt*?'

I rolled my eyes. And promptly passed out.

Going towards the light

I could hear someone calling my name. And there was a comforting beam shining just ahead of me that I felt I wanted to draw near to. The light flashed off. Oh. Is this how it was supposed to go? I was to find my way in the darkness? The light flashed on. I strained to see ahead and suddenly the light was blinding me.

'Please, Dr McCabe, move your torch from my

daughter's eyes. That can't be good for the retinas.'

The light went away. I blinked blearily and made out my mother, just at my shoulder, staring down at me. She was wearing a Hawaiian-print caftan in blues and golds, and I could see she'd trimmed her own hair again, though it didn't look DIY this time, thank frik. Somewhere, not far away, someone was belting out a catchy rhythm and I could hear familiar lyrics:

> *Oh whoa whoa whoa baby*
> *You're my kind la-la-lady*
> *Don't leeeeeeeave me in this turmoil*
> *Don't go swiiiiiiiitching me on to boil*

'I've died and gone to hell,' I whimpered, squeezing my eyes shut with a shudder.

'Oh, she's awake!' squealed my mother.

My eyes shot open again. Aha. It was definitely my mother, and I was alive. Blue was holding her hand. I could just see her eyes peeping over the mattress.

'What is that noise?' I whispered. 'Tell me that's not Dad singing.' My eyes began to water. 'Tell me he's not onstage singing. With the handbag.'

'I took care of it.' I turned my head in the direction of Pen's voice. She was sitting on a high stool to my left, still in the trisuit, still looking great. 'He's on the drums, the bag is behind the bass, but he's still man of the moment *cos guess who's singing?* Dizzee!' She squealed and clapped her hands. Then a serious look crossed her face. 'But you've got to get out there for the hula dance. Mrs Baldacci will be as mad as a snake. Not to mention Alex – you don't want to pee off Alex. Hey, you okay?'

'Is Dad –'

'Oh, yeah yeah. Dad. Dad is fine. Don't worry. Blue has been getting him loads of water whenever he feels thirsty.'

'Yay for Bluebird.' A smile cracked across my aching face and I tried to sit up.

Dr McCabe hove suddenly into view. 'Down!' he commanded. 'You've still got half a litre to go.' And he fiddled with a bag of liquid hanging above me, the tube snaking its way down to my arm.

'Whoa,' I said. 'I needed that?'

'Yes, so make sure you do exactly what Doctor Mac says, okay, Lula?' Mum looked stern and wagged a finger. 'Well done on the race, love' – a kiss to the cheek – 'I'm going to check on your father.'

We waited till Mum had exited the tent before shrilling queries at each other. We would have gone on forever: *Who? What? Did you see –? And then there was this THWOCK! Did the girls cycle past him? Was it –?*

But then, 'Enough!' Sergeant T's voice boomed round

the first-aid tent, and it takes some doing for a voice to boom in a tent, I can tell you.

Sergeant T! Who? What? Did you see –? And the THWOCKs! Did the girls cycle past him? Healey? Was it him? Was it you phoning Jack?

'If you don't stop now,' she said, raising her hand, 'Tallulah won't have a chance to get cleaned up in time for the hula dancing. Dr McCabe says you're good to go, Lula.'

'Oh no,' I said in mock dismay.

'Mrs Baldacci . . .' began Sergeant T.

'Okay, okay,' I mumbled, and elbowed myself up into a half-sitting position. The drip was nearly empty, and I was almost ready to leave, but I needed to find out . . .

'Did you get Healey?' I asked.

Sergeant T smiled and nodded. 'We got him, thanks to Mr Kadinski. Gavin rang us to say he'd overhead his mad grandfather going on about "taking down that girl", and he gave us all the information. I'm sorry we didn't get there sooner, though I guess we have Mr K and six police officers now to give evidence that he was shooting across the river. Honestly, I don't know what that old man thought he'd achieve by killing you, Tallulah.'

Pen shuddered, her hands coming up to her face. 'It was so terrible,' she said, her voice shaking. 'So, so terrible.'

'You totally saved my bacon,' I said, and pulled my little sister into a hug. 'And Sergeant T, and Mr Kadinski.' I offered Arns's mum my hand. 'Thank you.'

Sergeant T smiled and shook my hand. 'You're welcome. That boy Jack was ready to dive in and apprehend Healey himself too, you know.'

I bit my lip. 'What stopped him?'

'Mr Kadinski got there first,' said Sergeant T. 'Followed shortly by my team. And I'd better get back to them before they let Healey throw his wig in the river or some other ridiculous disaster. See you later, girls.'

'This is perfecto, Pen!' I said, squeezing Pen harder. 'Those fibres will match up and they'll get him for murdering Parcel for sure, won't they?'

'Get your scabby arms off me,' said my sister, sniffing and dropping her hands. 'And don't second-guess the law. It's too complex for the likes of your blunderiness.'

I shot her an amused *Oh yeah?* look.

She set her jaw, narrowing her eyes. 'PLUS! Enough with the mysteries and the violence and the crazy people, Lu. Enough.'

'Oh, please,' I mocked. 'You love it really.' Sergeant T's revelations about Jack had made me feel a little happier, though I still wondered why he hadn't called since yesterday. I swung my legs off the bed. Maybe it was time to wash some blood away and get out there to hula.

Oh, frik. The hula.

Chapter Forty-three

Bandages + track marks in veins not a good look for a hula dancer onstage (and you don't wanna *know* how bad a Pot Noodle tum looks in a bikini top and hula skirt), 6.30 p.m.

The curtains were drawn and the band was tuning up. I could hear Dad doing plinky plonky irritating things on the piano, and someone laughing heartily. My eyes narrowed. I would never laugh heartily again. Not after this public humiliation. Never. Never ever.

'I'd rather be shot at by bad men with guns than hula on this stage,' I hissed at Alex.

'Hey!' she trilled, looking fabulous in her luau get-up. 'Did you hear about Jazz?'

'What about Jazz?' I asked, though I really didn't want to know. In the wings the Hambledon boys stirred nervously, all pale bare hairless chests and surfer shorts. 'Why don't they have to wear bikini bottoms?' I grouched. '*We've* got to expose all!'

'Oh, Tatty, stop moaning. You look great! I'd love a pair of bikini boulders like yours, and I thought you said there was a Pot Noodle Pot going on?' Alex gestured at my naked midriff. 'No Pot. No Pot at all. Much lusher than Jazz, who let me tell you is totally humiliated after Esme accused her of messing with your seat in the boat.'

'No! Why'd she do that?'

'Esme says she saw her, but Jazz said she has no proof.'

'I bet Esme wasn't pleased.'

Alex shrugged and turned to face the front as Mrs Baldacci ran on to give us our last instructions.

'Who's my hula partner?' I hissed.

'Well, it ain't Arns, that's for sure. Mona would decapitate him.'

I was startled. 'What's that supposed to mean?'

'You haven't seen the portraits?'

'What portraits?'

'Hoo boy.' Alex laughed quietly.

'You'd better tell me now, Alex Thompson, or I'll untie your bikini top in the middle of the routine.'

'You would not!'

'I would and then I'd throw it to the roaring crowds.'

'Since you asked so nicely,' said Alex, her smile fading rapidly, 'old Tufty put the portraits you and Arns did of each other up in the gallery tent.'

'Right. So?'

'So, it's just . . . they're a little revealing.'

'Revealing of what? They're faces, for heaven's sake.'

Alex shrugged lamely. 'Oh, I don't know, Tatty Lula. They're just kind of looking at each other, and both are laughing . . . and they really do look like the two of you . . . They're . . . kind of intimate.'

My face coloured. I knew what Alex meant. About my portrait of Arns, anyway. And I knew how I felt about Arns. I *really* liked him. Maybe even loved him a little. But not like *that*. I know it's totally corny to say I loved him like a brother, but truly that's how I felt. He's the kind of boy that knows I dabble in motor mechanics without having to ask and without me having to tell. The boy that you can kiss and hug, and punch and push around, and tease and bully, without there being any of that *will she won't she* boringness going on. We were getting to know each other, to know each other *well*, and it was . . . *fun* . . . totally stress-free . . . and dare I say it, kind of soulmatey, without the lust.

Mrs Baldacci hurried over to us. 'One minute!' she hissed. 'One minute and you're on! You!' She pointed at me. 'Stay in the back row!'

'Ohh yes,' I said.

She threw me a threatening glance, and hurried off as the band kicked into serious luau mode.

'See you on the dark side,' I muttered to Alex. 'I've got a bad feeling about this.'

'Just follow my moves,' hissed my friend, 'and you'll be fine.'

And with that the curtains swished open. If I'd hoped that most of Hambledon and the lovely seaside folks of Port

Albert would be congregating at the bar, or the riverside, or near the boats . . . well, those hopes were dashed. They were all in THIS HERE TENT to see the girls in bikinis.

'Oh, frik,' I breathed, wiggling and shimmying, doing the wavy wavy thing with my hands and praying for a flash flood, a meteor strike, YES, even a wayward bullet. Is that bad? Yes, very bad. Be glad to be alive-a.

Thor T. Birtley's voice floated over to me from the wings. 'Why do I have to stand in for Jason Ferman? Why me? . . . Which girl is mine? . . .' Someone clearly told him something he didn't like because there was some scuffling and I'm sure I heard him squeal.

Then there was a really plinky bit, while Dad jigged about on his piano stool and the crowd clapped enthusiastically and that was the cue for the boys to come shimmying on.

Which they did. Including Thor T. Birtley who, it seemed, had been thrown onstage to land in front of me. Watching Alex carefully, I did a little raised arm thing and a bit of a twirl, catching Thor a little on the ankle with my big toe. 'Ouch,' I said. 'Sorry . . . sorry you drew the short straw,' I murmured sweetly to him.

'Oh,' he said. 'What have you heard?'

Plinky plinky shimmy shimmy.

'Oh, you know, you in the wings. Not wanting to be my partner.'

Thor's eyes bugged out and his shimmying got a little

crazy. 'Don't hurt me,' he begged. 'Please. I have a family.'

I gritted my teeth and smiled a particularly lovely stage smile. 'Oh, really?' I ground out.

I'll admit the smile must have been a little scary, and Tam says the front row of the audience did step back a little, but that was no reason for Thor to shimmy himself right offstage.

Oh no. Not now. Now I've got to go wiggle waggle to the front for eight seconds before assuming back-row position again. Partnerless for the front row 'moment of glory'? Too much to bear. I looked across at Dad, working the piano, and he turned to look at all of us, smiling happily, clearly having a good time. My throat tightened. *Good on you, Dad.* His eyes caught mine and he winked.

I started moving forward, on my own, and heard sharp laughter over to the right. I looked in that direction and there were Jack and Jazz with cameras and sound booms, Jazz most definitely focused on me. On me on my own.

My cheeks stung with the crimson that flooded them, and suddenly I felt every graze that had been bandaged and strapped and hidden under luau flowers. I felt all the soreness of muscles pushed too far, and tendons stressed for too long. I felt . . . defeated.

But not for long.

On to the stage pounded Esme Trooter, and she shoved Dad on his twirly piano stool so hard that he scooted two metres across the boards and the music stopped abruptly.

'That girl!' shrieked Esme, pointing a shaking finger at Jazz, 'fiddled about with Tallulah Bird's boat and we all saw how that ended up.'

She gestured to my puffy nose, and I bit my lip as the noise in the tent fizzled away in embarrassed murmurs, shuffles and flaps of canvas. Everyone was looking from me to Jazz, from Esme to me, to Jazz.

'Now, Esme,' said Jack. 'I'm sure that's not –'

'Oh, be quiet, you stupid boy,' cried Esme. She looked towards the audience. 'Did anyone else see this girl doing things she shouldn't have out at the Hambledon Girls' boat? If I'd known then that she was up to no good . . .'

Jazz lowered her camera, shaking her head in outraged wonderment.

There were murmurs from the crowd, and I leaned over to Esme. 'Um,' I said, 'I don't think –'

'Ah,' she said. 'Arthur.'

Mr Kadinski came through the tent doorway, holding a black leather bag. He walked quickly up to the stage, the handles dangling off an extended index finger. 'I was just coming over to see the lovely dancers' – he smiled at me, now walking up the steps to the side of the stage – 'when I noticed this bag had been left lying around. I thought while Esme had you all as a captive audience we could make sure it got back to its rightful owner.'

Jazz handed her camera to Jack and stepped forward. 'That's mine,' she said crossly. 'But I certainly didn't leave it lying about. I –'

'Oh!' I gasped as Mr K tripped up the last step. His arms flailed more wildly than I would have thought possible of a secret agent with incredible reflexes, and the bag sailed into the air, scattering its contents across the stage.

'Oh!' gasped the audience as Tampax Super Absorbent went skittering for all to see, along with a reel of fishing line, spare knickers, a packet of laxatives, a spanner and five washers . . .

'It *was* you!' shrieked Esme. 'And here is the evidence!'

I know it wasn't dignified, but I could not help but smile. Not smugly, you understand, just with the sheer joy of sweet, sweet . . . um . . . *something*! The tent erupted into an outraged buzz, and Sergeant T went over to where Jazz was protesting loudly. I'm sure it wasn't quite a police matter, but she went with Sergeant T regardless, leaving Jack looking horrified.

I helped Mr Kadinski to his feet, dusting off his fedora for him. 'Mr Kadinski,' I said, very formally, 'I love you.' Then, turning to Esme, 'And, Esme, I owe you soooo big!'

'I'll take a makeover,' said Esme promptly, 'thank you very much. Like you did for the sergeant's boy last month. He's looking very fine these days. I need to look fine too, what with all my telly appearances.'

She kissed me decorously on each cheek, then exited with Mr K stage right while Mrs Baldacci rushed back on to kick off the dance again.

So, I thought, *this is how it is. How the mighty Jazz has fallen. But I'm still on my own.* I glanced across the audience. No Jack. He'd probably gone to help Jazz deny all allegations. But you know what? *Who cares*, I thought, blocking the resounding answer – *me me me* – from my thoughts, and I took a confident step on my own towards the front row as Dad did an impressive crescendoey thing before heading into a plinky plonk tune all over again.

Only I wasn't on my own. Where Thor T. Birtley had appeared so briefly, there was now another figure.

Tall.

Dark.

Handsome.

'Huh,' I said, ungrateful wretch that I am. Shimmy, shimmy, two steps forward, two back, a little twirl. 'Where's Jazz?'

'Getting a bollocking,' replied Jack, a lazy smile wrenching my stomach down to my knees.

'Oh, yeah?'

'Yeah. I wanted to say sorry to you, Lula.'

I was surprised, but not shocked. Another two steps forward and twirl twirl, hold on to partner's forearm, ignore ridiculous plungey stomach at the feel of his skin beneath my fingers, twirl. Don't think about incredible naked chest. 'Huh,' I said again.

'Apparently, Jazz . . . well . . . I've just had an earful about how she hates all of you girls,' said Jack. 'She . . . she did mess around with the boat, hoping for blood and drama on film, and, you know, I can't – I just can't believe –'

'Can't believe what?' Another two steps forward and we're at the front. Smile and shimmy, hold forearm of incredibly handsome boy and smile again at the crowd because, actually, this isn't so bad. Look! There are Arns and Mona and they're *both* grinning and waving. Tam and Gianni are looking cosy . . . Is Carrie flirting with Forest? She is!

Jack curls my fingers into his palm and my heart goes into overdrive. 'I can't believe I didn't see it myself,' he murmurs. 'I'm sorry, Lula.'

Hip swing left, hip swing right, aaand turn. Oh, fantastic! Sergeant T is yelling at a sulky Jazz who is – gasp! – looking a little cowed! And Mum is twirling with Blue – aww! Pen is dancing with both Angus and Next-Door Dan, little minx. And Hambledon's police force is gawping – yes, well, forget them, and – okay, eight seconds is up. Twirling back now . . .

'Jazz doesn't like us girls?' I asked, a smile beginning.

Jack sighed. 'Please forgive me for my terrible stupidity,' he begged quietly.

I shot him a look. 'Only if you can forgive me for telling tales.'

443

He twirled me a little closer than he should. My fingers trailed across his chest, totally by accident, totally his fault. He cleared his throat. 'Tell me you weren't worried about talking to Sergeant T.'

I cleared mine. 'Er . . .'

'But you had to. There was no other way, was there? I was trying to tell you that at the hospital, but –'

'But you were rushing off with Jazz.'

'Well, yes,' admitted Jack. 'I'm sorry. I was just trying to stay out of your way and make sure Emily Saunders was all right. I . . . should have been with you.'

'So *will* you be with me? Will evil Jazz move from your homestead, from your life, from your thoughts? No more Jazz? Please?'

'I'm sorry?' Jack threw me a confused look. 'To whom do you refer? Who is this Jazz?'

Plinky plinky twirl shimmy ohhh how lovely this dance is. How joyful the music. It's all too too good . . . I think I'm going to explode with dizzy wonderfulness . . . my face hurts from smiling . . . I have a feeling Jack will be kissing it better . . .

'All that Jazz,' he murmured as the curtains swished closed to thunderous applause, 'is gone. What I've always wanted was just a hula with Lula.'

'That is totally cheesy,' I said, trying hard not to laugh. Alex says laughing at boys is an absolute no-no. Alex also says that the only thing boys want is . . . 'If you weren't such a lovely person, Jack, I'd be thinking that actually what you *really* wanted –'

'All right,' growled Jack, pulling me close, 'there's no fooling you, witch girl. You're reading my mind right now, aren't you? Or having a second-sighty thing?'

I sighed with happiness, my stomach a total butterfly house and my heart pounding like a pahu.

Clearly it was too good to be true, because suddenly Alex appeared at my elbow with a loud cough – 'Ahem!' – just as Jack's lips were nearing mine.

I jumped in fright.

She waved her index finger at me. 'Good thing your dad is on the other side of that curtain, Tatty Lula!' she admonished. 'And no, Jack, Lula has no second sight at all.' She lowered her voice, looking round at the dancers leaving the stage. '*Don't be starting any rumours with idle chit-chat!*' Thor T. Birtley was stage left, looking admiringly at my friend in her bikini and grass skirt, but Alex was not appreciative. 'Nothing to see here, Birtley Boy!' she snapped. 'Nothing to see!' and she hurried him offstage, disappearing with an indignant swish of her fragrant lei.

Jack turned back to me, pulling me closer. I yelped as he inadvertently pressed against the bandage on my arm, and then watched the smile fade from his face. 'Tallulah,' he said, then stopped. He took a breath, tracing the edge of the dressing with his thumb, and my skin went hot and shivery. 'Lu, you . . . you totally . . .'

'Dodged a bullet?' I finished.

'Hey,' he replied, gazing at me with serious eyes. 'You have no idea how I . . . If you'd been –' He stopped and shook his head, then hugged me close. I leaned my cheek on his chest. We stood like that for a while as the stage lights went out, one by one.

'Well,' I said at last, listening to his heart thud against my temple, 'you have no idea how close I came to having a dead boyfriend.' I leaned back and raised my eyebrows with a hint of a smile. 'In fact, I may still have one.'

Jack looked quizzical, then he just looked at my lips. 'Don't joke . . .' he said.

'I'm not!' I replied. Light from under the curtains drenched him in a honey glow, leaving his eyes dark and inscrutable, though I could just see he had eyes for nothing but me. I took a shaky breath. 'But let's not talk about that now.'

'No,' he agreed, still gazing at my mouth. 'Let's not talk. No talking at all.'

I closed my eyes and Jack's lips met mine as a slow ballad began to play on the other side of the stage curtains. All the hubbub quietened. We were centre stage in a world of our own, with no audience. I remember thinking that it was good we'd agreed on no conversation because, in between pounding hearts, shivery skin and liquid insides, words had completely failed me. Except for maybe . . .

Oh. Wow.

Acknowledgements

Heartfelt thanks to the incredibles who keep Lula in a state of hula, especially Pippa le Quesne and Charlie Viney of the Viney Agency, and all at Egmont – Ali Dougal in particular, who has a pure Lula heart and soul; Tim Deakin, who takes the pain out of copy-editing; Jo Hardacre, publicity expert; Jenny Hayes, crisis-averter-in-chief; Jane Tate, perfect proofreader; Tom Hartley, cool creative; Charlotte Moore, unflappable productionista; Sian Robertson, Rachel Bailey and Mike Richardson, marketing moguls; and Leah Thaxton, without whom Lula would not be on these printed pages.

Big hugs to Alison Lowry, Helen Suzor, Nicola van Rooyen and Candice Wiggett at Penguin Books SA for the excitement of Lula in South Africa.

I couldn't do it without the wonderfuls who keep me in my day job – thank you! – and the lovelies who crit my scribbling/have my kidlets to play/let me snivel on their shoulder – big kisses.

And I'd never have had the chance to write the first draft in one glorious go without the help of Celeste Mackintosh, who came to look after my family while I ran away to my hometown (the roads of which Lula tirelessly sprints). Thank you so much, Celeste.

Dad, I'm so sad you didn't get to read what I spent our last days together writing, and, Marzipan, as you can see, this one's for you, with all my love.

Another interview with Samantha Mackintosh

in which she reveals all tha—

Samantha: Ali? Is that you?

Ali from Egmont: Oh, hey, Sam! How are you?

Samantha: [*Looking around anxiously*] Okay . . . thank you . . . I guess. What were you saying just now about revealing stuff?

Ali: Oh, y'know, just chatting to the readers . . . [*Ali starts doing I'm-Totally-Innocent whistling tune*]

Samantha: Readers? Chatting to *readers*? Nooooo! I know your game, Missy Ali! Last time you told the readers how I got my dress all hoiked up one fine summer's day and walked across Waterloo Bridge showing the whole world my grey granny knickers! YOU CANNOT BE TRUSTED!

Ali: Sam! *You* spilled the beans! Not me! And you've just spilled them again! *I cannot be trusted*? [*Eyes all big and woeful*] How can you SAY that? I'm devastated!

Samantha: [*Looking suddenly worried*] Devastated? You are? [*Hugging Ali so hard she goes a little blue in the face*] No! I'm sorry. I didn't mean that. You are entirely trustworthy and lovely.

Ali: [*In a small voice*] Thank you. [*Cough*] How do you decide what to write about?

Samantha: Ha! A trick! This is another interview, isn't it?

Ali: [*Fully recovered*] But of course.

Sam: [*Sighing heavily*] Okay. Well, for me it's always about the characters. They'll start off resembling a certain person – maybe just someone I saw in the street or on the bus – and then they get a life of their own and REFUSE to conform to plot, and WILL NOT do as I tell them, and INSIST on texting their mates for pages on end thinking they're really funny instead of just doing something interesting . . .

Ali: Okaaaay. Have you been taking medication for that problem?

Samantha: Is that, like, an interview question, or a personal question?

Ali: Yes. No. Shh, you! Um, okay . . . Why do you write for young people?

Samantha: I abide by that rule: write what you know. I look like I'm ageing fast, but actually I never moved much past sixteen/seventeen.

Ali: [*Hiding a smile*] Really? Nooo. I would never have known. Anyway, where was I . . . Oh yes. Can you write anywhere or do you have a special place where you work?

Samantha: I can write anywhere – it can even be quite noisy.

Ali: What do you do if you get writer's block?

Samantha: Writer's block? No! The concept is too terrifying to admit to, but if the people in my head won't do what they're told I go for a challenging run with tunes in my ears. Or I invent a totally new character just to mix things up a little.

Ali: Describe yourself as a teenager in five words.

Samantha:

1. UNKISSED.

2. Totallyuncoolbutsomehowitwasokay.

3. Regularlydepressed.

4. Toosensitive.

5. GSOH.

Is that last one cheating?

Ali: They all are! [*Shakes head in despair*] If you could give your teenage self one piece of advice, what would it be?

Samantha: Don't stop writing just because it feels like too big a dream.

Ali: Do you think today's teens are different from how young people were when you were a teenager?

Samantha: Yikes! It wasn't that long ago! But I guess a lot has changed. I think today's teens have heaps more to cope with, and heaps more expected from them. (Chocolate helps.)

Ali: Have you ever kept a diary? Do you still keep one?

Samantha: I've kept a diary now and then. I'm not really a journal keeper, more of a corresponder.

Ali: Which fictional character do you most relate to and why?

Samantha: Probably Tallulah Bird, surprise, surprise . . .

. . . because she does stuff I always wish I'd been brave enough to try

. . . because she's a lot like me (except for her fine physique, ohhh for a bit of her fine physique, oh and her hair, I love her hair)

. . . because she can fix cars. Is that totally random? Yes. Sorry.

. . . and because she's just got sisters, no brothers, and goes to an all-girls' school so has ZERO boy contact. Which was pretty much my life growing up.

Ali: What do you like the most/ least about being an author?

Samantha: The thing I like most is the writing. The thing I like least is the cold, dark, insidious dread that no one will want to read that writing. The *other* thing I like most is hearing from readers. They're always cool and funny, and make me laugh.

Ali: You are totally sucking up to the readers!

Samantha: Am not! I thought this was all about trusting and truthfulness and blah blah! Readers are an unexpected bonus of writing something. It's true. I never actually believe that anyone will ever read anything I've written. I'm constantly surprised that people know who Boodle is.

Ali: Okay. I get that. Have you ever been inspired by your readers?

Samantha: They're mainly in my head because my books are quite new and I haven't met very many yet. So mostly these imaginary people are just very encouraging. Like at 5 a.m., I'll be going 'Sleeeep,' they'll be going, 'Get up! Move your saggy ass! Tallulah is hanging by her fingertips from a fraying tree root on the edge of a cliff and only you can save her!'

Ali: Moving swiftly on . . . How long does it take you to write a book?

Samantha: That depends on how busy my day job is, and how cRaZy it is at home, so, y'know, could be a few months, could be a few years. Sorry. I know that's not helpful.

Ali: What is your preferred genre of writing and do you write across any other genres? And how is Boodle?

Samantha: Pardon?

Ali: I mean . . . is her back okay?

Samantha: Wait! I thought this was all about me?

Lula: Sam, it's never about you. Ali, Boodle is fine.

Ali: Um, thanks. [*Whispers*] *Does Sam know you're here?*

Samantha: OF COURSE I KNOW SHE'S HERE! SHE'S IN MY HEAD. Well, not *now*. Now she's out in the open. [*Waving hands around head like a freaky freak*] Back inside, Lula! Back inside!

Lula: As if. I always have to come out here and set the record straight about stuff.

Samantha: I am perfectly capable, thank you very much, of answering interview questions.

Lula: Not true.

Samantha: TRUE! Answer to Ali's complicated question about genres? I like writing for girls – that sixteen-year-old voice is a lot of fun, and seems to speak to everyone from twelve to twenty-hundred.

Lula: That's how old Blue thinks Sam is. Twenty-hundred. [*Falls about laughing*]

Samantha: [*Cheeks a little flushed*] And! AND! I'll have you know that I'd like to have a go at other things, though, as there are quite a few other people in my head that have been yelling to get out.

Lula: That's true, actually. It's a little mad in here.

Samantha: Excuse me! Do you mind? Ali and I are having a conversation.

Ali: Um, I could come back later? Give you guys a chance to –

Samantha and Lula: No!

Lula: No need. I'll be good, promise.

Ali: [*Hurriedly*] Okay, um, describe the perfect kiss.

Samantha: Whoa! Where'd that come from? We were all, like, genres and characters and . . .

Lula: Now aren't you glad I'm here? Nobody wants to hear about your Stephen Measey experience. Because that really was not the perfect kiss, even if it was the first.

Samantha: [*Head in hands*] Oh boy. Actually, I'm so glad you're here. I am. So glad.

Lula: Remember that question you saw on the internet the other day?

Samantha: Oh, horrors, yes. That was excruciating.

Lula: So, Ali, this girl says: *I've never kissed anyone before. I am fifteen years old, and am obviously waiting for that special someone.*

I am nervous, like many inexperienced people, and I want to know what are some turn-offs when you kiss someone. A very wet kiss? Opening your eyes while kissing? Breathing through your mouth while kissing? Making weird noises with your lips while kissing?

Ali: Eek! Seriously?

Samantha: Seriously. I had to call Lula up straight away.

Lula: Though this is more Alex's area of expertise than mine.

Ali: So did this girl get any answers?

Lula: Not really. [*Shudders*] I mean . . . all of those are pretty awful. And there are countless other things to make kissing a nightmare.

Ali: Like?

Lula: Really? You want me to go into things like halitosis and

younger siblings and rumbly tums and –

Samantha: Enough! [*Head back in hands*] Please . . .

Lula: Okay, so, perfect kissing requires:

1. Lovely boy
2. Frisson (that's a French word meaning, really, he likes you and you like him, but the dictionary won't say that)
3. Soft lips
4. Fresh breath
5. No wet kissing/open eyes/breathing through mouth/weird noises/unwanted audiences/halitosis/interruptions from parents (and/or anyone)/fits of the giggles/rumbly tums – I think you get the picture.

Ali: Too much information.

Lula and Samantha: [*In unison*] You asked!

Ali: I'm going to stop asking. Just one more thing we need to know, though. What do you think is the hardest part of growing up?

Samantha: Boys. Definitely. And the fact that there's no end to growing up. It goes on and on. But I guess that's the best bit too.

Lula: Unless you get to twenty-hundred. That's way too much growing up. [*Falls about laughing. Again.*]

Ali: And on that, I'm outta here!

Samantha: Bye, Ali. I'm going to go and explain to Lula how easy it is to murder a fictional person.

Lula: Hey! I –

EGMONT PRESS: ETHICAL PUBLISHING

Egmont Press is about turning writers into successful authors and children into passionate readers – producing books that enrich and entertain. As a responsible children's publisher, we go even further, considering the world in which our consumers are growing up.

Safety First
Naturally, all of our books meet legal safety requirements. But we go further than this; every book with play value is tested to the highest standards – if it fails, it's back to the drawing-board.

Made Fairly
We are working to ensure that the workers involved in our supply chain – the people that make our books – are treated with fairness and respect.

Responsible Forestry
We are committed to ensuring all our papers come from environmentally and socially responsible forest sources.

**For more information, please visit our website at
www.egmont.co.uk/ethical**

Egmont is passionate about helping to preserve the world's remaining ancient forests. We only use paper from legal and sustainable forest sources, so we know where every single tree comes from that goes into every paper that makes up every book.

This book is made from paper certified by the Forestry Stewardship Council (FSC), an organisation dedicated to promoting responsible management of forest resources. For more information on the FSC, please visit **www.fsc.org**. To learn more about Egmont's sustainable paper policy, please visit **www.egmont.co.uk/ethical**.